THE ~~LIFE~~ *Murder* OF
BINDY MACKENZIE

by Jaclyn Moriarty

SCHOLASTIC INC.
New York Toronto London Auckland Sydney
Mexico City New Delhi Hong Kong Buenos Aires

*To my Mum and Dad,
to Liane, and to Colin
with love.
—J. M.*

Text copyright © 2006 by Jaclyn Moriarty. All rights reserved. Published by Scholastic Inc. SCHOLASTIC, the LANTERN LOGO, and associated logos are trademarks and/or registered trademarks of Scholastic Inc.

ISBN–13: 978-0-439-74052-4
ISBN–10: 0-439-74052-5

Arthur A. Levine Books hardcover edition designed by Elizabeth B. Parisi, published by Arthur A. Levine Books, an imprint of Scholastic Inc., October 2006.

12 11 10 9 8 7 6 5 4 3 2 1   8 9 10 11 12 13/0

Printed in the U.S.A.   40
This edition first printing, May 2008

PART ONE

i have never spoken to Bindy,
but i am sure that behind her extremely annoying
personality she is a beautiful human being.

A bit too smart.

You can't help who you are, Bindy, and maybe
you will change this year? Good luck with Year 11.
I think you will change.

BINDY MACKENZIE

BINDY WEARS HER HAIR WEIRD EVEN tho
PEOPLE tAlk ABOUt it BEHIND HER BACk.
i'D CHANGE MY HAIR, BUt tHAt'S BiNDY FoR YOU,
SHE'S Got GUtS.

She's a fast typist.

Well, what can you say about Bindy? Hmm. Did someone say
the word 'SMART'???? Bindy! You have words in your
head that would be too long to fit in anyone else's head!
Because you have SUCH A HUGE HEAD!
Just kidding!! (kind of)

Bindy Mackenzie talks like a horse.

PART TWO

I.

*Resolutions from the Heart —
This Week, Bindy Will . . .*

1. Begin Year 11!
2. Consider her future.
3. Read the book: *How Did I Get This Dysfunctional and What Can I Do to Change?* (Britney Brillson, Ph.D.). Photocopy extracts and distribute to fellow students.

× × ×

*As Wednesday wends its winsome way,
so Bindy goes to*

1. Maths
And Bindy, pay heed to . . .
Lucy Tan — she was a close second last year and rumor has it she's had advanced tutoring over the holidays. May well be a threat.

2. Biology

And Bindy, pay heed to . . .

Tonja Slavinski — her sudden flashes of genius last year were disturbing (to say the least).

3. English

And Bindy, pay heed to . . .

The teacher — it was to be Ms. Lawrence, but I hear she took flight at the last minute. Hence: a substitute named Miss Flynn. Substitute teachers, like student teachers, rarely reach the *heart* of a lesson. Find a way to guide her to the essence?

4. Form Assembly

And Bindy, pay heed to . . .

Nothing — ignore their clichés! Use time to recite strong German verbs in a whisper.

5. Friendship and Development ("FAD")

And Bindy, pay heed to . . .

The point — this is a new self-awareness course and, quite frankly, what is the point? Can it be the best use of our time? Seems unlikely.

6. Free Period

And Bindy, pay heed to . . .

YOURSELF! Go directly to the library, begin homework at 2:30 p.m. precisely, and continue until the final bell. DO NOT GET CAUGHT IN REVERIE.

× × ×

The Philosophical Musings of Bindy Mackenzie

Wednesday, 2:32 p.m. (in the library)

As with a knocked funny bone, so with life at large. Wait. Simply wait. Let the moment pass and your elbow will be yours once again.

2:35 p.m.

Consider a dirty window. If life seems suddenly dirty and smeared, simply *wash the window*. And life will sparkle once again.

2:38 p.m.

But how to wash the window?

2:39 p.m.

Nay, how to *smash* the window? And where to buy fresh glass?

2:40 p.m.

Turn from the window and consider this: People are generally good and kind and it is right that they inhabit the earth.

2:42 p.m.

Of course, some people have venom in their hearts. But venom is nature's defense mechanism and who are you to find fault with nature?!

2:43 p.m.

If certain venomous others — a certain Venomous Seven — have spoken ill of you, what is the *antidote* to that?

2:44 p.m.

Kindness is the antidote to cruelty!! Be kind to yourself! Behold! I will try it right now!

2:57 p.m.

And what, pray tell, if the antidote fails? What if the poison courses through my blood, already seeping into my bones?

---

3 p.m.

The solution, Bindy, is: Move on! Why waste your time on seven troubled people? Think of them as grimy dinner plates arranged in a row in a dishwasher. You, Bindy, are the dishwasher's fan. Set way *above* the seven grimy plates, you spin through the soap bubbles of life.

3:08 p.m.

Bindy, stop your reverie! Chew on a carob-coated energy drop and turn to your homework at once. Even if you just get five min —

3:10 p.m.

Oh, who am I trying to fool? My entire study period has been wasted. It seems to me that my entire career at Ashbury has also been wasted! I have been so helpful to my fellow students: I've offered free private tutoring! I've offered lunchtime seminars for troubled teens! I *realize* that my academic record may be intimidating, so I wear multicolored nail polish to show that I'm approachable — a free spirit! I hang little sprigs of tinsel from my spectacle frames each December! I know the birthday of every person in my roll-call class, and I *always* lead the class in "Happy Birthday"!

3:12 p.m.

Secretly, I admit, I find many of my classmates annoying. I've often thought to myself, "Good grief, these people are five-year-olds. Why must I spend my days amongst them?" But have I ever *said* such things aloud? No. I have been nothing but generous to them, and have kept these thoughts to myself.

And how have they repaid me? Have they been grateful or kind? Ho NO!

3:14 p.m.

They have leaped at the chance to *attack* me! Perhaps the following crossed their minds: "Here is a sheet of paper with Bindy's name in the center. Shall we write something complimentary?" But the answer came at once: "Why no, let us write vicious comments! Let us be the Venomous Seven! What do we care for *her* feelings?"

3:14 p.m.
What, indeed?!

3:15 p.m.
Well!

_____

3:16 p.m.
It has come to this.

A decision has been made.

Pay heed, Venomous Seven! You thought that I was bad before? *Wait until you see what I can be.* You think that your words are incisive and cruel? Wait until *I* speak my mind.

You had your chance with benevolent Bindy.

Ruthless Bindy just arrived.

2.

Nighttime Musings of Bindy Mackenzie

Thursday, 2:47 a.m.

My strategy is simple. First, I will contact the highest authority and expose the travesty, nay, the crime, of Friendship and Development. Second, I will decipher the true nature of each of the Venomous Seven, and will hold up a mirror to their souls. (The bloodcurdling screams that will follow!) (It will do them good.) Third, I will attend the next Friendship and Development class and *I will speak the truth*. Words that have been left unsaid throughout my life will *roll like a rich red carpet from my tongue!*

I can scarcely wait.

They all disguised their handwriting, but I know who wrote that I talk like a horse. Me? The girl who had voice training between the ages of 7 and 11? Third speaker on the debating team? *A volunteer to sing at the School Spectacular each year!* The girl who approaches those who seem distressed, and offers a shoulder to cry upon! (An offer rarely taken up, I admit, but never once made in the voice of a horse.)

This is surely a joke or a bad dream!

I have known him since infants' school, and he always elevates his "r"s when he joins them to "s"s (so that "horse" looks almost like "hotse").

His name is Toby Mazzerati.

Toby Mazzerati is a cane toad. But here is what I wrote (generously) under his name today:

I admire Toby. He has struggled academically (and perhaps with his weight) over the years, but has found his niche in woodwork. He likes to keep up a low-voiced commentary on life, so perhaps he has a future in radio?

Here is what I ought to have written:

Toby Mazzerati should die.

3.

Bindy Mackenzie
24 CLIPPING DRIVE, KELLYVILLE, NSW 2155

The Director
Office of the Board of Studies, NSW

Dear Sir (or Madam),
I am a student at Ashbury High, the finest school in Sydney's windswept Hills District.

Or, at least, it *was* the finest school.

It is my odious duty to inform you that the Ashbury gleam has been tarnished. Nay, I will go a step further: This year, the gleam is *gone*.

This year, Ashbury (in all its wisdom) has decided to offer a Year 11 "self-awareness" course entitled Friendship and Development, also known as "FAD." (You need not hear my views on the acronym.)

As you no doubt know, this course is not listed on the Board

15

of Studies Web site. Indeed, it seems that the course does not exist. It is an *"experimental* course." It will take up an hour of my time each week but *it will not count toward assessment.*

Well!

As a student embarking on the stormy seas of her final two years of high school; as a student determined, with all due modesty, to achieve the best marks in the state; *nay, as a student who believes with all her heart that this year will determine her WHOLE LIFE* — I write to express my concerns.

Sir (or Madam), what can be done to save Ashbury?

I am enclosing a report that I have just prepared, describing the first session of FAD. It took place yesterday — Wednesday. It is now the next day. Several hours have passed. I have tried to be accurate in my report, but I may have forgotten some details.

I thank you in advance and I remain:

Bindy Mackenzie

P.S. Please note that the address printed on this stationery is no longer current. I have just moved in with my Aunt Veronica and Uncle Jake (for reasons that do not concern you). I'll write my new address on the back of this page.

P.P.S. A note of caution! I assume you do not wish to be offended. I have therefore removed the disgraceful language spoken by my fellow students from this Report. I've replaced this language with words of my own choosing — these words appear in small capitals LIKE THIS.

× × ×

REPORT ON FRIENDSHIP AND DEVELOPMENT (FAD),
PREPARED FOR THE OFFICE OF
THE BOARD OF STUDIES, NSW

By Bindy Mackenzie

Session 1

The session took place in the storage room at the back of the gymnasium.

I could not believe this either.

But there it was, on my timetable: STORAGE ROOM, GYMNASIUM.

When I arrived, five other students were already there, but not the teacher. These five students had each unstacked a chair for him- or herself.

The chairs are straight-backed with curved iron legs, and are impossible simply to sit in. So:

- Briony Atkins (round face, blinking eyes) was tipping her chair back and forth, each time tipping farther as if tempting the chair to crash;
- Sergio Saba (dark hair, burn scar on cheek) had turned his chair around and was straddling it, his arms embracing the chair back;
- Toby Mazzerati (cane toad) was hunched forward, legs wide apart, hands dangling between his knees;

- Astrid Bexonville (green slanting eyes, black hair in high ponytail) had her legs folded beneath her and was chatting with:
- Emily Thompson (drama queen), whose feet were resting on the bars of Astrid's chair.

I put my laptop down and unstacked a chair of my own.

I also unstacked several further chairs and set them out ready for others who might arrive. This is the kind of thing I like to do.

"Wa-hay," said Toby Mazzerati. "It's Flying Fingers Mackenzie. We got lucky. We got Flying Fingers Mackenzie. Whaddya say, maestros and *messieurs,* bindi-eyes troubling your feet?" He continued talking in this nonsensical way. He is always doing this.

The others ignored him. I sat down next to Briony.

Astrid, her ponytail swinging, was telling Emily a story about a friend at another school whose boyfriend had ended their relationship "on the *first day of school!*"

She kept repeating "on the first day of school!" as if this had significance.

But why not the first day of school? I thought.

It makes perfect sense. Astrid's friend had had the summer for romance. The school year could now be for study.

I wondered if the others would reflect on this, but:

"FLAX that," said Emily. "Why didn't he do it on the holidays so she'd have the chance to adapt herself to her anguished new environment?"

"Wait, but," said Astrid, "you want to know how he did it?"

"Well, *yeah,* we want to know," said Sergio, joining the conversation, although no one would have known that he was listening.

"She walks into her homeroom," said Astrid, pleased to have Sergio's interest, "and her guy is just kind of like standing there and he has, like, his iPod connected to speakers? And he's kind of like staring at her and looking kind of like sad, and a song's playing out of the speakers, and guess what song it is?"

"What song is it?" said Sergio.

"It was a song called 'It's Over.'"

At this, there was silence.

Astrid whispered a dramatic (and unnecessary) explanation: "He was telling her it was over by playing a song called 'It's Over.'"

There was an outburst of disgraceful language from Emily. (As far as I could tell, she didn't even know this other girl. Her reaction seemed excessive. That is Emily for you.)

But even Sergio looked impressed. "This guy breaks up with your friend," said Sergio, "by playing a FOXGLOVE song?"

Now, that is something about Sergio. When he told Astrid he wanted to hear her story, he was just making fun of her. (She knew that, and he knew that she knew. It is a form of flirtation.)

But when he *reacted* to the story, he was genuine.

Emily stopped swearing to wonder what song Astrid meant. She didn't know a song called "It's Over." Nor did Sergio. Astrid admitted she did not know it herself. Next thing, all three were trying out different musical renditions of the phrase "It's o-o-over" while Toby Mazzerati announced their songs and described them. He used different voices and accents and sounded much like a frog.

Briony tipped her chair back and forth more quickly.

"You know who it's over for?" Astrid said suddenly, in a voice that cut through the chaos. Obediently, the others ceased their tomfoolery and turned to her. Astrid continued: "Ms. Lawrence."

"Oh yeah?" said Sergio easily. "I always liked the Lawrence."

"You can't just not show up for a new school year," explained Astrid, "and expect to keep your job."

"You've got to have commitment," Emily agreed.

"You know where she'll be?" said Toby. (His regular voice is surprisingly well-modulated.) "She'll be stuck in a traffic circle somewhere. I was out at Dural way last week, and I've seen the Lawrence doing loops around the inside lane of a traffic circle, and I've said to myself: That's not pretty. And I'm here to tell you now, it was not."

"Eventually she's gotta find a break in the traffic," said Sergio.

"No," reflected Toby. "I don't think so."

"She's not on a traffic circle," Emily declared. "She's in Thailand, surfing. I heard the principal going into anaphylactic shock about it. It was funny."

"Good-bye, Ms. Lawrence," said Astrid, and then: "Merry Christmas."

And they all began to sing Christmas carols.

At this point, to my relief, the teacher arrived.

Now, the storage room where we were sitting is separated from the gym by a sliding concertina wall. Mostly the room is approached by crossing the gym and pushing open the wall.

This teacher approached from a *most unusual* direction.

The fire escape.

She must have had a delicate step, for nobody had heard her climb the metallic stairs.

I sensed a reaction among us. Some of us were surprised. Some were curious (*I have never seen this teacher before. She must be new — so how did she know about the fire escape?*). Some distrustful (*The fire escape! I didn't even know it was there!*). Some were pleased. Some impressed. Some pointedly indifferent. Some were nervous —

I suppose there were only six of us.

But now as this teacher stepped into the room, paused, and looked about, I sensed the reaction change.

It was her appearance.

She was so small.

She sprang across to us like a lively fawn.

I saw the glint of a belly button ring as she sprang. (She was wearing hipster jeans and a short tank top.) Her hair was threaded into many fine plaits, held loosely at the neck by a bandanna. She stood behind a chair and beamed.

I knew at once that the whole thing — the jewelry, the hair, the smile — all of it was a disguise.

She was trying to hide her smallness.

She could not!

She had an accent, I observed. She was perhaps American. "Well, hiya everyone," she began, speaking through her smile. "My name's Try Montaine, yes, you heard me right — Try — it started as a nickname, but I've just about forgotten my real name!"

She waited for us to laugh but I heard small noises of confusion. *She's forgotten her real name!* the noises seemed to say. *Maybe she should ask her mum?*

Try hitched up her jeans, but they fell back into place around her hips.

"Okay, there's one, two — six of you here, so we're waiting for two more, because there's eight in all these groups except I think one or two groups got — you don't need to hear that, do you? Listen to me babbling, would you? Step one, make sure you're babbling to the right people, I guess. This is Year 11, and this is Friendship and Development. Am I right? Also known by the acronym 'FAD'?"

She was clinging to the back of the chair and rising on her toes.

Briony's face beside me seemed bewildered. I remembered that she sometimes fails exams. "An acronym is a kind of abbreviation," I whispered to her helpfully. Briony stared, and a moment later she shifted her chair away from me.

"You're in the right place," confirmed Toby Mazzerati. "But are you at the right time? Is anyone ever really *at the right time*? Who can tell?" He shrugged.

"Thanks, wow, this room is kind of claustrophobic, isn't it?" Try looked around at the chairs and gym mats stacked in the shadows, and then at the cobwebbed windows. "Can we open — ? You think we can open that wall between here and the gym? The gym's empty, right?"

People agreed and I started up to help, but Try waved me back and pushed open the heavy wall herself. It was a slow and noisy process. Toby began his commentary again ("It's Try the tiny teacher trying tiptoe tintinacity, it's Try the —"). "Excuse me?" said Try, looking back at him confused, but he only shook his head.

Just as she finished opening the wall, letting in a burst of light and space, a crowd of Year 8s arrived at the gym, a sports teacher shouting behind them.

Try looked crestfallen.

"I'll close it," said Sergio, and he did so in an instant.

Now the room was small and dark again.

"Huh!" Try sat down in the circle. She looked around, smiling while the Year 8 gym class thudded and shrieked through the concertina wall.

Everyone gazed at her.

"You probably want to know what Friendship and Development is all about?" she declared. "You were surprised to see it on your timetable?"

"I was surprised," I agreed. "I phoned the Board of Studies, and they said it's not on the official curriculum."

"You phoned the Board," repeated Toby Mazzerati. "She phoned the Board," he murmured to himself.

Try became enthusiastic. "Well, *this*," she said "is a new course. It's kind of experimental. Year 11 is a tough year. Assessment begins. You've got your Higher School Certificate looming next year. You're deciding on your future. And sometimes you might feel like you're drowning in all that worry. Your FAD group is going to be a life raft."

Then she reached into her handbag and took out some papers, which she passed around the group.

The papers showed a cartoon of a boy jumping out of a class-room window and into a life raft.

Everyone looked at it politely and then looked up at Try.

"So," she said, embarrassed. "This is just something I did on my computer for you last night . . . but anyway, you have to see this group of people here as your life raft —"

Emily and Astrid interrupted to exclaim, "*You* did this? This is *amazing!*"

To be perfectly honest, the art was not that great.

Try was blushing, and had started pulling the fine plaits out of her bandanna, one at a time. "Anyway," she said, folding up her own cartoon, but she was interrupted again.

Someone was pushing back the concertina wall. Everyone turned as Elizabeth Clarry (athlete) walked in, pressing the wall closed behind her.

She seemed surprised by our circle.

"Is this the Friendship and Development class?" she said. "Sorry I'm late."

Elizabeth Clarry is always late and often misses lessons. She is a distance runner and disappears to train or to compete.

I had hoped she was planning to focus on her schoolwork this year.

"Sit here," ordered Emily, pulling out the empty chair beside her. "That's our new teacher, Try, and we're the life raft." She gestured at the circle, her eyes lingering a moment on me. "You have to use your imagination," she added.

"Show her the picture," suggested Astrid.

"Forget about it," said Sergio, inexplicably, in a New Jersey mafia accent. He passed Elizabeth the cartoon and tapped on the life raft. One, two, three taps. Then he looked at her meaningfully.

"Is that art like FOXGLOVE great or what?" said Astrid. "Try did it herself."

"It's Flying Feet Clarry, we got Flying Feet Clarry, we got —"

That was Toby again.

Try did not seem to mind any of this. "So, one more to go," she said, counting again, and glancing at Elizabeth. "I was just explaining that it's tough to be in Year 11, so this course is going to cover issues like self-esteem, stress management, career planning, study management —"

Study management.

I interrupted (politely) to tell everyone that I had downloaded the syllabus for each of the courses offered this year, together with a set of past HSC exam papers and notes from the Marking Center. I said I would happily distribute these to anyone willing to cover the copying costs.

Try looked surprised, but said, "Thank you."

Then she said that she had taught English back in the U.S. for several years, but this year she was going to develop and direct the FAD course. It was her invention, she said, and she'd be supervising other teachers and doing general administration. Also, she said, she hoped we could forgive her if she forgot our names. "I'm terrible at names," she said, at which point I thought: *Well, you might want to work on that.*

"Could we start," she said, "by going around the circle and all of you tell me your names and what animal you'd be if you were an animal?"

She blushed again.

"One thing about that game," said Elizabeth Clarry, who was drumming the heels of her running shoes on an empty chair. The chair would soon be dirty. "I always wonder if we're meant to say what kind of animal we want to be, or what kind is most like our character?"

I was pleased by Elizabeth. She had pointed out, subtly, that this game is played so often it is a cliché.

At least, I think this is what she was getting at.

"Either," said Try, blushing even more. "Or, if you prefer, we could do the type of food you'd be, or which cartoon character or which —"

At that moment the final student arrived and the life raft was complete.

He was a new student, this final student.

I had seen him in some of my classes earlier that day and that week — Biology and Economics — but had not yet heard his name.

He had obviously come through the gymnasium, skirting around the Year 8 gym students, to push back the concertina wall — and the light that beamed upon us seemed to emanate from him.

It seemed like a halo or an extension of his golden hair.

For you see, he was very blonde and here is the remarkable thing:

His name turned out to be Blonde.

Finnegan Blonde.

He sat down and introduced himself.

Finnegan Blonde!

"Finnegan Blonde," he said, and he touched his blonde hair, unconsciously. He said almost nothing else that class, besides the name. And he mentioned that he had come from Queensland.

Now, I must interrupt myself to predict that the girls in the group — at least Emily and Astrid, perhaps Elizabeth too — will be head over heels in love with him before long. He has that mysterious air. Girls of their nature adore that.

And so we played the game in which we each declare an animal. I will not go into details. Now and then, I made some informative comments about the animals the others chose: feeding, hunting, mating habits, and so on. Finnegan Blonde said he would be a zebra. But he did not explain why that was.

"A zebra finch?" I said. "A zebra mussel? A zebra shark? Or a zebra longwing butterfly?"

I was trying, lightheartedly, to point out that the word "zebra" appears in the names of many animals.

He turned and fixed me with his gaze. "No," he said. "Just a zebra." Then he turned away.

I said I would be a giraffe, but, much like Finnegan Blonde, I did not explain.

Anyway, after the animal game had finished, Try said we had one more game to play. She said it was a game we'd play regularly throughout the year. She called it the Name Game. We had to write our names in the center of a blank piece of paper and pass the paper around the group.

"Each new name you get," said Try, "write a small comment about that person on their paper. You're new, aren't you?" She looked at Finnegan Blonde. "Sorry, if you can believe it, I've already forgotten your name — I remember you come from

Queensland, but I can't — anyway, it might be tough for you to write comments about the others because you're new, eh? But maybe you noticed something just in this class today? Do you think you can get by?"

And so we all wrote our names in large letters and we surrendered the Names to the group.

I beg your pardon.

We surrendered them to our life raft.

After some time of passing the papers around, the Names arrived back at their owners, and we learned what the others thought of us.

For your information, I have typed out the comments that the seven others wrote, and this is attached to my report.

I could tell that the others were pleased with their Names (as I was with mine). There was much laughing, gasping, even some teary eyes about the room.

The bell rang.

As we packed to go, there was talk of a party at Emily's house this Saturday. Who was attending? Why was it being held? Was it somebody's birthday? (I am paraphrasing, of course.) Had Sergio not heard? He was invited! General hilarity; disgraceful language; and so on.

I left without saying good-bye.

As I did, I heard a voice croaking behind me like a cane toad in mating season. It was Toby Mazzerati: "Flying Fingers Mackenzie, folks, there she goes, the talking dictionary, and where does she go, to the library, folks, is she off to the library to learn some new polysyllamogononsense words? Or . . ." And so on.

Then I heard another voice. It was Try, the teacher, beside me. She came up to my shoulder.

"Bindy," she said, "I like your nail polish."

She was smiling at my fingernails, which I paint in multiple colors — red, green, purple, and so on.

At least she had remembered *my* name.

***Attachment to Report on Friendship and Development: Sample of
the "Name Game"***

Bindy is a kindhearted, caring human being and none of us could ever do without her.

Bindy earns our respect by getting marks in the 99.9th percentile. That must take work and dedication!

There is nothing I would change about Bindy. She is perfect. Bindy, stay exactly as you are.

Bindy's hairstyle (and nail polish and wacky glasses) say: "I'm a fun and zany girl! Don't be afraid to say hi, nor to ask for some help with Economics."

BINDY MACKENZIE

Bindy takes time from her busy schedule to represent the school in debating and oratory. And she's a fast typist.

Bindy is never conceited or "big-headed." On the contrary, when she does well on an exam, she immediately offers to share the paper around, so that others can learn from her success.

Bindy's voice is like the dawn chorus of a flock of nightingales.

A Memo from Bindy Mackenzie

To: Toby Mazzerati
From: Bindy Mackenzie
Subject: Cane Toads
Time: Friday, 10 a.m.

Hi Toby,

I believe you chose the animal "cane toad" at the FAD session on Wednesday? I thought you might like to know a few fun facts about yourself:

- You were introduced to Australia in 1935 to control beetles that were eating sugarcane roots. That was a disaster. You got out of control. Now there are just *too many of you*.
- You are poisonous! People have died after eating you in soup.
- Your poison oozes out of your glands. Also, you squirt people in the face with it.
- In the mating season, you grow lumps on your fingers that help you hold tightly to female cane toads.

All the best,
Bindy

× × ×

As Saturday sings and skips along, so Bindy unwinds from her busy week by:

1. Kmart — morning shift (7:30–12:30) — (Womenswear)
2. Maths homework
3. Biology assignment
4. Reread *The Duchess of Malfi*
5. Piano practice
6. Musicianship preparation
7. Household tasks (laundry/vacuuming)
8. Baby-sitting — Brentwoods — (6:30 p.m. until midnight) (BRING JOHN DONNE)
9. German translation
10. Visualization
11. Prepare Sunday list of things to do
12. Go to bed

× × ×

FROM THE TRANSCRIPT FILE OF BINDY MACKENZIE

Saturday

12:45 p.m., Castle Towers food court, after work. I sit near Mister Minit, where keys are cut and bracelets are engraved. There is an occasional horrible shrieking sound from Mister Minit. Single lines of conversation float into my hearing.

A man says to his wife: And all this is real? Because, you know, it doesn't seem all that plausible.

A girl rushes by with a group of friends, concluding a story with the words: It was a great big giant head of cabbage!!

✕ ✕ ✕

Here Are Some Lines from a Book That Caught Bindy's Eye Today . . .

On the etiquette of shopping:

"In inquiring for goods at a store or shop, do not say to the clerk or salesman, 'I want' such an article but, 'Please show me' such an article, or some other polite form of address. . . . It is rude to sneer at and depreciate goods, and exceedingly discourteous to the salesman. . . . Whispering in a store is rude. Loud and showy behavior is exceedingly vulgar."

From *Our Deportment, or the Manner, Conduct, and Dress of the Most Refined Society; including Forms for Letters, Invitations, etc, etc. Also, Valuable Suggestions on Home Culture and Training* by John H. Young (1881), pp. 150–151.

✕ ✕ ✕

Nighttime Musings of Bindy Mackenzie

Monday, 4:30 a.m.

I have awakened in a feverish state.

Strange, strange how my heart crashes about like a sneaker in a clothes dryer.

There are just two days until Wednesday.

Already, I have written to the Board (step one), and have begun to expose the Venomous Seven's poisonous souls (step two).

I have exposed the poisonous soul of Toby Mazzerati, anyway.

I think that was a success. On Friday, I put his soul in an envelope and stuck it to the outside of his locker.

Later that day, I saw him leaning against a classroom door. "Hey, Bindy," he said, as I passed by. "Thanks for your note."

Everything about his words had a careful, uncertain tone. As if he were seated at a piano, trying out a difficult new piece.

"You're welcome," I said mysteriously, and I smiled.

"Uh," he said, "but, by the way, I didn't say I was a cane toad. In the FAD class? I didn't say cane toad."

"You didn't?" I feigned surprise.

"No. I said wolverine."

I laughed then, a waterfall of laughter, and continued on my way.

Emily Thompson is next.

35

As for the weekend? My first weekend in Year 11? I think it went well. At Kmart, I was on the changing-room door and had to give out the plastic numbers: 1, 2, 3, 4 or 5. (It is forbidden to try on more than five items at a time.)

I like to imagine that I am the Gatekeeper to the Kingdom of Changing Rooms. The plastic number is my gift to shoppers. A magic key that will reveal its purpose at an unexpected moment. Perhaps it will slay a dragon or open a secret door?

I have noticed that shoppers do not see the plastic number in this way.

Anyway, I survived Kmart, and I ticked off everything on Saturday's list. But I encountered my downfall again:

reverie

This is what happened.

When I arrived at the Brentwoods' to baby-sit on Saturday night, Maureen Brentwood gave me TWO BOOKS.

She runs a secondhand bookshop called Maureen's Magic, and she has been promising to set aside a book that I might like. I have never believed her promise. Why give away books when you could sell them?

Seriously, it's just not the secret to success. There is flaking paint on her front door and mold spots on her bathroom ceiling: I believe she could use some success.

36

Yet she gave me two books as she ran out the door, her husband waving from the car.

Now, I was *planning* to spend the evening reciting John Donne poems to Rebecca (aged 3) and Sam (aged 1), to help me memorize the poems (and for the good of the children's vocabulary), but instead, I watched them play with their finger paints.

And as I watched, I thought to myself: *What a lovely person Mrs. Brentwood is,* and *What a rare thing it is, to meet a thoughtful person in this cruel world,* and also: *How did she know that I love history?* (The books are about etiquette in the nineteenth century.)

Next thing I was caught up in reverie about books, history, clothes, rules, manners, kindness, and so on, and all the time I was so happy that Mrs. Brentwood had thought of me, I wanted to cry.

After I put the children to bed, I played Mr. Brentwood's PlayStation all evening.

I don't know.

So much for the night of John Donne!

Last night there was baby-sitting for Eleanora — no chance of working there, of course! (*She* knows of my fondness for history, but I cannot imagine her giving me books.)

How do I expect to maintain my position (first) in all my classes, if I don't use every moment? People say that Year 12 is important because that's when you do the HSC, but it's in *Year 11* that your rank is set in stone. If I slip down a rank or two this year, I doubt I will be able to climb back up and I will end up living on the streets with a cardboard sign: $1 FOR A SMILE.

Now, it is my belief that character flaws should be imprisoned to stop them from spreading. But I'm tired of writing the word "reverie" and putting it into a box.

$$\boxed{\textbf{reverie}}$$

I must think about Emily Thompson.
It's lucky I don't need much sleep.

$$\boxed{\textbf{reverie}}$$

$$\boxed{\textbf{reverie}}$$

$$\boxed{\textbf{reverie}}$$

I believe that Emily Thompson is a vampire.
Also, I believe that Emily Thompson wrote the following on my Name Game:

*Well, what can I say about Bindy. Hmm. Did someone say
the word "SMART"??? Bindy! You have words in your head
that would be too long to fit in anyone else's head! Because
you have SUCH A HUGE HEAD!! Just kidding!! (kind of)*

Let me explain why I think that.

Emily Thompson is a walking exclamation mark.

She is always opening her mouth and her eyes in astonishment.
She reminds me of the face at Luna Park, or a set of swinging
double doors. Life bursts out of Emily's face just as people burst
through swinging double doors.

She *adores,* nay, she *devours* (sucks the blood of) the people
she likes (such as her two best friends — who, along with Emily,
spent the summer with my mother, by the way. Did I spend the
summer with my mother? Why, no, actually. Thanks for asking.
She was busy with Emily Thompson and Emily's two best
friends).

And she *hates* and *despises* (nay, she *demolishes!*) the people
she dislikes.

I am a person Emily dislikes.

Lucky me.

What else? She wears too much lip gloss. She talks in capital
letters (her voice is so loud, you can hear her from the front
gates of the school).

And, strangest of all, she is obsessed with doing well at
school.

Strange because she is a moron.

She will never do well at school.

Yes, there is no doubt.

She is the one who wrote that comment on my Name Game. All those exclamation marks and capitals. Poor girl, she can't stand how well I do, so she tells herself I am big-headed. Jealousy, thy name is Emily.

So, how to describe her true nature?

I will reflect upon it and before this week is up, *I will show her.*

But, more to the point, by Wednesday afternoon, I will show them ALL my own true nature.

At last, I am going to speak my mind.

I wonder how to slow my beating heart?

Resolutions from the Heart —
This Week, Bindy Will . . .

1. Live until Wednesday afternoon (that is, do not have a heart attack before then).

The Dream Diary of Bindy Mackenzie

Tuesday, 5:20 a.m.

I dreamed that I was lying on my stomach, somewhere dark and warm. My eyes would not quite open. *This is good,* I thought. *I deserve this rest.* I smiled to myself and pressed into the warmth. Flower petals brushed against my neck. It was a tropical sauna.

But something heavy was resting on my back. What was it? Some kind of a backpack? My computer? I shifted, trying to tip the weight, but it only pressed harder and heavier.

Then a voice moved against my ears. It was not a backpack, but a person on my back!

"It's Flying Fingers Mackenzie," said the voice. "Wo-ho, we got lucky, we got Flying Fingers Mackenzie, it's okay, Mackenzie, I got lucky, I got Flying Fingers too —"

The flower petals brushed more quickly — they were sticky, they were *sticking* to my neck. There were not flower petals, they were fingers! What's more, they were lumpy and were clinging to me!

This was not a sauna but a swamp! I was a cane toad! There was a *cane toad on my back.*

It was so shocking that I had to wake at once.

A Memo from Ernst von Schmerz

To: Bindy Mackenzie
From: Ernst von Schmerz
Subject: Summonsing You
Time: Wednesday, lunchtime

Yo Bind,
Looked for you in the library, looked for you in the tuckshop, looked for you on the lawn. Nevertheless: Whassssup? Why have

we not crossed paths to date this year, my dirty ho? More than a week has passed. *Have we no single class together?* Howzat possible? *Perchance you is INVISIBLE this year?!?!* How was your summer holiday, anyho?

Me? Oh, thanks for asking. Went to a science camp, Penrith way. *Sweet as.*

To the point. Mrs. Lilydale wants to see us. She fastened her evil eye on me and said, "I need you and Bindy." *Find Bindy,* she said, *and bring her to me. The mission is yours,* she implied, *should you choose to accept it.*

And guess what, Bind, I accept.

So, where's YO ass, girlfriend?!!

No doubt she wants to talk to us about someone new for the debating team, given the loss of our second speaker to the vortex of international exchange. Think on ideas for recruitment, woncha, and track me down, hokay?

Just had a thoughtflash and philosophized. Here it *is*, for your infotainment:

The Philosophical Musings of Ernst von Schmerz
Where is Bindy?
Seems that I am alone this year
Like a tear that falls from a candlestick
(No, Ernst! That's wax, I fear, not a tear)
(Oh fear is the tangling horsewhip)
Can this be right?
It's a gangsta night so
It can't be right: *this darkness.*

The Philosophical Musings of Bindy Mackenzie

Wednesday, 1:46 p.m.

At last I am at FAD! Here I am at FAD! And I shall keep *nothing* to myself!

I am the first to arrive. Here I sit in the storage room at the back of the gymnasium. I have unstacked the chairs and they speak to me: *Speak the truth, Bindy! Do not fail!*

Also the chairs murmur: *Why has Bindy unstacked us?*

The chairs are right.

I will restack them. Why should I help the Venomous Seven to their seats?

No. It is too late. Here come Emily and Astrid. *Let it begin.*

4.

Bindy Mackenzie
24 CLIPPING DRIVE, KELLYVILLE, NSW 2155

The Director
Office of the Board of Studies, NSW

Dear Sir (or Madam),
I am a student at Ashbury High, a mediocre school in Sydney's windswept Hills District, and I wrote to you last week.

I am surprised that you have not replied. Did you receive my letter? Did you read the enclosed report?

I suppose you may be busy. You are, after all, responsible for the education and future of this state. (I had assumed that my own education and future would therefore be relevant to you. But perhaps I have mistook.)

Now, when I sent my report last week, I thought that it spoke for itself. I thought there was no need for me to direct you to the obvious. But perchance on this topic too my thoughts were

amiss? For instance, when you read the report, did you happen
to notice that:

1. We spent most of our first FAD session opening
   and closing the concertina wall.
2. When not manipulating the concertina wall, we
   talked about animals.
3. When not talking about animals, we passed papers
   around the room.
4. The reason we talked about animals, and passed
   papers around the room, was to help the teacher
   remember our names.
5. The teacher was utterly unable to recall our names.
6. By contrast, we all remembered her name.
7. Her name is Try Montaine.

Furthermore, please note that the course is entitled *Friendship
and Development.* Yet our friendships have already been formed
and set in stone. And *my* development is quite complete, thank
you very much. I can't speak for the others on that issue, but as far
as *sex* is concerned, I believe they have developed off the charts.

I am enclosing a report of the second session, which took
place today. I draw your attention to the fact that:

1. I have no time to take a kickboxing class.

And I remain:
Bindy Mackenzie

× × ×

REPORT ON FRIENDSHIP AND DEVELOPMENT (FAD),
PREPARED FOR THE OFFICE OF
THE BOARD OF STUDIES, NSW

By Bindy Mackenzie

Session 2

The session took place, once again, in the storage room at the back of the gymnasium.

I arrived first and sat in the circle of chairs; the others arrived in a flood, viz.:

- Emily and Astrid, in a frenzy of talk;
- Sergio joining them with a single ironic line (which I could not quite hear) that made Emily and Astrid laugh;
- Toby, talking to himself and doing a curious ostrich-style walk;
- Briony, daydreaming such that she almost bumped into Toby;
- Elizabeth, bright-eyed in T-shirt and tracksuit pants, and alongside her:
- Finnegan Blonde, actually taking Elizabeth's tracksuit pant cloth between his fingers, tugging it slightly — and letting it go.

When Finnegan touched Elizabeth's clothing in this way, he

said something solemn in a low voice. Elizabeth nodded like a mystic.

Just as this group poured through the concertina wall, the tiny teacher emerged from the fire escape.

She rushed toward the others, as a stream might rush to join a river.

They blended together and chatted excitedly like rapids.

I stayed in my chair like a rock.

It turned out that the excitement was about the summer storm brewing outside. The day had turned heavy with darkness. It would *pour rain* any moment, they all agreed (in some amazement).

There would be thunder!

There might be lightning!

"And these are things you've never experienced before?" I queried (cuttingly).

But Elizabeth was speaking: "There's a rainbow out there." She was pointing through the window to a faint curve of pink amongst the gray. A charm bracelet jangled faintly on her wrist.

"What does it mean?" Emily said, in a low, panicked voice: "What does it mean if a rainbow comes before rain?"

"You know what those clouds remind me of?" said Astrid, and Emily dropped her wide-eyed look at once. She took a Toblerone out of her pocket and peeled back the foil, while Astrid declared: "Those clouds remind me of a knee."

Every head tilted in surprise. Emily, biting off a pyramid of chocolate, said, "Astrid, what the FLAX?"

"Okay, remember when we went on that school trip to Hill End in Year 8? And we had to, like, gold-pan in the creek?" Astrid began. "And so, Sergio was kind of like running through the water, 'cause he wanted to get to the best gold, like acting like he knew where it was? And the rocks were like, *so* slippery. So he goes flying and lands on his knee on these rocks and there was like *blood* just like *bleeding* everywhere, and then later? His knee was so bruised. It was like FOXGLOVE blue and FOXGLOVE yellow and even FOXGLOVE *purple*."

"What a great way of describing a stormy sky," said Try serenely. "Like a bruised knee."

"You remember that?" Sergio stared at Astrid. "That was three years ago."

"I forgot we even went to Hill End," said Toby, and then began a nonsensical chant about gold-panning in Hill End.

"And yet your lyrics suggest that you remember it well," I said to him (acerbically).

But Astrid and Sergio were dancing in time to Toby's chant and his focus was not on me, it was on them.

"We were so like trashed that day?" Astrid said nostalgically, breaking away from the dance. "And I always remember everything that happens when I'm trashed. It's kind of like a thing about me, like a reversal? Because I remember FOXGLOVE nothing from when I'm not trashed."

I took a deep breath. "You would have us believe," I began (scornfully), "that inebriation enhances recollection?!"

Astrid glanced at me with an expression I have seen her use in

Maths when she does not comprehend what her textbook is saying and, further, holds the textbook responsible.

Meanwhile, Sergio had placed his foot up on the chair beside mine and was rolling up his trouser leg to reveal his knee. Everyone moved in closer. The knee was white, knobbly, and hair-sprouting.

"Did you imagine the bruise from Hill End would still *be* there?" I laughed (bitingly).

But Sergio was pointing to a fine white line, which he said was his "wicked-ass" scar from that very fall, on the rocks, in Hill End.

There was the slightest pause.

I think we were all thinking the same thing: If that fine line on his knee was a "wicked-ass" scar, what was the scar on his face? Sergio has a burn scar, you see, which begins just below his right eye, dips down toward his mouth, and extends out to his ear. It takes the form of raised white bumps with tangled red threads between them.

"Maybe you should have got stitches?" suggested Try, touching the small scar on his knee.

"It's not too late," suggested Toby. "Alls I need's a needle and thread."

And they all stepped back to talk about the storm once again.

"Well!" said Try, in a teacherly voice, and *Finally*, I thought to myself as we sat down in our circle.

It seemed that Try had changed. Her hair, with all its fine plaits, was twirled into a bun at the base of her neck this week.

She was wearing more straightforward jeans and a shirt that covered her belly button ring. Instead of a handbag: a blue wicker basket. Even her *accent* seemed stronger.

She held both hands flat in the air and said, "Okay, before we get started, I just want to say I have a bunch of ideas for how this course should run." She placed her basket on her lap.

"And," she said, "I want *our* group to have *more* fun, and be even *closer*, and just *way* better than all the other FAD groups, okay?"

Obligingly, the group responded by embracing the discourse of the television franchise *Survivor*. That is, they talked about tribal names, immunity challenges, and voting people out of the storage room.

Try waited patiently, and then she continued.

"As well as these Wednesday afternoons"— she said —"and I've got a surprise about *those,* which I'll save for now — I want us to have nights out, camping trips, weekends away, ski trips, pajama parties, séances, you name it!"

She was taking neat piles of paper from her basket as she talked, and was setting them out on her knees.

The papers, I could see, all began in large bold print: **Dear Parents.**

Things had gone much too far.

"Well, look," I said. "Are we really going to have time for extracurricular activities this year? I mean, maybe we should just limit ourselves to these Wednesdays? And actually, we could think about meeting every *second* Wednesday? We could use the alternate weeks as study periods." I had a flash of inspiration. "That way, we *would* be the best FAD group because we'd have the academic advantage. We'd get the best marks in the year!"

I noticed a strange quiver on that final word, which is why it became "YEAR!" I had meant simply to say "year."

After my speech, there was a moment's silence and then there was a burst of applause.

Or so it seemed, for a moment, to me.

Actually, the rain had begun outside.

"That's just rain," explained Astrid.

There was a chuckle from Briony, and we glanced at her in surprise. "How about that!" our glances seemed to say. "Briony's in the room!"

Briony folded her arms, so we looked away and forgot her again.

"Well," said Try, biting her lip and frowning down at the papers on her knees. "Well, I guess you might be right, Bindy, about . . ."

"Let's see," Emily interrupted, and almost fell off her chair as she reached toward the papers. Try gave me an apologetic shrug, and began to pass the notes around.

"These are permission slips," she said, "relating to the . . . extracurricular activities I'd like us to . . . but, anyhow, let's see what your parents think before we take that any further! And for *today*, let's start the Buddy Plan!"

The *Buddy Plan.*

"The Buddy Plan?" I said. "Is this a recruitment session for McDonald's employees?"

"No," said Astrid. "I doubt it."

"Remember," said Try, "remember how I said that school — that being a *teenager* — is a bit like drowning? So your FAD group is your life raft? Well, when you're out at sea, I think you need a buddy. A person whose special job it is to keep an eye on you — and it's your job to keep an eye on —"

"I am not," I announced, "a teenager."

"Excuse me?" said Try.

"You said that being a teenager is like drowning," I explained. "But I want to make it clear that *I'm* not drowning because I, personally, am not, and never have been, a teenager."

Once again, everyone turned to me in silence.

"How old are you?" Finnegan asked eventually.

"That's not the point," I said. "The point is that being a teenager is just a cliché. Teenagerdom is a social construct with all these related *teen problems*, which are just not a part of my life! Problems like *sex* and *drugs* and *eating disorders* and *broken families* and *divorced parents* and *vandalism* and *glandular fever.*"

"Sex is a problem?" Sergio looked surprised.

"What I'm *talking* about —" I tried.

"I thought we were talking about the Buddy Plan." Elizabeth leaned over to retie her running shoes.

"We were," Emily agreed. "Bindy, why don't you wait until you get your buddy and then you and your buddy can really

FOXGLOVE get *in* to the topic of your social construction site or whatever it is you're talking about, okay? And let Try get on with — with her renovation?"

I stared, confused, and then laughed aloud. "I assume you mean her innovation?" I said (witheringly).

"No, she was making a connection with the construction site metaphor," Sergio explained. "Nice, Em."

Try was talking over him: "Bindy, you're saying some interesting things here, and I'd love to discuss them. Please know that you — or, for that matter, *any* of you — can come and see me in my office anytime you like. Why not swing by for a chat about these issues of yours, Bindy? And in the meantime, is it okay if we talk about the Buddy Plan today?"

Construction site? These issues of *mine*?

Had they all misunderstood me completely?

Certainly, I will not be "swinging by" for a chat!

I simply stared.

"The Buddy Plan," repeated Try, resuming her enthusiastic accent. She ran her eyes around our circle. "I'm going to start by putting you in pairs," she explained. "So! You and you are a pair." She pointed at Emily and Astrid. Emily kissed the top of Astrid's head and Astrid, ceremoniously, did the same to her.

"And you two," Try continued, pointing at Elizabeth and Sergio, who nodded at each other gravely, "and *Bindy*, you can be with . . ." She paused for the first time, her eyes traveling around the circle. "Bindy can be with Finnegan."

53

I did not look at his face, so I don't know how he reacted. Certainly, he did not kiss the top of my head.

"So that leaves you two." She pointed at Toby and Briony, and Toby, inexplicably, picked up his notebook and slapped Briony across the knees. Briony seemed unsurprised.

"You must always be available for your buddy," said Try, "and from now on, if anything is worrying you, please go straight to him or her."

"Astrid," said Emily. "I finished my Toblerone."

Astrid stood up at once, knocking over her chair, and looking about her, one hand on Emily's shoulder. "STAY RIGHT WHERE YOU ARE," she shouted. "I'M GETTING YOU A NEW TOBLERONE." She began lifting gym mats and climbing stacks of chairs.

"That's the way," said Try, laughing. "Anyway, you can sit down now, Astrid. I *had* planned to start off with some trust exercises — you know, you fall backward into your buddy's arms and trust your buddy to catch you; you tie your hands together and lead each other around blindfolded? But these are things to do outside and that's not in the cards today! Astrid, okay, that was pretty funny. Sit down for now. As I was saying, we'll do trust another time."

Now she was taking out *another* set of papers.

It was entitled "Buddy Contract," but it looked like a questionnaire.

"Now and then," said Try, "I'd like you to write a few

paragraphs — a kind of Buddy Diary — about how the Buddy Plan is working for you. For now, I'm going to send you off to fill in these contracts. But where to send you? If only the gym were empty . . ."

Then she tilted her head and said, "Hey. *Is* the gym empty? Weren't there kids in there doing a gym class last week?"

Everyone stared at the concertina wall.

"If they're in there," said Toby. "They're *very, very* quiet."

"Maybe they're sleeping?" suggested Emily.

"That reminds me," said Sergio, turning to Try. "When do we all start sleeping together?"

"I doubt we'll sleep together," said Astrid. "We'll SORGHUM each other's brains out though."

"Well now, hang on," said Try.

"Check in Try's basket," suggested Toby. "She'll have the paperwork."

"Permission slips for our parents," murmured Elizabeth.

"Don't worry, Try," Emily said. "We'll be *way* better at it than every other FAD group."

"Do we get to sleep with everyone or just our buddy?" Sergio wondered, at which Elizabeth crossed her legs (once), Toby slapped Briony's knees (again), and Briony began to bite her nails.

(Now, can I just point something out? During our Year Assembly last week, the Year Coordinator welcomed us and said this: "When you left us at the end of Year 10 last year, you were kids. Today, you sit before me as adults."

I must give him a copy of the above conversation.)

Fortunately, Try jumped to her feet, opened the concertina wall, and revealed that the gym was empty.

"Find a corner with your buddy," she said, "away from everyone else, and fill in these forms. Come back in twenty minutes and I'll tell you my surprise!"

There is a raised stage at the front end of the gymnasium, with a small flight of steps leading up to it. Finnegan Blonde led me there. He has a comfortable walk. His hair continues to surprise me by being such a pale, golden blonde. It's rather like the sunshine on white sand. I suppose he comes from a sandy place — the beaches of northern Queensland.

He sat on the edge of the stage, and I sat on the staircase next to him. There were other pairs in various places around the gym, but we couldn't hear their voices for the rain. Meanwhile, the storm made the gymnasium eerily dark.

We both looked down at the form in our hands.

"So," said Finnegan. "You want to start?"

I need not bore you with the details of the form-filling, or with everything that Finnegan said. I need only say that I now have to take a class in kickboxing.

Finnegan must improve his marks.

Try called us from the opening of the concertina wall, "Okay, come on back now! I have to tell you my surprise!"

I felt relieved to be finished with the "Buddy Session."

I walked back quickly, not looking at Finnegan Blonde.

There was a strange scurry to sit down, as if this were musical chairs.

"Okay, are you ready?" Try's eyes sparkled excitedly.

Even I became intrigued.

"Here's the surprise! Okay, this storage room is really no place to meet, right? It's small, it's dusty, it's ridiculous." Everyone nodded. "So, I've got us another room and wait until you hear where it is? You ready? *It's in Castle Hill!* No, I'm not kidding! I've checked your timetables and turns out you all have a free period directly after FAD. So, we've got plenty of time to get back to school before final roll call. *And* I've found this great café in Castle Hill called the Blue Danish which has this room that groups can use, and they've said we can use it every week! *What do you think?!*"

This was preposterous.

I could not believe what I was hearing.

Outrage billowed within me, even as the others were congratulating Try, and laughing at her (because everyone knows the Blue Danish already — it's one of their favorite cafés) and Try was sitting back with a grin.

"Excuse me," I said in a strident voice. "I assume this is a joke?"

Try's smile began to fade.

I noticed with alarm that my own mouth was trembling. I pressed my feet firmly on the ground and continued: "A free period is not a *free* period, it's a study period. Getting back to school from Castle Hill every week would cut that study period in *half,* nay, it would *devour* that period! You don't realize how important that is?"

Now Try was biting her lip, while the others fell silent one by one.

The bell rang.

"Hey Bindy," said Emily, as if I had not been speaking. "Have you talked to Mrs. Lilydale this week?"

The others took the opportunity to gather their bags and leave. I heard the following comments: "See you at the Blue Danish next week," "They have the *best* coffee," and "You gotta love their raspberry friands." I even heard someone say: "What's up Bindy's ARROWGRASS?" and someone else respond: "She's always like that."

I turned to Emily.

"No," I said calmly. "I haven't seen Mrs. Lilydale this week. Ernst said she wanted me, but I couldn't find her at lunchtime — how did you know she was looking for me?"

"She's going to tell you who the new person is on your debating team," Emily said. She was swinging her bag from arm to arm as she spoke.

"FLAX me," said Astrid grimly, as Emily's bag smacked her in the stomach.

"FLAX," said Emily, "are you okay?" But Astrid had already recovered and was taking Emily's elbow to drag her toward the door.

"How do you . . . ?" I began.

"It's me," said Emily, over her shoulder. "I'm going to be on your debating team."

Then she and Astrid were gone.

My head began to ache.

× × ×

A Memo from Bindy Mackenzie

To: Mrs. Lilydale
From: Bindy Mackenzie
Subject: The Death of Debating
Time: Wednesday, 2:40 p.m.

Dear Mrs. Lilydale,

I tried to find you at lunchtime and I've just looked for you again, but no luck.

I guess you want to see me to discuss a new second speaker? Coincidentally, Emily Thompson has mentioned that *she* wants to join the team! I assume this is some kind of misunderstanding.

As you know, debating is very important to me — I probably won't stay on the team next year, because of concentrating on the HSC. So this is my last chance to win the Tearsdale Shield (again).

It would be great if you could clear up this confusion as soon as possible! Ernst and I are happy to discuss a new member, and naturally, we would *consider* E.T. — along with all the other options.

Sincerely,

Bindy Mackenzie

× × ×

A Memo from Bindy Mackenzie

To: Ernst von Schmerz
From: Bindy Mackenzie
Subject: DISASTER
Time: Wednesday, 2:45 p.m.

Dear Ernst,
EMILY THOMPSON THINKS *SHE'S* GOING TO BE SECOND
SPEAKER.

(I know.) (Say no more.) (Me neither. I can't believe it either.)

I went straight to find Mrs. Lilydale, but she's still not in her office so I put a memo under her door. But I could hardly come right out and say that Emily is too stupid, could I? (Mrs. L. surely knows that already. Or at least she has access to Emily's class records?)

What does Emily think she's doing, anyway? Isn't she too "cool" for debating? Why would she sink to our level?

Come and find me in the library as soon as you get this! I'll be there for a while after school, but not too long as I have to baby-sit.

I'll keep trying Mrs. L.'s office sporadically through the afternoon. If I find her, don't despair, I will convince her of her folly.

Best,
B.

P.S. Your "philosophical musing" poem was great. Very funny.

× × ×

A Memo from Ernst von Schmerz

To: Bindy Mackenzie
From: Ernst von Schmerz
Subject: And Yet
Time: Wednesday, after school some time

Yo Bind,
Emily Thompson on our team? Rock my kingdom like a cradle, Bind, that's total. Why you trippin? Emily is flippin and fly. I dig that chick.

Take some serenity, B: If Em joins our team, it will be both gangsta and inspired. That's my view, anyhow, so fry it up anyway you like.

Would love to chat, nevertheless, I must leave this at your locker. And will blog on the issue of Emily some time, so check it out should you like to. If only I had time to seek you in your dominion, but I don't as I must run thru the rain to my transcendental chat room.

Ernst

P.S. But what do you mean about Emily "sinking" to our "level"?

$$\times\ \times\ \times$$

A Memo from Bindy Mackenzie

To: Mrs. Lilydale
From: Bindy Mackenzie
Subject: Apologies
Time: Wednesday, 4 p.m.

Dear Mrs. Lilydale,

I must apologize for my slight outbreak of temper in your office just now. I'm sure you understand: It was just that I feel very strongly about this issue. And I was so surprised that you couldn't see my point of view!

As I said to you, I *really* think it's a mistake letting Emily on the team. It spells DOOM for debating! It spells SPONTANEOUS COMBUSTION for the Tearsdale Shield! (It's mainly made of wood, remember.) Think about it: When has Emily even shown the slightest glimmer of interest before? I doubt she even really knows what debating is. Don't you remember how disrespectful she was to *you* when she played at being a "lawyer" last year? She'll never show up, you know — she'll disrespect debating too, preferring parties, shopping, or some other phenomenon of teenage life.

Let's choose someone else for the team. I'm sure Emily won't mind, and I hope with all my heart that you agree.

Bindy Mackenzie

× × ×

FROM THE TRANSCRIPT FILE
OF BINDY MACKENZIE

Wednesday

4:25 p.m., on the bus, on the way to "baby-sitting" for Eleanora.

Boy in the aisle speaks to a girl: 'Cause that's why you eat chocolate, 'cause serotonin gets released in the brain.

Girl replies: Yeah, I was thinking, if you, like, ate chocolate and then gave someone a hug? It'd be like sensory overload. (*She shakes her folded umbrella, holds it up, and says*) Are you umbrella aware?

× × ×

TO: cecily.mackenzie@mackenzieworld.com.au; mackenziepaul@mackenzieenterprises.com.au
FROM: bindy.mackenzie@ashburyhigh.com.au
SENT: Wednesday, 9:30 p.m.
SUBJECT: Permission . . .

Dear Mum and Dad,
Hi there! How are you both? I'm well, thanks, though busy — we've already got a superabundance of homework. The teachers must think we have access to alternate universes in which we can draw on unlimited resources of time! And somehow

I have to find time for Kmart, baby-sitting, and piano practice (and lessons) as well!

Meanwhile, life here is chaotic. Auntie Veronica and Uncle Jake are great, and Bella is adorable — but that family has the vocal powers of kakapo birds!

Auntie Veronica and I have breakfast together every day, because we both get up early, and both like pink grapefruit with a light dusting of sugar. And I'll tell you something funny. Sometimes, Veronica will suddenly drop her spoon onto the table with a clatter, and then she will half shout: "Bindy Mackenzie!"

At this, I gasp with fright, and then I say hesitantly: "Yes?"

But she simply picks up her spoon again, shakes her head to herself, and says, "Bindy Mackenzie at my breakfast table. How superb."

Uncle Jake sleeps in every day and hardly ever goes to university. He locks himself in his study with a sign on his door that says NO ENTRY. Despite the sign, Bella wanders in all the time. And the other day I heard Jake say: "Bella, can't you read?" and Bella replied, "Yes, Daddy, I can read, but the words fall out of my head."

She's so funny.

She really can read, you know. And she's only four years old. Veronica and I both think she's ready for school, regardless of whether the words fall out of her head.

Anyway, how are things in the city?

I hope your ventures are succeeding beyond your wildest dreams.

Could one of you do me a favor? I'm supposed to get permission to go on some excursions for a new course called Friendship and Development. It isn't assessable, and I cannot see its point. I'll scan in the relevant notes. I'd be grateful for your feedback.

Best,

Bindy

TO: bindy.mackenzie@ashburyhigh.com.au
FROM: cecily.mackenzie@mackenzieworld.com.au
SENT: Wednesday, 9:30 p.m.
SUBJECT: OUT OF OFFICE AUTO-REPLY

Cecily Mackenzie will be unable to read your e-mail until Thursday of next week. If your message is urgent, please contact Cecily's assistant, Megan, at megan.donahue@mackenzie world.com.au.

TO: bindy.mackenzie@ashburyhigh.com.au
FROM: mackenziepaul@mackenzieenterprises.com.au
SENT: Wednesday, 9:55 p.m.
SUBJECT: Re: Permission . . .

Dear Bindy,

Hi there, yourself.

Permission granted, as requested.

Best,

Dad

5.

My Buddy Diary
By Bindy Mackenzie

Wednesday, Midnight
How is the Buddy Plan working for me? Why, perfectly, thank you. I don't know how I ever got by without it.

Of course, the Buddy Plan only began today, so it might be too early to tell. But I'm convinced my life will change for the better having Finnegan Blonde for a friend. He's new at the school and has already made some "buddies" of his own, and yet . . . something tells me he'll rush to me whenever he needs someone to talk to. I expect us to have midnight feasts, ride on seesaws together, and tell each other our secrets. (I also expect the sky to rain silver pennies, and fairies to dance on my windowsill.)

Am I being honest with my buddy? Well, today, he asked what "troubled" me. I said that I excel at so many subjects I worry my talents may be diluted.

He tried to look sympathetic, but when your eyebrows want to jump up off your forehead, there's not much you can do to stop them.

At least, when he asked about a "happy time" for me, I told him about how sometimes, when I play the piano, my little cousin comes in and dances around the living room, and shouts, "Keep the music! Keep the music!" as soon as I stop playing. Finnegan's eyebrows calmed at this. I showed him the photos of Bella that I keep on my mobile phone. Bella has a sweet, round face. She has dark hair cut into a short, shiny bob, and she always wears denim overalls: some with flowers embroidered at the knees, others with brightly colored patches. Finnegan scrolled through the photos patiently.

"And what's going on here?" he said, at one point.

"That's just an illusion," I explained. "My brother, Anthony, was walking down the stairs when I took the photo so it looks like he's kicking Bella in the head. But he's not. My brother would never do that."

"Your brother would never kick Bella in the head," Finnegan repeated, nodding. I noticed the mist of a smile.

The strangest thing happened at that moment: I almost told him the secret about Anthony. It has been troubling me. But I was silent.

When it came time to set me a "Buddy Challenge," he told me I had to take a kickboxing class.

The Buddy Contract

1. *What is your buddy's Name?*

Finnegan A. Blonde

2. *Ask your buddy for his/her phone number—now program the number into your mobile phone!*

3. *What is something that troubles your buddy?*

He forgot to bring an umbrella today.

4. *When is a "happy time" for your buddy?*

Nighttime.

5. *Ask your buddy a question of your choosing. Put the question and his/her answer here.*

I asked Finnegan how his marks were at his old school last year. His response was as follows: "Last year was not a great year."

6. *Set your buddy a worthwhile challenge for the year ahead. Write the challenge here.*

I have challenged Finnegan to improve his marks this year.

7. *Get your buddy to add his name and signature to this declaration:*

I, Finnegan A. Blonde, *solemnly and sincerely promise that I will always turn to my buddy when I need someone to talk to — night or day, rain or shine, thunder, lightning, or avalanche . . .*

Signed: *Finnegan A. Blonde*

8. *Now get your buddy to add his name and signature to this declaration:*

I, Finnegan A. Blonde, *solemnly and sincerely promise that I will always be available for my buddy if he/she needs someone to talk to — night or day, rain or shine, thunder, lightning, or avalanche . . .*

Signed: *Finnegan A. Blonde*

6.

A Memo from Bindy Mackenzie

To: Emily Thompson
From: Bindy Mackenzie
Subject: Komodo Dragons
Time: Thursday, 5 a.m.

Dear Emily,

As you are considering joining my debating team, I thought you ought to know about our traditions!

First, we give all team members practice debates every couple of days until the season begins. Accordingly, please prepare the affirmative argument for the following topic:

That those who employ foul language are staining the fabric of our society.

Please deliver your argument to me as soon as possible.

Second, we give each of our speakers a token animal. This helps to build team spirit.

I have decided that your token animal is the *komodo dragon*.

You are so very similar to a komodo dragon! From now on, you must be known as Emily the Komodo Dragon.

Some information for you to keep in mind:

1. You are the largest lizard in the world.
2. You are cold-blooded and vicious.
3. You kill other animals by biting them, which gives them blood poisoning.
4. Why does this give them blood poisoning? Because your mouth is full of filthy, diseased bacteria.

I suggest you walk around the school in the style of a komodo dragon: Drop to your hands and knees and slither along the corridors; stick out your tongue whenever an insect flies by; and so on. Use your imagination.

Best wishes,

Bindy Mackenzie

× × ×

TO: mackenziepaul@mackenzieenterprises.com.au
FROM: bindy.mackenzie@ashburyhigh.com.au
SENT: Thursday, 5:10 a.m.
SUBJECT: Re: Re: Permission . . .

Dear Dad,
Thanks for trying, but I'm afraid an e-mail is not enough. The school needs "written permission" for extracurricular activities.

More to the point, did you read the notes? What do you think of these FAD activities? A terrible waste of time, perhaps? Let me know.

On an unrelated matter, I have two funding applications, first, for driving lessons (you may recall that I got my learner's permit over the holidays), and second, for gym membership (I need to take a kickboxing class for the FAD course — see my last e-mail for details of this course). May I please use the credit card for these activities?

Thanks and
Best,
Bindy

TO: megan.donahue@mackenzieworld.com.au
FROM: bindy.mackenzie@ashburyhigh.com.au
SENT: Thursday, 5:20 a.m.
SUBJECT: Message for My Mother

Dear Megan,
Hello, how are you? I'll never forget how much fun we had at Mum's office Christmas party that time when I was seven and you brought along the Slip 'n' Slide.

Anyway, I understand my mother is out of town and I wondered if you were passing on messages to her? I e-mailed her yesterday and it would be great if she could see that e-mail (and its attachments).

Thanks so much and best wishes,
Bindy Mackenzie

× × ×

The Philosophical Musings of Bindy Mackenzie

Thursday, 5:30 a.m.

How simple it is to right the world when it seems to fall askew! A sleepless, dreamless night gives way to a flash of inspiration: *three letters*. One need only write three letters (a memo and two e-mails) to find oneself again! Three letters written and o-n-e is found! Ready for a full day of work!

5:40 a.m.

And yet, how the world seems to jangle and jar when one's head is empty of sleep.

---

6 a.m.

Even if one feels exhausted and ill, and even if one's head aches, yet to succeed one mu

× × ×

A Memo from Bindy Mackenzie

To: Auntie Veronica
From: Bindy
Subject: Today
Time: Thursday, 6:02 a.m.

Dear Auntie Veronica,

This note is at the breakfast table rather than me, because I am going back to bed. I'm not feeling that great and I think I'll have to miss school today.

Love,

Bindy

× × ×

Nighttime Musings of Bindy Mackenzie

Friday, 11:30 p.m.

After a day of illness (yesterday), I returned to school today.

The first thing I did was take out my memo to Emily Thompson and tape it to her locker.

Then, at lunchtime, I happened upon Emily with her two best friends. Their names are Lydia and Cassie. The three of them were sitting with their legs stretched out before them, leaning against the wall in the lower courtyard. They like to sun themselves there.

Allow me to digress for a moment to admit some confusion: Why is a friendship flourishing between Emily and Astrid in our FAD group? Astrid is not part of Emily's threesome! And what need has Emily for a new friend? (More than a friend now — a *buddy*.) What do Emily's two best friends think of her new alliance? Does it not irk them?

For let me say this: The threesome of Emily, Lydia, and Cassie is such a close-knit one that it breathes new life into three-related words such as:

triplication

trisection

triumvirate

In short, I cannot look at Emily and her two best friends without thinking at once of optional triangulation and its effect on the symmetry of three-dimensional quasi-crystals.

(I mentioned this to Emily once and found her response quite cutting.)

(You know, I once saw a pair of substitute teachers arguing about the talents of a Polish exchange student. When one lost her temper and slapped the other, I handed my card to the victim, saying: "I should be honored to act as your witness." That teacher used precisely the same cutting words as Emily.)

But enough digression. Today, at least, the threesome seemed cozy as ever, despite Emily's betrayal.

I had a wall of schoolwork to catch up on, since yesterday had been lost, and I should have crossed directly to the library. I hate losing a day of schoolwork, and lunchtimes are valuable to me.

But I could not resist.

I had to know Emily's response to my memo.

So I slowed my steps slightly as I passed the reclining trinity.

"Hey, Bindy?" said one of Emily's two friends (Lydia) just as my shadow crossed her.

I looked at her, apprehensive.

She put one hand to her forehead to shield her eyes from the sun. "Say hi to your mum for me, would you?"

"For me too." Cassie smiled sleepily. (Sunshine makes the three girls drowsy.)

"Your mum's so cool," added Lydia, apparently without a trace of irony. She sighed and stretched her arms, much as a cat would stretch its arms, if you could picture for a moment a cat with slender brown arms.

Here I must point out that Emily and her two best friends spent the summer at my mother's sailing school.

"How curious," I almost said, "that you three spent the summer with my mother, whereas I did not."

But I kept my mouth closed. (So much for the new, ruthless Bindy. Is she afraid of the triumvirate?)

Emily was staring. I wondered, my heart beating wildly: Had she got my memo yet? Had it rendered her, of all people, speechless?

But just as I myself lost courage and continued on my way, promising to say hi to my mother ("Or at least to her assistant," I added — "What?" they said — "Nothing," I replied) — just as I'd passed by with that exchange, Emily said the following: "Bindy."

It was a command.

I turned.

She held her hand out to me, and I looked at it, confused. Did she wish me to help her to her feet? So she could punch me in the nose? I would not!

"See my wristband?" she said.

There was a strip of red paper curled around her wrist. And some kind of animal was sketched, in squiggly black ink, onto the red.

"It's a komodo dragon," Emily explained. (It was not.)

"Is it?" I ventured.

"Yeah. I'll do that speech thing you want me to do, the one about stain removal? I'll do it on the weekend. But I made this as a tribute to the team. Because *I am the komodo dragon*." She assumed a hoarse, dramatic voice, and Cassie giggled. Now she touched the wristband, and Lydia leaned over and tightened it for her.

"You like it?" said Emily, holding it up toward me again.

There was no doubt about it.

She was proud.

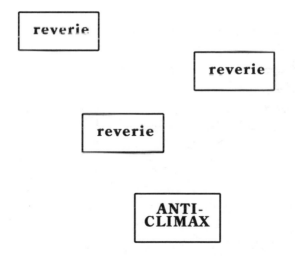

7.

TO: bindy.mackenzie@ashburyhigh.com.au
FROM: megan.donahue@mackenzieworld.com.au
SENT: Monday, 9 a.m.
SUBJECT: Message for Your Mother!!

Dear Bindy,

Great to hear from you! Although I have to say, I have no idea what you're talking about — a Christmas party with a Slip 'n' Slide? I have a vague memory of Christmas parties, but what's a Slip 'n' Slide? Well, I guess I'll take your word for it . . . glad you had fun at the party.

I've told your mum you'd like to speak with her. She actually does check e-mail while she's on the road — that auto-reply is just for the sake of clients — so she would have got your e-mail the other day. I'm sure you'll hear back soon!

Cheers,

Megan

Assistant to Cecily Mackenzie

Mackenzie World Pty Ltd

TO: bindy.mackenzie@ashburyhigh.com.au
FROM: mackenziepaul@mackenzieenterprises.com.au
SENT: Monday, 10:30 a.m.
SUBJECT: Re: Re: Re: Permission . . .

Dear Bindy,

If your school needs "written permission" for "extracurricu-blahdy blah," why don't you just print out my previous e-mail and take that along?

Re: your funding requests: Driving lessons do not fall into the terms of our agreement (required education expenses), so they'll have to come out of your own pocket.

Assuming gym membership is compulsory for school, that's fine, use the credit card.

When can I expect your next Business Proposal?

Best,

Dad

TO: mackenziepaul@mackenzieenterprises.com.au
FROM: bindy.mackenzie@ashburyhigh.com.au
SENT: Monday, 1 p.m.
SUBJECT: The Point of Permission

Dear Dad,

I think the point is that we need to get your *signature* for per-missions. A printed-out e-mail won't suffice. Perhaps I should resend the FAD notes, so you could print them out and read them?

At least then you'd know what you were permitting. You might even exercise your right to *refuse* permission! Who knows?

With respect, I believe that a case can be made that driving lessons are directly related to my education. If I had my license, I could drive myself to school each day, and to Kmart, baby-sitting, and piano, thus saving time now wasted on public transport. I would therefore have more time for study, and my education would benefit accordingly.

(Furthermore, I could drive into the city to visit you and Mum.)

Best,

Bindy

TO: bindy.mackenzie@ashburyhigh.com.au
FROM: mackenziepaul@mackenzieenterprises.com.au
SENT: Monday, 2:30 p.m.
SUBJECT: Re: The Point of Permission

Nice try, kid. But nobody likes a smart aleck.

You know you can visit your mum and me anytime. Just give a shout.

Get your Auntie Veronica or Uncle Jake to sign the permission forms for you. You have my permission to treat them as *in loco parentis*.

Best,

Dad

P.S. How's your brother, anyway? Do I assume he lives and breathes? I never hear from him. All getting along there?

TO: cecily.mackenzie@mackenzieworld.com.au
FROM: bindy.mackenzie@ashburyhigh.com.au
SENT: Monday, 3:30 p.m.
SUBJECT: Hello

Dear Mum,

I know you're on the road, but Megan tells me you still check your e-mail. Did you get my note last week about permission? And do you think you could talk to Dad about driving lessons? He thinks I should pay for them myself. I'm sure he's only saying this because he does't fully understand the economic benefits of my being able to drive. If you could just explain . . . ?

He also asks about Anthony a lot, and I don't know what to do. I wish we didn't have to keep this secret.

How was your weekend? Mine was just fine. On Saturday night, I baby-sat for my favorite client, Maureen Brentwood. Have I mentioned her to you? She's a new client, but she's already started giving me historic books as thoughtful gifts. I read them all the time. Furthermore, when I arrived on Saturday, she pointed out a plate of apple-and-cinnamon muffins, hidden at the top of a cupboard, and said they were for me!

"Word to the wise," she whispered, as she grabbed her keys. "Keep them hidden 'til the kids are safe in bed — turns out they've both got wheat allergies, and I'm sure you don't want them throwing up all night!"

I didn't know what to do, because, actually, I didn't feel like a muffin. I've been a bit unwell lately — I even stayed home from school last Thursday, and it's taking me a while to recover. In fact, I feel awful again today — but enough school was missed on Thursday. I will ignore these symptoms.

Anyhow, I crumbled the muffins into pieces and sprinkled them onto the lawn. Hopefully the birds will spot them.

On Sunday night, I was "baby-sitting" again, and you know, there is such contrast among people! Because this was for another new client, a woman named Eleanora White. And the reason I put "baby-sitting" in quotes is that *she doesn't go out*! She leads me through to the kitchen (where a bird perches in a cage), sits at the table, and makes *gnocchi*!

Apparently, I am there in case the baby wakes up while her hands are sticky. We sit opposite each other, drink tea, eat ginger biscuits, and talk. She asks about my interests and education, but her manner is so cold and distant! It's just as if the questions were a *test* rather than a conversation.

And here's something funny. I have been going there on Sundays and Wednesdays for a few weeks now, and the baby has never woken once.

Once, Eleanora looked at me sharply (mashed potato spilling from her hands). "Don't go into the baby's room," she said. "She's in that phase where she's terrified of strangers."

Now, do you see a logical flaw?

If I am not to go into the baby's room, then what, pray tell, is my purpose?!

At any rate, I spent the night reciting John Donne's poems to Eleanora and her budgerigar.

Best,

Bindy

TO: bindy.mackenzie@ashburyhigh.com.au
FROM: cecily.mackenzie@mackenzieworld.com.au
SENT: Monday, 3:30 p.m.
SUBJECT: OUT OF OFFICE AUTO-REPLY

Cecily Mackenzie will be unable to read your e-mail until Tuesday next week. If your message is urgent, please contact Cecily's assistant, Megan, at megan.donahue@mackenzieworld.com.au.

8.

*Here Are Some Lines from a Book
That Caught Bindy's Eye Today . . .*

On Mothers and Daughters:

[W]ho should hear of the daughter's aspirations, hopes, and secrets if not the mother? She it is that can safely and carefully direct the daughter's thoughts as they turn to the mysteries of life or the joy of youthful affection. Is not the mother rich in the experience of a tender love?

From *Twentieth Century Etiquette: An Up-to-Date Book for Polite Society, Containing Rules for Conduct in Public, Social and Private Life, at Home and Abroad, embellished with nearly half a hundred full-page engravings and numerous drawings,* by Annie Randall White (1900), p. 105.

9.

The Philosophical Musings of Bindy Mackenzie

Tuesday, 5:08 a.m.

Think of an aeroplane preparing for departure. It taxis into take-off position and aligns itself with the runway center line. The throttle advances smoothly; the plane accelerates; the engines roar — any moment there will be lift-off! And then, quite suddenly, everything stops.

The takeoff has been canceled.

What becomes, pray tell, of that buildup and acceleration? Nay, where does the roar and the energy go if denied its embrace with the sky?

5:15 a.m.

Now think of a girl approaching Wednesday afternoon. (Last Wednesday afternoon, to be precise.) She has spent a lifetime biting her tongue at the moronic behavior that surrounds her — responding to stupidity with sweetness — but now a decision has been made. She will no longer feign indifference. *Speak the truth!* she decides. *Keep nothing to yourself!* She is exhilarated,

85

terrified, on fire! She has advanced to takeoff position! She is aligned with the runway center line! Her engines roar — *let it begin,* she says.

And the Venomous Seven arrive.

5:18 a.m.

Oh, they were as stupid as ever. They were amazed that it was going to rain! They reflected on foolish accidents from a *stupid* school excursion to Hill End several years before! (I'm not surprised *Astrid* remembers that excursion.) They danced and climbed on furniture!

No, stupidity is not the problem. It's as rife as ever.

The problem was this: Their words looped between them and bound them tight. They formed a kind of ring that she could not penetrate. They were much like a circle of musk-ox protecting their calves from wolves.

She was cutting, biting, withering, acerbic, and scornful! Yet, they scarcely heard her, and when they did, they paid *not a flicker of heed.*

The inanity escalates — the teacher thought they should meet in Castle Hill! Emily Thompson thought she should debate! — but the girl's efforts to inject the light of truth led to nothing but vacant stares. . . .

5:22 a.m.

It is a canceled takeoff, a postponed pyrotechnic display . . .

So where did the girl's rapid heartbeat go? Where are her hopes and expectations?

5:35 a.m.

WELL, ALL I KNOW IS THIS:

I awoke the next morning with stomach cramps and a head-ache, feeling exhausted and ill. I threw up several times. And it seems pretty clear to me that my hopes and expectations, finding no relief, had turned themselves backwards onto ME.

5:43 a.m.

Of course, Auntie Veronica came down with the same symptoms the next day. She thinks we just caught the same flu.

5:45 a.m.

But NO!!

I do not believe that it was simply the flu!

I believe that I had suffered an acute attack of:

ANTI-CLIMAX

10.

Bindy Mackenzie
24 CLIPPING DRIVE, KELLYVILLE, NSW 2155

The Director
Office of the Board of Studies, NSW

Dear Sir (or Madam),
I am a student at Ashbury High, a loathsome school in Sydney's windswept Hills District, and I am writing to inform you that I will not write again.

I have written two letters to date and I have not received a reply. Although I find this astonishing, outrageous, and unforgivable, I will refrain from comment.

Enclosed is a brief report on the third session of FAD. It is more brief than my previous reports because I do not believe you are reading them. Nay, I do not imagine you even cast your eyes over the *envelopes*!

I considered *not even preparing this report*, but I am the sort of girl who follows things through.

Accordingly, I will continue to write reports, but I will not send them to you. I will keep them in my drawer at home, and, should you wish to peruse them, you had better get a search warrant. No, that is bitter humor. You need only contact me. But I will not hold my breath.

Disappointed, dismayed, and disbelieving, nevertheless, I remain:

Bindy Mackenzie

✕ ✕ ✕

BRIEF REPORT ON FRIENDSHIP AND DEVELOPMENT (FAD), PREPARED FOR THE OFFICE OF THE BOARD OF STUDIES, NSW

By Bindy Mackenzie

Session 3

Little happened of note in this, the third session of FAD, except that:

(A)   I missed the first fifteen minutes.

The session took place at the Blue Danish café. The bus to Castle Hill was surprisingly crowded and most of us had to stand in the aisle, occasionally grabbing at the back of a seat or someone else's ponytail for balance.

Prior to the bus trip I had found Try and explained that I did not have permission to leave the school grounds. "I'll just have to work in the library," I sighed apologetically.

"Good news," said Try, with a slow, shrewd grin. "Your mum mailed the slip in to me. Bindy, will you give me a chance?" Her tone slipped to a gentler key, and she added: "It must be rough on you, living away from your parents. Your mum mentioned it in her note. If you ever want to talk —" But we were standing in the senior common room. (I had been surprised to locate Try there — most teachers stay out of that student domain.) A crowd of Year 12s had just arrived and wanted to get past us to the coffee machine. I used the distraction to flee.

Upon arrival at Castle Hill, I excused myself to go to the bathroom, as I felt a little odd. I then became disoriented. I turned past an ice cream parlor that was certainly not there when I arrived; it must have been installed in the few moments while I was in the bathroom.

Eventually, I asked a woman in a pet supply shop for help.

The woman smiled and said, "This place can get confusing!" which almost made me cry. Her voice was so kind. She gave me directions, also pointing out a center directory, in case I got lost again.

I found my FAD group at the back of the Blue Danish, in a section made private by a richly brocaded curtain brushing the floor. They were seated on low, worn-looking orange armchairs, either perched on the very edge of the chair or slouching back into the springy cushions, legs stretched out and feet up on the coffee table.

Try had chosen a simple footstool to sit upon, leaving the last orange armchair for me. She is so tiny that the footstool seemed just right for her, like one of Bella's doll chairs. She had asked the group to describe an important event from the last week. "No events of note," I responded, when it came to my turn.

(B)   We discovered that Astrid is reincarnated.

Try explained that the next few weeks are going to be all about *us*. We are going to find out who we are.

"Well, I'm reincarnated," declared Astrid, her green eyes gazing around the group. "I know that much about me."

We all looked at Astrid with expressions that said: *Pray tell.*

She gave a modest shrug, so Sergio asked: "Who did you used to be?"

"Not 'who,'" said Astrid, shaking her long dark ponytail. "*What* did I used to be. That's the question."

"Okay, what did you used to be?" Toby obliged.

"A carnation," said Astrid. "I'm a reincarnated carnation. It's something I've kind of like always known." She shrugged modestly.

Finnegan examined Astrid's face. "I don't see it," he said, after a moment.

"Are you sure you weren't the fertilizer used to *grow* the carnation?" I said. "A trick of your memory there?" (Astrid, I should point out, is probably the most vicious girl in my year.) I hoped to make the group laugh with my comment, but it seemed to go unheard.

"That's a pretty flower," murmured Try. "The carnation."

"When did you — bloom?" said Sergio.

"Where?" said Elizabeth. "In a garden? Or a carnation farm?"

"Okay," said Emily. "Good. This is what I want to know: At what *exact* point did you die? If you just grew and then died, okay, fine, but what I want to know is, did someone pick you and put you in a vase, and if they did, did you get to be alive while you were in the vase and see the inside of the person's house or did you die as soon as you were picked and did that hurt?"

"Or were you in someone's lapel?" suggested Try.

(C)   **Toby behaved like a rock star.**

Try handed out questionnaires to help us find out who we are. She assured us that she did not want to see our answers.

"So you don't want to know who we are?" I asked.

"It's not that, it's just —" She was flustered.

Astrid rolled her eyes at me and said, "Confidentiality is *vital,* Bindy."

"In*deed*," I said meaningfully. I was not sure what I meant.

A sample page from my questionnaire is attached. It gives you the idea.

While we were filling in the forms, resting the papers on folders, or on books, or on our laps, Toby Mazzerati spoke in a low hissing voice and said: "Is everybody having a good time?!!" He cupped his hands around his mouth and made an urgent breathing noise.

I realized he was imitating a rock star at a concert. The breathing noise was supposed to be the sound of cheering.

We all continued writing.

(D)   Briony spoke three times.

At one point during the session, I observed that the tiles on the wall had a cylindrical pattern that reminded me a little of cucumbers.

"Sea cucumbers," I reflected, "have no brain. They live on decayed material that floats in the water, and they are poisonous."

Then I turned toward Briony and fixed my gaze upon her.

Immediately, I noticed a fly buzzing around the light-shade.

"That fly's big," I said.

The group regarded me uneasily.

"It puts me in mind of a Queen Alexandra's Birdwing," I continued. "That's the largest butterfly in the world. It's poisonous too." Now I turned toward Elizabeth and fixed my gaze upon *her*.

There was a moment of thoughtful silence in the group.

Then an extraordinary thing happened. Briony spoke. Her words sounded gravelly at first, but she cleared her throat and tried again, and what she said was this: "Sea cucumbers are related to sea stars and sand dollars."

"Really?" said Finnegan, his whole body turning toward her.

It is strange enough for Briony to speak once.

But guess what happened next? She spoke again.

"Also," she said, this time focusing on Finnegan's golden hair. He nodded his encouragement. "Also," she said, "sea cucumbers vomit out their own internal organs when something wants to eat them."

Astrid put down the friand she had just picked up.

"Wow," said Try, nodding with polite amazement. "How about that?"

And just when we thought that the wonders would never cease, Briony spoke a third time. "My mother's a marine biologist," she explained. "I don't know anything about butterflies, though." And looking at me, she concluded: "Sorry."

She grabbed her cappuccino, slurped from it, and blushed.

(E)   **Finnegan went to get sugar for Elizabeth, but Elizabeth explained that she didn't take sugar in her coffee, which led to some confusion as Finnegan had understood her to be *asking* him for sugar. It turned out that *Emily* had been the one asking, but Finnegan had mistook her voice for Elizabeth's.**

The above is self-explanatory.

(F)   **Everyone drank coffee.**

I suppose it *was* a café.

(G)   **Try invited everyone to her home for a "get-together" on Saturday.**

Extremely short notice, no?

Certainly, she is the only teacher I've known who has invited a class to her home.

I explained that I drew the line at spontaneous, unplanned, impulsive Saturday "get-togethers" and could not possibly attend.

(H)   **Try asked for my mother's phone number.**

I pretended not to hear.

Attachment to Report on Friendship and Development:
Sample page from my "Who Am I?" ("confidential") questionnaire

a) *The first thing I see when I wake up in the morning is . . .*
aus außer bei mit von nach zu zeit gegenüber
(German prepositions that take the dative case.) (They're on my wardrobe door.)

b) *The last thing I think about when I go to sleep each night is . . .*
hydrogen helium lithium beryllium boron carbon nitrogen oxygen . . .
(The periodic table.) (I recorded myself reciting it and play the tape every night.)

c) *Something I enjoy doing is . . .*
eavesdropping on strangers. I do this on the bus, around school, in shopping centers, and in libraries. I type up transcripts of their conversations on my laptop. I find transcripts intriguing.

d) *My favorite person to talk to is . . .*
my brother.

e) *A person I admire is . . .*
my father. He is ruthlessly ambitious and always succeeds.

f) *A person I miss sometimes is . . .*
Kelly Simonds. She was second speaker on my debating team last year, but has moved to Austria as an international exchange student.

My Buddy Diary
By Bindy Mackenzie

At the end of today's FAD session, I held the door of the Blue Danish open because I believed my buddy, Finnegan Blonde, was behind me. However, when I turned back, he was actually at the register, buying an extra takeaway coffee. Realizing my error, I let the door swing closed.

Another thing: After school, I joined the Castle Hill Gym to take kickboxing classes. This was in accordance with my buddy's challenge. The classes are on Tuesday afternoons, at the same time as my piano lessons. I am therefore unable to attend. I might try a hip-hop class instead.

× × ×

The Dream Diary of Bindy Mackenzie
Wednesday, 11:45 p.m.

Just got home from "baby-sitting" for Eleanora, and fell asleep at my desk. I dreamed I was wading, barefoot, knee-deep, through inky black mud. It was one of those dreams without much light — perhaps a lantern hovered at my chin, otherwise grim darkness. I tried not to mind the slow, warm ooze of the mud between my toes, but when it curled around my shins it seemed malevolent. And then I panicked as my foot landed on something coiled and hard — *just a root,* I thought, but my ankle brushed against skin. *Just a corpse*, I thought, and woke with a clamp around my chest.

× × ×

Nighttime Musings of Bindy Mackenzie

Thursday, 1 a.m.

Still can't sleep. My mind has wandered far from images of inky black mud. I am thinking, instead, of open doors.

Often I hold a door open because I think someone is behind me, and then I discover they are actually a long way back. There was the incident with Finnegan, but also, at Kmart the other day, I held a door for my supervisor, who has a knee-brace and walks with a cane. It took light-years for her to limp over, even though she tried to hurry so as not to hold me up. "Thanks," she panted, but I heard something *other* than thanks in her voice.

I therefore believe that I am not very good at:

judging distances

× × ×

Further Nighttime Musings of Bindy Mackenzie

Thursday, 2 a.m.

I have stomach cramps.

I wonder if training in archery or firearms might help to improve my ability to:

judge distances

Further Extended Nighttime Musings of Bindy Mackenzie

Thursday, 3 a.m.

At least, there is this: Today I revealed the poisonous souls of two more people — the sea cucumber and the Queen Alexandra's Birdwing butterfly.

Second Further Extended Nighttime Musings of Bindy Mackenzie

Thursday, 3:05 a.m.

Wait, no, it was not today, it was yesterday! Now it is the next day. It's early the next day, of course, but it is the next day. The Thurs-day. Thor's day. Thor is the Norse god of thunder and so am I, I just realized, the god of thunder, the goddess of storms, for I know how to bluster and I know

Oh, what am I talking about?

Let me say this. I treated my symptoms of anti-climax by *doubling* my efforts at FAD yesterday. It was like getting *two* planes on the runway instead of just one, or *twice* as many engines, or *twice* as many flight attendants, oh what I am talking about.

Anyway, two poisonous souls instead of one. And I spoke their souls *to their faces* instead of just writing them down.

I felt a shadow of guilt as I did this and here is why: There is a difference between poisonous and venomous.

A poisonous animal is one that has toxins inside it. It doesn't attack you, but let's say you eat it? You die (or you get sick).

But a venomous animal has something like *fangs* that it uses to *attack* you — to *inject* you with its venom. You don't have to eat it, you just have to get in its way.

Briony, Elizabeth, and Sergio are merely poisonous. They don't mean to do harm. Like a sea cucumber or butterfly, their poison is really a defense against predators. They are not so culpable as the venomous ones: Toby and Emily and Astrid.

And so I felt the shadow of guilt when I turned on Briony and Elizabeth today, and yet I wonder now: Why feel guilty? Remember what Briony wrote on my Name Game? I believe she has just the right mix of stupidity and manners to write something as nasty as this:

> *"You can't help who you are, Bindy, and maybe you will change this year? Good luck with Year 11. I think you will change."*

She probably believed it would encourage me.

Elizabeth Clarry, meanwhile, is often short and sharp. I therefore conclude that it was *she* who wrote:

"A bit too smart."

Too smart for what, Ms. Clarry? Too smart for you? Can't run fast enough to keep up with my brains?

So.

No guilt.

They ought to know the nature of their souls, and I have revealed them. (Although, it was disconcerting to discover that Briony already knew about her soul. Her mother is a marine biologist! Who could have predicted?)

Next week, I will complete my task.

The final victims are Sergio and Astrid.

Sergio is innocent enough, but, like a platypus, he can surprise you with a spurt of venom. (I suppose that technically makes him venomous, since he can *attack*, but not very often, and not in the same league as the venomous three. *None are in the same league as Astrid.*)

I believe it was the platypus who wrote that I wear my hair "weird" and suggested that it takes "guts" to do so. Sergio has laughed at my hairstyle before, and is just the sort of person to twist cruelty into "compliment."

There is no doubt in my mind that Astrid — the sea wasp — wrote this:

"I have never spoken to Bindy, but I am sure that behind her extremely annoying personality she is a beautiful human being."

100

I have two things to say about Astrid:

1. She lied when she said she had never spoken
   to me.
2. She is the most venomous of all.

Third Further Extended Nighttime Musings
of Bindy Mackenzie

Thursday, 4:03 a.m.

Strange, after a day like today — I mean yesterday, of course — a day when I revealed two souls, and furtheralsomore, what a strange and wonderful word! Furtheralsomore. I love it. Anyway, furtheralsomore, I refused to attend their Saturday "get-together" at Try's house — *they* will be wasting time, filling in foolish "confidential" questionnaires and talking about *themselves*, but I will have a wondrous Saturday! After Kmart, I'll get homework done, maybe summarize my history notes, work through Hanon's *The Virtuoso Pianist, Complete Piano Exercises,* match up some of my odd socks. I'll write my speech for English next week. I always win that speech contest. I'll feed the ca —

But where was I?

Ah, yes, strange. Strange that my symptoms of anti-climax persist even after revealing two souls.

I still have the headache, my stomach hurts, and I'm *so tired.* Yet I cannot sleep tonight — perhaps I fear a return to that dream of corpses and tree roots. My arms are so heavy and numb I scarcely believe that I can lift them.

Auntie Veronica said at dinner that she feels the same way

herself, so I suppose we still have that virus, but how long can it last?

"What a coincidence," Uncle Jake said. "You two having the same thing!"

What does he mean? Why should we not have the same virus? We live in the same house! I don't understand him.

And more to the point, and furtheralsomore, he doesn't pronounce the word correctly. A university professor.

"Co-inky-dence," he says, and it makes me want to kill him.

Further Final Extended Fourth Night Musing Times of Bindy Good Night Mackenzie

Thursday, 4:52 a.m.

Oh, I must confess it.

The Venomous Seven,

What seven? What seven?

What Venomous Seven?

There are the poisonous (Briony, Elizabeth, and Sergio), there are the venomous (Toby, Emily, and unforgivable Astrid), but even the poison and the venom adds up only to six — and all along I have lied when I have called them the Venomous Seven

I did it because of its intense half-rhyme. The assonance of those recurrings *v*'s and *e*'s.

They are only Six, and

Finnegan

Finnegan

Finnegan Blonde

IS NOT AMONG THEM!

Why did I disgrace him by including his name in that number? Oh the number seven, it disgraces him! And just for the sake of the rhyme!

But why does he disgrace *himself,* I perplex me, by mingling with the musk-oxen?

I do not know him well, of course, but I know this for-certain-sure: He is neither poisonous nor venomous.

No. I see it in his eyes: kindness.

That rare and valuable — it was *he* who wrote those simple words, the only kind words, the jewel among the mud, on my Name Game:

"A fast typist."

My breath stops at the sight of them.

He is an enigma, a mystery. How did he come to float into our FAD group, the sunlight at play in his hair? Nay, how does he *continue* to float? I fear his toes must brush against the tops of their heads — I fear he must tarnish his toes. He is in danger! Every moment he spends among them his sweet pink toes are in danger! In danger of inky black mud!

(I have never seen his toes and must admit, I do not know that they are pink.)

As his buddy I should advise him to drop out of FAD. It behooves me, nay, it is my *duty* to give him this advice!

(Maybe he and I should drop out together? We could spend FAD session time engaged in joint study sessions. It's not a bad idea.)

For now, at last, I fall asleep yet my eyes blur with tears at the thought of his words: *a fast typist.*

He must have seen me typing earlier that week, the week of the very first FAD session.

How generous of him, to have noticed me, before we were even introduced.

11.

A Day in the Life of Bindy Mackenzie . . .

Monday.

Worst day of my life?

It began with this:

Uncle Jake, in the kitchen, with the box.

Usually, it's just Veronica and me at breakfast — sometimes chatting quietly, sometimes spooning out our grapefruit wedges, lost in thought.

But there was Jake in his blue flannel pajamas, ripping up a cardboard box.

"Bind, you look as bad as I feel," said Veronica, and immediately dropped her head onto the table with a clunk. She closed her eyes and appeared to fall asleep. Sometimes Veronica is much like her four-year-old daughter.

I ate my grapefruit. Jake ripped up his cardboard box. Veronica dozed, her head resting on the table. Now and then she

105

sat up, looked at her teacup, blinked, and rested again. We heard the sound of Bella shouting in her bedroom: "I have *not* been playing with the remote control! It's not a *toy*!" Bella often defends herself in her sleep. There was a grunt from Jake as he tugged at some masking tape on the box.

"Jake?" I said. "What's that box you're tearing up?"

Veronica sat up and slapped her own cheeks.

"Finally she asks!" Jake beamed at Veronica. "Go look in the living room, Bind, and you'll see what was inside the box."

I did as he asked.

Standing in the center of the room was a shiny, bright-white baby swing. It was decorated with dolphins.

I returned to the kitchen in confusion.

It was much too small for Bella. Had they lost their sense of proportion?

But Veronica's eyes shimmered, Jake dimpled and grinned — and suddenly I understood. "You're having a new baby," I whispered.

"It seemed like a good idea at the time," said Veronica.

"We weren't going to tell anyone for a couple more weeks," explained Jake excitedly, "but we saw that swing on sale yesterday and guess what, Bind, you're the first person we've told!"

I stood in the center of the kitchen and exclaimed: "A *baby*!" I'd never been the first to be told about a baby before. I tried to dance my hands about to show excitement.

But I had a strange sensation, as if there were some problem I'd forgotten.

"I don't know if Bella's going to like this news," Veronica was saying, "but I've got to say, I feel just like I did when she was on the way. I'm so tired and —"

"Wait a minute," I interrupted, realizing the problem. "This virus that we've both got — isn't *that* why you feel like this . . . ? I mean, are you sure you're . . . ?"

Veronica and Jake looked at me.

"Well, there are one or two other indications," Veronica began gently. "And the doctor —"

"But haven't we got the same symptoms?" I persisted. "I mean, I thought we had the same —"

Uncle Jake stepped in.

"Isn't it a co-inky-dence!" he cried. "You two have the same thing!"

Now at last his "joke" made sense.

"Hey Bindy," he continued, "you must be pregnant too!"

They both burst out laughing.

That's when I lost my mind.

"WHAT'S SO *FUNNY*?" I shouted. "WHY DO YOU ASSUME THAT I'M *NOT*?!!!"

And I ran from the room.

As I pounded up the stairs I was conscious of silence from the kitchen. Then, as I reached the landing, I heard Jake murmur something, and they exploded into laughter once again.

At school, my subjects rolled grimly by, much like a convoy of tanks.

In German, the room blurred with regret. I recalled the

image of myself in the kitchen, dancing my hands to show excitement. I must have looked like a tree, stolidly fixed to the ground, its branches tossed by the wind. Shouldn't the tree have uprooted itself, rushed to Veronica, and hugged her? Why had the tree lost its temper and sprinted from the room? Was *that* an appropriate reaction for a tree, when told news of a pregnancy?

My face burned with shame. (And with confusion. Was I a girl or a tree?)

I was so regretful that when Ernst leaned over, his bangs in his eyes, to say, "Bindy, you've gotta check out my blog — I've been riffing on the topic of Emily debating and —", I interrupted him.

"Ernst," I said coldly, "isn't it time you got yourself a new name?"

He was startled into silence.

In Biology, I couldn't really concentrate. I was wondering at my announcement that morning that *I* could be pregnant too. (I couldn't.)

At recess, I happened upon Toby, along with Briony and the evil Astrid, standing outside the tuckshop.

I tried to skirt around them, but they noticed me and embraced me with their conversation. They were talking about the FAD event I had missed on Saturday. The one that took place at Try's house. They wanted to tell me about it.

They said that Try lived in an enormous house with no furniture. This house, it seemed, faced onto Castle Hill Heritage Park, and Try had taken them into the park for a picnic. She had brought coconuts along. She had instructed each "Buddy Pair" to work together to get milk out of the coconut, using nothing but the objects found in the park.

"Finnegan had to do it on his own," Astrid informed me. "He looked so lonely. Just kind of wandering."

"He was wandering lonely as a cloud," Toby explained.

"A cloud with a coconut." Astrid was wistful.

"Astrid and Emily tried to strangle their coconut," said Toby.

"They used the ropes from the climbing equipment." (That was Briony. I am always surprised when she speaks.) Astrid shrugged proudly.

It seemed that nobody had got the milk out of their coconut. There had been a sudden downpour, and they had all run back into Try's house, where she offered them towels and freshly baked banana bread.

"You should have been there, Bindy," said Astrid. "Try's got this massive-big dictionary? You would have just gone off when you saw it."

"I would have gone off?" I repeated acidly. "Like old cheese?"

"Excuse me?"

But before I had a chance to explain, the three of them had launched into an animated discussion about their favorite kinds of cheese.

In Modern History, our assessment tasks were handed back (and a new case study was assigned). I got 18/20. Fine, I thought, the scale must be tougher than usual. But I happen to sit behind

Elizabeth Clarry, and there at the tilt of her shiny white page was her mark:

19/20.

I closed my eyes and that beautiful red number shimmered. *19*. What was it doing on *her* assignment? Surely it was *my* 19! I checked to see that the papers hadn't got mixed up, but no, this was my paper, and Elizabeth Clarry had hers. Yet, there was no doubt: Elizabeth Clarry, long-distance runner, Elizabeth Clarry, Queen Alexandra's Birdwing — Elizabeth Clarry had my mark.

I spent recess looking for the teacher, Ms. Walcynski, to demand an explanation, but could not find her.

In Maths (Extension 1), Ms. Yen was writing up a theorem on the board.

I noticed a flaw in her logic and called out a correction. She turned, she frowned, and *Lucy Tan announced that I was wrong.* There was no flaw in Ms. Yen's logic, said Lucy primly, *but,* she reassured me, *she could see where I'd got confused.*

Ms. Yen smiled, thanked us both, and carried on.

At lunchtime, in the library, I opened my Maths textbook and considered the theorem. No matter how many times I reworked it, I could not escape the conclusion that Lucy Tan had been right.

I was mortified.

I flicked through the textbook to a later chapter. I would learn all about quadratic polynomials! One day, Ms. Yen and Lucy would humbly ask *my* opinion on the relation between roots and coefficients! "Ah, Lucy," I would smile tenderly. "I can see where you've got confused."

The prospect of Double English did lighten my heart somewhat. To my surprise, our "temporary" teacher (Miss Flynn) has continued to show up each lesson. And she gets to the *heart* of the texts. She is softly spoken, inclining toward knee-length skirts and pastel cardigans. She often refers to the notes on her desk as she teaches, squinting down at them ferociously. And she has a trick of drumming the fingers of one hand onto the palm of the other when anyone talks nonsense for too long. This is an effective way of cutting the nonsense off. (I admit, I have begun to hope that our missing teacher, Ms. Lawrence, will never return from her surfing trip.)

More to the point, this English lesson was to be the final day in our oratory contest.

The last few students would speak on topics of their choice, and Miss Flynn would declare the winner. (Winners from each class then compete, and the champion represents the school.)

Each year, it is *I* who represent the school.

I had given my speech yesterday, and was quietly confident.

But today, Emily Thompson spoke, and may the planets spin like marbles, may the sun slip like egg yolk from the sky — Emily Thompson was a hit.

She was informative and entertaining, and she had the class in fits.

And guess what her topic was?

That those who employ foul language are staining the fabric of our society.

The very topic I had given her as a "practice debate." She even *mentioned* that I had come up with the topic. (Everyone tittered.) She then proceeded to treat it as a joke, offering a satirical survey of "swearing" and "cursing" through time.

"Why are people afraid of swearing?" she cried. "It's only words. It's only letters of the alphabet!" Then she took up a box that she had placed on a nearby desk, opened the lid, and tipped a noisy pile of white squares onto the floor. The box was a Scrabble game and the squares were letter tiles. (She did this for dramatic effect.)

"Can these letters hurt you?" she cried, pointing her toes at them and almost slipping on one. ("Apart from when they break your leg?" she joked.) She said that people who want to ban swearing make the swear words more powerful. "If the words were used all the time," she argued, "they would be harmless." (There is a flaw in Emily's logic, but my head is too tangled to figure out what it is.)

"In conclusion," Emily concluded, "I suggest a new school rule. All students must replace three common words — let's say, 'classroom,' 'bus,' and 'tree' — with three extremely rude words. Let's save the fabric of society! Let's everyone use as much bad language as we can!"

"Let's everyone not," remarked Miss Flynn, but in a good-humored way.

Nobody was surprised when the announcement was made

at the end of the class: The winner of the contest was Emily.

Emily Thompson, drama queen, Emily Thompson, komodo dragon — Emily Thompson had my prize.

At the bus stop after school, I happened to pass Emily, Toby, and once again the unpardonable Astrid. As I approached, Emily broke away from the others and thanked me for the topic she had used in her speech. She seemed genuinely grateful. She tried to be matter-of-fact, as if her success meant nothing to her, but her eyes sparkled and her mouth kept breaking into smiles.

Astrid was scratching her ankle with her bus pass, but she straightened up to ask what we were talking about. When Emily explained, both Astrid and Toby congratulated her enthusiastically.

It occurred to me that, in all the years that I had won the oratory contest, no one had congratulated me once.

On the bus trip home, I thought about ways you could break open a coconut, using nothing but the objects in a park.

✕ ✕ ✕

Here Are Some Lines from a Book
That Caught Bindy's Eye Today . . .

"The school days to a young girl are usually full of pleasure and freedom from care or anxiety."

From *Twentieth Century Etiquette: An Up-to-Date Book for Polite Society Containing Rules for Conduct in Public, Social and Private Life, at Home and Abroad,* by Annie Randall White, 1900, p. 101.

$$\times \quad \times \quad \times$$

A Day in the Life of Bindy Mackenzie . . .

Tuesday.

Worst day of my life.

Astonishingly, the day began, once again, like this:

Uncle Jake, in the kitchen, with a box.

This box was smaller and he was tearing it more quietly. In fact, the kitchen itself seemed smaller and more demure. Veronica sat up straight and smiled, "Hello there, you!" as I walked in the door. Jake looked up and announced, "Bindy Mackenzie!"

I wanted to make a joke about the cardboard box. I wanted to say something clever like, "Don't tell me. Twins." Something that would show I was not an adolescent, running from the room in a temper, but a sophisticated person who took babies in her stride. But all I could do was say, "Hello."

"This time he's found a car seat on sale," Veronica tilted her head at Jake's cardboard box. "Can you believe this guy?" Next, she tilted her head at me. "You feeling okay, Bindy? That flu you had is hanging around longer than it should be."

"No, no, I'm fine," I assured her. I was trouble enough for them without complaining about my health.

I reached around Jake to get to the fridge, and noticed a crust of toast peeking out of the hem of his pajamas.

"Hey Bind," he said.

I stopped.

A premonition — a flailing heart.

"I hear you're after driving lessons," he said. "Your mum called while you were out the other day — you should call her back; she's been trying to reach you — and she tells me you want to learn to drive. Anyway," he continued (slow, tearing sound), "I reckon I could give it my best shot." He looked up, a fresh square of cardboard hopeful in his hand.

I sat at the table, poured myself juice, and tried to thank Jake for his offer.

It was clear to me — and my heart broke a little at the thought — that they were both being generous and kind. They wanted to make up for laughing at me yesterday. It made me want to shout again: *Stop it! I don't deserve it! You should be ANGRY at me!*

Meanwhile, I have to admit, my mind was consumed with an image: a plump young woman nods, a dimple in her chin, a key swinging gently on a chain around her neck. I was seven years old, and this woman was my first piano teacher. Her name was Penny. I think that the key around her neck was engraved with the number 21, but it should have been engraved with the number of her prison cell.

Penny should have been in jail.

For, you see, *she was untrained in the art of piano teaching.*

It took my next teacher, my current teacher, *months,* nay, *years* to unravel the habits that Penny had instilled. My wrists were at an ungainly angle! My fingers curled too tight! The pressure I applied, the clunking of the pedals, oh, I need not go on . . .

Who knows? If I'd begun with a qualified teacher, I could perhaps be a concert pianist today. (As it is, I don't do *quite as well* at my piano exams as I would like.)

And now the same thing was going to happen with my driving lessons!

With the right instructor I might become a racing car driver and win the next Grand Prix! With the *wrong* instructor, who knew what dangerous habits I might (unconsciously) adopt? I pictured myself in the driver's seat: hunched forward, wrists oddly bent, fingers curled too tight around the steering wheel. I pictured Jake beside me, brazenly unaware. At the very least, I wanted *professional* driving lessons. But how could I refuse such an offer without seeming rude?

Perhaps if I just stayed quiet, his offer would slip into a void, much like the forgotten piece of toast in his pajama cuff.

At school, I walked around trying to think how to get out of driving lessons without offending Jake. I would have to avoid him, I thought, whenever the car was in sight. I would have to lose my learner's plates, or accidentally burn my *Guide for New Drivers*.

Or I could say that my father wanted to teach me to drive. I could say that!

Only, would Jake believe me?

I could *convince* my father to teach me how to drive.

More plausibly, I could sell my father a new business proposal and earn myself the money for professional lessons. But what would my proposal be?

I was engrossed in the problem and scarcely noticed what was happening around me. But curious things kept happening that day, and these I could not help but see.

First, in Economics, Mr. Patel opened the lesson with a rhetorical question ("What makes the Australian dollar rise and fall?") and a boy named Jacob Kowalski raised his hand. He spoke in a complete paragraph. He used words like "export" and "reserve bank." Mr. Patel raised his eyebrows. He shot a few more queries at Jacob. Jacob responded to each with the same eloquence. Now, Jacob Kowalski is someone who has always drifted in the shadows at Ashbury: a small, skinny boy; shoulders violin-thin; hazy; an average student who never contributes in class. But today, as Jacob spoke, Mr. Patel's head tipped sideways in wonder.

"I'll just step out and have a smoke," he said. "And Jacob will take this class."

He did step out and have a smoke, too, but Jacob didn't take the class. Everyone talked amongst themselves.

Afterwards, I heard Jacob admit to a friend that he had sub-scribed to the *Financial Review* for a while. I turned, amazed, and noticed something else: He was no longer small and skinny. His head reached to just below the door frame. And his shoul-ders were cello-broad.

Then, in the library at lunchtime, I saw Miss Flynn encircled by some people from my year. They were planning an online student newspaper. Why was a substitute English teacher start-ing a school newspaper? It seemed a bit forward to me. Playing around with our intranet. A high-pitched giggle bubbled from the group. That was surely not Gabby Riley? (She's in all the lowest classes, and was suspended seven times last year.) And yet it *was* Gabby Riley. It emerged that she wants to write the paper's gossip column. She would do it as a kind of daily blog. I had no idea she even knew the alphabet, let alone a word like "blog."

In Biology, I noticed that Finnegan was absent. I knew he was at school, as I'd seen him in Economics earlier. About ten minutes into the lesson, I had to leave the room to get my Ping-Pong paddle (for an experiment), and was just turning back when I saw him. He was emerging from Mrs. Lilydale's office. Why had he been speaking to Mrs. Lilydale? She doesn't teach any of his subjects. I wondered if I should point that out to him archly. He would walk toward me now to reach Biology. His lateness might go unnoticed if we entered the science lab together. I would point that out too.

But, as I watched, he spun on his heel and walked in the

opposite direction. I kept my eye on the door for the rest of the lesson, but he never turned up.

Why was everyone behaving so strangely? I pondered this as I entered the Year 11 wing just before final roll call. People seemed to be emerging from curious places — from anonymity, from serial suspension, from Mrs. Lilydale's office. And then the final curious event occurred.

A group of people were standing by the window at the far end of the room.

Six people.

Toby, Emily, Briony, Elizabeth, Sergio, and Astrid.

I continued on to my locker, opened it, and turned back to look.

There they were. The Venomous Six.

Cane toad, komodo dragon, sea cucumber, Queen Alexandra's Birdwing, platypus, and sea wasp.

As I watched, the cane toad leaned over and murmured something into the ear of the sea cucumber. The Queen Alexandra's Birdwing began to giggle. The platypus clapped his hand onto the arm of the komodo dragon. All seemed to dance around the darkness of the sea wasp. My vision speckled and the animals tumbled together. It was just as if they had been placed in a crate, and someone had lifted that crate into the air and given it a good strong shake.

Something seethed within me.

Something pressed at the back of my teeth and stung the inside of my nostrils.

What did they think they were doing? Chatting and laughing, blissful and ignorant? After all my work, could *none* of them see who they were? Was I the only one who could truly see them?

I stood by my open locker taking short, shallow breaths. I could hear myself wheezing and knew I should get out my inhaler, but my arms were folded too tight. My fingers, meanwhile, were drumming hard onto the arms — I realized they were playing the piano. They were pounding out Mozart's "Rondo in D" — a clamor in my mind.

I wanted to scream with the force of my whole body. I wanted to run to that group of six, shake each by the shoulders, and cry: "Can't you see who you are? *Can't you see yourselves?*"

I looked around at other students opening lockers, spilling out books, slamming lockers, dropping things to the floor — all unaware of the animals dancing in the corner.

And that's when the plan came to me.

It swooped into my mind, complete.

A simple plan to reveal their venomous souls.

I would do it.

Tomorrow, just before FAD.

I managed to unclasp my arms, take a puff of Ventolin, and turn to my locker. I calmed my breathing, but inside my head something seemed to bubble and steam. I could feel engines burning. Firework wicks were being lit.

Which is why, when I arrived home from school, I sat at the piano to relax my wrists.

I used my left hand to lift the right wrist high in the air, and let it flop down onto the keys. I did the same with the left wrist. The keyboard jangled and jarred.

I sensed a shadow behind me.

"Nice technique," joked Uncle Jake, through a mouthful of stewed apples. (He still buys himself the jars of baby food that Bella used to eat.) "Some kind of modern jazz?"

"Ha-ha," I responded, mildly.

"You've got your piano lesson today, haven't you?" he continued. "What's say we drive you there?"

"Thanks," I said, "but that's okay, I like to walk." In order to politely signal the end of our conversation, I played the scale of E flat minor, *pianissimo*.

"Your first driving lesson," announced Uncle Jake, and he dropped the car keys onto the piano top.

Now I understood.

But I did not know how to argue.

I scarcely had time to review my copy of the *Road Users' Handbook*. I grabbed the *Guide for New Drivers*, but that turned out to be a waste. I gave it to Uncle Jake, pointing out the section called "Information for Supervising Drivers," and he took it with a flourish and read a random line. "Feeling stressed, Bindy?" he said. "If so, we've gotta reschedule!" Then he laughed and headed out to the driveway.

My learner's plates were so bright! Black and yellow, like cartoon bees. Vaguely, I wished I had put them through the washing machine, like my brother does whenever he gets new jeans. If only they were faded and frayed, I thought, then I might look like I could drive.

I felt embarrassed, placing the learner's plates on the front and back of the car, and even more so sliding into the driver's seat. I had never sat there before. It seemed such a crowded and serious place. To calm myself, I held the steering wheel and jiggled it a little.

Uncle Jake sat in the passenger seat. His eyes had the careful, squinting appearance of someone who is trying not to laugh. I stopped jiggling the steering wheel.

"What's this?" Jake wriggled his bottom. Then he pulled out my Log Book. He had sat on it, bending the top right-hand corner.

I explained about the Log Book: how I had to complete at least fifty hours of supervised driving before I could take the DART (the Driving Ability Road Test); how it was Uncle Jake's job to sign off on each driving task as I completed it; how I had to record the time, date, and location of each practice session in the Log Book, along with the number of kilometers covered, the road, weather, traffic conditions . . . I suppose I may have talked on a bit.

"Daddy?" said a voice. "When is Bindy going to drive?"

I spun around so fast the seat belt snapped and pulled a muscle in my neck.

Bella was in the backseat! Strapped into her child-safety seat, straining forward to get my attention, an earnest expression on her face.

"Bella!" I said. "I'm sorry, darling. You can't come with us now. I'm learning to drive!"

Bella tilted her head like a little bird.

"Bindy," she said. "When are you going to drive?"

Beside me, Uncle Jake burped.

When he burps, he twists his mouth to the side and blows the burp out slowly, like cigarette smoke.

"Excuse you, Daddy," said Bella.

"Come on, Bell," I pleaded. "Run inside to your mum."

"She'll be all right," said Uncle Jake. "Let's get going."

And then *he* began to talk.

He said I should imagine the steering wheel as a clock, and place my hands at ten to two. He mentioned the ignition, the rear view mirror and the dashboard. He talked about the handbrake. He talked about *getting the big picture*, about *defensive driving*, about *indicating*, about *communicating with other drivers*. He shifted around, pointing here and there as he talked, while Bella sang the national anthem and kicked the back of my seat.

I cannot explain what happened next.

I truly cannot say.

There is a blur or a buzzing in my mind, perhaps from the cartoon bees, perhaps from Uncle Jake's voice.

I remember the voice fading in and out. I remember thinking, "Surely he doesn't expect me to remember all *this*?" I remember thinking, "Ten to two? But perhaps he is wrong? What if it is quarter to three? What if it is half past six!" (But half past six would make no sense. You'd have both hands together at the bottom of the steering wheel. I missed a whole section of Uncle Jake's speech as I reasoned this through.) I remember saying, "But in the handbook, it didn't —" and Uncle Jake cut me off.

"Bindy," he said, "forget the handbook."

(His voice, as he said this, put me in mind of a commander in a military movie, addressing his elite swat team. "Forget the drills," the commander says. "This is where you prove your worth. This is it. The real thing. Crunch time.")

I missed another chunk of Jake's speech, thinking up the commander's speech, and lingering over the phrase *crunch time*. (It made me oddly hungry.) When I tuned back in, Jake was asking some rhetorical questions. "Am I just following the rules? Am I just driving in *theory*? Or am I *one with the car*? Am I, Bindy Mackenzie, one with the traffic on this road? That's what you've got to be asking yourself."

Then Bella interrupted her singing to inquire when Bindy planned to drive.

I remember turning the key, resting my foot on the accelerator, and breathing in sharply as the car gave a growl. Uncle Jake, I recall, was still talking: He was instructing me on what to do when we reached the stop sign at the end of our street.

As it happened, there was no need for that instruction.

There was a car, I noticed vaguely, parked on the curb opposite our driveway.

I edged to the end of our driveway.

I switched on the right-turning indicator. A small green arrow blinked at me.

I proceeded out of the driveway.

At this point, I thought to myself: *Once I have turned the corner, I will remember to switch off the indicator.*

And then I reconsidered.

No, I thought, *it will turn off by itself.*

The strangest panic struck me: *Do I need to turn the indicator off, or will it turn off by itself?!* And then: *Hang on, did I need to put an indicator on AT ALL?! There is no car behind me! There is just a house! Uncle Jake is squinting with laughter at me!*

This is it, I thought. *CRUNCH TIME!*

I gripped the wheel, pressed the pedal hard, and crashed into the parked car.

The noise of the crash was like a giant taking a bite out of a brick wall. Above that crunching sound was something louder and more penetrating: It was Uncle Jake barking out a series of swear words.

I sat and gaped in amazement.

Jake stopped swearing. His voice took on a firm, controlling tone. He instructed me to get out of the car and, once I had done so, he slid over to the driver's seat, reversed into our driveway, and stopped the car.

Bella unstrapped herself and tumbled out of the car in a strangely excited state. She began dancing around the front lawn. I stood in the middle of the road, my arms folded tightly, trying not to tremble.

The front fender of Jake's car was hanging loose. The other car had an apologetic, crumpled look. It was an electric-blue

Nissan Pulsar, and Jake told me that it belonged to a neighbor. We stood and stared at it. Jake became quite friendly with me, chatting about the particular neighbor and how he always disobeyed water restrictions, hosing down his lawn night and day. Auntie Veronica emerged from the house, frowning into the sun, and then ran across to us.

The owner of the car was not home, but a few other neighbors were available and, handily, so was a gang of tattooed men from a nearby building site. They all wanted to examine the damage and to hear the tale. They looked at me expectantly.

Why had I crashed into this car? they asked.

Why accelerate toward a parked vehicle?

Why, said one kindly, had I not turned the steering wheel?

Several of the builders pronounced the Nissan Pulsar "a write-off." Something about damage to too many panels. An irritating woman wondered if the police ought to be called. A bearded man with a hammer examined the road for skid marks. He could not find them. Had the brake locked up, he wondered, when I tried to stop?

All I could do was stare.

I had no idea what had happened.

I hadn't even touched the brake.

Later, after I had phoned to explain my absence from piano, Veronica put an arm around my shoulder and offered me a cup of herbal tea. "Everyone crashes at least once," she said. "Look at it this way: You've gone and got your turn over early."

But later still, when I was not in the room, I heard her say quite clearly to Jake: "What was Bella doing in the car?"

"She was only —" Jake began.

Veronica interrupted: "You don't bring a four-year-old along when you're teaching a beginner how to drive, Jake."

"It was only around the block —" he tried again.

"Whatever," she said. "You just don't."

I tried to phone my mother, but only got her voice mail.

12.

By Bindy Mackenzie

Session 4

I shall not tell how I arrived at FAD: late, alone, breathless, my outstretched hand pressed against the door, fingers smudging the cold of the glass, brushing the rough, white paint of the "u" in the "Blue" of "Blue Danish." I was abuzz, nay, *agleam* with an ecstasy of agitation. For I, Bindy Mackenzie, was an aeroplane taking off. I was a firecracker, fuse freshly lit (the air quivered still with the memory of the snap of the match).

I was a person who had *done something*. I had ensured that my climax — my elusive climax — would *finally take place*.

This is why I was late.

But I shall not tell of that.

And nor shall I tell how the door swung closed behind me, and there was Emily, alone at the counter.

I joined her there, but I shall not tell how Emily, gazing straight ahead at the girl behind the counter, spoke in one smooth sentence to say: "Can I have a hot chocolate, please, and I'm going to need my gratitude back."

It took a moment to realize she was talking to me.

"What gratitude?" I said.

"The gratitude I gave you on Monday afternoon." She counted out change, refusing my eye. "For that speech topic. I have an ice-cold heart today, Bindy, and guess who froze it? You. Because I was talking to Ernst about debating this morning, and I mentioned the tradition of practice topics and token animals. And Ernst said, 'Girl, you make my head spin like a mixmaster.' And I said —"

Emily paused, frowning, and now she glanced at me.

"I've never really heard Ernst speak before," she confided. "Why does he talk like that? Anyway." She remembered her icy heart and turned away again. "He said that it was all untrue. There are no practice debates or token animals. So I guess you made that up to play some kind of joke on me, and even though I won the contest with your topic, it is now an empty victory, in my mind. Because it started with a trick. And so, Bindy, I withdraw my gratitude. Unequivalently."

"When you say 'unequivalently,'" I said (stalling), "do you mean 'unequivocally'?"

"You do whatever you want," she said. "I'm taking it back and you can't stop me."

"Okay," I agreed.

And without so much as a sideways glance, Emily swept her hot chocolate up and flounced across to the curtain.

But I shall not tell of that.

No, and nor shall I tell that behind the curtain, the FAD group sat as they had the week before, shoes and sneakers resting on the table, laces lost amongst napkins and coffee mugs.

Try welcomed me, saying they had all missed me at the event on Saturday, and expressing her hope that I could join them next time. Meanwhile, Emily, realizing her chair was next to mine, wheeled it theatrically back and around the circle. Everyone watched as she jostled her chair into a new position. She ended up next to Finnegan, who gave her a curious look.

I only smiled to myself.

Don't worry, Finnegan. I sent him a thought-message. *Soon, you will see how your buddy takes care of herself. Wait until we get back to school! You will see how she floats above them all!*

I was a kite flying high in the blue. *They* were nothing but cold, wilted lettuce, spilled from a sandwich to the sand, unwanted even by the seagulls.

Try had her basket on her lap, as usual. And, as usual, she was drawing out piles of papers. Doing this seems to make her blush and talk too quickly.

"So, I've just put together a couple more cartoons for you," she chattered, "just silly things for fun, and I've written a schedule for the rest of the term, and I've got these exercises, and some forms to fill in and, oh, these other cartoons too —"

"Well," I said, in a friendly voice. "It's great that you're practicing your art on us, Try, but don't use up the *entire* Ashbury paper supply!"

The following sounds were emitted, simultaneously, from the group:

Gasp
Uh!
Oh!!
Ga-a-asp.
Eu-u-mh.
Tuh.
FOXGLOVE *hell, Bindy.*

I laughed, to indicate to my sensitive friends that my remark was intended as a *joke,* or as some friendly advice. Try herself also laughed, leaning close over her basket, busying herself with papers.

"Okay, fair enough." She allowed some little plaits to spill over her eyes. "I'll cut back on the paperwork and spare a few Aussie trees!"

At this, Emily and Astrid launched into a passionate attack on Australian trees.

Apparently, such trees are *worthless* compared to the value! the magic! the talent! that came shining through in a single one of Try's cartoons. Even Sergio said he'd been thinking she should syndicate them. And Toby pointed out that Ashbury uses recycled paper.

Try hushed them all, still laughing.

But, of course, I shall not tell of that.

No, and nor shall I tell how Try asked us each to describe an important event from our week.

On Monday, said a clear, chiming voice inside my head, *my uncle and aunt told me they're expecting a new baby. I'm not sure where they'll keep this baby when it arrives. Seeing as I live in their spare room.*

And the clear, chiming voice went on: *But don't worry. I've made myself invaluable to them. Just yesterday, I crashed their car.*

Aloud I replied, "No events of note this week, thanks."

Astrid made her contemptuous *euumh* sound again.

As for the others? Important events of the week? Well, Elizabeth had learned to Rollerblade. Sergio had taught her. Toby had discovered a snail on his bedroom floor. Finnegan had stayed up all night last night, watching *The Sopranos,* season five. Emily had decided to end her diet. Astrid had been chased by the police, but had escaped by hiding in some rose bushes.

"Not carnation bushes?" I said. "Shouldn't you turn to relatives in times of need? Or what would you call them, ancestors?"

Before anyone had a chance to launch into a chorus of gasps again, Try cut in with her topic for today's session.

The topic was FLAWS.

She wanted to know what we *didn't* like about ourselves —
what we would change if we could.

But I shall not tell of the confessions, the jokes, the despair of
my "friends" in response to this query.

Partly, I admit, I shall not tell because I did not listen.

I was thinking of the topic.

I was thinking of my own three flaws:

   (1) a tendency toward

> **reverie**

   (2) difficulty coping with

> **ANTI-
> CLIMAX**

and (3) occasional trouble

> **judging distances**

These three flaws were safe in their boxes. Why on earth
would I reveal them? Release them from the boxes? Risk their
expansion?

The idea was astounding.

But let me tell you (or no, I shall not tell), what was even more astounding: the eagerness with which the others (all except Briony) wanted to share!

Their chatter floated around me like soap bubbles. Now and then a word brushed against my arm and quietly popped. They spoke and I looked from face to face and thought of their manifold flaws. They seemed to me to be nothing but *collections* of flaws! (Except for Finnegan, of course.)

But, oh! I knew their faces (except Finnegan's face, which I have scarcely glanced upon). I knew their faces because today I had studied each in turn. At lunchtime, I had tracked down their school photographs, photocopied each, and blown them up to poster size. And just before FAD I had taken these posters, and —

But Astrid was speaking.

"Well, for *me*," she was saying, "*my* problem? I think, well, this is my flaw. I seem kind of bad in the way I treat guys? I mean, I have this habit of making them fall for me, I know that sounds conceited, but I kind of use my, whatever, seduction powers, and get them to fall in love with me, and then I just hurt them. It's like I want to hurt them. Like a compulsion or something."

"Strange," I murmured. "I'd thought of her as a sea wasp, but now I see she's more a poisonous princess."

Astrid spoke quickly.

"Seriously," she said. "I know it sounds conceited and everything, but I'm really, truly not saying I'm a princess. I know I'm not beautiful or —"

"Sure you are," said Toby.

"No," I declared. "I'm referring to the mythical poisonous princesses. The legend is that certain little girls were fed poison all their lives, so that when they grew up into beautiful young women, the first man they kissed would die. You're just like them."

"Oh!" Astrid laughed. "Ha-ha. Okay."

There were sharp intakes of breath; one or two people simply sighed.

And then (but I shall not tell this), silent Briony spoke.

"Sea wasps," she said, "also known as box jellyfish, are one of the deadliest animals in the world."

Ah.

The marine biologist mother again.

Sergio swiveled to look at her. "Yeah?"

Briony nodded and spoke a second time.

"I think Bindy just mentioned sea wasps," she explained. "So, anyway, they've got these long, almost invisible tentacles, up to three meters long, and they can kill you in minutes. If they sting you, you feel like you're suffocating."

"Huh," offered Elizabeth.

Briony spoke a third time.

"They usually come out in the summer, up north, so you can't go swimming then," she said, "unless you wear nylon stockings."

The others looked at her, expectantly, but Briony was finished. She was drinking her coffee, and looking through the plate-glass window at the traffic outside.

"The sea cucumber speaks three times," I whispered to myself.

Apparently, the whisper reached Toby. He turned sharply toward me, and his eyes seemed to burn into my skin.

I raised a protective hand, pretending I needed it to rest my chin.

Just wait, I thought, *until you see the Year 11 wing.*

No, but I shall not tell of any of these things, not of Emily nor Try, not of Astrid nor Briony, not of Toby and his scalding eyes. I shall not tell any of this, for these things do not count.

The only thing that counts is this: Sergio shared a theory.

Sergio, the boy with the burn scar on his face, the boy who taught Elizabeth to Rollerblade this week, the boy whom I took to be a platypus — Sergio began to speak.

(This is not unusual, actually. Sergio talks a lot.)

Today he shared a theory about adrenaline.

"That's like this theory I've got," he began. "You gotta ask yourself: Why does anyone swim at all when there's killer jellyfish in the water? Not to mention sharks. There was a fourteen-foot shark off Collaroy the other day; it took a chunk out of this guy's surfboard that I know. But he's back out in the water the next day. It doesn't make sense but, check it out, *maybe it does.* Because, see, what if we're *supposed* to scare ourselves SPURGE-LESS every couple of days? Because we've got to get our rush of adrenaline? Keep our fight-flight response kinda tuned, like when the saber-toothed tigers were after us. That's why I myself am dedicated to extreme sports and rock climbing and . . ."

Sergio continued and I stared at his face, the burn-scarred

face I knew so well from a poster I had held in my hands, less than an hour before. I watched his mouth, and as I watched, his chin turned into a platypus bill.

I blinked a few times.

But there it was: Sergio's face, growing a shiny black beak. His eyes, meanwhile, were shrinking, turning round and bright, and thick fur was crawling from his eyebrows down to his cheeks. I forced myself to look at the floor, but the carpet had become a rushing stream. Sergio's armchair itself was awash with mud, bark, and leaves, and Sergio was the size of a small cat. He was lying flat on his back on the chair, balancing on his tail, four webbed feet splayed out around him. The hind feet, I noticed, kicked against the chair now and then, to emphasize a point. I saw the little slits of his ears, and remembered that the platypus closes its ears when it dives underwater. How adorable Sergio was! Protecting himself from ear infections by closing his little ears! How sweet, and unique, and harmless he was! I wanted to hug him!

But — no! I remembered in a panic. He was not harmless at all! There were hidden spurs just above his heels! He was *not* kicking for emphasis, he was kicking to release a spurt of venom! Venom strong enough to kill a dog!

Elizabeth, seated beside him, gazing at his sweet little platypus face, was oblivious to the danger.

Someone had to save her!

Of course, I remembered, calming slightly, Elizabeth was not a dog. Sergio's venom wouldn't kill her.

She was just a girl.

No! She was a butterfly!

At this, my thoughts hit a large stone wall and collapsed in a shameful puddle.

What on earth was I thinking?

What madness had beset me?

I dug my nails into the palms of my hands and turned my attention back to Sergio.

To my relief, he was a boy again.

His feet were firmly planted on the carpet, which itself was perfectly dry.

"This is why," he was saying, "this is why speeding tickets should be outlawed. We've got to speed when we drive to keep ourselves alive, or we're all gonna end up dead. See my point? We've got to get ourselves that rush. Me? Whenever I get behind the wheel, I've got to gun it. I'm kind of pathological about it. I've got to put my foot down to the floor. Now it might be that my mother refuses to —"

"Well, Sergio," I thought, in a clear, chiming voice, "is it any wonder you have that terrible *burn scar* on your face with an attitude like that?"

And then there was the silence.

Such a silence.

It seemed that the entire café had paused, but for the sound of a single plastic teaspoon tapping on the side of a mug. Outside, a row of cars stood in suspense at the traffic lights.

I looked up, surprised.

What had happened?

Uneasiness curled tentacles around my heart.

Every person in that circle of chairs — every person except Sergio — was staring directly at me.

Surely I had not said those words aloud?

Please don't let me have said those words aloud.

But just as one knows for certain that the buzz of an alarm clock is not a dream, so I knew with a sudden twist that I had spoken those words aloud.

"Well, Sergio," I had said, "is it any wonder you have that terrible *burn scar* on your face with an attitude like that?"

The silent faces were worse, far worse, than any of their gasps or murmurs. These faces no longer blended together. They did not have the faded, vacant stares of blown-up paper photographs.

These faces were sharper than the fangs of a saw-scaled viper.

Furthermore, these faces were ready to launch themselves at me in a single, unified attack.

I admit this:

I did not believe I could survive the attack.

My only chance, as far as I could tell, was to leap over the back of my chair, spin on my heel, dive through the curtain, and run. While running, I would have to scream and knock over tables, in order to create confusion.

In all honesty, I was drawing my knees up, ready to spring, when I noticed Sergio.

He was grinning at me.

"You got me there, Bindy," he said, broadening the grin. "To be fair, I didn't pick up this particular scar in a high-speed car chase. But, okay, Bind, I could have got it that way, and you got me."

His tone was playful, wry, and mock-gallant all at once, and he settled himself into his armchair, in a deliberate gesture of repose. Scuffed black shoes landed with a thud on the coffee table. Arms stretched up and folded themselves behind his head.

The others seemed to take his behavior as a cue. As one, they altered their positions. Chairs creaked. Toby Mazzerati scratched his ear. Elizabeth breathed in deeply through her nose. Finnegan shifted a mug that was dangerously close to Sergio's foot.

Try, who sits on a low footstool, looked up around the group and began to speak.

She was nervous. She spoke rapidly. She spoke nonsense.

"Well, ya see," she began, her accent stronger than ever, even taking on a southern twang I had not noticed before. "Ya see, I'm just glad I got you guys to talk about *flaws* in your character today. Because, I'll tell y'all what I was thinking when you talked. I was thinking: These are not *flaws* talking, these are *teenagers*! And one day, sometime soon, I want to tell you *my* theories about that species. The species of teenager. Ha-ha."

I held my head perfectly still.
I thought: *What have I done?*
I thought: *Sergio just won me a reprieve, but for how long?*
And a smaller voice in the back of my mind: *You think they*

140

want to kill you now? Wait until they see what you've done to the Year 11 wing.

Try's voice sounded over my heartbeat.

"So, just to finish up," she was saying, "I want to take another shot at that Name Game. You remember the Name Game? Where you write your names in the center of a paper and pass it around the group? I want to do that again today, now that you've all got to know each other better. Who knows? You might be in for some surprises!"

She studied each face in turn as she spoke, but did not even glance in my direction.

PART THREE

Bindy, maybe you should seek advice from a mental health professional.

She's kind of insensitive.

I used to think that you couldn't help being the way you are, Bindy, and so sometimes I forgave you. Now I realise you do it on purpose so I never want to see you again. Thanks.

BINDY MACKENZIE

NO OFFENSE, BUT SOMEONE NEEDS tO ARRANGE A SLOW AND PAINFUL DEATH FOR YOU, BINDY.

Bindy, you have to try to learn that you're not superior to every other person in the room.

Bindy, I'm not sure if you realize it, but today you've upset almost every single person in the FAD group including Try! Have you ever considered USING that huge brain of yours?

Bindy Mackenzie has poison running through her veins.

PART FOUR

I.

The Ashbury Online News
Gabby's Gossip Column

Mysterious goings-on in the **Year 11 wing** today! **Students** headed to afternoon roll call, unaware of the transformation that awaited them. Soon, they would become aware!!

As the **students** flooded into the wing, aiming for their lockers, a gasp of horror rose up. It was a gasp that could probably be heard as far afield as the Castle Hill Pub!

(Which reminds me of a certain **last Friday night**... Did someone say the words "fake ID"? Not mentioning any names, but try borrowing your *sister's* ID next time, Flick — not your boyfriend's!)

Anyway, back to the **Year 11 wing.** The gasp was for this reason: The room had been *transformed*! The walls, windows, lockers, and doors were *covered* in HUGE color photographs. The photos were of certain **Year 11 students**. They were the size of enormous posters! And they had WORDS written across them in red letters! "Huh?" (is what we all said to ourselves).

If that shock weren't enough, further excitement was about to unfold. **Bindy Mackenzie** (famous for having a computer instead of a brain, and for her popular [?] lunchtime seminars of yonder years, on "Taming the Teen Monster Inside You" [did someone just say the word "Huh?"]) . . .

Anyway, enough of the asides, **Bindy Mackenzie** came storming in with a crazed expression on her face, and started ripping the photos down!! This led to **chaos** as some of us hadn't had a chance to look properly and wanted a bit more time. "Hang on," we said, reasonably enough, "let us look." But **Bindy** was a machine!!! To everyone's amazement, she had the posters crumpled up into spitwad-sized balls before you could say the word "blink."

(Which reminds me of a certain **last Saturday night** . . . Did someone say the words "stolen property"? Not mentioning any names, but Marty, how many pint glasses do you reckon you can fit down your pants before somebody "blinks" and notices? You're not *that* much of a legend!!!)

ANYWAY, as I was saying, your trusty gossip columnist has asked around and thinks she can confirm that the following faces were hanging from the walls of the Year 11 wing. And these words were splashed across the faces:

Toby Mazzerati — frog (or maybe cane toad)
Emily Thompson — dragon (or maybe kimono)
Briony Atkins — sea cucumber
Elizabeth Clarry — butterfly?

Astrid Bexonville — sea wasp
Sergio Saba — platypus

So far, no one has claimed responsibility for this **strange photographic display.** Our beloved Year Coordinator, **Mr. Botherit,** was heard commenting, "I don't know who put the posters up. I expect it was some kind of natural phenomenon that we'll never explain, like a cyclone or Stonehenge. Anyway, they've come down now so it's not serious. Let's forget about it."

Mrs. Lilydale, our beloved (?) Year Coordinator from *last* year, was heard commenting: "Well, how can he be sure it's not serious?" She then added thoughtfully: "Thank goodness for the quick wit and good citizenship of **Bindy Mackenzie.**"

2.

Nighttime Musings of Bindy Mackenzie

Wednesday, midnight

This is how it feels to stand on the street and look at cars that you have broken. To look at steel, crumpled and bent. To know that you alone inflicted that damage, but you alone can never fix it.

It's like seeing this: Emily's wounded pride at having been tricked. The tilt of Try's head over her cartoons. A startled glance from Astrid. Disappointment drawing over Finnegan's face. Sergio's wide-eyed grin.

It's like tearing down a series of posters, and seeing it all again: their crumpled faces in my hands.

3.

Thursday

*10:30 a.m., Auntie Veronica and Uncle Jake's place. Veronica and Jake are in
the hallway by the open front door. Jake is tossing his car keys gently in the air.
I am in the kitchen.*

Veronica: Watch out for that speed camera down by —
Jake: Yep. Gotcha. You just slow down when you get near —
Veronica: Okay, well, but don't get distracted by talk radio. I
had to pay Maria in two-dollar coins today, it was all I had. She
didn't seem to mind. She did Bindy's room for me this morning,
and the bathrooms.
Jake: All that while I was sleeping? She must've done a shocker
of a job. What's up with Bindy, anyway? Why's she home from
school?
Veronica: She's got a sore throat, poor kid, I don't know, I think
she overworks herself. I said to her, I said, "Bindy, you can't

153

burn a candle at both" — *hello* there, you. I thought you were in the TV room watching TV.

Bella: I *am* in the TV room watching TV.

Jake: Well, Bella-baby, it looks like you're standing in the hallway.

Friday

7:28 a.m., on my shadow seat, just outside the school library.

A woman's voice: No, no, it's perfectly fine. I *lied* in mine. But the rest of them should just go through.

A second woman's voice: Do you think that's wise? I mean —

The first woman's voice: There's someone sitting there — oh, it's Bindy Mackenzie. [*The first woman is Mrs. Lilydale. I hadn't recognized her voice. The other woman wears a hat tipped forward over her sunglasses. She slips away as Mrs. Lilydale speaks to me.*] Bindy, we didn't see you there! Good that it's you, I was looking for you yesterday, but it turned out you weren't at school. . . . We've got to talk debating and this problem that you have, I mean to say, the Tearsdale gets under way after . . . Oh, and I heard about those pictures in the Year 11 wing on Wednesday, and how you took them — Bindy, you look tired, have you been taking those carob-coated energy drops I gave you, let me give you some more —

Later in the morning, 8:55 a.m., still on my shadow seat. I see Astrid and Sergio arriving at school together. Astrid has a lime-green ribbon in her hair, which sets off the darkness of her high ponytail.

Astrid: I guess I just ask myself, why would someone choose the personality she's chosen? You know what I mean? I mean, *why* would you choose to be a really annoying, like, insensitive, self-centered b-i-t-c-h?

Sergio: Nice spelling. Maybe she didn't choose it? Maybe she can't help being that way. Didja think of that?

Astrid: Well, who else would have chosen it? She's got to accept respons —

Sergio: *Shhhhh,* she's sitting right there.

Astrid: She can't hear me. Don't worry about it. She can't hear us.

Sunday

4:30 p.m., at the kitchen table in Veronica and Jake's place. Jake is at the stove, staring into a saucepan. Bella is on the floor, quietly reading, her little finger sliding slowly across the page. There is a recipe book open on the table beside me.

Jake: [*talking to himself*] What, so that's it? It can't be right. No, there's got to be more than this. [*raising his voice*] Bindy, is this right? I'm just stirring this with a wooden spoon? And that's it? Can you read it out again?

Bindy: You're doing it right. It's just chocolate, cream, and butter. You just stir like you're doing.

Jake: Would you check out this melting chocolate, Bindy? Look at it spilling from the spoon, see that? Like a chocolate waterfall — it's like that kid in the chocolate factory movie who goes up the pipe [*makes a slurping noise*], he goes up the pipe like [*makes the slurping noise again*] — I can't believe this is it. This is how you make truffles? Veronica's going to be over the — why don't I do this all the time? Oh, sorry, Bindy, you're trying to work. I'll be quiet.

Bindy: It's okay, Jake. Keep talking.

Monday

8:07 a.m., on the school bus, surrounded by Ashbury students. From a few seats back, I hear the conversation of two people I know. It is Astrid and Elizabeth — why is it always Astrid?

Astrid: What do you reckon's wrong with her? I mean, it must have been her that put up those photos with the animal words? She keeps going on about animals in FAD, and like describing them, so it must have been — and then she takes them all down like some kind of — I mean, what's *up* with her?

Elizabeth: Maybe we should ask her?

There are two boys in the seat behind me. They are taking out their lunches.

One of the boys: What have I got today? A ham sandwich? That is so *random*.

Tuesday

9:15 a.m. I am in Economics. Mr. Patel just handed back our essays. I got 16/20. I have never received 16/20 on anything before. Mr. Patel has asked Jacob Kowalski to read out his essay. Jacob got 20/20. Someone giggles.

Mr. Patel: Hang on, Jacob, until the giggles stop. I know you're texting, Celia, don't try to hide that phone! There will be no multitasking in this room!

[*But I can't stop staring at the number 16: such a strange, unfamiliar number.*]

Wednesday

11:30 a.m., Year 12 students coming out of an English exam, passing my shadow seat.

Girl's earnest voice: I think it's like, if you've got a good feeling at the end, that's the best indication? That's what Kara said anyway, and I was like, okay.

Another girl's voice: Did you do that third question? I was like: *Excuse me?* And that's even though I ate fish fingers last night.

Girl's voice: I asked Try for some help yesterday, with the themes and that, 'cause she used to be an English teacher and she's like the f . . . n life raft? You could tell she was really trying but she didn't have an effin' clue. Anyway, I guess, why would she, she's from Ohio, so they'd have different English there. Do they even speak English in Ohio?

Boy's voice: Do you want to go to Mackas and not talk?

Later, still on my shadow seat. It's almost 2:00 p.m. Mr. Botherit, our Year Coordinator, is rushing by.

Mr. Botherit: Hey there, Bindy Mackenzie, hard at it as usual. That's what we like to see. [*He rushes on — hesitates — turns* *back*]. Bindy, don't you have your FAD class now? [*Taking a few steps closer*] Bindy? Lunchtime ended an age ago, didn't you hear the bell? Shouldn't you be at FAD? And call me old-fashioned, but shouldn't you stop typing when a teacher speaks to you?

4.

A Note from the Desk of Try Montaine

Dear Bindy,
This is a note to let you know some of the things that I'm
hoping . . .

- I'm hoping you're not planning to give up on your FAD
  group.
- I know you think FAD is a waste of time, but I'm *hoping*
  you can give us a second chance   to prove you
  wrong . . .
- I'm hoping, most of all, that you'll come and chat with
  me anytime you feel like it — I'll be in my office most of
  today and tomorrow, so maybe we could talk before you
  all go off on holiday?

Best wishes,
Your FAD teacher,
TRY

P.S. I'm also hoping you don't think this note is totally corny. I was so disappointed when you didn't come to FAD yesterday — our last session before the break! I had a sleepless night thinking about it. This lame note is the result!

×   ×   ×

A Memo from Ernst von Schmerz

To: Bindy Mackenzie
From: Ernst von Schmerz
Subject: Always with the Summonsing
Time: Thursday lunchtime

Yo Bind,

Cos equals adjacent over hypotenuse, girl, who died and made me the messenger? Mr. B. wants to see you. Mrs. L. wants to see you. That small teacher with the plaits and a name like *Attempt* wants to see you. And where you at? Trapped inside your own auditory canal? The PA is phat with your name today, Bindy: *Bindy Mackenzie, please report* — ; *Bindy Mackenzie, please* — . I deduce that you ignore their pleas because the plaintive keep on pleading. You want they should come pleading to me?

Nice.

But I don't know where you are, shadow-girl, you are *elusive*.

You want to talk? Post me a message with the subject line HELP on my blog bull-board, and I will be there. Enter a chatroom and converse! (You never engage in IM.)

Or give me a call. Maybe we could meet up on the break?

Otherwise, Bind, I'll leave you to your intervisibility. And next time a teacher asks me where you are, I'll say, "Bindy? There is no such girl."

It's your choice.

Catch,

Ernst

× × ×

Thursday afternoon

Dear Bindy,

Welcome home from school. How's your health? Sorry, I can't find that "Messages for Bindy" paper you gave me, but I do have two messages for you. Do they still count if they're not on the right paper?

One message is that Maureen Brentwood called. You remember Maureen. You baby-sit for her. She said she wants you to phone her about an idea she has for your holidays. "You mean about a baby-sitting job?" I said. "No," she said firmly, "an idea." She had a mysterious air.

The other message is that your mum came by today, and we had a catch-up and a cup of tea. She waited on the porch, hoping you'd come home from school earlier than usual, but then she had to leave. She wants me to ask you the following: Are you coming to visit her during your break? Why don't you ever answer your phone? (She says she's been calling you a lot the last few weeks.) How is your health? Does she need to make a doctor's appointment for you? (I told her you'd been unwell.)

Your mum also had a few letters for you, which I've left on your bed — apparently, they arrived at your old address a few weeks back but your mum's only just picked them up. Looks like the Board of Studies is after you. Maybe they're bored of study (ha-ha), and want to conduct experiments on your mind?

Speaking of minds, I'm off to the park with Bella, to see if I left mine on the swings.

Lots of love,
Auntie Veronica

✕ ✕ ✕

LETTERS FROM THE BOARD OF STUDIES
[Letter 1]

Office of the Board of Studies, NSW

Ms. Bindy Mackenzie
24 Clipping Drive
Kellyville NSW 2155

Dear Ms. Mackenzie,
Thank you for your letter.

We have conducted inquiries on your behalf, and we are happy to confirm that Friendship and Development (FAD) is a course currently offered at Ashbury High. The course is to be taken by senior students for one lesson each week. It covers personal development issues such as self-esteem, stress management, career planning, and study management.

We trust that this has been helpful.

Please do not hesitate to contact us if you have any further queries.

Yours sincerely,

George Sutcliffe

Student Liaison Officer

Office of the Board of Studies

[Letter 2]

Office of the Board of Studies, NSW

Ms. Bindy Mackenzie
24 Clipping Drive
Kellyville NSW 2155

Dear Ms. Mackenzie,

Thank you for your letter.

It appears that you did not receive our previous letter. A copy is attached.

We understand that you are now concerned about a "concertina wall" that needs to be "opened" and "closed" during the course of your "FAD" lessons. We have contacted your school to inquire about this wall.

We trust that this has been helpful.

Please do not hesitate to contact us if you have any further queries.

Yours sincerely,

George Sutcliffe

Student Liaison Officer

Office of the Board of Studies

[Letter 3]

Office of the Board of Studies, NSW

Ms. Bindy Mackenzie
24 Clipping Drive
Kellyville NSW 2155

Dear Ms. Mackenzie,

Thank you for your letter.

It seems you did not receive our previous two letters. Copies are attached.

We are always pleased to hear when a student is enjoying a course at his or her school. If you would like to continue providing us with "reports" on your "FAD" classes, please feel free to do so. All future "reports" should be sent to Mr. Cedric E. Constantine (Assistant to the Student Liaison Officer).

We trust that this has been helpful.

Please do not hesitate to contact Mr. Cedric E. Constantine (Assistant to the Student Liaison Officer) if you have any further queries. I have given him a copy of your file.

Yours sincerely,

George Sutcliffe

Student Liaison Officer

Office of the Board of Studies

× × ×

A Memo from Bindy Mackenzie

To: Ernst von Schmerz
From: Bindy Mackenzie
Subject: Thanks and Sorry
Time: Friday recess

Dear Ernst,

Thanks for your memo. Don't worry, I'm taking steps to ensure that those teachers won't bother you again. Well, I can't be sure of that. They might bother you for other reasons. Other messages, other notes. They might bother you to blow up a balloon, or to rescue a tiger from a tree.

Forgive my insanity. I think it is temporary. I think I will return to myself one day soon. Maybe we can meet up on the holiday, as you suggest, but of course they only last for two weeks, and I'm sure you are busy. I'll be busy with Kmart, baby-sitting, some extra work I've just been given at a bookshop owned by one of my baby-sitting clients, assignments, essays, revision, advance preparation for next term, etc., etc. You understand.

However, in relation to the teachers who want to see me: You may be pleased to know that I have arranged to meet with Mrs. Lilydale at the start of lunch today, and with Mr. Botherit at the end of lunch. I am just about to write to the other teacher: the small one with the plaits and a name like *Endeavor*. She wrote me a note herself, so I'm replying.

So! Thank you very much and I hope you won't be bothered again.

Best,

Bindy

✕ ✕ ✕

A Memo from Bindy Mackenzie

To: Try
From: Bindy Mackenzie
Subject: FAD
Time: Friday recess

Dear Try,

Thank you for your note full of hope. I didn't think it was corny or lame at all. I think it was kind of you to write it, and beyond the call of duty.

I'm very sorry, but I'd prefer not to come to your FAD classes again. It's not that I don't want to give the FAD group a second chance. It's just that I think you and the others will get along much better without me!

If I am technically required to continue taking the course, perhaps I could do it by correspondence?

Yours sincerely,

Bindy Mackenzie

Hi Bindy,

So sorry — had to rush off at the last minute so can't be here to meet you as planned. I wanted to see you so I could talk about debating. It starts in the third week after the break, so decision time! Listen, I'm sure you've heard that Emily T. was a hit in the oratory contest? (Runner-up at district level but knocked out at the next round — not bad!) And she's been going great guns with mock trial! Her Legal Studies teacher raves about her! You know, her parents are both successful lawyers, too. . . . So shall we assume you're happy, after all, to have her on your team? Back on track? A team player again? Raring to get up and at 'em? We need you, Bindy! The team needs you!

Have fun on your break!

So long!

Mrs. Lilydale

The Philosophical Musings of Bindy Mackenzie

Friday, 1:47 p.m. (by a window in the Year 11 wing)

If a teacher can be absent from a meeting, can a student then be absent from a class? Perhaps the student should have left a note at the classroom door: "Hi, Ms. Yen. So sorry — had to rush off at the last minute so can't be here for your Maths class as planned."

1:49 p.m.

Of course, Mr. Botherit *was* there at *his* meeting. Does he cancel Mrs. Lilydale out?

1:50 p.m.

Now, there is a question. Does Mr. Botherit cancel Mrs. Lilydale out? A Year Coordinator like Mrs. Lilydale! I used to knock on her door last year, and she would trill, "Ah-hah! A Bindy viewpoint!," beckon me into the office, offer a cup of tea, and sit back happily, waiting for my viewpoint. (I had viewpoints on many things last year: my teachers, global dimming, Iraq, reality TV and the associated decline of civilization, alcohol abuse among teenagers . . .) Today, I climbed to the top balcony, knocked on Mr. Botherit's door, and he glanced up from a spilling pile of paper. "Oh!" he said in surprise.

1:54 p.m.

"Oh!" he exclaimed, and he gathered his papers together, and gave me a thoughtful frown. "Sit down, sit down!" he remembered himself, and I sat. There is a window behind his head, filled with bright sunlight. It was difficult to look at him.

"Bindy," he said, "yes, I asked you to come and see me, didn't I?" And he began to spill papers again.

(It is worth pointing out that this is Mr. Botherit's first year as Year Coordinator. He joined our school two years ago as an English teacher, and has stirred up controversy in the past — he started a pen-pal scheme with the wayward students of a nearby school. As far as I can see, the only step he has taken toward embracing his new role as Year Coordinator is the "rousing" speeches he gives at our weekly assemblies.)

"Now," he said, finding the paper he wanted. "Ah yes, this is why I wanted to see you. Looks like you've been busy writing letters to the Board!"

1:58 p.m.
Betrayal!

The Board of Studies had contacted him! That ridiculous Student Liaison Officer! He had replied to my letters in a manner that suggested he must have failed Primary Comprehension. He had replied to my letters without *actually* responding to a single word that I said. (His replies, quite frankly, made me despair for the future of this state.) *Meanwhile*, secretly, he had contacted Mr. Botherit to pass on my complaints! He had contacted Mr. Botherit to say: *What shall we do about this girl?*

2:03 p.m.
Well! I could not believe it.

While I was not believing it, Mr. Botherit wasted several minutes of my life gently suggesting that I come to *him* in the future

169

if I have any concerns about my school. No need, he reasoned, to go straight to the Board! He wondered why I hadn't come to him first on this occasion. (It didn't seem right to point out his inexperience as a Year Coordinator, nor his errors of judgment in the past, so I simply smiled enigmatically.) More minutes passed as he explained the *multitude* of benefits of FAD. He could see exactly why I doubted that I needed it, but he was sure my group would bring me around.

"And your group," he said earnestly, "I looked it up — and they seem like a fine group, as far as . . ." He turned to his computer.

And something extraordinary happened.

2:08 p.m.

He turned, as I said, to his computer.

He squinted at it. Turned, with irritation, to the window behind him that was obviously lighting up his screen. He hit a few keys. "FAD, FAD," he muttered to himself. "This newfangled software," he apologized. "We seem to be doing a trial run with some tricky new software, and *I* can't get the hang of — hang on, here we go. Yes, here's your FAD group. You're in with a great bunch of people! Terence Brickhill, Sky Morrell, Ernst von Schmerz — he's a friend of yours, isn't he? Oh, look, and you've got Ashlee, she's a great girl!" He faced me again, smiling broadly, and I simply stared.

2:12 p.m.

I'd been attending the wrong FAD group all this time.

Somehow I'd misread my timetable! And those names he just mentioned — those were *my* kind of names, those were *my* class, *my* level of people! I had slipped into the wrong universe! Somehow I had made a terrible mistake and now I was mortified. I sat in Mr. Botherit's office feeling as if I had come to school in my pajamas.

"That?" I whispered, after staring a moment. "*That's* my FAD group? Because I thought . . ."

Mr. Botherit turned back to his computer, nodding — and then he frowned.

As he frowned, his eyebrows seemed to jump.

"Oh, sorry, Bindy. No. Look at that!" He bit his lower lip, concentrating. He ran his mouse to the edge of his desk, looked down at the mouse with surprise, and returned it to the mouse pad. "My mistake. You're not with that FAD group at all! Here we go. Bindy Mackenzie. You're with Emily, Astrid, Sergio, Toby — that lot. Does that sound right?"

"That sounds right," I breathed. I felt a strange wave of relief. I was properly dressed, in full uniform, and not in my sleepwear after all.

"Sorry about that," he repeated, still gazing at the screen. "See, I was looking at an older version of the FAD groups — it appears that you *were* with that first group, originally, but someone . . ." He tapped at a key or two and then shrugged to himself.

"But someone," he repeated, "moved you."

And now here I am, in the Year 11 wing, reflecting on Year Coordinators and FAD groups. The meeting concluded when the bell rang. Mr. Botherit was still talking, but I stood up and shouted, "I'd better get to Maths!"

"Promise me you'll give your FAD class another go?" He raised his voice a little himself, as if trying to keep up with my shout.

"Maths!" I sang again.

And now here I am, in the Year 11 wing — not in Maths at all.

I am new to this. This "skipping a class." I see why they call it skipping. My heart skips a beat every now and then, when it remembers that it should be in class. Actually, I think I might contact Mr. Patel later, apologize, and ask for a copy of his class plan for today, along with suggested additional reading so that I can catch up.

Is that common practice for those who "skip" a class?

Of course, they might not call it "skipping." What is the current slang for educational absenteeism? (I do not mingle with the sort of student that practices this art.) Do they call it "skiving off," "playing hooky," "wagging"? I have heard the word "jigging," but perhaps I have mistook. Isn't that a sort of Irish dance?

The technical term is "truancy," of course. The original meaning of "truant" is a person who begs by choice. That is, a person who doesn't need to beg, but chooses to do so anyway. An "idle rogue," says my dictionary.

2:24 p.m.

I am an idle rogue.

2:25 p.m.

I was an idle rogue on Wednesday, of course: I missed my FAD class.

But isn't that something different? Not idleness at all? If you know that a group despises you, are you not *compelled* to stay away? Even if someone once *moved* me into that group (assuming Mr. Botherit is right about that, and wasn't just confused by his new software) — even if someone wanted me once, they certainly don't want me now.

2:27 p.m.

Strange.

I know I have been lost in

reverie

but this wing has been whisper-quiet. I could have sworn I was alone. Yet, just now, I turn toward my locker and there I see a bulky yellow envelope! It is taped to the outside of my locker. How did it get there? Are others, like me, shadow people? I will stop my and get it.

× × ×

A Note from the Desk of Try Montaine

Dear Bindy,

Well, I've given some thought to your creative suggestion that you do your FAD course by correspondence. And I'm afraid I can't get my head around it . . . I don't think a life raft *works* that way.

You've got to at least be in the same room!!

But you've given me an idea — how about some homework for over the break, to catch up on the FAD class you missed?

The homework is simple. It's this: *Tell me what makes you who you are.*

Take a blank sheet of paper and write down anything— your favorite colors and foods, the moments that changed your life, some things you've seen and heard that have affected or surprised or concerned you. Be as honest as you can, Bindy. Don't think about the impression you're making. This can only help you if you're honest. Be honest.

Let's have the story of *you*. The story of Bindy's life! (The group had fun doing this task while you were absent the other day — I think they found it invaluable.)

To be honest, Bindy, I missed you at FAD — you and your multicolored nail polish. Which brings me to your gift! I'm enclosing some wonderful, sparkling nail polish in this envelope. It's especially for you, from a member of your FAD group. (I've promised not to give away *which* member — you'll just have to guess.)

Look at it as a bribe if you like. Look at it as secret code for: *Your FAD group wants you back!*

Best wishes,

TRY

PART FIVE

Bindy Mackenzie:
A Life

INTRODUCTORY NOTE

The following Life has been prepared by me (Belinda "Bindy" Mackenzie) for the purposes of a course entitled "Friendship and Development."

Now, I had planned to present this Life as a "collage." I wanted to answer the question "What makes me who I am?" by scanning in various documents: my birth certificate; health records; my parents' tax returns; Kmart superannuation documentation; photos of my father with a chisel in his hand . . . and so on.

However, most of these documents are now in a padlocked storage area at our old house in Kellyville. The house has tenants living in it.

(I contacted the real-estate agent to request her assistance in procuring consent to access landlord chattels, but she said she didn't "get what I was on about.")

Accordingly, sections (1) and (2) of this Life are written in straightforward narrative. They describe my early years to the best of my recollection.

However, good news!

I *do* have my special box with me. This is a box that contains my old diaries and a few other select items that are precious to me, such as merit awards, prizes, and copies of correspondence with the Ashbury school principal.

Hence, sections (3) to (12) of this Life will be made up of the contents of my special box (along with occasional explanatory notes). As you will note, the diary entries are rather scarce. I have had little time for diary writing in the past (this year, I seem to write too much). In fact, looking through these scarce diary entries, I notice that they do not truly represent my life. Please keep this in mind.

I now invite you to enter the Life of Bindy Mackenzie. . . .
Please enjoy.

1. Bindy Mackenzie: The Early Years
(Age 0–3)

I was born on a cold, blue Wednesday in the middle of the month of July.

I was two weeks early, and my mother likes to say that I've been in a hurry ever since.

My father, Paul Mackenzie, was working in construction at the time. The day that I was born, he suffered a concussion when a hammer fell onto his head. Indeed, he was en route to the hospital, in the front seat of an ambulance (he refused to cower in the back), blood dripping into his eyes, when my mother felt her first contraction.

My mother, Cecily Mackenzie, had started an MBA while pregnant with me. According to family legend, she distracted herself from the labor pains by writing an assignment on the Application of Financial Ratio Analysis to Assessment of Profitability in Small- and Medium-Sized Businesses.

A single photograph was taken that day. It shows me in my mother's arms, my father leaning over both of us. My father is

Bindy Mackenzie: A Life

wearing a hospital gown that falls open at the neck, showing the hair on his chest. There is a white gauze bandage protruding from the side of his head. I have studied his face for indications of concussion, but his pupils seem normal to me. He must have made a speedy recovery.

I appear to be a sweet baby: a round face and squinty little eyes.

My parents brought me home from the hospital, to live in their rented apartment.

My father sued his employer for the falling hammer, accepted their settlement check, and bought a dilapidated house in Winston Hills.

My mother received a High Distinction for her Financial Ratio Analysis assignment.

One year later, my brother, Anthony, was born.

To be honest, I have no memory of any of this.

2. Bindy Mackenzie: The Shadowy Years
(Age 3–6)

My father fixed up the house in Winston Hills, sold it, and bought a house in Seven Hills.

This became the pattern of his life — indeed, it *remains* the pattern of his life. He buys a house, we move in, he renovates it, and he sells it (or he rents it out while he waits for zoning laws to change, so he can demolish the house, subdivide, and make a tidy fortune). He is a property developer. He runs a business called Mackenzie Enterprises, which currently has a portfolio of twenty-five properties, mostly in the Hills District. The longest we have stayed in any one house is seven months. The shortest is seventy-two hours.

Most recently, we lived in Kellyville. At present, however, I am staying with my aunt and uncle. (My parents wanted to live in/renovate a one-bedroom apartment in the city and there was no room for Anthony and me.)

But back to my childhood!

By the time I turned six, my family had moved eleven times.

I have a few, shadowy memories of my life between the ages of three and six.

I remember, when I was four, looking at a run-down building with my dad and saying, "That house looks so crestfallen."

Dad laughed and told me that the land was more valuable than the house. The very existence of the house, he said, *reduced* the value of the land.

"So it's an impediment?" I said. "To your profit margin?"

Dad laughed again.

I remember the preschool teacher saying to my mother, in some awe, "Is she like this at home?"

I remember reading *Around the World in Eighty Days*, in a sandpit, and the glorious way it made me feel.

I remember my first asthma attack. I was five.

Dad was reading a newspaper, elbow on the kitchen table, chin resting on his fist. Each time he turned a page, he half stood up from his chair, so he wouldn't have to move his chin from his fist.

I began to explain that it would make more sense if he simply

Bindy Mackenzie: A Life

changed his position, returning the elbow to — but I realized he was not listening.

Mum was at the sink, washing spinach. She turned the tap full blast. Water rebounded and splashed her in the eyes. She jumped back in surprise and tripped over my father, who was standing up to turn a page.

Together they fell to the floor in a foolish tumble.

My brother, four at the time, saw this from the hallway, and took a flying leap. He landed on my father's stomach. All three shouted with laughter.

I took large, careful steps over my family.

I stood on my toes and turned off the tap. I tipped Dad's chair upright. I stared at my family, wondering how to get them off the floor.

I started to wheeze. I began to cough.

I was pointing to my parents, to the sink, to the newspaper, and chair — but the more I tried to speak the more I coughed.

I grew out of asthma after several months, but some years later, it returned.

3. Bindy Mackenzie: The Year of the Fountain Pen (Hills District Primary, Year 2, Age 7)

DIARY ENTRY
Tuesday, 16 April
Dear Diary,
Have you met Anthony? He is my younger brother and he has dark brown hair. Anyway, Anthony has a headache today. Daddy

said, "No, you don't." Anthony said, "Yes, I do." Daddy said he has no respect for headaches. They don't exist. Six-year-olds do NOT get headaches, he said. He said Anthony has to talk himself out of his head.

Later, I saw Mummy give Anthony an aspirin. I didn't know if Daddy knows.

Friday, 14 June
Dearest Diary,
I am learning to play the piano!!! My teacher is Penny and she's fat but she's really nice. My favorite part is the treble clef. And there are really, really interesting sentences for remembering the notes. They are:

- Every Good Boy Deserves Fruit.
- All Cows Eat Grass.
- Grandma Brings Doughnuts For All.

I keep saying the sentences to Anthony, and sometimes I keep getting out apples, oranges, bananas, excetera —(FRUIT, I mean), and saying, "*Every* good boy deserves fruit, Anthony," in a serious voice and I give him the fruit. We both keep laughing. It's funny.

Wednesday, 7 August
Hi Diary,
I stayed home from school today. "Felt a bit under the weather." I started reading a book called *Wuthering Heights* by Emily

Bindy Mackenzie: A Life

Brontë. I need to use the dictionary quite a lot and sometimes it's confusing BUT it has a great atmosphere. I think it's called gothic. Mummy gave me a book of crosswords. But they were too easy. I told her maybe I need cryptic crosswords instead because I wasn't being challenged.

Sunday, 1 September
Dear Diary,
Today Daddy let me help with the wallpaper!! He's pulling it off my bedroom wall. But I said, "Daddy, it's *beautiful*," because it's got roses on it. But Daddy just laughed. My job was to go along in front of him with a bucket of water, and maybe some other product is in the water, and wipe a sponge over the paper to make it wet. I could not reach some bits so Daddy did them. I got sopping wet. And then Daddy gave me a fountain pen to say thank you. It says "Delta Hotel" in nine-karat gold on the side.

Tuesday, 15 October
Oh My Darling Diary,
I just had the WORST day of my life. I lost the fountain pen that Daddy gave me for being his special girl!!!! I was not ever going to lose it. I KNOW I left it at school, on the windowsill outside the music room, but Mum drove me back and it WASN'T THERE anymore. SOMEONE MUST HAVE STOLEN IT.

I don't know how I'm going to tell Dad. He will be so disappointed in me. I know it.

But he could not be as disappointed in me as I am in myself.

Friday, 25 October

Hi Diary,

Well, I finally got brave enough to tell Dad about the fountain pen. He wasn't mad at all!

He just said be careful with your stuff because I'm not made of money, okay? And then he said, you use fountain pens at school? Don't you use pencils? And then I started explaining about how Miss Carmine only lets us use pencils but I'm allowed to use the fountain pen for special sometimes, because it's special, only after big lunch and how I am the best at printing and we are all working on our posture, and we already did our pencil grip, and some kids need to work on their rounded letters, and I need to work on my pointed letters, and we get to do cursive now, sometimes, and all that.

Later on, Daddy said he wanted me to begin voice training, in addition to piano lessons, to help me modulate my voice.

Friday, 20 December

Guess what, Diary,

Last day of school!!! I asked Miss Carmine for some extra work for the holidays so I could get a head start on Year 3, but she just laughed and said, "Bindy, learn to relax!"

Bindy Mackenzie: A Life

4. Bindy Mackenzie: The Triumphant Year
(Hills District Primary, Year 3, Age 8)

DIARY ENTRY

Tuesday, 18 February

Dear Diary,

Today, Mum's car won't start and there's a summer storm outside, so Mum said we could stay home from school. Dad said, "They won't get an education staying home from school." But Mum said, "Okay, *you* drop them off. Your car works." And Dad said it's too far out of his way. Mum said, "I'll get the neighbors to give them a lift." (We don't even know the neighbors. We just moved in.) So Dad went to work and Mum didn't even think about asking the neighbors.

Mum's now on the phone trying to get a business name registered. Anthony's singing a song about telephone electrocution. He made it up. He tried to stop Mum using the phone because of the lightning, but she ignored him. So now he's singing the song.

I'm here on the living room floor behind the couch.

I'm reading *Pride and Prejudice* by Jane Austen. I don't know what prejudice is yet, but Jane Austen seems quite witty.

BINDY MACKENZIE'S SPECIAL CLIPPINGS FILE
Hills News, *Thursday, 27 February*

Local student, Bindy Mackenzie, aged 8, has been awarded first place in the under-10 division of the *Hills News* "I Care about My World" competition with her innovative design for a hat.

The hat has a broad, plastic rim that collects rainwater and funnels it into an attached drinking bottle. (See picture.)

"I would like to thank my father," said Bindy, "for being an inspiration to me. He is a person who sees possibility lurking behind every shadow. He has taught me to be the same."

DIARY ENTRY

Friday, 2 May

BEST DAY EVER!! Won the School Spelling Bee. It is the first time that anyone from Year 3 has ever won it. The Year 6 girl who was runner-up ran out of the room crying.

Also discovered William Faulkner. Such haunting prose.

BINDY MACKENZIE'S SPECIAL CLIPPINGS FILE

Sun Herald, *Monday, 16 June*

Children's Poetry Competition

A Reflection on Blue

Blue is the color of my

Mum's nail polish today

For a party trick,

She said.

Blue is the sea

But not always

It's only the reflection of the sky

And the refraction of blue light

From the sun which is a

White ball of light containing each of the colors

Some of which

Bindy Mackenzie: A Life

Are absorbed, including the color red
And also the sea contains particles of dirt and
Plants and animals, dead and alive,
Which make it look a bit
Blue.
Blue is the Blue Mountains
Which my brother,
Anthony,
Can see from
His window
In his bedroom
If he stands
On his drum kit.
Blue is the way my friend
Toby
sometimes feels
because
other kids
call
him
fat
Even though he's not
Really, not very,
And I said,
"Toby,
You're not
that fat, you're
Just

a
bit
plump"
And I
bought him
a blue
Chupa Chup.
To cheer
him up.
Blue is the name of my Auntie Veronica's dog:
Blue.
Blue likes it
If you throw him an ice cube
He crunches it
He likes to fetch
A blue rubber ball
But he won't give it back
He just offers it to you
And you try to pull it out of his mouth
And he holds it with his teeth!
But Blue got sick.
And he threw up a bit
On the laundry floor
And the vet said,
"There's nothing we can do
For Blue"
And he died,

Bindy Mackenzie: A Life

Just yesterday,
And this
poem
Is a
Special Gift for
Auntie Veronica
In memory of her dog:
Blue.

    — *Bindy Mackenzie* — *First Prize (Junior Division)*

DIARY ENTRY

Wednesday, 13 August

Well, Dear Diary,

Today I needed $10 but I only had $2.

We had to bring in $10 for the Sausage Sizzle next weekend.

Anthony and I forgot to ask for the money last night, but I remembered on the way to school. And I was thinking about how Dad always says, "There is a solution for every problem," so this is what I did.

I bought a bag of 10 cheap pens for $1.50 and some colorful stickers for 50¢. I put one sticker on each pen, then I said they were super sticker pens and I sold them to some kids at school for $1 each. So then I had $10.

When I got home I was telling Mum what happened, and she was going, "Oh, goodness," and Dad heard and he said, "What did you do?"

I told him the story, and he started laughing until he couldn't stop. Then he goes, "Give me five!" which is this thing where you slap your hands together.

And then he goes, "Bindy, that is an important lesson for you — always remember that you are the shepherd and all the other kids are sheep."

He asked Anthony what he did about the $10, and Anthony said he just did what other kids did who forgot their money. He told the teacher he'd bring it tomorrow. Dad went into his study.

5. Bindy Mackenzie: The Reflective Year
(Hills District Primary, Year 4, Age 9)

DIARY ENTRY

Thursday, 5 March

Reflections on being Number One

Being Number One is strange. Where can you go from here? Nowhere except down.

Last year, when I was *attaining* first place (design competition, spelling bee, poetry contest, etc.), I was thrilled. But this year . . . ?

Well, let's just say I arrived on the first day of Year 4 with terror in my soul. What if I could not live up to the standards I had set last year? What if I began to slip down?

Others might laugh: "Oh yeah," they might say, sarcastically, "it's *really* tough being Number One."

But each Friday, when we get out weekly tests back, I don't feel *glad* to get 100%.

I feel relieved.

Bindy Mackenzie: A Life

Friday, 3 April

Reflections on the Human Condition

I think it's a good idea to imagine that everyone you meet is having a bad day. So, it's YOUR job to cheer them up.

ACHIEVEMENT AWARD

To: Bindy Mackenzie

For: 100 Gold Stars

Top work, Bindy!

Nobody in my class EVER got 100 gold stars before!

And it's only May! ☺☺☺

Saturday, 27 June

Hi Diary,

Just back from a friend's birthday party. (Toby Mazzerati.)

There were eleven boys at the party, and three girls. The girls banded together: We were allies in a world of boys! The boys wanted to play computer games, but Mrs. Mazzerati made us go outside and play "traditional" party games.

There was also something called the Chocolate Game which I thoroughly enjoyed. The group sits in a circle around a block of chocolate. A dice is passed around the circle. (I told everyone that "die" is the technical singular of "dice" but that "dice" is acceptable these days.) If you throw a six, you have to put on an apron and begin eating the chocolate, by cutting it up with a plastic knife and fork! You should hear the screaming and shouting when you get a six! "SIX!" they all shriek. And they rush the dice around the circle, hoping to get *another* six to stop the first person's attack on the chocolate.

I got six more often than anybody else. I felt so proud. I can't explain it — I know it was only luck.

I admit, there was a point when I thought: *Really? I have to eat more chocolate?*

But I always did.

Now, two hours later, back home again, I have the strangest feeling. I can't describe it. I guess I just feel sad that the party's over. I feel tired and confused and cranky. I wonder if I'll ever have such fun again? I mean, it just seemed to *work* so beautifully — could that party, that chocolate game, have been the high point of my life? Is it all downhill from here?

I think Keats put it best when he wrote:

My heart aches, and a drowsy numbness pains
My sense, as though of hemlock I had drunk,
Or emptied some dull opiate to the drains.

Sunday, 16 August
I've been struggling a bit with *Ulysses* by James Joyce. I think a good editor might have made a world of difference to this book.

Saturday, 31 October
Today we moved to another new house. It's a wreck. Anthony and I walked in the front door, straight down the hall, and out the back without stopping. We looked at each other and laughed.

Bindy Mackenzie: A Life

We sat on the porch for a while, talking about the universe, and watching some kids play in a swimming pool next door.

Next thing, one of the kids climbed out of the pool and ran over to the wire fence. He was shivering and asking us over to swim!

Mum found our swimmers for us (how did she know which box they were in?), and we swam all afternoon, played Red Light/ Green Light, played Crocodile, Crocodile, played whirlpool, et cetera.

The boy who invited us is named Sam, and he and Anthony are the same age, and Sam's coming over to watch a movie at our place tomorrow.

Thursday, 19 November

As soon as Mum got home from work last night, I handed her my history exercise book and said, "Ask me." Because there was a test coming today.

But this morning I woke up and at first I felt fine but then I was eating my breakfast and I opened up my history book to look one more time and SUDDENLY I got the WORST headache and such a bad tummyache like I couldn't stand up.

Mum said I had to go back to bed and she'd stay home with me today. I made her promise to phone Mr. Inglewood and ask if I could do the test tomorrow instead. She said only if I promise to take a day off today and not think about history.

After I slept a bit, Mum came in and had a talk with me. She said I had to learn to relax and who cares if I mess up a history test sometimes? "Nobody," she said.

Then she went out and I was thinking, Well, I *care, aren't* I *somebody?* and Dad came home and I heard them fighting in the hallway. Dad was saying Mum should have sent me to school anyway, "because you've gotta sand back those neuroses." And Mum was going, "If a ten-year-old's having a nervous breakdown about *school*work, that's a problem," and Dad was going, "If I know our Bindy, she'll be out of bed any moment, demanding you take her to school, and she'll be right because you can't let fear get in the way of progress."

So I waited a moment then I got up and went out and said I need to go to school now.

Dad goes, "That's the spirit."

Mum goes, "Bindy, you promised."

I said, "That promise was contrary to my own interests and you should not have exacted it from me."

Dad goes, "Ahaaah!"

So I went to school and the history test was easy and we got it back in the afternoon and I got 20/20, *Excellent Work.*

6. Bindy Mackenzie: The Year
I Learned the Facts of Life
(Hills District Primary, Year 5, Age 10)

DIARY ENTRY

Saturday, 6 February

Just read a book called *Lady Chatterley's Lover* by D.H. Lawrence. Rather repetitive and overwrought. I don't understand why the

Lady is spending so much time with the gardener. And what exactly are they doing? It should be made clear.

Mum took us to visit Auntie Veronica today. Anthony brought Sam along. I'm impressed that they've managed to stay friends even though we've moved several times since we lived next door to him and his pool.

Thursday, 20 May
Reflections on Velcro

Lately, I've been reading the myths of Ancient Greece. I have just finished a story about a hero named Herakles who had to undertake twelve "labors" (which means challenges, like killing many-headed serpents and stealing apples).

As I read, I felt as if pieces of Velcro were being torn apart in my chest. For I could not stop the despairing "rip" of this thought: *When did he get to take a break? Why, after each of these labors, did Herakles have to do ANOTHER one? When did this poor man get to take a break?*

Saturday, 17 July
Reflections on Realists

This morning I overheard Mum and Dad fighting. (I was on the floor behind the couch.)

Dad was going, "Cecily, listen to me. You're not hearing me here. Hello? Am I speaking to a rock?"

Afterwards, I hovered around Dad a bit, in case he wanted *me* to hear him. We were taking some doors off their hinges, and Dad said something interesting.

This is what he said.

"Bindy," he said. "What would you call a person who walks into a takeaway joint and makes her choice by looking at the glossy pictures on the wall above the counter? Rather than at the *actual* food which is sitting right in front of her? Right there in front of her, underneath the glass? What would you call such a person? Do you hear what I'm saying?"

I assured him that I did.

Hills District Primary School
Half-Yearly Report: BINDY MACKENZIE
General Comments

Bindy is a pleasure to have in the class. I can honestly say I've never had a student as bright, conscientious and cheerful as she is. No doubt, she will eventually win over her classmates — she's a little too advanced for most of them at the moment, but she tries very hard to engage with them.

DIARY ENTRY
Monday, 6 September

I think Toby Mazzerati and I may be drifting apart. We were both in the purple group but today I heard him ask to move to the green group. Why? My only hope is that I did not cause offense this morning, when I tried to tell him about this "five food groups float" that I saw at the Orange Blossom Festival. I suppose I thought he might benefit from some clear nutritional information — his weight and so on.

Bindy Mackenzie: A Life

Sunday, 5 December

Oh Dear Diary,

I have spent the day reading some books by young people's authors, including Judy Blume. I found them in a box of Mum's things that I was unpacking (we moved here just yesterday), and I am now a different person.

It has been a revelation.

I now know exactly what's going to happen to me, physically, in the next few years. (I also know what is going to happen to boys — things called wet dreams and erections. It seems impressive.)

I think I even get what S-E-X *really* is!

I feel very odd, but also strangely elated. At last I have learned the facts of life.

7. Bindy Mackenzie: The Surprising Year (Hills District Primary, Year 6, Age 11)

DIARY ENTRY

Sunday, 2 January

Dear Diary,

Today may have been a perfect day.

This morning, Mum was out doing a newspaper interview, because she won Business Woman of the Year again, and when she arrived home Dad had a bouquet of flowers waiting for her! It was so sweet.

I spent some time weeding in the front garden and helped Dad paint the front fence. The people next door have a boat lying facedown in their front garden. Dad and I made some jokes about the boat. Sulfur-crested cockatoos flew about the eucalyptus trees. Mum came out with some sandwiches and fresh-squeezed apple juice and suggested we take a break. So, I sat on the grass and read *An Enquiry Into the Human Mind on the Principles of Common Sense* by Thomas Reid.

Hills District Primary School Talent Quest
FIRST PRIZE TO BINDY MACKENZIE
For her valiant rendition of Beethoven's
Sonata No. 23 in F minor

DIARY ENTRY
Tuesday, 7 March
Today, I presented another submission to Dad that we should get pocket money. (Mum does give us money sometimes, as a surprise, but I don't think Dad knows about that.) I pointed out that if you give a child a limited amount of spending money, you will help him or her to learn sound financial management.

As usual, Dad said that he only pays out his hard-earned cash if there's something in it for him.

But then he looked at his wrists for a while and said something amazing. If Anthony or I develop a business proposal — something that might make a profit that we could then share with him — he would consider investing in that business. Our share of the profits would then be our "pocket money."

Bindy Mackenzie: A Life

200

I am going to work on my first business proposal right now!!!

BUSINESS PROPOSAL
by BINDY MACKENZIE

To Dad,

My proposal is to buy skipping ropes cheaply and then sell them to the other kids at high prices. So, Dad, I humbly ask you to invest money so that I can buy skipping ropes.

Yours sincerely,

Bindy Mackenzie

Response to Bindy Mackenzie's Skipping Rope Business Proposal: APPROVED

Please provide regular reports on the progress of this business.

Paul Mackenzie

DIARY ENTRY

Wednesday, 12 April

Reflections on Transformation

Today I was watching some people play hopscotch, play elastics, chat, and skip with the ropes that *I* sold them — and somehow the games and the conversations began to blur and transform before my eyes. They seemed to become quavers, crotchets, and semibreves (and I was the composer); next they were harpsichords, violins, and trombones (and I was the conductor).

Saturday, 15 July

Today is my birthday!!! I am now twelve years old.

I got *The Compleat Workes of William Shakespeare*, Beginner French and German CDs (I'm hoping to learn basic French and German before I start at Ashbury next year), and some glitter glue.

Moreover, I'm elated because we're having Party Pies for dinner, and chocolate mousse for dessert!!

HILLS DISTRICT PRIMARY "SMILE AWARD"
Presented to *Bindy Mackenzie*
"The Friendliest Girl in Year 6"

DIARY ENTRY

Monday, 7 August

Anthony did a business proposal today. He proposed that Dad give him ten million dollars so that he and Sam could make a horror movie.

Dad wrote "REJECTED" in red pen across the page. He said Anthony was welcome to waste his own time but shouldn't go around wasting others'.

"Your loss," said Anthony.

Saturday, 16 December

Reflections on Existence

Today I was helping Dad sand back the paint on the kitchen cupboards.

Bindy Mackenzie: A Life

As we worked (and the lightest film of dust settled onto our bare arms), I told Dad about Sartre's views on nothingness. I said that starting at Ashbury next year made me feel that I was going from *existence* to *non-existence*. I would be a *nobody* at Ashbury.

Dad said something interesting. "Bindy," he said, "that's not the attitude. Hold on to the idea that *you* are Number One. Those other kids? Nothing. You? Something else. You tell yourself that while you're sanding there."

And so I did.

8. Bindy Mackenzie: The Feverish Year
(Ashbury High, Year 7, Age 12)

DIARY ENTRY
Wednesday, 31 January
Reflections on Beauty — 3:45 p.m.
Today was my first day at Ashbury!

I was struck, most of all, by the beauty.

Excuse me, I cannot reflect on beauty any further! I would like to get a head start on my homework.

Bindy's Reflections on Beauty (Part 2) — 11 p.m.
The beauty of my fellow Year 7 students!

It almost made me weep to be one with them! Nervous eyes, polished shoes, and neatly brushed hair! From all four corners of the Hills District we came — yet we were all the same. For we all wore the Ashbury blue, and carried the regulation Ashbury bag, stamped with the Ashbury crest.

There is an especially beautiful "group of four" in my home-room. They obviously come from the same primary school as they are already close friends. They walked into the classroom, a smooth, graceful step, talking and laughing, as if this were just an ordinary day — not the first day of Year 7 at all! Two girls with long dark hair; one skinny boy; one boy with blonde hair past his shoulders. The skinny boy caught me staring, and raised his eyebrows up and down, up and down. I laughed and he turned back to his friends.

Monday, 5 February
To the Principal
Ashbury High

Dear Sir,
Good morning, my name is Bindy Mackenzie and I am in Year 7 at your school.

I would like to congratulate you on the excellence of your school. I know I have been here for only three days, but the academic standards seem rigorous, the lessons begin and end on time, and the teachers seem stern but fair.

I have a small suggestion to make and it is: Do we really have to move around so much?

In primary, we used to stay in the same classroom all day. Here, almost every subject is in a different place and Art is right across the oval!! It seems like a waste of time and energy, and I

Bindy Mackenzie: A Life

have found myself lost more than once. What if the students stayed in one room and the teachers *came to them*!?

Just a thought . . .

Yours sincerely,

Bindy Mackenzie

DIARY ENTRY

Dienstag, Februar 6

Heute hatte ich zum ersten mal Deutsch studiert! Und von jetzt werde ich EINFACH auf Deutsch schreiben, auf Deutsch denken, und auf Deutch leben! Von jetz bin ich *einfach* Deutsch! Ich werde mit meiner Familie auf Deutsch sprechen. Ich werde Alles auf Deutsch machen! Also, guten Nacht! Ich schreibe weiter Morgen!

Wednesday, 14 February

Had to stop speaking and writing only in German. The other teachers didn't appreciate it.

It had seemed to make sense to me, to immerse myself in German, but my parents refused to pass the pepper even though it was *clear* what I was asking for — pepper, in German, is *pfeffer*.

Anthony was the only good sport. He listened to what I said with an intense expression on his face and then he nodded vigorously and replied in his own nonsense German: "Munchen, wonchen, gebrunchen! Ganz begobbleston! Schnell! Ja schnell!" He made me laugh, despite myself.

Anyway, it's over now.

I suppose one must make compromises.

DIARY ENTRY

Thursday, 12 April

Lately, I've been staring at the Group of Four more than usual. I've smiled at the skinny boy a few times, but he hasn't done his bouncing eyebrows thing again. Actually, he doesn't seem to notice.

I hope, one day, to make friends with the Group — perhaps even make it into a Group of Five?

The more I stare the more *strangely familiar* the Four become. As if I had met them somewhere before. Is that just wishful thinking?

Their names do not seem familiar. The prettier of the two girls is Astrid Bexonville. She wears her hair in a French braid, and I have watched in awe as she reaches back to unplait her hair, shake it out — *and then casually rebraid it*! Now, there is talent.

Sunday, 22 April

Reflections on Choice

Mum and Dad were fighting this morning. Mum was saying she wants to stay in this house for a few more years now. She said she was waiting at traffic lights behind a moving truck today, and the sight of that truck gave her stomach cramps so bad she had to do a U-turn and pull over.

Bindy Mackenzie: A Life

Afterwards, Dad said something interesting to me. He said, "Bindy, when you're renovating a house, you're always making choices. The choices aren't that tough — keep the good and chuck out the bad. Keep the original moldings, rip out the shag pile carpet. You hearing me?"

I nodded to reassure him, and he went on.

"And I reckon it's the same with your genes," he said. (I thought he meant *jeans* at first, and explained that I do not wear these.) "Now," he said, ignoring me. "You've got a mother with a good head for business, but a tendency toward hysterics. You might have inherited both, but you've gotta make the choice which you keep and which you chuck. My advice, keep that business head but toss aside the hysterics. Okay, kid? It's your choice."

I told Dad a little about the Danish philosopher, Søren Aabye Kierkegaard, and what he has to say about choice.

Hills District Oratory Contest

Year 7

Adjudicator's Notes

Bindy Mackenzie

This girl is dynamite! You can just see that talent crackling! And that noble toss of her head when she makes a point — it just killed me! Wonderful! First place!

DIARY ENTRY

Monday, 30 April

GUESS WHAT? *I've figured out the Group of Four!!* I KNEW they looked familiar!

I've been gazing at them, trying to trigger my memory. The skinny boy kind of widened his eyes at me the other day, and I realized it was not meant in the spirit of bouncing eyebrows. It was more: *"Why do you keep LOOKING at me?"*

So, I did some research — school administration office, school library, other students, local library, etc.— and discovered that the Group of Four all attended Kellyville Primary. I flicked through that school's public archives, and noticed their regular participation in the Twilight Parade at the Orange Blossom Festival.

And *bling! bling! bling!* went my mind.

Two years ago I had watched the Twilight Parade, and had fallen in love with a Kellyville Primary "Food Groups" float!

Frantically, I flicked through newspaper reports, and there it was: a photograph of the very float. And there *they* were, the Group of Four, amongst a larger group of children. The four were dressed up as a banana, a cauliflower, a cheese slice, and a lamb chop.

As soon as the time seems right, I mean to congratulate the Group of Four, on their marvelous and educational float.

Wednesday, 9 May

Toby Mazzerati was a good friend in primary school, but we drifted apart in the last couple of years. However, now, here at Ashbury, he is friendly again. Is it loyalty because we've known each other so long? Today he gave me a jewelry box that he had made in woodwork. It has beautiful gold hinges and the lid opens and closes smoothly.

Bindy Mackenzie: A Life

I accepted the box gratefully, and told him how much I loved it, and I lavished praise upon the craftsmanship. His cheeks turned pale pink, and he gave me a big smile.

Then I offered him help with his algebra. I'd heard him talking to himself in Maths the day before. "What is x?" he was murmuring. "If x equals x equals x, then what is y equals y equals y? If you were my x, would you also be my x, and who would be my y and why is y my y?" He was saying this in a sort of chant.

"I'd like to pay you back for this," I explained, "and I know that Maths is something of a challenge for you."

He said he'd give that a miss, but thanks for the offer.

**B.H. Neumann Certificate for Perfect Score
in Australian Mathematics Competition
for the Westpac Award**

To: Bindy Mackenzie

Hey Bindy, congratulations on this! Interested in signing up for the Australian Mathematical Olympiad Program? Cheers, Ms. Yen

---

DIARY ENTRY
Friday, 15 June
I think I might have been wrong about Toby being friendly again. He hasn't really spoken to me since he gave me the wooden jewelry box.

Saturday, 11 August

Reflections on Humor

Today, Anthony and Sam were watching *Raising Arizona* — they're working through the Coen Brothers' films — and I took a break to join them.

The three of us laughed hysterically, and afterwards continued to laugh as we made ourselves sausages and chips for dinner, and recalled the funniest moments from the film.

Now, Anthony and Sam are only in Year 6, but they often make me laugh. So, you would think that the humor of my Year 7 classmates would be even more impressive. And at times, I must admit, I am surprised into laughter by the quick wit around me.

But sometimes that humor bewilders me. The other day, I overheard a conversation between Emily Thompson and her two best friends. The three of them had fallen out about a month ago — I don't know why, but I had been watching with interest. On this day, however, they seemed to make up. They were hugging and crying together — *all* of them crying! (I don't believe I have ever cried in front of another human being.)

One of them said tearily, "And I was eating waffles last night, and I couldn't stop thinking . . ." Another interrupted: "Waffles?" she said, in a tragic voice. "Waffles," agreed the first. "Waffles," the third repeated, in her own tragic voice. And before you knew it all three were shouting the word "WAFFLES," laughter exploding around them.

I suppose they just found the word amusing at that moment. But I did not see that it could possibly be.

They are so strange, young people.

Bindy Mackenzie: A Life

Ashbury End of Year Report Card
Bindy Mackenzie
MATHEMATICS

Bindy is an extremely talented student, who has excelled in this class. Most gratifying, however, is her diligence. If she doesn't understand a problem, she will work and work at it — such ferocity! She's a delight to teach.

DIARY ENTRY
Tuesday, 11 December
Amazing news!! The Group of Four seems to have split up!! It is Astrid and blonde boy versus Nicole and skinny boy! Astrid and blonde-hair have merged with another group. Astrid seems cocky and defiant. Wish I knew what the fight was all about.

Thursday, 20 December
My last day of Year 7 today.
Very strange day.

For much of the year, I waited for the opportunity to tell the Group of Four that I had seen them before.

Today, I thought I had an opportunity, at last, to speak.

The Group has not made up — they remain splintered. Astrid *has* seemed happy enough with that, but today, on the Year 7 balcony, I happened to see her crying. Now, I know that Nicole has been spreading a rumor that Astrid was the one who caused the breakup, by stealing a guy from Nicole, even though she knew they liked each other. I guessed that this was why Astrid was crying.

Now, I thought, was the time to speak to her.

"Astrid?" I said, approaching gently. "You know, I saw you on a float in the Twilight Parade at the Orange Blossom Festival back in Year 5?"

A few people were walking along the balcony, and they paused and looked at us with interest. Astrid's eyes were puffy. She stared at me.

I realized it was the first time I'd ever actually spoken to her. I found my voice trembling, but was determined to go on.

"It was the 'five food groups' float," I explained. "And it was really wonderful. I loved it! And listen, I *know* the kind of person who would be on a float like that is *not* the kind of person to steal a boy from her friend! I know you didn't do what they're saying you did. I can't believe Nicole is spreading those rumors!"

Astrid's face was doing something odd. It was as if the face wanted to find its own center. Her eyes seemed to crease downward, toward her nose; her nose crinkled upward; her mouth curled in on itself.

"And you were so great in the Orange Blossom Festival!" I continued, in something of a panic: Why wasn't she speaking? "You really look *superb*," I said, "all dressed up as a lamb chop!"

At last, Astrid spoke.

I cannot write the words that she spoke.

They are not in my vocabulary.

Let's just say that she spoke in these unwritable words to say some cruel things about my appearance, about the sound of my voice, and about the fact that I exist. She told me to "get out of her face."

Then she turned towards the passersby and laughed. (They laughed too.)

I noticed something — Astrid might be beautiful, but when she laughs, she sometimes gives herself a double chin. She leans down to laugh, you see, lowering her chin to her neck. It makes her look a little plump.

She will be fat one day. She will go from vodka to anti-depressants to marijuana, and she will find herself on the slippery slope to crack cocaine.

I feel sorry for her.

I'm confident she'll be in and out of rehab.

9. Bindy Mackenzie: The Unremarkable Year
(Ashbury High, Year 8, Age 13)

Explanatory Note

I have looked through my special box, but can find nothing at all relating to this year. It must have been completely unre-markable.

I do recall that my asthma returned during an incident that took place on our school trip to Hill End. I did not enjoy that trip. I have been a chronic asthmatic ever since, and take preventative medication every day. I always carry an inhaler, and only wear clothes that have pockets, and my hand is always checking in a pocket to ensure that the inhaler is there. When I moved in with Auntie Veronica this year, she scattered inhalers all over her house (high enough so Bella can't reach them). Now I catch sight of them in unexpected places — on the windowsill, in a china cabinet. It's like an Easter egg hunt for inhalers.

10. Bindy Mackenzie: The Friendship Year
(Ashbury High, Year 9, Age 14)

Feel like a MORON?
Think you might be MALFUNCTIONING?

BINDY MACKENZIE CAN HELP!

Come along and learn how to
"TAME THE TEEN MONSTER INSIDE YOU!"

Bindy's advisory sessions will take place in the relaxed, convivial setting of the locker room, every second Tuesday this term.

Free to all students! Real Indian tea will be served.

Bindy Mackenzie: A Life

DIARY ENTRY

Monday, 3 February

I am excited about Year 9. I intend to embrace it. I will *erase* Year 8 from existence. It didn't happen! Poof! It's gone! (I saw Astrid today, back from her summer holiday with a ridiculously dark suntan. She will erase her*self* from existence if she keeps that up. Somebody should tell her there's a hole in the ozone layer.)

Anyway, I will gather Year 9 into my arms and squeeze it tight. Press it close to my body and curl my legs around it.

In that spirit, I have registered for the School Spectacular, the School Representative Council, the Duke of Edinburgh Award Scheme, the Tournament of Minds, a C-grade netball team, and the squash comp.

Also, debating! There's a contest called the Tearsdale Shield that our school has never won. The debating coach, Mrs. Lilydale, seems friendly. We chatted for a while (she knows of my academic record), and I told her about my "Tame the Teen Monster" plans. She wished me heartfelt luck with my first session tomorrow.

I wonder if anyone will come?

Tuesday, 4 February
To The Principal
Ashbury High

Dear Sir,
I am writing about a matter of grave concern.

Today, I held the first session of "Taming the Teen Monster Inside You." This course is based on several books about juvenile delinquency and teenage self-esteem that I read over the summer.

My aim is to help the socially malfunctioning amongst us to realize their full potential.

I am delighted to inform you that three students attended this first session.

They were all new to the school this year. Their names are Ernst von Schmerz, Kelly Simonds, and Joshua Lynch. I have no complaints about their conduct: They listened attentively, and Ernst promised to write it all up on his blog!

No, my complaint is more important — a grave issue, nay, an issue of life-or-death. I am sorry to say, at the end of the session, Joshua Lynch reached into his school bag, to take out his books for the next class, and *I believe I glimpsed something like drug paraphernalia.* Or, at least, something like drugs. A large plastic bag containing a greeny-browny plantlike substance.

I do not believe in "telling tales" — but I was frightened by the size of that bag. I fear that my new friend may be heading for a fall.

I hope that you can find a way to help him.

Thank you,

Yours sincerely,

Bindy Mackenzie

DIARY ENTRY

Wednesday, 5 March

I now have two new friends at Ashbury: Ernst von Schmerz and Kelly Simonds.

Bindy Mackenzie: A Life

I also have a new debating team.

I confess there is a link between the above two facts. . . .

Today, I mentioned to Ernst and Kelly that I would not be able to lunch with them, as I had to see Mrs. Lilydale about debating, which begins next term.

Ernst tipped his head to the side.

Kelly said, "Whuh?" (That is her way of loading the word "what?" with confusion — a kind of cross between "what?" and "huh?")

And it turned out that *they* also had to see Mrs. Lilydale.

Because *they* are my debating team!

They had always assumed that I knew this! Indeed, they had been to see Mrs. Lilydale the very same day that I had, to ask her about debating. And it was Mrs. Lilydale who suggested — nay, insisted — that they attend my first "Tame the Teen Monster" session! To get to know me, and each other, their debating team!

I felt embarrassed to have been mistaken — I had thought it was my posters that brought those two along.

(I don't know who told that other boy, Joshua Lynch, to come along. I suppose he must regret his decision now.)

ASHBURY CITIZENSHIP AWARD
To: *Bindy Mackenzie*
For: *Adopting the Music Courtyard and adjoining paths as her part of the school to keep clean.*

DIARY ENTRY

Saturday, 19 April

Sam went to the wrong house to visit Anthony today. He'd been thinking about something else, and knocked on the door of the house we had lived in *two houses ago*. It was so funny. Sam can be vague. He and my brother are both so artistic and creative. They plan to make films together, and I believe they have every chance of success.

At the moment, they are going through films written by Charlie Kaufman. I watched *Being John Malkovich* with them. I think it's my favorite film of all time.

Especially, I liked the scene in which everyone has to crouch and hunch down, because the ceilings are too low. That scene spoke to me, because I think I have to crouch and crawl my way through my days. I feel a lot like a giraffe.

<u>*Explanatory Note*</u>
The above may look like a blank, white square, but it is actually a receipt for a CD — the only "rock music" CD I have ever purchased. The receipt has now faded to this white, blank state.

Bindy Mackenzie: A Life

DIARY ENTRY

Thursday, 14 August

Reflection on Names

Today at lunchtime, Ernst von Schmerz told me that his real name is Kee Dow Liang.

His parents moved to Sydney from Malaysia when he was six, and changed his name to Harold Brown to help him fit in. When he turned thirteen, he decided to go back to his real name but the kids at his school "did not react well."

"What did they do?" I asked, but we were passing the tuck-shop at that moment, and Ernst said, "Hang a links here" — that is his way of saying, "Let's turn left here."

After we had bought ourselves salt-and-vinegar chips, I asked Ernst again about the kids at his old school. He said (cryptically) that they'd tried to teach him that a person should *never* change his name, especially not to something "funny" like Kee Dow Liang.

So Ernst decided he would change his name as often as he could. At the moment his name is Ernst von Schmerz. In the future, he said, it could be anything.

Certificate for Most Improved Team Member
Grade C, Netball
To: Bindy Mackenzie

Bindy, congratulations on this — from our first game you were jumping like a little bean, and you finally learned to catch the ball! A joy for a coach to watch!

DIARY ENTRY

Thursday, 21 August

I would have liked to talk to Kelly Simonds about Ernst and his name: ask her if she thought he was doing the right thing. Or was he hurting himself to defy those other kids? Did he really *want* to be Ernst von Schmerz? If so, what had become of Kee Dow Liang — and of Harold Brown, come to think of it? And if Ernst changes his name again, who will he be? Will we really know him any longer?

But I do not speak to Kelly much these days. Although she is an excellent second speaker, and is friendly with us at debates, she has been drifting away during school days, and often she sits with other groups.

Kmart
Casual Employee of the Month — August
Bindy Mackenzie

Explanatory Note

In Year 9, I commenced work as a casual employee of Kmart Australia Ltd., and by August, I was Employee of the Month.

I befriended another new employee: a girl named Leesa, a student at Brookfield High. Considering that she was a Brookfielder, Leesa seemed nothing like a criminal.

Late at night, when the store had closed and we were reshelving and tidying, Leesa would take breaks to visit me. (She was in Appliances; I was in Womenswear.) She'd roll up on the back of a shopping trolley.

Bindy Mackenzie: A Life

220

We'd chat about our ambitions to rise to the position of Store Manager one day (we were being ironic and made each other laugh). And one day, Leesa asked for my phone number. She wrote it on the back of her hand, apparently oblivious to ink poisoning.

Now, a few days after this, Leesa actually telephoned. This happened early one morning. She told me she and some friends had tickets to see a band called Powderfinger the following night. Did I want to come along?

I explained that I had a piano exam. Leesa did not seem to mind.

Later that night, I admitted to myself that the piano exam was at four and there was plenty of time to get to a concert. In truth, I had been alarmed at the idea of meeting Leesa's Brookfield friends. Even if Leesa could not see through me, I knew that her friends would. (And how did one go to a concert? What did one do? Dance? How? Sing along? But I didn't know the words! I would surely fail!)

The next day, after my piano exam, I went into HMV and bought a copy of a Powderfinger CD — the only rock CD in my collection.

But when I returned to Kmart the following week, Leesa was not there. I suppose her trolley riding might have lost her the job.

DIARY ENTRY

Monday, 15 September

Today, in Art, I overheard Emily Thompson talking with her two friends, Lydia and Cassie. Lydia is going out with Sergio Saba at the moment — and she was telling the others that he'd met her at the time he was supposed to last night (he's usually late).

At this, Emily said wryly: "That's a turnip for the books."

She honestly said "turnip." She thinks the expression has something to do with vegetables.

I have serious concerns about the stupidity levels in my year.

Thursday, 2 October

Guess what, Mum secretly bought Anthony a Super-8 movie camera! (He's been asking Dad for the money for one, and Dad keeps refusing.) Anthony and Sam have already written their first movie. They want me to play the victim. All I have to do is get stabbed twenty times and climb a tree, covered in red paint. I've been going to drama classes on Saturdays, for the skills component of the Duke of Edinburgh Award, and to First Aid (for the service component) on Thursday nights — so I think I am prepared for the part.

Thursday, 6 November

Reflections on Glandular Fever

Astrid Bexonville has glandular fever.

I overheard her friends saying she's going to miss all the exams, but she'll be allowed to do them on her own later, probably in the principal's office.

As for glandular fever, I don't believe in it. I don't think it exists. It's one of those "teenage" ailments that students invent to get themselves extra study time. I have no respect for it.

---

11. Bindy Mackenzie: The Year of the Important Error
(Ashbury High, Year 10, Age 15)

Saturday, 14 February

My Dearest Diary,

I thought it best to warn you: I won't have time to write very much this year. I will write even less than usual. I hope you will not take offense.

You see, this is the most important year of my life to date: Year 10. A year that will shape my academic future. The Year of the School Certificate. I must focus all my energy on study — I must avoid the "pointless reverie" of diary writing.

I have to write now though, because I am in a flutter. It turns out that the first few weeks of Year 10 have been surprising, nay, they have been *exciting*!

Things have been happening!

Here is a list:

1. Kelly Simonds is friendly to us, as if she had never drifted! She sits with Ernst and me at recess now, and she has lunch with her other friends. That's a compromise we accept. Often I am in the library over lunch anyway, working.
2. Ernst is going to set up an online study group.
3. A boy in our year, Sergio Saba, spoke to me. He recently broke up with his girlfriend (Lydia), and might just be feeling lonely.

But he genuinely spoke to me. He was walking by at lunch-time and he said "Hey, Bindy, [. . .] is heaps good." I couldn't quite hear what was "heaps good." I smiled enigmatically. He has a scar on his face, but is handsome, and there is something compelling about his eyes.

4. I am waiting to see if he speaks to me again. If so, I will try to respond! I hope he says something I can hear.

5. There is going to be a Spring Concert, and I am secretly planning a solo!

So, you see, "It is all happening," as people say.

Monday, 1 March
Well, Diary,

I feel like a fool.

The lesson is this: When you think things are exciting, they probably are not.

Nobody signed up for Ernst's online study group except me.

Sergio, the boy with the burn scar, has not spoken a word to me again. He's already got a new girlfriend. I still don't know what was "heaps good."

Also, Kelly Simonds says she's applying to be an exchange student next year. She wants to go to Germany or Switzerland.

I urged her not to be foolish.

"Don't squander an important year of your education!" I said.

But she snorted. She says I'm just worried that she'll come back speaking better German than I do.

Bindy Mackenzie: A Life

And, finally, I went to see Mrs. Lilydale today. She now greets me with two hats on — her debating coach hat, and her Year Coordinator hat — she is our Year 10 Coordinator, you see. (She likes to use the old-fashioned term "form mistress." I admire her fondness for the past.)

But I was there about the Spring Concert.

"I'd like to sign up for the concert," I said. "I'd like to sing a solo."

Well!

The wave of doubt that crossed Mrs. Lilydale's face!

Immediately, I withdrew: "Or not," I said. "Or maybe not, after all."

"Oh," she said, quickly realizing her error. "No, no! Bindy! If that's what you want to do, you must do it! Here, see, I'll put your name down now. Sing a dozen solos if you like!"

"No, that's okay," I said proudly. "Please cross off my name."

Friday, 19 March

Cassie Aganovic spoke to me today. She is one of Emily Thompson's triangle of friends. I know it is wrong to be enthused by contact from the "upper class," but she spoke to me so casually, as if I were a regular acquaintance! She was asking if I knew a boy named Matthew Dunlop, who apparently goes to Brookfield High. I wonder why she thought I knew him? Anyway, I told her that I do actually have a friend at Brookfield, a girl named Leesa, and I said I'd ask Leesa for her.

Well!

That was strange.

It was as if I had completely forgotten that I do *not* have a friend named Leesa! I haven't spoken to her since last year when she phoned about the Powderfinger concert. Then she left Kmart and that was it. I don't even know her full name. . . .

Of course, I then worried that Cassie might be patiently waiting for me to ask Leesa, on her behalf, and I knew I couldn't do that. I began to wish that I just knew who this Matthew Dunlop was. If only I happened to know him all on my own, the problem would be solved.

Suddenly, an amazing thing happened. I realized I *did* know him!

I ran and found Cassie — I tried to slow down as I approached — and I told her that I had met someone of that very name at the School Spectacular last year! Well, I had not exactly meet him. But I had distinctly heard the announcement: "Matthew Dunlop of Brookfield High on the trumpet!"

Cassie seemed very pleased.

Friday, 2 April

You know, I hope I had the right person. "Matthew Dunlop," I mean. When I told Cassie last month that I knew him.

To be honest, there were *hundreds* of people playing or performing at the School Spectacular. And hundreds of announcements through muffled microphones. I suppose I might have heard *Michael* Dunlop, rather than Matthew. Or possibly Marcus Dunhill.

I wonder if I should say something to Cassie?

No, I must learn to be "cool."

Bindy Mackenzie: A Life

✕ ✕ ✕

Thursday, 3 June
The Principal
Ashbury High

Dear Sir,
I am writing to you about a matter of some concern.

My friend, Ernst von Schmerz, has mentioned to me that certain Ashbury students have installed file-sharing software on the school intranet, and are using it to "share" and "exchange" music files. (Ernst, I should point out, is highly computer literate.)

I wanted to draw your attention to this fact, as I would be distressed if our school were vicariously liable for copyright infringement.

Kindest regards,

Bindy Mackenzie

P.S. Also, do you realize that the reserve behind our school is positively *teeming* with students who are engaged in underage drinking/drug-taking and should actually be in class? Why on earth are supervisors not stationed at key points throughout the reserve?

DIARY ENTRY
Thursday, 17 June
Reflections on Romance
There is much fanfare at school at the moment about the Formal Dance to take place at the end of this year.

Not until the end of the year — but already the fanfare!

People are crying and fretting about theme, decorations, location and, most of all, about the state of their "romantic relationships."

As I said to Mrs. Lilydale today (she and I have made up and I often drop by for a chat) — I believe romance has no place in the school system.

I myself have always planned to avoid romance until the summer between Years 11 and 12. During that summer, I plan to meet and fall in love with a handsome young man, and we will spend our days sitting side by the side on the sand at the beach, reading prescribed texts for the following year and testing one another on their content. We will fall asleep over the texts as the sun sets. The young man and I will then *separate* for the course of Year 12 so as to concentrate on schoolwork, reuniting *only* at the end of the year for the Graduation Dance.

I had forgotten the Year 10 Formal, of course.

Saturday, 19 June

Reflections on History

I hear there will be dancing at the Formal Dance at the end of this year. I wonder what to do about that.

I believe life was perfect in Victorian England.

In those days, young ladies had maids who fixed their hair, their petticoats, their jewels, and their swirling gowns. They rode in silken carriages through lush, green fields, along cobbled laneways, toward elegant balls. They did not feel afraid as they emerged from their carriage because they knew

Bindy Mackenzie: A Life

exactly how to dance — they had taken lessons from a very young age.

Handsome, well-dressed gentlemen converged upon the ball-room, hoping to find ladies with intelligent eyes, who could sing, play the piano, and recite poems. They looked for young ladies who cross-stitched and reflected on life. They asked these young ladies to dance.

BUSINESS PROPOSAL

To: Mr. Paul Mackenzie (Dad)
From: Bindy Mackenzie
Subject: Personalized School Stationery

Mr. Mackenzie,
Please find attached my latest, exciting "Business Proposal."

(1) Bindy Mackenzie: A Background
Bindy Mackenzie is a small business operating in the highly profitable *schools* market. (See www.bindymackenzie.com for past ventures.) The manager (Bindy Mackenzie) has run the business since she was eleven. Her overhead costs are low as she operates out of her bedroom.

(2) Business Opportunity
There are three major forms of communication used by students in a school: They (A) talk (in person or by phone); (B) write notes; and (C) Instant Message.

I believe there is an opportunity to sell a *standardized* form of *personalized* stationery to students for the purposes of (B).

(3) Proposal to take Advantage of Opportunity
Operating Plan
Offer personalized stationery for each member of Year 10.

Market Segment
Year 10, Ashbury High.

Competitors
Newsagencies, school supply shop, parents who provide stationery for free.

Marketing Plan
- Notice in School Newsletter
- Notice on School Intranet
- Grassroots campaign — I will print up a set of stationery for myself and use it to communicate with other students and teachers. Word of mouth will do the rest. . . .

Sample Products
See attached samples of Bindy Mackenzie's Personalized Stationery for the Busy Teen, including:

- Memo from [student's name]
- Philosophical Musings of [student's name]

Bindy Mackenzie: A Life

- Telephone Messages for [student's name]
- The Short-Term Scholarly Goals of [student's name]
- Must-Haves for My Soul: A Spiritual Shopping List for [student's name]

DIARY ENTRY
Thursday, 12 August
Feeling low.

Dad invested in my personalized stationery but I am forlorn about its success (one customer — Ernst von Schmerz).

I wonder if Anthony is right. He refuses to take business proposals seriously. The other day he proposed that Dad invest $35 million so that he and Sam could start a chain of independent movie cinemas.

It's true that I never actually make much money from the proposals, but they seem to impress Dad. He always laughs. Sometimes I wish I could concentrate on schoolwork, and my part-time jobs, without also having to create business opportunities.

$$\times \quad \times \quad \times$$

The Philosophical Musings of Bindy Mackenzie
Wednesday, 15 September (in my bedroom)

I may as well use some of this stationery. I have printed so much for myself! Sigh.

I'm not sure how this is "philosophy," but Emily Thompson hates me. It turns out I did get the name wrong, back when I told Cassie Aganovic that I knew someone called "Matthew Dunlop of Brookfield." It now turns out (Emily tells me, sparks shooting from her ears), that there is *nobody* at Brookfield of that name. Some wicked boy was using a false name to deceive Cassie! I was in error. And for some reason this was a matter of life and death. Good grief. Can a *name* be so important?

Cassie herself does not seem angry with me. I apologized to her, and explained that I must have misheard (or misremembered). She just smiled and said I shouldn't let it get me down. Meanwhile, her two friends, Emily and Lydia (especially that wildfire Emily) absolutely HATE and DESPISE me.

The loyalty between those three!

It is close to appalling.

Hi Bindy,

My, you do have speedy fingers! What a marvelous job you did typing up the transcript of that *fiasco* today. I must admit that Emily Thompson did a rather good job as a "lawyer," but how sweet of you to come by my office to offer comfort afterwards.

Now, you might have noticed some *papers* on my desk as you walked in — tell me, *did* you see anything curious? Do be a team player and tell me what you saw — so I can explain!

So long!

Mrs. Lilydale

× × ×

Bindy Mackenzie: A Life

A Memo from Bindy Mackenzie

To: Mrs. Lilydale
From: Bindy Mackenzie
Subject: Papers on your desk . . .
Time: Monday afternoon

Dear Mrs. Lilydale,

You know, I enjoyed typing the transcript at the fiasco so much, that I've opened up a "transcript file" on my computer. I can't seem to stop typing the transcripts of conversations around me! I suppose it is not a good habit, but it is teaching me about humankind.

As for the papers on your desk, you'll just have to *guess* what I saw!! But don't worry, your secrets are always safe with me.

Best wishes,

Bindy Mackenzie

The Philosophical Musings of Bindy Mackenzie

Thursday, 5:05 p.m.

Mum and Dad are not speaking to each other — they're fighting because Anthony wants to go to a performing arts school with Sam next year, and Dad says the idea is absurd and the fees are extortionate.

I could play the piano — that might cheer everyone up. But here I sit on my piano stool, lost in a sort of reverie.

Feel odd about music generally. Last term, there was a dramatic conflict between Ashbury and Brookfield High, culminating in a sort of legal hearing, at which I typed the transcript. (Afterwards, I was with Mrs. Lilydale in her office — saw nothing at *all* on her desk, but she *thinks* I did. Couldn't resist keeping her guessing . . . I wonder what was there?)

5:07 p.m.

I should have made these notecards bigger. Have to keep starting a fresh one.

Anyway, after the "hearing," the Spring Concert became the "Spring for Unity Concert," bringing together Ashbury and Brookfield (a fruitless attempt at reconciliation). Cassie Aganovic made everyone weep at the concert. Nobody knew she could sing, but it turns out she has a voice as sweet as a gray singing finch, and as haunting as the song of the hermit thrush. The standing ovation that followed her performance went on for about twenty minutes. (I was so glad I pulled out of that concert myself.)

I could not explain, even to myself, how Cassie's singing made me feel, until much later that day — when I was almost asleep — and a single word crept into my mind. It was the word *pride*. I felt so proud of Cassie. A hall crowded with people, and all of us listening in wonder to someone from *my* year, someone who belonged, in a way, to *me*.

5:15 p.m.

Afterwards, everyone was saying she has to go on *Australian Idol.*

Bindy Mackenzie: A Life

I said, "It would be a tragedy if Cassie went on *Australian Idol*," and people sneered at me. They thought I was being jealous. But I only meant that she is far too unique and special for reality TV.

5:22 p.m.

Later, I saw that I had no right to feel proud. Cassie is not my friend, and in no way belongs to me. She might be in my year, but she's in a whole other class.

Typically, my mother is oblivious to issues of class. You see, Emily, Lydia, and Cassie are all going to Mum's sailing school (her latest business venture) over the summer. It happened this way: Mum offered places at the school as prizes for the concert. Cassie was the winner, of course, and Lydia, by chance, was runner-up. Emily's parents will pay for her to join her best friends.

Mum thinks I should come too — she doesn't have a clue! I could hardly spend a summer with Emily Thompson. She HATES me. I am still in trouble for that error I made about a name.

Are mistakes not allowed once in a while?

DURAL LADIES SOCIAL CLUB

Scholarship for Outstanding Achievement
By a Student in Year Ten
Textbook Allowance for All Year Eleven Textbooks
Presented to:
Bindy Mackenzie

DIARY ENTRY

Friday, 19 November

Dearest Diary,

Some funny things happened today, and it would help, I think, to unravel them here in your pages. I hope you do not mind.

It was shortly after school had finished for today.

I was sitting on a garden seat, which nobody else seems to know about. It's in the shadows of the Japanese maple outside the library. It's my favorite place to sit on these warm days, and sometimes I type transcripts of conversations floating by.

Anyway, the first thing that happened was that Toby Mazzerati "floated" by. He noticed me — people usually do not — and I felt oddly proud of his excellent eyesight. He made a humorous comment about how quickly I type on my laptop. I did not mind.

And then the strangest thing happened: I was suddenly convinced that Toby was about to ask me to the Year 10 Formal. I widened my eyes, my mouth dropped open, and I stared straight at his face. I suppose I may have terrified him.

Toby smiled and continued on his way, talking in that strange poetic style he has, and I dropped my eyes again.

Now, if that were not enough, a few moments later, two substitute teachers came striding by. They did not notice me at all. They were arguing about the intelligence levels of a Polish exchange student.

And an extraordinary thing happened! One of the teachers became so upset she *lost her temper and slapped the first*! It was a hard slap. The victim cried out, her hands rushing up to protect her face (too late), and the folder she was carrying thudded to the ground. Loose papers were taken by the breeze.

I rushed to collect the papers, and offered my details to the victim. I said I would be glad to testify on her behalf, should she wish to take legal action for the assault.

I will not sully my diary by recording the teacher's response.

I will only say that I now feel in a state of shock — as if my heart has been subject to too much today: The quivering moment when I thought Toby would ask me to the Formal; the surprise at the raised voices of teachers; the shock of a violent attack; the cruel rejection of my offer to help . . .

I suppose I will be all right.

$$\times \quad \times \quad \times$$

Hi Bindy,

The school year is winding up and the time of exams and cleanup is upon us. The time of celebration too! It gladdened my heart to see you and Ernst attending the Formal as "friends" last night. Perfect! You were both so dignified. If only others took their cue from you!

I just want to wish you well for Year 11, Bindy. I'm sure you will continue to shine — over the last few years, you've been such a hit, both academically and with your extracurricular activities. Such successes with the Duke of Edinburgh Award, the Tournament of Minds, and debating. Such a strident voice in the School Representative Council, despite howls of protests from your classmates! And I hear you're not too awful at netball and squash anymore either!

On a more personal note, you were a ray of light in this difficult year, and I will miss your visits next year. Drop by whenever you like, won't you — and *do* take these carob-coated energy drops. I'm enclosing a box for your summer, but come by early next year and I'll give you another. They'll help to ensure that you keep up your dazzling performance in your senior years.

So long!

Mrs. Lilydale

DIARY ENTRY

Thursday, 16 December

Only one more day of school. And only one more page of this Diary . . . What can it mean? Will life thence come to an end?

Tomorrow, we get our report cards. (I received Band 6 results in each of the five courses I took for the school certificate. Still, I'm always fearful about report cards.)

Next year (if life does not end), all will be different . . .

No more Mrs. Lilydale as Year Coordinator.

No more Kelly Simonds. (She's going to be an exchange student in Austria.)

Ernst and I had a farewell party for Kelly at recess. (Her other friends had a cake for her at lunch.) It's a small thing, but at one point during the party, I asked Kelly what the time was. She raised an eyebrow archly. "A hair past a freckle?" she said, holding out her hand to show me that she didn't have a watch.

Bindy Mackenzie: A Life

I don't know. Perhaps the people of Vienna will appreciate Kelly's wit, but I'm not sure it's her best feature.

Next year, no more parents either! They've decided to move into the city and leave me behind. I'm trying to see this in a positive light: Veronica, Jake, and Bella are great, so I'll be fine. Besides, I expect we'll write lots of e-mails to each other. I like, very much, the idea of correspondence with my parents. I can tell them things I might not otherwise. It will take my relationship with Mum and Dad to a different, better level.

The final lines of this diary . . .

I will miss you, sweet Diary.

I am going on to Year 11 now, a whole new domain. The most important year of my academic life so far.

I am afraid.

(Note: Band 6 is the highest you can get in the school certificate.)

12. Concluding Remarks

The Life you have just read is merely a *piece* of a larger work in progress. Each day, each hour, each *moment*, something new occurs in life . . .

I am now in Year 11. How to capture my first term, and beyond?

Well, I am not the sort of girl to give up.

I have decided to *continue* this Life in private.

Hence, I have started a fresh document on my laptop and have scanned in various notes, papers, and correspondence from *this* year — as with this Life, I have tried to be as honest as possible, including that which does not show me in my best light. I have begun with the Name Game we played at the very first session of FAD, scanned in my philosophical musings, memos, and notable correspondence, and copied in Nighttime Musings, e-mails, and various transcripts I have collected this year.

I will continue to add to this document, scanning in items as I write them. I will even include this *very* project!

And then I will begin a new "Part."

And with a new Part, I will begin a new term, *a new life*: I will begin a new Bindy Mackenzie.

PART SIX

I.

*Here Are Some Lines from a Book
That Caught Bindy's Eye Today . . .*

"[A new school term] is the time when resentments are laid aside, friendships are renewed, and the pages of life are freshened . . ."

(Note: The book actually refers to a new *year*, but I think the author would have said the same thing about a new school term.)

From *Our Deportment, or the Manner, Conduct, and Dress of the Most Refined Society,* by John H. Young (1881), p. 165.

A Memo from Bindy Mackenzie

To: Try
From: Bindy Mackenzie
Subject: Bindy Mackenzie
Time: Monday, the First Day of Term, 5:36 a.m.

Dear Try,
I hereby attach, with trembling stapler, a printout of my FAD assignment. It is entitled, "Bindy Mackenzie: A Life."

I also attach, with trembling heart, my gratitude. By asking me to prepare this Life, I believe you may have saved my life. Nay, not merely saved it, but *formed it afresh*!

You see, before I put this Life together, I was in a desperate state. I thought I had always been generous with my classmates, yet the Name Game we did at the first FAD class revealed that I had *failed* to win their hearts. So I chose to be ruthless instead, and I *completely* lost their respect. (You've probably noticed that.) All this has caused me such despair that I think it has made me ill.

But preparing this Life over the last few days has revealed a truth to me. My generosity of the past few years has been tinged with darkness! I see that now. Although I tried to *help*, I thought that my classmates were "teen monsters": people with drug and alcohol addictions, people who infringe copyright . . . No wonder my classmates have not liked me! And no wonder I exploded into *ruthlessness* this year. I thought I was surrounded by monsters, and was fed up with trying to help them.

And yet, in my distant past, I had *loved* my classmates. I thought

244

that they were *beautiful*. It seems to me, when I study this Life, that *Year 9* marks a turning point. (Perhaps some strange event took place in Year 8?)

This term, I will draw on my childlike self. I will *love* my classmates again. I will focus on the positive features of fellow human beings, and most especially my FAD group. I'll point these positive features out to them. I'll help them to reach their potential!

Will I have *poison running through my veins*?! Nay! I'll have *affection* spilling from my every pore.

And I'll spill every drop that I can on the members of my FAD group.

With much gratitude,

Bindy Mackenzie

P.S. Can you please thank the FAD member who gave me the glittering nail polish? I wear it every day now, and am trying harder than ever to stop chewing my nails! I've also been trying hard to figure out who it is from, but I simply cannot. Any clues are welcome.

P.P.S. Here, along with my Life, is a small gift for you — I have gotten one of your cartoons framed.

P.P.P.S. I'm nervous about returning to FAD, but I see that it is vital. I must win their forgiveness and their hearts. It is only in such a way that I will find myself again. Only this, I think, will cure me of my despair (and the associated physical symptoms).

The Philosophical Musings of Bindy Mackenzie
Monday, 5:49 a.m. (in my bedroom)

If the slow but steady melting of the polar ice caps can cause such meteorological events as the weakening of the Gulf Stream and consequent dismantling of various ecosystems, can it really be surprising that the sudden thaw in a girl's icy state should be followed by a headache?

✕ ✕ ✕

TO: mackenziepaul@mackenzieenterprises.com.au
FROM: bindy.mackenzie@ashbury.com.au
SENT: Monday, 6 a.m.
SUBJECT: Decisions . . .

Dear Dad,
Hi there! It's the first day of school after the holidays, and I've decided to catch up on correspondence before the term gets under way!

How are you? Anthony and I were sorry to miss you when we visited during the holidays — I know you've been interstate a lot, so I understand. Anyway, as Mum said, the apartment is not really big enough for two people, let alone four, so it was probably best. (We ordered Hawaiian pizza the first night, so I bet you're secretly glad you weren't around!)

My holiday was busy — I spent a lot of time on a school assignment for FAD. I also spent several evenings helping one of my baby-sitting clients. She runs a secondhand bookstore and we reorganized the store together. Actually, she was so impressed that she offered me a full-time job, Saturdays and Thursdays.

Can I have your advice? Do you think I should quit Kmart to take up Maureen's offer? It's less money, but more fun, and I do have another regular job to supplement my income (I sit with a woman named Eleanora while she makes pasta on Sunday and Wednesday nights — I think she does this for a local Italian restaurant).

Another thing: If I take the job, I might surprise Maureen by secretly renovating the back rooms of the store — a disastrous storeroom and bathroom — so any advice on renovation would be appreciated. I know that's your field of expertise.

Best,
Bindy

× × ×

My Buddy Diary
By Bindy Mackenzie

Monday, 6:15 a.m.

A long time ago, my buddy set me the challenge of attending kickboxing classes. I am sorry to confess that I did not meet this challenge last term. (I was a different person then.) (And the classes were on at the same time as my piano lessons.)

However, yesterday, I discovered a new Sunday class, at 2 p.m., and so I took it. I found the other students to be vastly more coordinated than I am. I could not kick and punch at the same time. (Interestingly, as a child, I was never able to rub my tummy and pat my head at the same time.) And I felt too embarrassed to shout "Ha!" each time I kicked.

Accordingly, I do not think that

> **kick-boxing**

is my thing.

As I mentioned before, I might try a hip-hop class instead. I hope that my buddy will understand.

$$\times \quad \times \quad \times$$

Bindy Mackenzie
24 Clipping Drive, Kellyville, NSW 2155

Mr. George Sutcliffe
Student Liaison Officer
Office of the Board of Studies

Dear Mr. Sutcliffe,
Thank you for your letters, in which you "respond" to my complaints about a course at my school called FAD.

I am writing now to withdraw those complaints. I suspect that you did not fully understand them, and I know you have already spoken to my Year Coordinator. However, I am concerned that

248

someone else in your department might read the file and take action.

I hereby confess that I was mistaken.

FAD is a revelation, and my FAD teacher, Try Montaine, is a genius.

Accordingly, please destroy my file, along with this letter.

With muted appreciation,

I remain,

Bindy Mackenzie

✕ ✕ ✕

A Memo from Bindy Mackenzie

To: Ms. Walcynski
From: Bindy Mackenzie
Subject: Modern History Case Study
Time: Monday, the First Day of Term, 7:02 a.m

Dear Ms. Walcynski,

I am writing to request an extension for my case study, *Compare and Contrast the Lives of Martin Luther King and Malcolm X.* I have examined the recommended reading, read several additional articles, watched Spike Lee's film, and written a draft of the assignment, but I believe I need more time to polish it.

I am truly sorry to be making this request. As you no doubt know, I have never in my life asked for an extension, or handed in a late assignment, in this or any other subject.

I believe the circumstances are exceptional: I had a FAD assignment to complete over the holidays and it took up most of my time.

Thank you so much for your patience,

Kind regards,

Bindy Mackenzie

× × ×

The Philosophical Musings of Bindy Mackenzie
7:10 a.m.

Bindy, ignore your splitting headache, and embrace the thrill of the new term — a new era, a new Bindy Mackenzie!

Pay heed, FAD group, I am going to discover the *true and thrilling nature of your souls*!! I am going to find the nobility within you, and reveal that nobility to you!!

Affectionate Bindy has returned.

2.

A Portrait of Toby Mazzerati

Here I sit in Assembly, the first Wednesday of the new term.

Mr. Botherit is welcoming us back to school. He is so enthusiastic I begin to wonder if we have only been gone for two weeks.

His voice fades into a hazy distance, and I focus on Toby Mazzerati.

He must be here somewhere in this assembly hall, but I cannot find him. So I will record my memory of him.

Toby Mazzerati is faintly freckled all over. You cannot tell that he is freckled unless you see him up close on a bright day or perhaps beneath a sunlamp.

Toby has reddish-blonde hair, thick and soft.

He has small eyes, the color of red-brown rust, but rust is flat and dull, whereas Toby's eyes gleam.

He is short and plump.

There is something puffy and swollen about him — I often think of pastry, the lid of a pie, slowly ballooning in the oven.

Excuse me, Mr. Botherit's voice is growing loud.

He is explaining that *anyone* can *change*.

Well, that is good news! I myself am hoping —

Oh, Mr. Botherit, hush.

He has gone too far.

He always does.

He is saying that people who have done poorly in schoolwork before can pick themselves up in Year 11 and come first in the year! He is recommending tutors, study schedules, meetings with course advisers, etc., etc.

He is going to play havoc with the bell curve. He should leave it alone.

It is later.

I am in my room at home.

This afternoon, I attended my first session of FAD since the disastrous session last term. I will not lie. I was terrified.

But! I caught the bus with the others into Castle Hill. It was less crowded than usual, and we all found seats, most of us alongside strangers. I was near the front, and turned around to give each of the FAD group an affectionate smile. Sergio was the only one to return it properly. The others pretended not to see me, or widened their eyes, raised their eyebrows, curled their lips, or snorted like angry horses.

Finnegan Blonde offered a faint, inscrutable smile; the mildest creasing at the corners of his eyes, and then turned toward the bus window. He seemed then, as I watched, to have a private thought, and to smile, amused, at this thought, and he knocked against the window gently, with the knuckle of his right index finger.

I smiled warmly at Try too, but I turned away at once, not wanting to see her reaction. My greatest fear was that she had read my Life and not liked it. I did not want to see disappointment in her eyes. But perhaps she had not yet had the time. I only gave it to her two days ago! I assume she was grateful for the framed cartoon and has it hanging in her front hallway. (She hasn't mentioned it.)

They ordered their coffees (Astrid, I noted, had switched to herbal tea) and found their armchairs behind the curtain. Emily insisted she had post-traumatic stress disorder from a Legal Studies exam she had done that day. "Seriously," she was saying, "what are the symptoms?" Toby and Finnegan mocked her. Astrid mentioned that she had a mild concussion from running into a telegraph pole while being chased by the police after a party on Saturday night. Toby and Finnegan turned from Emily to mock Astrid instead. Briony was timid. Sergio and Elizabeth leaned close together to talk about Elizabeth's new Rollerblades. His breath caressed her cheek. Her eyes sparkled like raindrops. He touched her elfin ears. She drew her legs up into the couch and gathered her arms around those legs.

Ahh! I thought. *That's one thing that has changed — Sergio and Elizabeth: an item. It must have happened over the break.*

But I had predicted that.

Try was as tiny as ever, and she perched on the same footstool. She explained that today we would talk about fear.

Blushing, she produced a bright purple ball, the size of a basketball, but made of soft cloth and containing a jingling bell.

"We throw the ball," she explained, "and whoever catches it must tell us the things they fear."

Finnegan brought the coffees in, as usual, and I turned to consider Toby — and found myself in shock.

Has every single person in Year 11 changed so dramatically?

I'd seen him sitting on the bus, and around the school, but simply had not noticed. Toby had *stretched* like an elastic band.

What was I thinking when I said he was swollen and puffy?

His skin sits firm on his bones, a pleasant, pale brown. His arms are smooth as they reach for his coffee; he blinks once or twice and his thoughts ripple out across the well-defined structure of his face.

What was I thinking when I said he was short? *He has grown tall.* His head sits up above the top of the couch, and his feet stretch out to the floor.

(What is happening to the boys in Year 11? Some, I must say, remain short. Some have terrible acne; many have bristles of hair on their upper lips; but many — many! — have grown smooth, bronzed skin, muscles, legs, and forearms!

I find it hard to look at these "men" without feeling something —

I feel like a passenger in an accelerating car, a hand on a gearstick that keeps changing, ever faster. But where does it end?)

I continued to watch Toby in quiet amazement as the FAD session went on. I saw him glance at me a little uncomfortably once or twice. I believe he sensed my gaze.

It was easier to stare when he was talking — and the ball seemed often to land in his hands. He leaned forward to talk. The conversation, as usual, strayed away from fears — their fears ranged from exams to careers to concern about the vulnerability of their little brothers and sisters to parents' marriages and parents' health to global warming to sharks to terrorist attacks. But somehow ended up at conspiracy theories.

Toby is fond of conspiracies. He believes that all sunglasses have built-in hidden cameras, which see what you are seeing, while a central agency watches every frame. Similar, he said, to computers — there is a department recording every tap of your fingers on a keyboard.

He also believes that most robberies you read about in newspapers are fictional — planted there to make people buy insurance.

He threw the ball to Briony then, and she declared that electricity companies make it darker outside so we have to use more lights. It took us all a moment to realize she was joking, and to laugh.

It is Thursday now.

I'm trying to find a positive animal for Toby to replace the cane toad. Some kind of chattering monkey? I Googled "chattering monkey," and it seems to be a metaphor for the taunting voices in the back of your head. The voices that insist you will fail.

I don't think that is what Toby's chatting intends.

Thursday, 11:53 p.m.

Worked at Maureen's Magic tonight and remembered this:

Whenever Toby threw the ball at FAD yesterday, he threw it to Briony. He did this casually, glancing at others first as if considering them, and then tossing it, always, to her.

I remember thinking, almost crossly: *Why throw the ball to Briony? She's too shy!*

But Briony always caught the ball, held it tightly in both hands, and spoke. And each time her voice grew louder and her sentences became more complete. Sometimes she even made jokes.

I think that Toby knew what he was doing.

I think he was chipping away at her silence, constructing a place where she could speak.

Friday, 4:10 a.m.

There is determination behind Toby's lighthearted chat. I have heard rumors that he is building a snooker table as his major work for Design and Technology. People are amazed at the ambition. But the message seems to be: If anyone can build a snooker table, Toby Mazzerati can.

I believe that Toby is a kind person.

I remember when he gave me a wooden jewelry box.

(Nobody threw the ball to me at FAD.)

× × ×

A Memo from Bindy Mackenzie

To: Toby Mazzerati
From: Bindy Mackenzie
Subject: YOU
Time: Friday, 11:30 a.m.

Dear Toby,
Once, I left you a message in which I said that you are a cane toad.
Today, I write to assure you that you are not.
No, Toby, I was mistaken.
You are not a cane toad, but a woodpecker!
Woodpeckers enjoy working with wood. So do you!
Woodpeckers keep up a constant, tapping noise as they beat their little beaks against the bark. So do you! (If not "tapping," at least a sort of "chatting.")
A woodpecker is beautiful, and you have grown into a dashing young man, far removed from the plump little boy I used to know in primary school.
Most importantly, a woodpecker's work is vital for other birds — the holes they make in trees become nests for smaller birds, such as bluebirds, wrens, and chickadees.
I believe that you are just the same.
(I understand that woodpeckers also have extremely long tongues, shock-absorbers in their heads, and stiff tail feathers. Perhaps you do too!)

I hope you will forgive me for mistaking you for a cane toad. I am enclosing a small gift: a complimentary set of personalized memo stationery.

Very best wishes,
Bindy Mackenzie

3.

A Memo from Bindy Mackenzie

To: Try
From: Bindy Mackenzie
Subject: FAD Study Management Session
Time: Monday

Dear Try,
Congratulations on your excellent FAD session on fear last week. It was thought provoking! I was glad you persuaded me to return to FAD.

I am writing now to make a humble offer.

Would you like *me* to present a FAD session on study management? Perhaps it would give you a break?

I admit, I have never wanted to share my personal study strategies before. I've always guarded them closely. But now, this term, for you, for FAD? It would be my honor.

Kind regards,
Bindy Mackenzie

×　×　×

A Note from the Desk of Try Montaine

Dear Bindy,

Great idea! Come by my office and let's discuss.

    Best wishes,

    Try

×　×　×

TO: <u>bindy.mackenzie@ashburyhigh.com.au</u>
FROM: <u>mackenziepaul@mackenzieenterprises.com.au</u>
SENT: Wednesday, 10:30 a.m.
SUBJECT: Re: Decisions . . .

Hi Bindy,

Sorry for the delay — still interstate as we speak. By all means, quit Kmart. Diversify. Managing a bookstore sounds like a step up the ladder to me — assume it pays better too.

    How's your brother? See him around the house much? I never hear from him.

    As for renovating tips: cheap chrome shelves from Ikea, white towels, scented candles, imitation clawfoot tub — you know the tricks. Have coffee brewing when buyers come by, & bowls of green apples everyplace.

    Best,

    Dad

P.S. Hey, if you're in the mood for renovating — that old place on Gilbert Rd. — closer to you than me. Drop in whenever you feel like it and work on the wallpaper? I've stripped back about five layers so far, and looks like we're down to the last. You know the one? Key's in the pipe above the door. Big help.

TO: cecily.mackenzie@mackenzieworld.com.au
FROM: bindy.mackenzie@ashburyhigh.com.au
SENT: Thursday, 3:30 P.M.
SUBJECT: Dad and Anthony

Dear Mum,
Dad keeps asking about Anthony. What should I do? Maybe we should just tell Dad?

I took the day off school yesterday to go to the doctor's, as I've still been feeling tired, cranky, headachey, etc., and I couldn't get your suggestion out of my head. You know when you said it might be glandular fever? (I apologize for shouting at you about that.)

I was sitting in the waiting room for half an hour, looking at the chairs. They have green upholstery patterned with four-leaf clovers. I looked up at the frosted glass walls, at the posters about cholesterol, at a woman with a baby on her lap. But I could not resist looking back at those green chairs. And each time I looked, I thought: *Those are not four-leaf clovers, those are little fat hands. Those chairs are covered with little fat hands.*

Then I felt the glands around my neck and they didn't seem very swollen to me.

So I got up, canceled my appointment, and went home.

Anyway, if I do have glandular fever, I'll just talk myself out of it.

Got to go, I'm late for Maureen's Magic.

Best,

Bindy

TO: bindy.mackenzie@ashburyhigh.com.au
FROM: cecily.mackenzie@mackenzieworld.com.au
SENT: Thursday, 6:05 p.m.
SUBJECT: Re: Dad and Anthony

Bindy Mackenzie, answer your phone! Why do you *never* answer it?! I'm calling you right now!

Love,

Mum

$$\times \quad \times \quad \times$$

A Memo from Bindy Mackenzie

To: Frau McAllister
From: Bindy Mackenzie
Subject: German translation
Time: Monday morning

Dear Frau McAllister,

Just a note to apologize for not handing in my translation today.

I will get it to you tomorrow. I'm afraid I've been very busy over the weekend putting together a PowerPoint presentation for another course.

Best wishes,

Bindy Mackenzie

✕ ✕ ✕

FROM THE TRANSCRIPT FILE OF BINDY MACKENZIE

Wednesday

8:45 a.m.: Students arriving at school, passing my shadow seat. There Astrid and Emily.

Astrid: Can you effin' believe she's taken over the whole f . . . n FAD group now, after what she said to Sergio, and how she tried to get you off her debating team and everything, and how she called us all names on posters, and then she just doesn't turn up the next week, and now she's back she thinks she can *teach* us.
Emily: I know.
Astrid: And I'm like, are you kidding me? Excuse me? You think you can just, like, take Try's place? And I had a really good talk with Try about it, and she was being so *nice* about Bindy, which, can you believe it? We talked about other stuff too, like where Try comes from and that? And you can tell she's really trying to change her accent so she can fit in, can't you? It's so cute the way it goes all over the place? Cause she traveled so far to get here to us, and it's like, Bindy's making us go to her *place* instead of the Blue

Danish cos she wants to do a *Power*-f . . . n-Point presentation, and
it's like, Try's already traveled far *enough*, hasn't she? To get here?
From America, I mean. We're not going, are we?

Emily: Yeah, no, I know . . . Um, but when you think about it, it's
kind of the main thing Bindy has to offer. I mean, her brain. Aren't
you kind of interested to see what she does to get marks like she
always gets, and maybe get some ideas?

Astrid: Sergio said practically the same thing yesterday cos
he wants to get into uni and shit. I'm, like, a lost cause, but —
shut *up*, she's right there again. She's always effin' sitting on
that seat.

(I might have to work rather hard to win their hearts.)

× × ×

Nighttime Musings of Bindy Mackenzie
Wednesday, 11:25 p.m.

Today, here at Aunt Veronica's house, I taught the FAD group
study management. I was terrified that no one would show up.

But they did.

It was strange, seeing them in the living room, embarrassed
at first, but soon throwing themselves onto the couches, and bringing in chairs from the kitchen so they could put their feet up.
Finnegan set up the screen for me, and he found the light switch to
make it dark when I began.

I told Try she should take a break, so she sat out on the verandah and enjoyed the sun. (I wondered if she might mention my
Life, or the framed cartoon, but she did not.)

Most people listened! As I talked, I looked around and saw some

264

concentrating faces. (Some frowned, and others were lost in their own distant thoughts.) They did laugh, sometimes harshly, and when they grew bored, they simply talked amongst themselves.

At one point I told them that my favorite mathematical formula is

$$\frac{-b \pm \sqrt{b^2 - 4ac}}{2a}$$

That formula, I said, makes my heart sing.

There was silence.

"So, if a guy wants to get you going," said Sergio slowly, "he whispers the quadratic formula in your ear?"

"I guess so," I replied. There was laughter.

I was halfway through my Study Tips when Emily raised her hand. She did this for humorous effect, pretending I was a teacher.

"You really need to do all this," she said, "to get those marks you get?"

"I think so," I said.

Then she sighed, murmured, "flax that," and let her notes slip to the floor.

At one point, my computer froze up and I panicked. (I suppose the FAD group make me nervous: It is clear that they still resent me.) Finnegan moved behind me, leaned over my shoulder, restarted the computer, and found the file again.

Afterwards, Auntie Veronica passed around her coconut-cherry slice and tea. I could see they liked Veronica, but I wished that Bella had been home too, rather than at playgroup. *She* would have won their hearts.

Auntie Veronica wanted to slice some bread for Briony, because she confessed she's allergic to coconut, but Veronica couldn't find her chopping board. She opened every cupboard and drawer in the kitchen, and then looked up in amazement.

"It's been stolen!" she said. "Why would anyone break into a house, leave *everything else*, and steal the chopping board? It just seems, I don't know, mean-spirited?"

She has a sincere way of talking nonsense, and everyone hesitated before they realized she was joking. Then they began to search the *house* for her chopping board. Some ended up in my bedroom. Astrid and Sergio stood staring, silently, at the study notes that cover my walls.

I noticed something: Toby Mazzerati paused by my dressing table and touched my jewelry box. There was a glimmer of a smile. It is a wooden box that he himself made for me, many years ago.

It was Finnegan who found the chopping board, eventually, amongst Bella's toys.

Afterwards, when everyone had gone, Auntie Veronica looked thoughtful and said, "What's that girl's name? Astrid, is it? That silver stud in her eyebrow. Shouldn't she get it removed?"

I have always liked Auntie Veronica's sense of humor.

EFFECTIVE STUDY MANAGEMENT:
A GUIDE
By Bindy Mackenzie

OVERVIEW

- What do you hope to achieve today?
- Why?
- Why are you here?
- *Why are we all here?* (Meaning of Life, etc.)

Effective Study Management: A Guide © Bindy Mackenzie

WHO ARE YOUR FRIENDS?

- Library
- Board of Studies resources
- Ice water
- Fish
- Grapes

Effective Study Management: A Guide © Bindy Mackenzie

KNOW THINE ENEMIES . . .

- Sleep (Try gradually reducing the hours spent sleeping?)
- Parties (Consider canceling parties?)
- Reverie (What is it? When is it okay? Etc.)
- Intoxication

Effective Study Management: A Guide © Bindy Mackenzie

BINDY MACKENZIE'S STUDY TIPS #1

Never forget the Joy of Mnemonics; e.g.:
- "King Phillip Came Over from Germany Swimming" = Kingdom Phylum Class Order Family Genus Species
- "My Very Elderly Mother Just Sat Up Near Pluto" = Mercury Venus Earth Mars Jupiter Saturn Uranus Neptune Pluto

Effective Study Management: A Guide © Bindy Mackenzie

BINDY MACKENZIE'S STUDY TIPS #2

Think of maths formulae as your friends. Talk to them. Laugh with them. Choose a favorite. Buy them small treats.

Effective Study Management: A Guide © Bindy Mackenzie

BINDY MACKENZIE'S STUDY TIPS #3

Summarize your study notes and *talk* about them. Talk about your study notes to:

- Friends
- Babies
- Budgerigars
- Furniture

Effective Study Management: A Guide © Bindy Mackenzie

BINDY MACKENZIE'S STUDY TIPS #4

Put your study notes onto index cards. Scatter the cards through the home. Glue them to the back of cereal boxes and onto the side of the toothpaste tube. Mail yourself an index card.

Effective Study Management: A Guide © Bindy Mackenzie

BINDY MACKENZIE'S STUDY TIPS #5

Now and then, eat your study notes.

Effective Study Management: A Guide © Bindy Mackenzie

BINDY MACKENZIE'S STUDY TIPS #6

Rename your pets.

Say you have a dog and a goldfish?

Rename your dog Nicholas II.

Each time you see him, say, "Hello there, Tsar Nicholas! Thinking about the 1825 Decembrists' Revolt and the 1861 Emancipation of the Serfs and how they affected your reign? I thought so! How about Alexander II, eh? Swimming around in the aquarium there? What do you think of *him*?"

Effective Study Management: A Guide © Bindy Mackenzie

BINDY MACKENZIE'S STUDY TIPS #7

After every shower, use your finger to write a date, a formula, or a fact in the steam on the bathroom mirror.

Effective Study Management: A Guide © Bindy Mackenzie

4.

A Portrait of Emily Thompson

It is Friday afternoon and here I am on my shadow seat outside the library.

Tonight: our first debate of the year. It will take place at St. Mark's Christian Brothers. (Their team, last year, was solid but lacking in vocabulary.)

Emily will debut as our second speaker. It is the time to consider the nobility within her.

She is average in height, broad-shouldered. She is always eating junk food, but she is slim enough. I believe she likes to ride horses.

It is hard to recall the color of her eyes — I only see them flashing and sparking at me. I have also seen them brim with tears. I remember her crying when her friend Cassie sang at the Spring Concert last year.

I also remember her crying when the tuckshop discontinued stocking certain chocolates.

Like the boys at St. Mark's, Emily struggles with vocabulary.

Yet she seems ignorant of her own ignorance. She is always astonished when she gets a bad mark, gasping loudly, the tears brimming again.

She has never liked me much, and despised me last year when I made a mistake about a name.

To my surprise, she did take notes on Wednesday, when I ran the Study Management course.

It's much later — midnight.

What an extraordinary night!

The familiar flutter of the first debate of the year: My Ashbury uniform is freshly ironed, my hair neat in its coiled plaits. A St. Mark's boy greets us at the school building, polite and reserved. He points the way along empty corridors, where footsteps seem too loud. Fluorescent lighting in a staff room, tables set with cakes and sandwiches, milling adults, boys standing silent, girls with high-pitched giggles.

Ernst von Schmerz and beside him, Emily. (I had thought she would be late.)

Mrs. Lilydale approaches with sponge cake on a paper plate and presses this into my hands. Emily holds a chocolate cupcake but makes no move to eat it. She looks pale.

As usual, the small talk is forced and nervous until we get our topic. *That young people should be banned from participation in professional sports.* We look at each other, intrigued. Ernst says a few words that confuse the opposition (they cannot understand him). There is a coin toss. We lose. The others choose Negative; and we are led to an empty classroom, and given one hour to prepare.

And then the debate — Ernst and his superb opening. Emily's surprise that Ernst can speak plain English. The first speaker from St. Mark's — no match for Ernst. Me scribbling rebuttals on blank cards. Emily, white as paper, stumbling a little as she stands in the center of the room. Then: startling the room with a blaze of words — a shifting in the audience, a straightening of the adjudicator's shoulders.

Ernst and I turn to each other. It's an understatement to say it, but Emily knows how to speak.

She returns to her seat; now her cheeks are flushed, eyes straight ahead. I take one of my blank cards and write, "THAT WAS FANTASTIC." And slide it along the desk to her. She glances down and smiles.

And so it goes. The adjudicator stands to announce the results, and we have won our first debate.

Mrs. Lilydale rushes at us with excitement. We shrug, nonchalant. It is only the first round.

But now, later, it is not the debate that occupies my mind.

No, and nor is it our triumph.

What I recall most vividly is that hour of preparation time in the empty classroom.

It is Saturday. I wonder if Emily is a dog?

She is fiercely loyal to her two best friends. She bounces

around playfully when excited, but growls and barks viciously when mad.

Would Emily like it if I told her that she is a dog? Perhaps not.

I'd better go. I need to be at Maureen's Magic (that is, her bookshop) in ten minutes. I wonder if I should try to learn to drive again.

Perhaps not.

Sunday now, and I'm just home from my job at Eleanora's place. Also dropped by Dad's house on Gilbert Road and worked on the wallpaper.

But Eleanora's place — such a strange job. To sit opposite someone while she plunges her hands into wet dough. (She has moved on from gnocchi to linguini, winding wide white strips through a pasta machine.) If only I could meet her baby just once, it might seem a little less bizarre.

The baby's name is Calypso, you know. "Calypso!" I said.

But Eleanora did not seem amused. "Yes, *Bindy*?" she replied, presumably pointing out the strangeness of my name. But Bindy is a common abbreviation of Belinda! Nothing to do with the bindi-eyes on my lawn!

Mostly, we sit quietly, and I answer her queries about school.

I told her about the first round of the debating competition.

But I did not mention the hour in the empty classroom.

How the atmosphere changes at once when the door is closed. Plunging into a moment of relief — we are away from the opposition team and the formalities! — but even the relief is charged with tension. There is only an hour to prepare!

As usual, I rushed to the board and wrote up the topic, along with words and phrases to define: *Young people! Young! People! Banned! Participation! Professional Sports! Professional! Sports!* Frantically, I scribbled some ideas: *young bones; muscle damage; schoolwork!; pushy parents; eating disorders; is ballet a sport?*

There was silence behind me.

I looked back.

Emily Thompson was sitting on a desk, legs swinging, tears sliding slowly down her face.

3 a.m. now, Monday morning.

Feeling ill Might just —

Just threw up in the bathroom. Feel a bit better now, but can't stop trembling. How strange, this numbness in my cheeks. I sense it often, you know, and sometimes in my arms and legs — it's more than pins and needles — it seems to numb my mind.

I must keep working on my *character*. Eventually, *that* will cure me. As Dad always says, good health is nothing but good character.

I wonder if Emily might be a humpback whale.

That connection she has with her two best friends — I believe they could easily sing to one another, like whales, across hundreds of miles.

But, to my surprise, Emily's friends were not at St. Mark's to watch the debate.

In the empty classroom at preparation time, I found out why.

Emily hiccupped quietly when I turned from the board and looked at her. She blinked, turned away, and picked up a pen.

But it was too late.

I could not pretend I had not seen. I moved toward her and hesitated. Ernst, who had been looking discreetly from Emily to me and back, took my cue and he himself moved closer. We both waited.

And Emily confounded us.

She apologized, in a whisper, for joining the team.

She said she was going to let us down.

She would try her best, she said, but knew we had always won before, with Kelly Simonds on the team. With her, she said, we would lose. And she had made Lydia and Cassie promise not to come tonight, because she didn't want them to see her fail.

"You guys are just so professional at this," she whispered. "I'm not even, like, an amateur."

Well!

She felt *inferior* to Ernst and me!

It was a shock.

We assured her she could do it. She'd been a hit in mock trial with Legal Studies; she'd won the next stage of the oratory contest; she was famous for cross-examining Mrs. Lilydale last year — how could she doubt herself?

"But this is different," Emily insisted. "You guys are gonna be wishing the whole time that Kelly Simonds was here."

At this, *Ernst* surprised me.

"Who really liked Kelly Simonds anyway?" he said in a low voice.

"What?!" I cried.

But that was what he said.

Emily giggled, and I felt a weight, such a curious burden of weight, lifting slowly from my shoulders.

Who really liked Kelly Simonds anyway?

Not me.

And then, as I stood, as I floated on the spot, Emily Thompson rushed to the board and began to scribble ideas.

Now, much later, I am intrigued by a vision of a bank of elevators, one sliding down on its shafts, another shooting up toward the roof.

I had believed that Emily was slipping *downward* into the debating world. It turns out she had believed she was climbing — ascending to the echelons of intellect.

She had been terrified of looking up there, but, despite herself, she had tried.

Emily Thompson may be many things, but above all, she is loyal, determined, and brave.

Imagine if she were my friend.

× × ×

A Memo from Bindy Mackenzie

To: Emily Thompson
From: Bindy Mackenzie
Subject: YOU
Time: Tuesday, 10:30 a.m.

Dear Emily,
Once, I left you a message in which I said you are a komodo dragon.

Today, I write to assure you that you are not. (Unless, of course, you would like to be.)

I admit, I said it because I wanted to scare you away from debating. I was completely mistaken about you. You won our first debate for us on Friday night. I am honored to have you on the team.

You, Emily Thompson, are a northern hairy-nosed wombat.

A wombat is a strong, sturdy animal with short legs and short claws.

It likes to frolic when cheerful.

It will growl, snort, and screech when angry.

It loves chocolate.

And it is so tough and so determined it can push its way through any fence and dig under any wall.

I hope you will forgive me for mistaking you for a komodo

dragon, and I hope you will accept this small gift: complimentary personalized memo stationery.

Very best wishes,

Bindy Mackenzie

P.S. I chose a northern hairy-nosed wombat because these are more rare than the common wombat, and you, Emily, are unique.

5.

My Buddy Diary
By Bindy Mackenzie

Monday, 8 p.m.

This afternoon I tried another class at the gym, as I have yet to complete my buddy's challenge. I tried:

> **hip-hop**

I couldn't do it. Such strange undulations of the body! Such meaningless slappings of the shoulders and the thighs, while the head darts back and forth! As soon as I had figured out one of the patterns, they had moved on to another. And they kept dancing off in one direction while I danced in another. I was always bumping into people.

I still have some kind of a stomach flu, so that might be why it was so hard. There are curious twinges in my stomach, much like the small cracks and snaps you hear, late at night, in a stranger's house.

Wednesday, 11 p.m.

This afternoon, I tried a class called:

---

advanced step

I thought that would be simple. I know how to walk up steps. I have done it often. But oh no, they have to complicate things! First, you have to build a platform, and then you have to *dance* around the platform. Step, jog, jog, step, fall, jog, step. I always jogged while the others stepped, and I don't think you were meant to fall.

I was in no mood to watch Eleanora make pasta after that, and may have been a little snappy with her.

Still, I was already depressed, even before the class. At FAD today, Try taught her own lesson on "Study Management." She had already prepared it, she said. *Why didn't she tell me that when I offered to teach the class?* I felt mortified.

Her session was based on this book she likes, something about multiple intelligences. The book says there are seven different types of intelligences. They are:

(1) "Body" — which means you can dance, exercise, and do sports. Ha ha! I certainly have *that* kind of intelligence, don't I? Ha ha ha! Anyway, we gave it to Elizabeth, as she's an athlete. Sergio said she's already better than he is at blading.

281

(2) "Interpersonal" — where you are good at getting on with other people. I could tell Astrid wanted that one as she's a party girl — she was kind of twirling her ponytail with one hand and brushing cake crumbs off her knees with the other while we discussed it — but we gave it to Sergio.

(3) "Intrapersonal" — where you have *inner* brilliance, meaning you think deep thoughts. Secretly, I thought I ought to get that because of my philosophical musings, but I guess the others don't know about those. They chose Briony. Because she is so quiet, I suppose.

(4) "Mathematical" — which we gave to Astrid because you could tell she was "stressing" that she wouldn't get any of the intelligences. Also, she mentioned that she's got a maths tutor now, and it was working because she got 82 percent in the latest exam. I got 63 percent in the same exam. That was surely an error in marking, but I haven't raised it with Ms. Yen.

(5) "Musical" — Toby got that because he chants in an almost-musical way. (I hummed softly to myself while they discussed this one, and played a few arpeggios on my knees. To no avail.)

(6) "Verbal" — I thought of Emily, given her recent success in public speaking, but the others gave that to Finnegan because they'd heard he's doing really well in Computing Applications and was learning all these programming languages. They decided this equals verbal intelligence in the modern world. (I have not forgotten that Finnegan told me he got bad marks

last year. Has he met my challenge to improve them therefore? That is gratifying.)

(7) "Visual" — Emily told us she can read minds so she got that. (I'm not sure that's what it means — I think it might be referring to painting and the arts — but Emily does have a vibrant imagination.)

So that's the seven types of intelligence, and I don't know if you've noticed this, but Bindy Mackenzie is not there.

Nobody appeared to notice this.

And Try has not said a single word about my Life.

× × ×

The Dream Diary of Bindy Mackenzie

Thursday, 10 p.m.

Last night I had a dream that lasted through the night, or so it seemed. It lingered in my mind all day, like a tent of darkness, and all day I saw terrible visions — glimpses of decay and broken bodies. I kept remembering those two dead birds I once saw lying in the gutter near Maureen's place. The visions seemed connected to the pains in my stomach and my head. I threw up once, but it did not help.

I cannot clearly recall the dream. The mood was grim and shadowy, and I think it began in a living room somewhere. The TV was on and my father had his feet up on the couch. When I looked at his face, his eyes were bloodshot, so I knew that the

283

TV news was about my mother. I started sobbing, crying out, pleading with the dream to let my mother live — but someone moved quietly into the room and told me it was not just my mother, but also my brother, and probably me as well. There was something absolute in the news of our deaths. There was an ugly smell in the dream, and today, an ugly taste in my mouth.

✕   ✕   ✕

My Buddy Diary
By Bindy Mackenzie

Thursday, 10:20 p.m.
Today, despite my darkness and depression, I went to the gym after Maureen's Magic and tried to do a

spin class

I couldn't keep up. It just means going on a stationary bicycle, so I thought: *easy.* But it's not. They were too fast. My feet got tangled in the pedals. My face was still crimson when I arrived home, and, humorously, Auntie Veronica told me I was looking pale. Ha! If you think a fire engine can look pale! (I said to her.)

But she ignored me, and said she'd been noticing that I'm white as a ghost lately — or did she say *white as a corpse*? — and she said she'd got me some vitamin supplements, and wondered if I might not be exercising too much? And what did the doctor say about the gland — I interrupted to point out that *she's* the pregnant one, and should be resting on the couch, not running around buying me vitamin supplements.

That surprised her.

She is always asking about my health and arranging doctor's appointments for me. I'm tired of making excuses and pretending to go to the doctor. I feel unwell enough as it is.

× × ×

As Friday flits and flutters by, so Bindy goes to

1. Modern History
And Bindy, pay heed to . . .

Ms. Walcynski. Haven't done the assignment on Martin Luther King etc. yet. Move to a seat way down the back of the room? She might not notice me.

2. Economics
And Bindy, pay heed to . . .

Mr. Patel. Have not yet chosen financial article and analyzed. Do it on bus on the way to school? Remember scissors, newspapers, pen, etc.

3. Double English
And Bindy, pay heed to . . .

Miss Flynn. Essay on *Pride and Prejudice* due today. Can I write an entire essay during recess? Note that Miss Flynn talks a lot at the start of class — use that time to keep writing?

4. Double English
And Bindy, pay heed to . . .
See above.

5. Double Maths
And Bindy, pay heed to . . .
Lucy Tan, Saxon Walker, Marley Duncan, Kari Hutchinson, Ernst von Schmerz (traitor!), Arcadia Johnston, Chris McAdam, Natasha Bartosz, Deanna Waites, Nicholas Brunelli, Jose Mafio, Jane Ongaro, and *Astrid Bexonville.*

6. Double Maths
They all (apparently) did better than me in last week's exam.
I still cannot believe it. Must discuss with Ms. Yen.
Further note: Is this actually Bindy Mackenzie's timetable? Can there be such a dramatic change? When have I *ever* been late with an assignment?! At the same time there is something oddly exhilarating in the absoluteness of this change. In simply surrendering to perfect failure . . . All these years I have worked so hard and now I am very tired. Isn't it time for me to stop?

TO: mackenziepaul@mackenzieenterprises.com.au
FROM: bindy.mackenzie@ashbury.com.au

Dear Dad,

Now it's my turn to apologize for the delay.

Guess what, I've resigned from Kmart and am working in Maureen's bookstore! Thanks for your advice! (Although, I think you might have misunderstood — the pay is actually *lower* in the bookstore. And I'm not the manager. Just an assistant.)

My role is to catalogue and shelve new books. And, I think, to chat with Maureen during frequent breaks for apple muffins and coffee.

The shop, I should say, is veiled in a thin layer of dust. You can tell which sections are unpopular because cobwebs are strung from shelf to shelf. The light fittings are grimy and clouded with dead moths and flies.

And as for the rooms out the back! Let's just say that *you* would be calling in the demolition team! (I think renovation is beyond me but I *could* spring clean.)

No time though. Maureen's always around, and I'm always busy cataloging.

Now, there *is* a spare key, hanging from a ring behind the counter in Maureen's place. I *could* borrow it, when she isn't looking, sneak in late one night and get to work. . . .

What do you think?

Of course, I'm sure you prefer me to keep working on your Gilbert Road place. The walls are about half done now — I haven't given up!

Anyway, would love to stay and chat but Auntie Veronica is calling from downstairs — she, Bella, and I are going shopping before my debate tonight.

Best,

Bindy

TO: bindy.mackenzie@ashbury.com.au
FROM: mackenziepaul@mackenzieenterprises.com.au
SENT: Friday, 4:30 p.m.
SUBJECT: Re: Hi there

Hi Bindy,

Good news about new job.

You never answer my questions about Anthony. What's he up to? You two help out your Auntie V. around the house there? Tell me if he's not pulling his weight and I'll have a word. (Tell *him* to e-mail/call me so that I can.)

Best,

Dad

TO: mackenziepaul@mackenzieenterprises.com.au
FROM: bindy.mackenzie@ashbury.com.au
SENT: Friday, 11 p.m.
SUBJECT: Re: Re: Hi there

Hi Dad,

You'll be glad to hear that we won our debate again tonight.

The topic was *That every citizen of the world should be entitled to vote in U.S. elections.*

We were affirmative. We eviscerated them.

I was almost late because Auntie V, Bella, and I were having so much fun in Castle Hill. At one point, a giant blue cat approached with a basket of lollipops. Bella shrieked and sprinted away, and we had to chase her all the way to the car park!

You ask about Anthony. It seems like we hardly see each other — we're both so busy. And even when we're home, his room is downstairs and I'm upstairs, so we're a whole household away from each other. . . . As for helping around the house, well, Auntie Veronica likes to make a game of housework. She often leaves a basket of clean laundry on a chair in the entrance hallway. When you enter the house, you have to fold one item or match a pair of socks! (Bella tries hard, but usually mismatches.)

As I speak, Anthony is standing in the entrance hall downstairs folding clothes. He can never stop at just one.

Best,
Bindy

$$\times \quad \times \quad \times$$

The Philosophical Musings of Bindy Mackenzie
Friday, 11:30 p.m. (in my bedroom)
When you speak to a large blue cat, to whom do you speak? Do you speak to the cat or the person you know to be inside the cat

suit? Is he both? Does he stop being himself when he steps into the costume? Who is the large blue cat?

Am I inside a cat suit, trapped by my own name? Is it my costume?

And who is Ernst von Schmerz? He is trapped inside his name. (He says he can't change it again until his personalized stationery runs out. . . .)

And who, pray tell, is my brother, Anthony? The real Anthony? Or an imaginary boy who lives in a room downstairs? Who stands in the entrance hallway neatly folding clothes?

6.

A Portrait of Briony Atkins

It is Wednesday lunchtime, and soon I must join the FAD group on the bus to Castle Hill.

I missed last week's session because I was not well. (My mother and her crazy notion that I have glandular fever. She rang and insisted that I take the day off. She and Auntie Veronica are always on my case.)

For now, I sit at a window desk in the Year 11 wing, watching Briony Atkins.

She stands at her locker.

On the floor, to her right, is her schoolbag. To her left stands a black umbrella. It is leaning against the lower lockers and it puts me in mind of a crotchet or a semi-quaver.

Briony's uniform falls neat and straight. Her shoes, I see, glint under the lights above — so does her short brown hair with its auburn highlights.

Now I can see inside her locker. She has pressed the door open and is crouching down to reach inside her bag.

The inside of her locker is so neat! Her books and folders line up, *side by side,* in a row, as if on display! They are not helter-skelter atop one another as mine are!

Now she is standing again and her fingers are running along her neat row of books.

An image comes to mind: my mother ironing the pleats of my netball skirt, back when we lived in the same house. I remember how she would pause now and then, set down the iron, run a finger along the pleats . . .

Now Briony has found the folder she wanted, and is gone.

I turn to the book that I like to carry these days — one that Maureen gave me on etiquette — and I open it at a random page.

And there, if you can believe it, is the answer.

The reason that Briony troubles me; the reason she has *always* troubled me. I will type out the lines:

"A shy person will throw a restraint over a group of people, and cause the most sparkling conversation to flag; it is impossible to become friendly and chatty with such an individual."

How do I find the positive light within such a person as that?

Late Wednesday night.

Went to Eleanora's tonight. Still no sign of the baby. I asked to see a photo and Eleanora looked at me in panic, I'm sure. "But my hands!" she said. "I can't get the albums out!"

FAD was also intriguing.

It turned out that Emily and Astrid had secretly offered to run a session of *their* own. They had followed my lead! I suppose that is flattering.

The nature of the session was not, however, clear to me.

It seemed to consist of a series of questions, which we were supposed to discuss. Here is an example:

Okay, let's say there's a piece of machinery in a factory. If you get your sleeve caught in this machinery, your fingers will be mangled. But, okay, let's say it's not switched on, but it could be switched on at any moment, would you put your hand in it? Why? Oh, okay, why not? No, seriously, why not?

This set of questions was asked, with intensity, by Astrid, who looked at us in turn, and we looked at one another, perplexed, then tried, halfheartedly, to answer.

"No," we said, "because we like our fingers."

At which, Astrid turned hopefully to Sergio and said, "But *you* would, right? Because of your adrenalin thing?" And Sergio said, gently and kindly, "But Astrid, I'm not a COCKLEBUR."

"I don't really like that sort of language," said Try absentmindedly.

But Astrid was nodding slowly. She tilted her head toward Emily and stage-whispered, "Em, what was our point?" Emily shrugged and they both collapsed in giggles.

Other questions included: *Do you think staircases go as high as they could? No, seriously, don't you think they should go higher?*

Also: *Do you think we could fly if we truly believed in ourselves?*

"Elizabeth already flies," Sergio said, "when she runs." He gazed at her as he said this, and Elizabeth laughed, embarrassed.

I was trying to focus on Briony and yet, she is so easy to forget.

Such a silence!

When one remembers Briony, one finds the silence exasperating. A black hole in the armchair constellation.

I tried to dispel this notion, to focus on the *positive*. But I could not explain this: Finnegan and Elizabeth both tend to be quiet, yet neither of them has the same effect. Their eyes, faces, gestures participate. They are one with the group. Now and then they speak, and no one is surprised.

Briony is not one with us at all. She is separate. She sits awkward, her shoulders tense.

And I have noticed over and over: She only ever speaks three times.

Except when Toby is tossing the ball to her, forcing her to speak, Briony speaks three times.

Once her quota of three is used, she reacts even to questions with nothing but the murmur of a smile. Her eyes dart away. She hangs her head, unwinds the Band-Aid on her thumb, and presses it back down.

Thursday, 2 a.m.

Shall I say that Briony is a sweet white rabbit or a mouse? But she might not like that. I feel such curious tingling in my arms and legs these days, as if a mouse were chewing gently on my flesh.

Thursday, 8 p.m.

Strange.

Today we had Biology and I became conscious of some kind of fanfare across the room. It turned out that the teacher was lavishing praise on Briony. Something about her assignment.

(I must do that assignment myself sometime. It's some kind of environmental case study, I think.)

Briony has done something *brilliant* about contaminated water in Bangladesh. Something *superb*.

(Briony's name looks a bit like Biology. I wonder if that gave her an advantage?)

Later, I saw Toby in Economics and I mentioned Briony's success. Just to see his face.

It lit up like a Christmas tree.

And then I could not help myself.

"Toby," I said. "Have you noticed that she always speaks three times?"

The Christmas lights dimmed. Disappointment etched itself in lines around his mouth.

"I'm not criticizing her," I hurried to explain. "It's just

something I've noticed in FAD. It's never more or less than three times. If she can help it."

Now Toby breathed in slowly: the sigh you breathe when a child asks for a foolish favor.

And then he said, "You know how we had to give challenges to our buddy?"

I nodded.

"And Briony is my buddy?"

I nodded again.

"Well. I challenged her to speak three times each week."

I clasped a hand to my mouth.

"If I hadn't," he said, "she'd never say a single word."

Later today, while quietly shelving books in Maureen's bookstore, I realized this: *Briony always speaks three times.*

But this time I realized in a whole different way.

That is: She has never once failed to meet the challenge.

And Toby was right: *Without that challenge, she would not say a word.*

What must it mean to her to force herself to speak three times? Someone as shy as Briony? To do that *every week.*

She was so much more than a rabbit or a mouse!

Then, too, there was that day when Toby threw the ball to Briony. She began to relax. She turned into somebody playful and almost fun. She was no longer a black hole. She was simply herself.

Which means, of course, that normally she is not herself.

Imagine the loneliness of that: never to be yourself.

I flicked through the pages of a paperback, pretending to read, but meanwhile, I felt my face burning.

For Briony had met her challenge but *I had not*. Finnegan had asked me to take a kickboxing class. Such a simple challenge, yet the moment I saw that I would not excel — that I might look foolish in that class — I dropped out!

Well!

And look too at this simple challenge I set myself! That I would come into Maureen's shop late one night and give it a thorough clean. A surprise gift for a friend! And yet I had not even had the courage to take the key!

I decided I would do it. Maureen was chatting with a customer, so I walked (brazenly) behind the counter and took down the key.

And now, home again, I feel a little better when I touch the cold metal in my pocket. I have put it on my starfish key ring to keep it safe.

For now, though, I must think of Briony again. I turn to my etiquette book and flip through the pages. I'm not sure what I seek . . . but there it is.

"The person who is shy," begins the book:

> . . . needs the most delicate sympathy. He should
> be encouraged to talk, but it must be done in so careful
> a manner that he will not be conscious of your intent,

else will his pride take alarm, and he will retreat from the field.

I turn a page and the book recommends that boys and girls who are shy should be taught dancing, gymnastics, and boxing.

I will see what I can do.

× × ×

A Memo from Bindy Mackenzie

To: Briony Atkins
From: Bindy Mackenzie
Subject: YOU
Time: Friday, 11 a.m.

Dear Briony,

Once, I may have suggested that you were a sea cucumber. I may have whispered this in your presence.

(Indeed, I may have written the words SEA CUCUMBER across a large photographic poster of your face.)

That was wrong of me.

You are, in no way, a sea cucumber.

(Even though your mother is a marine biologist!)

No, Briony, I was mistaken.

You are a Fly River Turtle.

Like a Fly River Turtle, you appear to be timid — you dive under a rock at the hint of a stranger — but, in the right company, you are playful and at ease. You may seem gentle and vulnerable, but you carry a shell that is resolute and hard as rock.

I hope you will forgive me for mistaking you for a sea cucumber.

And please accept this complimentary set of personalized memo stationery.

Very best wishes,

Bindy Mackenzie

P.S. Also, you may like to know that I am a member of the Castle Hill Gym. Lately, I've been going regularly and sitting at the rowing machine. If you'd ever like to join me, I have some visitor's passes. They have classes in aerodance, aqua-gymnastics, and kickboxing. I wonder if these might interest you?

$$\times \quad \times \quad \times$$

The Philosophical Musings of Bindy Mackenzie
Monday morning, early.

Yesterday, at the gym, I sat as usual in my rowing machine, and I rowed.

As I rowed, I saw this: a personal trainer with three plump people. He was showing them around, pointing out changing rooms, equipment, and weights — and the three plump people, dressed in jackets and jeans, looked nervous, awkward, and self-conscious. They glanced at us — they glanced at *me* — and what they saw were *members* of the gym, people in sports attire,

299

pushing and pulling at various pieces of steel. Occasional grunt-ing and groaning. (I even grunted once a little myself.) They glanced at us with respect, and I realized, as I watched: *They are tourists*. They are tourists, *but I belong.*

And then I realized this: *I have never felt like this before.*

I have never, to the best of my recollection, thought to myself: *I belong.*

So that was a shock.

7.

Telephone Messages for Bindy Mackenzie . . .

While you were . . . in the shower just now.

You received a call from . . . a guy who says he works for a law firm (Elroy, Lexus & Thai [Tie?]). His name is Blake Elroy, so he claims. (He called on your mobile phone, and I answered it for you. Is that okay? Sorry.)

In relation to . . . something about an *incident* you witnessed at Ashbury last year?!! He wants you to call him and arrange to come in to give a statement! WHAT DID YOU WITNESS?

Further notes . . . Hey Bindy. Look, I found your phone messages stationery. Hope I used it right. Come downstairs and tell me what this is about.

Love,
Auntie Veronica

The Philosophical Musings of Bindy Mackenzie

Wednesday, not sure of the time. After recess? In the Year 11 wing, at a desk, by the window, amongst lockers.

My telephone message must be about that minor assault I saw from my shadow seat outside the library last year. (The substitute teachers arguing — one slapped the other across the face.) I remember it vividly! I will make an exquisite witness! I phoned back and left a message, assuring the lawyer that I would make an exquisite witness.

How strange, what a marvel, what a twist! Last year, when I witnessed the assault, I felt such a foolish outsider — so unwanted, even by the victim, who swore at me when I offered support. But now she wants me, after all! She has seen the error of her ways! All this time she must have *kept* my contact details! And now I am going to play a key role in the dance of the legal system.

I belong! Once again, I *belong*.

A shrill, strange sound tears through my head! High-pitched! A dazzle of noise! What is that?! What is that sound?!

Oh. It is the school bell.

I know it well.

And here the doors are thrown open, and students pour into my space, as if staging a surprise attack! An attack on the lockers! A lesson ends, a lesson begins. Or perhaps it is the start of recess? Or is it lunch?

A few minutes later . . .

Oh. Funny. It turns out it was neither recess nor lunch. It was just the short pause between two classes.

Just now, a hand landed on my shoulder. I gasped and jumped out of the chair. It was Miss Flynn, my English teacher. She waited, patient, while I calmed myself.

(Miss Flynn is, coincidentally, a substitute teacher, just like the fighting women I witnessed last year. And yet she does not seem to be going anywhere. Can a substitute remain for so long? *Why you are still here?* I almost asked.)

But I did not want to hurt her feelings.

She herself did not spare mine.

"Bindy, I just finished teaching an English class, and I'm sure you *belong* in that class. Just as you *belonged* in my class on Monday. What's going on? This isn't like you. And another thing, Bindy, see this briefcase of mine? Right now, it's full of *Pride and Prejudice* essays, and that means your essay *belongs* here too, and, as far as I know, it's not."

I explained that I have been distracted by FAD.

"I've been writing portraits of my FAD group," I said, "which has sometimes required me to *follow* the FAD member around, thereby forcing me to miss classes of my own."

It was a shame, I said, but could not be avoided.

I promised I would get to her essay as soon as I could.

As I spoke, I noticed that Miss Flynn was drumming the fingers of her right hand onto the palm of her left. There was something distracting about that. And then I looked at her face, at the sharp little curl of her mouth, and I remembered. She drums her fingers like that whenever somebody speaks nonsense. It's her technique. She meant I was speaking nonsense!

I have never been treated with such disrespect.

Anyway, she is gone now. I didn't really mean to miss English. But how could I tell her that I had simply been confused? That time has been rather curious of late? That I no longer know who I am? A person who does not write essays! A person obsessed with her FAD group! (Help! What of my future? Oh well. Never mind.)

How could I say that my arms and legs are heavy with exhaustion, that my head pounds like a beating fist, that my stomach is sick with something like the cousin of fear? (But what do I fear?) I saw a billboard ad for soft tissues today, which showed a puppy resting its neck on the edge of the package. The idea of pressure against my neck — a wave of nausea struck me like a cannonball. I had to run to the gutter and throw up.

Speaking of palms, mine are marvelously callused at the moment. From the rowing machine. I can't stop feeling the roughness of the skin there.

Which makes me think of those "trust exercises." It was months ago that Try mentioned them, at an early FAD session. It was when we were first given our "buddies." Try said she'd planned to give us "trust exercises," but it was raining. "We'll do trust another time," she said. And she explained. "You know," she said, "you tie your hand to your buddy's hand and lead each other around blindfolded?"

Imagine if we did that now! Finnegan would hold my hand, and he would feel the calluses on my palms.

He might not like that. He might prefer a soft and tender hand.

I have been using hand cream and moisturizers each day lately, just in case these trust exercises come up.

And yet, I picture this: Finnegan's hand closes around my hand. A buzzing sounds, that no one else can hear, as of a swarm of distant bees. This is our hands, communicating. Finnegan's hand buzzes, "What's this?" and my hand replies, ever so softly, "This? This is calluses from the gym," And Finnegan's hand says, "Ah, the gym that you joined because of my challenge?," and my hand whispers, "Yes." And then, although we both face resolutely forward, so that the gold of his hair is nothing but a light in the corner of my eye, so that his profile is nothing but a shadowy outline — although we look straight ahead, and not at one another — even so, our hands squeeze tight.

I have seen Finnegan's hands, so I know how they would feel;

they are much larger than mine. Cool and dry, I think, yet with something that softens as it presses.

I wonder what we will do in FAD today? I think we ought to do those trust exercises *some*time. Really, a teacher should not promise future exercises and then not carry them through. That just confuses the students.

I suppose I have missed a couple of FAD sessions. I suppose she might have done the trust exercises while I was absent. But what would poor Finnegan have done? Wandering lonely as a cloud, blindfolded, no buddy to guide him, bumping into trees.

I hope they didn't do something like take turns sharing buddies, so that Astrid tied her hand to Finnegan, or Elizabeth, or Emily, or Briony. That would have been wrong.

There was another trust exercise too. I remember Try mentioned something else. Falling into your buddy's arms and trusting your buddy to catch you. Imagine Astrid falling into Finnegan's arms. She is too quick and bony. I don't think he'd have liked that. Or Elizabeth. (He might have liked that — I think he is fond of Elizabeth — sometimes I feel sorry for him, as he must have noticed that Sergio and Liz are together.) Or Emily. But she is too hysterical — she wouldn't have trusted him, she would have collapsed into giggles.

No. It is right that I, his buddy, do the trust exercises with Finnegan. I would fall freely and neatly. I would not grow hysterical.

306

He would be pleased. And I would catch him, too, when he fell into my arms. He may be taller and larger than me, but I would focus, oh! I would concentrate, and I would catch him. I am sure of it. I suppose we might somehow tumble to the grass.

I suppose I should be at the Year Assembly just now. And yet why? I might just rest my head here on this desk and have a sleep.

Important to be awake for FAD later today.

I might just rest my head. I might just fall, inside my mind, backwards, into his arms.

× × ×

My Buddy Diary
By Bindy Mackenzie

Wednesday, Late

I write now to record an incident connected with my buddy. I call it the *Cincinnati Incident.*

It took place today, on the way to FAD.

Now, I should say that earlier, at lunchtime (after several hours of very strange reverie in the Year 11 wing), I had chanced upon my buddy, emerging from an office.

It was the office of Mrs. Lilydale.

Something sparked in my brain.

I had seen Finnegan emerge from that office before. And at that time I had wondered: *Why?* She is not one of his teachers.

She is not our Year Coordinator. Back then when it happened, the only reason I could think of was that Finnegan was seeing Mrs. Lilydale as debating coach. That he would be our new second speaker.

But although I waited patiently, I heard no such thing. And Emily became our second speaker and, as it happens, excels in this role. (We continue to win.)

So I had slowly forgotten the event — and yet, here he was again! Emerging from Mrs. Lilydale's office! But for what purpose?

I decided I would ask him when I had the chance.

And then, behold! A chance.

The FAD group walked as one today, after lunch, down to the bus stop. But we lingered because Astrid wanted to show us how she had given herself a black eye, climbing onto the roof of a house to hide from the police during a raid at a party on the weekend. She performed an elaborate mime on the front lawns of the school.

As a result, we missed the bus.

But nobody minded. It is not a long walk into Castle Hill.

We set forth.

The path begins along a highway, forcing one to walk almost single file, while trucks and cars speed by. As we turned onto a quieter street, I found myself beside Finnegan.

"Hey," he said.

I waited a moment, then realized it was his way of saying, "Hi."

"Hey," I tried, in response. I felt oddly pleased by my delay. There was an enigma to it. I kicked at a tuft of grass in a crack, and tripped slightly.

I saw you coming out of Mrs. Lilydale's office at lunchtime today, I rehearsed in my mind as we walked. I chanted it so many times that when I finally said it out loud, it had a curious, stilted tone.

"I saw you coming out of Mrs. Lilydale's office at lunchtime today," I sang.

"Did you?" Finnegan replied. I glanced at him. He raised his eyebrows. We continued walking.

Good gracious.

"Is she one of your teachers?" I tried, although I knew the answer.

"No," he said, in an easy voice. "But she's supervising me in an independent study that I'm doing for Ancient History. It's this thing I started at my old school last year, and Mrs. L. knows more about it than Mr. Ramekin, so that's how that worked out."

Huh!

A simple explanation.

The most mysterious circumstances — the mystery now dissolved.

Sometimes I prefer not to know.

We walked along the suburban path, quietly for a while. Junk had been set out for collection at various houses, and we had to step around or over curious objects. At one house, a paint-flaking rattan chair; at another, a stained computer monitor. Such pristine houses, I thought, with their window boxes and gardens — and yet they disgorge such junk!

I thought about saying this aloud, but was frightened of Finnegan's eyebrows.

We stepped around a box of foolscap folders, pages ruffled by the wind. I thought, *This is the discarded work of a Year 12 student! That student could be a genius! I could take this box of folders! I could transcribe the essays; I could borrow these ideas!*

But if I stopped and gathered the folders, Finnegan might find me odd, or immoral.

Worse, he might simply keep walking. Join Sergio, Astrid, and Emily up ahead.

So I continued.

An otter smiled up at me. Someone had put an otter out for collection.

But as I came closer, I saw it was only a rolled up piece of foam, tied with string.

Now we were descending, crossing at lights, reaching the Castle Towers car park.

Two men approached, dressed in suit trousers and shirts. They skirted around Astrid and Emily.

As they neared us, one said to the other: "There's two or three in Cincinnati."

And then they had passed.

I glanced back. *Two or three what in Cincinnati?* I wondered. *Factories? Skyscrapers? What?*

"I guess he means *n*'s," said Finnegan, beside me.

I looked at him, confused.

"In Cincinnati?" he explained. "There are two or three *n*'s in Cincinnati. Or maybe he means *i*'s?"

I laughed aloud. I could not stop. I erupted.

"What's so funny?" called some of the others, turning back.

"Nothing, nothing," I giggled.

Finnegan smiled. Then, as I continued giggling, he stopped smiling and raised his eyebrows.

× × ×

Philosophical Musings of Bindy Mackenzie

Tuesday

Have spent the last few days looking through dictionaries. Also, leaving messages for the lawyer who wants me to testify about the fighting teachers. At last I've got through to the lawyer!

Made an appointment for the Friday after next, at 2 *p.m.* His office is on Cleveland Street.

That's funny. Cleveland is a city in Ohio.

So is Cincinnati.

8.

A Portrait of Elizabeth Clarry

Here I sit in a small café in the Strand Arcade. It is Sunday. I am waiting to meet my brother.

Across the room: a burst of flames.

No, it is not flames. It is flowers wrapped in cellophane, lying on a table. The cellophane must have caught the light.

I am thinking about Elizabeth Clarry: how I have seen her as nothing but an athlete. I have seen her running shoes, sports clothes, the way she stretches her legs and reaches to her toes. I have seen reports in the newsletter about her success in competitions.

But I have always known there is more. I have known, for example, that she was once best friends with, and looked out for, a girl in our year named Celia, notorious for running away.

I have known that Elizabeth is shy but wry. I have suspected that she is bright. And indeed, the other day, Miss Flynn read out her essay on *Pride and Prejudice*.

As Miss Flynn read, I felt a strange compulsion to quietly

open my laptop and secretly type the whole thing. Then hand it in as my own.

Of course, I did no such thing.

(For a start, Miss Flynn would have recognized it.)

On Wednesday, our FAD group went to Castle Hill Heritage Park, rather than the Blue Danish café. The sky was a dark wintry blue.

The others pointed out Try's house to me as they all went last term — it overlooks the park, and is forbidding and foreboding.

Emily became hysterical when we entered the park because she saw a sign: WARNING: PINDONE BAITING UNDER WAY. It showed a cartoon picture of a rabbit, a red cross through its body. They were poisoning rabbits in the park, said the sign. It warned that the poison could be lethal to pets.

We walked, uneasy, along a path through bluegum, grey ironbark, and red mahogany trees. Sticks curled and twisted as if to camouflage themselves as snakes. Bellbirds chimed. A frog hopped over Sergio's foot.

Then we found the picnic grounds and sat.

Try began by telling us the history of the park itself: the Darug Aboriginals who first lived there and their violent banishment by whites. The stone barracks built to imprison convicts, who planted crops while secretly planning a rebellion. "Death or liberty, and a ship to take us home," was their slogan.

They failed. The rebels were hanged. The crops that the dead men had planted also failed, decimated by rust and blight. The barracks were shut down. Then reopened as the first lunatic asylum in the country.

All this is true.

I had read the history before, but as Try spoke today, a cloud crossed the sun, and deep shadows plunged into our circle.

We huddled closer together.

We talked of the sufferings of the past, of this very spot and the dark state of the world today. People banished from their homes, lost in new lands, imprisoned in barbed wire.

There was talk of terrorists and despots.

I decided to lighten the mood.

"If only," I said, "if only there were more people like Cincinnatus. Like Lucius Quinctius Cincinnatus."

"If only," agreed Sergio, a gleam in his eye.

He was a Roman farmer, I explained, but he became a dictator twice (458 and 439 B.C.). His friends persuaded him that his country needed him to take control. But he only stayed a dictator *just* long enough to restore peace and order, and then returned to his farm.

As I told this story, I lingered on the name: *Cincinnatus.*

"Isn't it a beautiful name?" I said. "Cincinnatus."

"Hmm," agreed Try.

"I found out about him the other day," I explained, "because I was looking up words that sound like Cincinnati. I like that word, *Cincinnati.*"

"Hmm," said Try again.

"I wonder what it's like," I said dreamily, "in Cincinnati?"

"I wonder," agreed Try, and changed the subject.

I glanced over at Finnegan as this conversation proceeded, but he did not appear to be listening.

After this, we talked about broken marriages.

Most people in my FAD group seem to have divorced parents. I felt grateful that my parents are together. Astrid said her father had recently moved out. He forgot to pack the Thermos that he takes to work each day, for coffee or soup, so he phoned Astrid's mother and asked her to leave it on the porch for him to collect. Astrid's mother laughed and hung up on him.

Sergio mentioned that his parents had broken up after his mother caused the scar on his face.

There was a stillness in the group.

His mother was sterilizing bottles for his baby sister, he said, by boiling them on the stove, and forgot that the saucepan had a metal handle. So when she picked it up she scalded her hand. She flung the saucepan away from herself. She didn't realize that Sergio, who was four at the time, and had been watching TV in the other room, had just crept up behind her to surprise her. The boiling water hit him in the face.

Sergio's father could never forgive his mother for her mistake, nor could she forgive herself. And the costs of treatment and skin grafts for Sergio was making them broke. So the marriage fell apart.

Nobody could speak after this; Sergio tried to grin. There

was something about the awkward tilt of his shoulder that suggested he wanted the subject changed.

I tried to think of something to say. But what?! Should I share some of my Cincinnati words — *cinnamon, cinema, Cinescope*?

Eventually, Briony spoke three times, each time referring to a cousin of hers who had cerebral palsy.

Finnegan said a cousin of his had been killed in an accident last year. They'd lived just a couple of streets away from each other when they were kids, and practically lived in each other's houses, so they were more like brother and sister. They used to ride their bikes to the beach almost every day, and chase cane toads, and play imaginary games, and his cousin had these imaginary names for both of them, which they used even when they were grown up. Then she'd moved to Sydney, but they Instant Messaged almost every night right until the night before it happened, and now he was in Sydney, seeing all the things she'd described to him and it was like her voice was in his head, describing it all. He spoke in an offhand voice to tell the story.

Elizabeth, beside him, placed a hand on his shoulder. It seemed to me she did this without thinking. I believe that Finnegan was comforted.

After a time, we were all silent. We had sunk into a shared gloom.

Somebody suggested we never return to this park.

Try mentioned a house she owns in the Blue Mountains. She became enthusiastic, trying to lighten the mood. She would arrange a weekend away! She would bring in notes for our parents!

We walked back to the entrance gate to the park, and somebody spotted a dead rabbit amongst the trees. Emily was inconsolable.

I thought perhaps Elizabeth was a unicorn: elusive and unique. I thought of unicorn horns, which were once collected and cherished. People believed they could protect you from disease, and could also detect poison. Of course, there is no such thing as a unicorn — the horns that people collected were probably just narwhal teeth.

A narwhal, I should add, is a small arctic whale. I don't think Elizabeth is a narwhal.

Oh, what am I talking about? I liked being in the park with them. Elizabeth smiles like a friend.

My meeting with Anthony will not be long. We will only have time for espressos. I have to return to Castle Hill to sit with Eleanora while she makes pasta. I wonder if there is a baby down the hall in Eleanora's house. I wonder if that door is closed on nothing but an empty crib?

× × ×

A Memo from Bindy Mackenzie

To: Elizabeth Clarry
From: Bindy Mackenzie
Subject: YOU
Time: Monday, 7 a.m.

Dear Elizabeth,

I once suggested that you were a Queen Alexandra's Birdwing.

That was wrong of me.

(Although, of course, if you would *like* to be a butterfly, flitting about the coastal rain forests of northern Papua New Guinea, by all means, go ahead. Please note that you will only have a life span of three months.)

However, I think you are a Camargue horse.

A Camargue horse is a wild, white horse that canters along the plains and marshes of southeast France.

And so do you!

Or, at least, if you were in southeast France, I'm sure you would canter along.

The Camargue horse has expressive, intelligent eyes. It has a sense of humor and fun! It is strong, beautiful, and brave.

I hope you will forgive me for mistaking you, a wild white horse, for a poisonous butterfly.

And here is a complimentary set of personalized memo stationery.

Very best wishes,

Bindy Mackenzie

9.

The Dream Diary of Bindy Mackenzie

Monday, 7:20 a.m.

I dreamed that I was on an iceberg, just outside Cincinnati. It was not cold at all: It was soft and warm as a pile of feather quilts. I was flat on my stomach, resting my chin on my hands. In the distance, two little narwhals were fighting. They were using their single, protruding teeth like swords. It was a sword fight!

Suddenly, one of the narwhals stopped, leaned over, picked up a fish, and tossed the fish in the air. The other batted the fish with its tooth. The first hit it back. Hence the fight became a cheerful game of tennis.

I smiled to myself. I knew they were competing for a female narwhal. I could see the very narwhal in question — she was on a distant iceberg of her own, across an expanse of silver-blue. She wore her hair in two coiled plaits, pinned to each side of her head.

I laughed out loud in sudden delight.

That was me!

I wear my hair like that!

I squinted back at the tennis players, but could not tell who they were. I thought that the cheeky one was Sergio. Or perhaps Toby. The other had bright blonde hair, and may have been Lleyton Hewitt.

I turned back to the female narwhal, but her iceberg had started up like a car and was zooming into the distance. She had disappeared.

Yesterday, when I met Anthony for coffee, I told him about my decision to devote myself to uncovering the beauty of my FAD group.

Anthony is a year younger than me, but sometimes his eyes are wise.

"Well, okay," he said, "but make sure you don't lose yourself. Don't let yourself disappear."

Before he could go on, Sam arrived, and the two of them began to take photographs of me for an assignment.

Also in the dream, another iceberg pulled up beside me, and there was Eleanora, the pasta maker. She was standing in the center of the iceberg, staring directly at me. Her arms were folded.

I know why I dreamed that.

Last night, at Eleanora's, I excused myself to go to the bathroom. Before I knew what I was doing, I was slipping past the bathroom door and on down the hall to the baby's room. I had to know. Was there a baby in there? Was it merely an empty room? My heart hammered. My hand reached for the door handle —

Something made me turn.

Eleanora stood in the hallway, staring at me.

"Oh!" I said. "This isn't the bathroom?"

She continued to stare.

10.

A Portrait of Sergio Saba

I am in Modern History.

I see Sergio. He sits diagonally ahead of me, to the right. He is therefore alongside Elizabeth, who sits in front of me. The two cast glances and jokes at one another all the time.

I believe Ms. Walcynski is speaking to me.

Ah yes, she just reminded me that we have moved on to the Romanov Dynasty, and I still have not submitted my assignment on American Civil Rights.

I hear some giggles, but mostly I sense a ripple of amazement. Faces turn, concerned, delighted, amused — to gaze at me.

Who is this Bindy Mackenzie? the faces seem to say. *A Bindy who does not do assignments! I do not know her!*

(I don't know her either. Why do I not seem to *care*?!)

I have witnessed this sort of thing before. I think it's called: *public humiliation by the educational establishment.*

Now I know what it is like!

I don't mind it so much.

I said, "Ms. Walcynski, I couldn't get into my room to get my assignment this morning because the cleaner was in there, vacuuming."

She was so startled her face shook a little. People giggled.

It was a lie! I haven't done the assignment yet.

And it makes no sense! You can get into a room if someone's cleaning it! You're allowed!

Although, it's partly true — Maria, the cleaner, *was* in my room this morning, vacuuming, and it was so loud it made my head explode.

But back to Sergio.

I see him clearly from here. I have always considered him attractive. Soft dark hair, golden-brown skin — such a keen, mischievous glint to his dark eyes. Girls tumble over themselves to catch that eye.

That tiny gold stud in his ear. I wonder if he ever wears silver?

His only flaw is the burn scar that tendrils across his cheek.

Without that scar, Sergio would be perfection.

But now, as I look, I see moles and pimple scars. There is a faint red patch on the right of his neck, as if he had just scratched himself. The collar of his shirt is smudged.

These things I only see because I stare, and, as I stare, Sergio turns, sees me and looks back, a flicker of something in the deep black-brown of those eyes. Somehow, I cannot look away. We stare for an eternity. I am typing now, as I stare. I am thinking of the narwhal — my face burns — I am —

"Bindy Mackenzie!"

That is Ms. Walcynski again.

"Do you have to type *every* word I say?" she demands.

I look up at her enigmatically, still typing. She thinks I'm typing class notes!

I haven't got a clue what she is talking about. Is she perhaps speaking Russian?

Sergio is neither tall nor particularly large, although his forearms resting on the desk there do have muscular definition.

I remember an event from last year. It was in a History class too. Sergio was staring through the classroom window and saw a gang of Brookfield students, arriving at our school car park. They carried cricket bats, hammers, and planks of wood. They circled around a student's car.

It was not Sergio's car.

But seeing them, Sergio shouted, leaped from his desk, scrambled out of the classroom window, and ran like the wind across the schoolyard. The rest of the class was slow to see what Sergio had seen.

Of course, when they did see, they rose as one and poured out the windows of the classroom (while the teacher yelled for them to stop). We ran, I remember, like a storm, toward those Brookfielders.

Seeing the storm, the Brookfielders retreated. But who knows what he had intended, a shortish boy like Sergio, confronting a gang like that? He could not have known the class would rise and join him.

I found the event exhilarating.

I return my gaze to brave Sergio: his hands and wrists on the desk. There is an elastic band hanging loose around his wrist. On the back of his right hand: smudged red ink. I think it might be a phone number. His nails are chewed and torn; his thumb-nail is black.

I drop my eyes to his shoes beneath the desk and feel a quick-ening pulse. Something so intimate about shoes. I can even see part of one ankle — the way he is sitting now. He is leaning back, elbows on the back of the chair, loose, almost disrespectful — and one trouser leg is slightly raised. There is a graze on the ankle. I think I see a small tattoo.

There is something I am seeing, but yet I do not see.

What is it about Sergio?

There is something connecting it all: that misbuttoned shirt, the slipping hem on his trousers leg, the tattoo, the cuts, grazes, Band-Aids, smudges. All tilt toward his brazen attitude. He leans, seeming amused, but joins in conversations — both at FAD and in class — at unexpected moments. Teachers and students light up when he speaks.

There is *attitude* in him, but when Sergio pauses and looks at you, he truly looks. He *embraces* you with his eyes. He is com-fortable with his world, and his words, when he speaks them, are honest.

He *looks*, I understand it now, because he refuses to be looked at. He defies you to look at the scar on his face. He defied the FAD group early on, when he folded up his trouser leg and pointed to a faint white scar, remnant of that terrible trip to Hill End.

When he looked at me just now, he saw my fears and my faults.

But I think, for just a flicker, he may have seen simply this: Bindy Mackenzie.

That is Sergio's charm.

So few people look and truly see.

Now I know why Sergio is so attractive to the girls.

In the past, I know, he has perhaps taken advantage of this — he has not been especially committed to his girlfriends. I hear he has cheated on them.

But this year, it seems, he has found strength. He has chosen one — Elizabeth Clarry. That he sees her unique beauty; that he sees the truth of Elizabeth. That is what I admire above all else.

When people stare, Sergio looks back.

He rises to the challenge.

For this he deserves to be nobody but himself. Enough with the animals. Sergio is simply a boy.

A Memo from Bindy Mackenzie

To: Sergio Saba
From: Bindy Mackenzie

Subject: YOU
Time: Monday, 2:30 p.m.

Dear Sergio,
I once believed that you were a platypus.

I apologize for that.

You are not a platypus, Sergio. You are an extraordinary young man.

I hope you will forgive my mistake.

Here's some personalized memo stationery.

Very best wishes,

Bindy Mackenzie

P.S. Sorry for staring at you in History this morning.

11.

Telephone Messages for Bindy Mackenzie . . .

While you were . . . at school today.
You received a call from . . . Eleanora.
In relation to . . . she wants to cancel Wednesday and Sunday nights until further notice . . .
Further notes . . . she's the one you sit with while she makes pasta, isn't she? Because she's worried that the baby will wake up while her hands are sticky? Maybe she's noticed the kitchen tap. Sorry about losing your job, Bindy, but it was a weird one, wasn't it? . . .

Also, that lawyer called again. Confirming your meeting this Friday. He was a bit pompous.

Love,
Auntie Veronica

× × ×

The Philosophical Musings of Bindy Mackenzie
Don't know what day it is. Tuesday?

Strange to see my income dwindle. Have left Kmart — and yesterday, the message: No more Eleanora. I suppose I shouldn't have walked down the hall toward the baby's room — but still, to cancel straightaway like that — it makes you wonder. Was I too close to the truth? Is there, in fact, no baby? Wonder if I should break into her house one day and check?

Suppose I should prepare another business proposal for Dad, but I should really get some schoolwork done. Or should I? Feel rather giddy with this fall.

Yes, I'm sure it's Tuesday.
And soon it is my birthday! Maybe someone will give me money? I wonder if my FAD group knows? This year it falls on a Friday, and the next day we're going to Try's house in the Blue Mountains. Wonder if they'll like me by then. Have sent memos but no response.

Strange sounds. Strange familiar school sounds.

Might just rest my head here for a moment.

Hi Bindy,
You're a tricky one to find. Have you not been hearing the messages over the PA? I need you to come and see me — still no history assignment!! And the assessment task on Tsar Nicholas is due this week.

Reminder: Exams are coming up and you'll need to get

cracking, Bindy, or you won't even understand the questions. . . . This is not like you at all!

Yours,

Ms. Walcynski

The Philosophical Musings of Bindy Mackenzie

Tuesday, midafternoon

How can I complete a history assignment when I'm so busy each
night? I've been busy each night. I can't remember why. Each
night, I am very busy.

Just now, the biology teacher told us all what amazing work
Briony's doing on some experiment, some extension of her pol-
luted water assignment, and Briony blushed.

"Look," I murmured, "she's turning cinnabarine."

The person beside me ignored me.

"It means red," I explained. But it was as if I had not spoken.

Yet I had spoken rather loudly, hoping Finnegan could hear.
(He sits two rows back.) I sense that he loves words that start
with *cin*. That's why I've been looking them up for him.

Still Tuesday

Last night I dreamt the word "Cincinnati." It was a banner
and it rippled through the sky.

The biology teacher is talking to me. He is using words. Local
terrestrial. Aquatic ecosystem. Biotic. Abiotic. Overdue. Exams.
What are these wonderful words?

I smile at the teacher, delighted. What does he mean?

I find that my heart hurts a little when I smile.

So I stop and turn away.

× × ×

Dear Bindy,

How about you pop up to my office today — if you don't mind the climb to the top balcony? I've been hearing reports that you're not quite yourself. I want you to drop by the sick bay too — I've told the nurse to look out for you.

Let's have a chat as soon as possible.

Best wishes,

Mr. Botherit

Year Coordinator, Year 11

× × ×

The Philosophical Musings of Bindy Mackenzie

Wednesday, almost time for FAD

MUST try to go to English class more often. Miss Flynn was talking to me again today, and I could not understand a word she said.

"Look at the sky, Miss Flynn," I said. "It's such an ashen gray! It's cinerulent!"

Then I looked at her and realized that Miss Flynn is not Finnegan. Even though there are F's and n's in both names.

Thursday, I think.

Yesterday in FAD, Try was handing out cartoons again, so I asked her in a whisper if she'd received my framed cartoon. "Oh, yes!" she said. "Thanks! That was so sweet of you." She seemed genuinely grateful, but no word on my Life. Anti-climax struck another blow to my rib cage. But what do I want her to say?

Still Thursday, I think.

I must remember to go to work in Maureen's bookshop today. Yet it is so familiar. I am tiring of it. The bookshop. I feel *cinct* by books.

Every night these last few nights, after midnight, I slip silently from the sleeping house, and I go there. I stop by Dad's Gilbert Road house on the way and tear down a few strips of wallpaper.

Then I am cinct by books, just as Australia is cinct by sea. Dusting, cleaning, polishing — I have dusted every book. I have climbed on shelves and taken apart the light fixtures. I have swept up piles of insects. I have scrubbed the walls until buckets of water turned black.

But today it will all be worth it. Today! Maureen will thank me! She will hug me and whirl me in circles! She will call me an *elf* and a *fairy*! She will shower me with more free books! She might pay me a bonus.

Telephone Messages for Bindy Mackenzie . . .

While you were . . . at your bookshop job this afternoon
You received a call from . . . your mum.
In relation to . . . she says she's left a thousand messages on your phone — she wants to know what the doctor said this afternoon. And she says she's been getting phone calls from your school.
Further notes . . . Bindy Mackenzie, did you GO to the doctor today? Your mum says she made an appointment for you at 4 and I'm sure you were at your bookshop then. Have you been to any of the appointments *I* have made for you? And what's going on at school?! Stop hiding in your room! Come talk to me! You look more sleepy every time I see you.

Love,
Auntie Veronica

× × ×

The Philosophical Musings of Bindy Mackenzie
Thursday, Late
What an unexpected twist.

Maureen did not notice.

A week's worth of midnight escapades. That bookshop gleamed! But she did not say a word. She said she'd been in Queensland these last few days, but she did not wear a suntan nor the air of one who had relaxed.

"Bindy," she said, sounding agitated, "have you noticed the

spare key? It usually hangs on this hook above the counter and I can't find it."

She was frowning, distracted. She was rummaging in her handbag, pulling things up and pushing them back down. A notebook fell to the floor with a slap, open at a page —*"Markus Pulie?"* said the page. Maureen jumped, swept up the book, and stuffed it back into her bag. She returned her gaze to the empty hook.

Thursday, Late

Does she think I stole the key? How dare she?!

Well, I suppose I did.

But who is *Markus Pulie*? A name in her notebook. Why the question mark? I have a strange conviction that he will replace me. She was so harried and distracted today. She hardly looked at me. Is she going to *fire* me? And hire this *Markus Pulie* in my place?

Thursday, Still late

Let us count our small blessings.

At least I don't need to worry about school tomorrow — I'm going into the city to see a lawyer.

And tonight I convinced Auntie V. that I am perfectly well — *I do not have glandular fever! I do not have glandular fever!* (That is my new chant.) I "confessed" that my problem is my eyesight.

"I can't read the board anymore," I explained. "My glasses stopped working months ago."

"What! Why didn't you say anything?!"

She's going to take me to the optometrist next week.

It was not a total lie. My eyes *are* blurry on occasion. And there is a buzzing in my ears. And I feel, sometimes, like I just got off a fast-moving Ferris wheel.

× × ×

Nighttime Musings of Bindy Mackenzie

Late Friday Night

Have you ever seen a burst of light explode?

It happened to me today, and everything fell into place.

I saw the lawyer. I took the train to Redfern and found my way to Cleveland Street.

I wore my school uniform. It seemed formal enough for a legal office.

But the legal office was nothing but a bare little room. An exposed electric light. A scratched table.

A young man in a suit.

Blake Elroy.

His face was puffy and his voice pompous.

He ushered me into the office — where was the receptionist? Where the glamorous harbor view?

But the office was at street level, and bedraggled men and women peered in, or bounced against the glass.

I sat opposite the lawyer, trying to ignore the bouncing.

"Now then," he said, straightening his shoulders. "You know what this is about?"

"I understand it's about the dispute between the two substitute teachers last year," I said, adopting his official tone, trying to show at once that I was more than a mere schoolgirl. *I would make an exquisite witness!* "They were arguing about a Polish exchange student," I declared. "The blonde woman struck the redhead with her right hand. This left a bright red mark on her cheek. The redhead dropped her books."

I sat back, waiting for the praise.

I realized something — I missed waiting for praise. It had been so long. In the past, I was *always* sitting back, waiting for praise. But at school these days there has been a drought of it, I suppose because I don't do any work. All this time I had embraced my decline, but really I'd never stopped believing I would soon climb back, that I would soon reclaim the praise. Now I thought: *But how? How could I ever catch up?*

"Very well," said the lawyer, pursing his lips. "But what makes you think they were substitute teachers, these two women?"

"Well!" I began. "It was clear — they were —"

Why had I believed they were substitute teachers?

"Because," he said, "they were not substitute teachers. The women you saw fighting were in fact computer programmers. Contractors. Working for the Board of Studies. Installing new software. But no matter! Tell me, what makes you think they were arguing about a Polish exchange student?"

On this, I was more certain.

"I heard them," I explained. "I heard the name."

"The name of a Polish student at your school? Hmm. An exchange student, you say?"

"Well —" I realized, as I spoke, "Well, I don't *know* that it was an exchange student. I just heard a Polish name. And I assumed it must be an exchange . . ."

He looked down at the papers on his desk. "And what was that name?"

"I don't know," I whispered. "I can't remember."

"Well, no matter. We'll get a list of the names of Polish students at your school and you can go through it. You don't happen to *have* a list on you, do you?"

I gasped, slightly.

It was like walking into the wrong exam.

"No matter," he sighed again. And then, sharply: "Are you sure it was a *student*? How do you know this Polish person was a student?"

I thought I might burst into tears.

I couldn't speak for a moment.

How did I know?

Then I rallied: "But why does all this matter?" I pleaded. "I clearly saw that woman hit the other one! Isn't that all you need for an assault charge?"

"An *assault charge*! Who said this was an assault charge?" The lawyer looked amused.

I chewed on my nails like a teenager.

"No, no," he said. "This is a copyright dispute. It matters not a *whit* that one struck the other. What matters is the *words* they spoke. Our client tells us that, when you were eavesdropping on them, (a) the copyright issue was being discussed, and (b) important admissions were made about that issue, which the other party now, of course, denies. So what we want from *you* is what you heard. Tell me. What did you hear?"

A copyright dispute?

My head seemed to me to be revolving.

"But all they were talking about," I murmured, "was a Polish exchange student."

He seemed, then, to pounce.

"That's all you heard?" he pounced.

I nodded miserably.

"Tell me precisely what they said about this Polish exchange student."

Helplessly I shrugged. I had no recollection of particular words.

We regarded one another for a moment. And then I whispered, "A copyright dispute?"

He lifted one of the papers on his desk, to reveal a disk in a paper envelope.

He held it up.

"Over this," he said. "Software. *Enlightenment,* it's called. A rather New Age name. Some educational software that the Board plans on rolling out. It's a consolidation tool for teachers, basically — brings together information about education in this state. You've got your student records, your teacher qualifications, your exams, your assessment tasks, your model answers, you name it . . ."

He droned on but my head had caught these words, and was chanting them: *your exams, your assessment tasks, your model answers.*

On that disk?

If I could just distract his attention!

If I could slip that disk into my pocket!

Exams, assessment tasks, model answers . . .

All there! The solution all there!

But the lawyer was raising his voice.

"See, your school's agreed to do the test run," he explained, waving the disk gently back and forth before my eyes. "It's loaded onto the teachers' computers there with a password. The teachers have the password."

Ah.

The password.

The disk, on its own, was useless.

What had I been thinking anyway?

Of cheating?

Never!

"But you're telling me you heard nothing about software?" he leaned forward, examining my face.

"No," I whispered.

An inscrutable expression seemed to flit across his face — something almost like triumph. Was he *pleased* that I was failing as a witness? As if he'd always known that a schoolgirl would be no help?

He continued to prod at my story for a while, trying to find a way into *copyright* and *software* when all I had to offer was a student and a slap.

At one point, he paused.

"Well, now — this Polish student — could that have been the

password, do you think? I can't *tell* you the password, but I *can* say that it sounds like a name — it might even sound a bit like a Polish name, I *guess*. Was it the password, do you think?"

And so the meeting went on.

My memory of the fight had been a neat wooden structure — and here was a lawyer, dismantling it, one plank of timber at a time.

"Well," he said, as the meeting closed. "You've got my number. I want you to spend this next week really *thinking* over the event, and let's say you remember anything at all? Give me a call."

As I caught the train home, the burst of light exploded.

I saw why I had been wrong.

I had believed the women were substitute teachers because *I* had never seen them before, and furthermore, *I* disapprove of substitute teachers. So I am always looking out for them, ready to disapprove.

I had believed they were discussing an exchange student because *I* was caught up in the issue of exchange — at that time, my friend Kelly Simonds was about to exchange me for Vienna.

And these last years I'd seen only the flaws of my classmates because I was caught up with flaws of my own. The events of Year 8 had caused me to obsess about those flaws.

My brother had warned me I might lose myself. The opposite was true.

I had been lost *within* myself. When you're lost within yourself, you make mistakes.

How fortunate that I had begun to change! That I was using my talents of observation now, to help my FAD group see the *good* within themselves!

12.

A Portrait of Astrid Bexonville

Ah, Astrid.

It has come to you at last.

The most important portrait.

The portrait I have feared.

The portrait that makes my heart flutter, nay, that —

Enough!

Here I sit, on the terrace at Castle Hill Public Library. It is late afternoon, and chilly. My eyelashes keep fluttering: Auntie Veronica took me to the optometrist yesterday afternoon. My eyes are no worse and I didn't need new glasses, so he gave me trial contact lenses. They seem to make me blink. Strange, though, to see the world without frames! As if I were a regular person with vision of my own!

I believe it is Tuesday. Three days until my birthday.

Tuesday?

I am missing piano!!

Ah well.

Obediently, I think of Astrid Bexonville.

I will not think of our conversation, near the end of Year 7, when I called her a lamb chop.

I will not think of the trip to Hill End — nor feel that tightening, those frantic gasps for air . . .

I will clear my mind of evil Astrid and see what makes her shine.

Astrid is like the speck of light at the tip of a sparkler. She is lively, agile, seems always to be climbing, hiding in gardens, running from police.

She is unafraid of spiders. In the FAD session at my place, an enormous huntsman appeared on the wall above the curtain rod. While Emily screamed, and the boys took large steps backwards, Astrid moved in, fascinated. She asked for a dustpan and broom, stood on the couch, captured the spider, and carefully carried it outside.

I remember in Year 9 when a teacher left the room for a moment: Astrid suggested that we all move into the empty room next door and sit down at the same desks. Everybody obeyed. The teacher was nonplussed. It was, in fact, amusing.

Oh, but there are so many ways I could help Astrid!

I could send her a checklist for alcoholics — how much *does* she drink? Does she understand the risks? I could recommend restraint and legal conduct. Why is she always running from the police? Perhaps if she stopped breaking the law? She has referred, obscurely, to shoplifting, drug use, and minor acts of vandalism.

She talks about fashion and makeup a lot. Encourage her to be less superficial?

Perhaps I will send her this quote that I found only this morning in my etiquette book: *"But a love of dress has its perils for weak minds."* (*Our Deportment*, p. 313.)

But see how I stray into her flaws! Just because I don't break the law!

(Well, but I do! I stole a key from Maureen's shop, and I'd better find a way to put it back soon, or else . . .)

I must focus on Astrid's qualities.

She is very pretty, that stud in her eyebrow glinting in the sun.

There, in the distance now, walking down the hill from Castle Towers, I see a girl and her boyfriend. Like Astrid, the girl has long black hair, and has tied it with a lime-green ribbon.

That green-and-black that Astrid favors — now, that is picturesque. Like pine needles scattered on inky mud. Like traffic lights in the rain. A black cow standing in a meadow.

The girl and her boyfriend have stopped at the lights now, waiting to cross the street. The girl turns toward her boyfriend. They embrace. They hold each other tight.

They glance back toward the terrace where I sit.

There is something —

That is not a girl and her boyfriend!

That is Astrid.

And that is Sergio.

13.

The Philosophical Musings of Bindy Mackenzie

Friday morning. My Birthday!

Since Tuesday, I have been lost and distressed, but the time has come to emerge from the gloom — it's my birthday!

Spin like a revolving door; pivot on your heel like a goal shooter! Face the sunshine again, Bindy — it's your birthday!

Friday morning. My Birthday!

It is time to see the bright side of life, and the bright side of life is this: *I might have been wrong!*

Maybe that was *not* Astrid and Sergio standing together at the lights? Maybe I *imagined* their embrace? (Look at the dismal state of my witnessing skills! That lawyer was amazed by my stupidity. *And* I was trying out new contact lenses!)

Another bright side: I have not seen any tenderness between the two these last few days. (I stopped schoolwork altogether to spy — but found nothing.)

Friday morning. My Birthday!

So! I will embrace my birthday and enjoy it. I will see nothing but the bright side. And tomorrow my FAD group goes to the Blue Mountains! (I wish I had something to wear.) Maybe I will finish my portrait of Astrid — I stopped it abruptly when I thought she was a traitor and so have not sent her a memo. I suppose I will give her some personalized memo stationery tomorrow.

Friday morning. My Birthday!

Tonight, Auntie Veronica and Uncle Jake will make a birthday dinner, with Mum, Anthony, Sam, and Ernst von Schmerz. Dad would be here too, of course, but he's still working in Tasmania.

There's my phone ringing now. Probably Dad. He likes to be the first with birthday greetings.

Friday morning. My Birthday!

Huh. It was not my dad. It was my piano teacher. She just got a cancellation and suggested I come by later today, to make up for the lesson I missed on Tuesday.

Generous woman!

I see the postman through the window! I might just run downstairs . . .

Friday morning. My Birthday!

THERE WAS A POSTCARD FROM DAD IN TASMANIA!!!! HOW DID HE TIME IT SO PERFECTLY!!! TO ARRIVE ON THIS VERY DAY!!

I will not read it now.

I will save it for later today.

For now, school! Let's see who remembers it's my birthday.

Friday afternoon. My Birthday.

Just home from piano and must do some visualization exercises to restore my birthday mood. Piano was disconcerting. I was somewhat shaken when I arrived anyway, as no one had remembered my birthday. (Except Ernst.) And teachers pleaded for overdue assignments as if it were an ordinary day. I am weary of their pleading. "Can't you just write it yourself?" I snapped at Ms. Walcynski today. The look that she gave me!

Friday afternoon. My Birthday.

But, piano. I arrived to find Mrs. Woolley on her front porch, chatting with another student's mother. We stood together for a moment and watched a woman push a baby carriage by.

Guess who the woman was?

Eleanora. My pasta lady.

She didn't look up as she passed: She was pushing the carriage quite briskly. And inside the carriage? A plump, happy baby, gurgling away at the world.

Friday afternoon.

And that's not all. Just after Eleanora passed, Mrs. Woolley murmured, "Oh, there goes that poor woman, Eleanora. Her husband left her just a month before that baby was born. She's a

347

nervous wreck about the baby, I hear, and terribly timid to boot — doesn't know a *soul* in this city. A woman in the corner store told me."

Friday afternoon.
There I sat at Mrs. Woolley's piano, scales and arpeggios trilling, while realization weighed heavy, heavy! in my stomach. There was no *mystery* about Eleanora! She was just lonely! She needed somebody to *talk* to. All those nights while she made pasta and threw questions at me — she had seemed so stilted and peculiar. I could see nothing but secrets and intrigue. But she was simply *timid*! I never really knew that a grown-up could be "timid."

Friday afternoon.
As you can imagine, I did not play the piano well. (It's been a while since I practiced, for a start.) Mrs. Woolley worked herself up into a fever. "Are you playing with your fingers or your *heart*, Bindy? Are you merely playing in *theory*? Or are you *one with the music*? Are you, Bindy Mackenzie, one with this piece and this piano?" She went on like this quite a bit.

Friday afternoon.
But Mrs. Woolley, I kept wanting to say, *it's my birthday.*

Friday afternoon. My Birthday!
And so it is! I can hear Auntie Veronica and Bella in the kitchen downstairs, clattering around, tins clashing, excited chat.

Must go down and offer to help.

But first, I will cheer myself up and read Dad's postcard!!!

Friday afternoon.

Oh. How funny.

The postcard was not to me.

It was to *Bella* from her *Uncle Dave*. (That's Jake's brother, I think.) It seems he's on holiday in Tasmania. What a coincidence. In the postcard, he promises to bring back a Tasmanian tiger for Bella.

Friday afternoon.

Good luck, Uncle Dave. Last I heard they were extinct.

Friday afternoon.

For heaven's sakes, who sends a postcard to a four-year-old?

Friday afternoon

I'm overreacting here.

Something to do with the disappointment, I guess, combined with feeling stupid about my mistake. I mean, who mistakes *Bella* for "Bindy"? Who reads *Uncle Dave* and sees "Dad"? *Why did I think this postcard was for me?!*

I guess I just glanced at the card and saw what I wanted to see.

Friday afternoon.

Can't stop feeling embarrassed for having this card in my room

349

all day. Can't stop thinking stupid thoughts like: *It's my birthday! Why should Bella get a card?* Keep trying to get up from my bed, to go downstairs, but can't stop crying.

✕ ✕ ✕

Nighttime Musings of Bindy Mackenzie

Friday, 11:00 p.m.

Well, it is over.

My birthday dinner is done . . .

I have waved good-bye to all the guests and helped Uncle Jake pack the dishwasher. Auntie Veronica went straight to bed — exhausted. I think you get tired more quickly when you're pregnant.

It was fun. Mum arrived with a huge bunch of helium balloons. Anthony and Sam brought their movie camera along and got Ernst and me to act out impromptu scenes with Bella's toys. Bella felt proud that her toys were in a movie.

Also, I got some great stuff — including jeans which appear to be pre-faded and pre-ripped and which you wear low down around your waist! And high black boots! And a jacket and some other tops which will be good for the mountains.

I pretended to be shocked by all these "fashionable" clothes, but I tried them on and did a parade around the kitchen, and everyone made so much noise about how great I looked, and secretly I thought maybe I looked kind of, I don't know, "cool"????

But then the telephone rang and I kind of jumped excitedly,

and ran to get it, but it wasn't my dad. It was Maureen from the bookshop, saying she's very sorry but she can't keep employing me at the moment, and she should really have looked at her turnover before she took me on. *Indeed,* I thought to myself acerbically. She promised to call me the moment she could afford to take me on again. Then right at the end of the conversation she mentioned, in an offhand way, that the spare key was still missing, the one from behind the counter?

"Oh, really?" I said. "Terrible!"

And hung up.

I believe she suspected me of dishonesty! I bet it's nothing to do with her profit margin! I bet she's planning to employ that name I saw on her notepad — she had looked so embarrassed when I saw it on the floor of the shop. Markus Pulie. I remember the name well. But imagine suspecting *me* of stealing a key!

Anyway, all this rushed through my head as I returned to the table. The others waited patiently and I explained I had lost my job.

"On your birthday!" they cried, outraged yet sympathetic.

I did not mention the missing key. I still keep it on my starfish key ring.

I rather enjoyed their outrage on my behalf, and became quite gleeful about how I had lost *all* my jobs — and the night turned pleasant again.

Halfway through the chocolate mousse cake dessert, however, Uncle Jake said the word "coincidence."

He said it in that way he does: "co-inky-dence."

And suddenly, I was *convinced* he was about to say "Cincinnati," and say it like this: "Cinky-natty."

I was TERRIFIED, because I knew that would ruin my word, Finnegan's word, forevermore.

(I had no reason to believe he was about to say "Cincinnati." I just suddenly believed that he would.)

I guess I must have looked pale or horror-struck because next thing everyone was saying, "What's wrong, Bindy?"

And they were suddenly urgent, saying, what's wrong *generally* with you? All looking at each other and agreeing that I've been acting strange lately, and Ernst von Schmerz, traitor, told them he never sees me at school anymore, and *Mum* said the school phoned her to say I've been missing classes, and *Anthony* said he thought I was kind of weird when we met in the city the other day, etc., etc.

Even Bella chimed in to say I'd been playing with her food a lot lately. That stopped the conversation for a moment. Bella explained that she meant her plastic picnic food. *I* thought we were playing together.

They were also asking me about my health, and saying they don't understand why I keep avoiding the doctor, and Mum was practically crying.

It was like an ambush!

It was like one of those *interventions* when they try to get people to stop taking drugs!!!

I could only calm them down by promising to go to the doctor as soon as I get back from the Blue Mountains.

But after that, the atmosphere had changed.

And I kept looking at the phone, waiting for my dad to ring.

And now it is after 11 p.m., and there's less than an hour of my birthday left.

To be honest, I'm tired of getting things wrong. When it first happened, at the lawyer's office, I thought: *Well, that's a good lesson*. But since then I've had enough of learning. Eleanora turning out to be a lonely lady with a baby. And Dad not being the one who phoned this morning, or sent that postcard —

Hey, an e-mail just came in — I won't have any expectations . . .

Ha! It's from my dad! He made it, after all, just in time. . . .

I'll read his birthday greetings, and then I'll go to bed.

$$\times \quad \times \quad \times$$

TO: bindy.mackenzie@ashburyhigh.com.au
FROM: mackenziepaul@mackenzieenterprises.com.au
SENT: Friday, 11:20 p.m.
SUBJECT: Your e-mail

Hi Bindy,

It was around this time a few weeks back that I received an e-mail from you. You may recall that you said Anthony was downstairs in the hallway sorting laundry.

353

Now, the funny thing was, Anthony himself phoned that very moment to say hi — he was calling from a party, he said, at Sam's place and hadn't been home all day.

That didn't bother me too much — thought you must have been mistaken — but it did get me wondering.

And today, I finally got back to Sydney from Tas., & didn't go straight home. Was driving by that drama school Anthony wanted to go to and, on a whim, stopped the car — and guess what? He's enrolled. Guess who pays the fees? Your mother. Recalled that Sam's family moved to the city to be closer to the school — so, when I got home just now, I called their place, talked to Sam's parents, and the truth came out.

Turns out your brother's not staying there with you and your Auntie V., Bindy. He's staying with his friend Sam and going to a school that I forbade.

I'll talk to your mother about this when she gets in. She wasn't here when I got home. That sounds like her car now. . . .

But wanted you to know right away —

Bad enough that your mum and Anthony deceived me.

Never thought my Bindy capable.

Dad

PART SEVEN

I.

My Buddy Diary
By Bindy Mackenzie

Friday, 11:30 p.m., My Birthday
I have just done something remarkable.

I have phoned Finnegan Blonde.

I did not know what else to do.

I have his number programmed into my mobile from our first buddy session. I pressed the button. I held the phone hard against my ear. The sound of his voice seemed to fling me across the room.

But it was just voice mail.

I left the following message:

"Hello. This is Bindy Mackenzie. I hope I have not disturbed you. I am phoning in accordance with the Buddy Plan. I'd like to request an appointment with you. Okay. Thank you very much."

Then I pressed END.

2.

Very late Friday — no, I suppose it is very early Saturday

It is 1:45 a.m. on the night of my birthday.

I am in a nightclub.

I sit at a round table that wobbles as I type. The table is on a balcony, just above the stage. From here, we watched a band perform — vanished now.

The music was a revelation — I felt it pound through my being. I believe I swayed, jigged, and tapped in my seat — I almost wished we'd chosen to be down amongst the audience rather than safe up here at a table. Still, from here I could see the band clearly. I saw sweat form and slide down the lead singer's cheeks. I saw a bearded man, dressed in black, in the shadows just offstage. I wondered: Why? And then, as I watched, the lead singer finished a song — and lifted his electric guitar from his shoulders. The bearded man slid forward from the shadows, took it in one hand, and offered, instead, an acoustic guitar. The lead singer accepted. He slung it over his shoulders. He tried it out. The drummer hit his drumsticks together, to beat in the next song.

The chair beside me is empty. Finnegan has gone to get drinks. From downstairs, I hear:

An excited voice: They didn't do that hanging tree song — do you want to get a taxi? — I don't want to wait for the bus — or do you reckon we should wait for the bus?

[*These are the voices of stragglers, wandering out of this nightclub now, under the bright, white lights, leaving crushed paper cups, cigarette stubs — now the room is almost empty — but look, it's the drummer and the bass guitarist! — They are smoking cigarettes (disappointing).*]

Drummer: Every week we rehearse, and there's never one rehearsal where everyone's —

Bass guitarist: On time. I know.

Drummer: Yeah, that, but I mean, every week there's some attitude. There's just — it's like the difference between the band and everything else is just — there's just no difference. It's like life.

Bass guitarist: Exactly. You've got to take life as it is. It's like when Zoe's here and, like, her vocals just don't tell us where to go? And I'm like, I'm like — you know. And like with Michael, I'm like, "You've gotta memorize it, man. You don't use sheets." To Michael, I mean. And it's like — you know, you gotta make that choice. Every day. It's like, you gotta stop it all manifesting.

3.

Saturday, 3 a.m.

Back home from the nightclub, and cannot imagine sleeping.

My ears still ring, oddly, from the music.

Strange, unexpected evening!

What happened was this: I left a message on Finnegan's phone. Once I had done so, I felt flooded with relief, as if, somehow, I had just fixed everything with my dad. When I saw Dad's e-mail, I felt my face freeze from the inside. I felt despair so pure it made me panic. I phoned Finnegan, rushed an entry in my Buddy Diary, and sat on my bed, calm.

Then, almost immediately, I wanted to shoot myself. I was no longer frozen, but burning with mortification. *What had I done?*

I had phoned Finnegan Blonde! At 11:30 p.m.! And he would get my message and think: *Aren't we seeing each other tomorrow at the Blue Mountains? Why is she phoning me now? Why didn't she just wait and talk to me tomorrow like a NORMAL person?*

But, I argued, defending myself, what else was I supposed to

360

do? My world was at an end. I could scarcely call my parents — they would be confronting one another, and I would only make it worse. I could not call Anthony — it was too late and I might wake Sam's family. Veronica and Jake were asleep. *I had to talk to somebody.*

And Finnegan had said he likes the nighttime! He said he likes to stay awake all night!

But every night?

He was probably fast asleep when I called! Because we're going to the mountains early tomorrow! I probably woke him up from a happy dream! And right now he was staring at his phone, thinking to himself: *Whoever phoned just then? Whoever left that message? I will kill them.*

I was wondering whether there was a way to contact a phone company and get a voice mail message deleted from someone else's phone — when my phone rang.

It was Finnegan.

"You want to meet right now?" he said.

I was surprised into silence.

"I'm on Gilbert Road. Just coming up to the lights on Old Northern Road. That far from you?"

I shook my head slowly, although he could not see me.

Then I gave him directions. I was still wearing my new clothes and felt relieved that I had not taken my hair down yet. I slung my laptop over my shoulder, slipped through the back door, and found myself, alone and trembling, on the cold, dark street.

A small white car slid up.

And there was Finnegan Blonde, leaning over to open the passenger door for me. His eyes widened when he saw my laptop, then the corners of his mouth twitched in a smile. I bring my laptop everywhere: I feel lost without it.

I had trouble with the seat belt and Finnegan glanced over as he accelerated away from the curb. This panicked me: He was glancing over and seeing me fail with the seat belt! I gasped slightly, wrenched the belt again, and plunged it into its clasp. Relief.

Then, as he drove, he began to chat in a low, idle voice — something about the streetlights around this neighborhood, about a possum he'd just seen running along a wire, about the band we were on our way to see, about the guy he knew who ran the club — glancing and talking, while at the same time *driving*. Turning the steering wheel, *changing* gears, switching on indicators — all of it!

Driving! Was he old enough to drive as well as this? I had seen no permit plates on the car. Should I remind him of the penalties for failure to display — I decided against this.

It occurred to me that he was talking to try to relax me.

I realized I must look anxious.

For some reason, I was sitting with my back straight, not allowing it to touch any part of the seat. As if I were afraid the seat would smudge my back. Also, I was holding my chin up, at a peculiar angle, looking out of the car window — as if I were intrigued by the tops of telegraph poles.

I knew I must look curious, yet I could not seem to make myself relax.

"Mm," I said, now and again, in response to Finnegan's words (I was still peering up out of the window).

Eventually, he stopped talking and we drove in silence for a few moments. My teeth began to chatter from the cold.

Actually, the sound of my teeth chattering filled the car.

Finnegan glanced over again.

There was concern, and confusion, on his face.

"You want —" he began, then changed his mind. "You can close the window if you like."

"No, no," I shivered, "it's fine."

But I was freezing.

A few moments later, I very quietly closed the window.

Generously, Finnegan switched on the heater then. I think the word for the expression on his face is "consternation."

Now, as my body warmed, I did relax a little, and my teeth slowly stopped their clattering.

Finnegan turned on some music.

"These are the guys we're seeing," he said, pointing to the CD player. "This is their demo CD. I used to kind of follow them up in Queensland."

Only then did I register what he had been saying — we were going to *see a band*. In a *club*. At *midnight*.

I stared at him in wonder.

But it was easy.

I went to a nightclub and saw a band. And it was easy!

Well, it helped that Finnegan knew the manager, I suppose. We did not go in the front door, where crowds were gathering, and where, I expect, they would have asked us for proof of age. I had been feeling fatalistic about that — I had decided to shrug slowly, open out my hands and say, "You got me. I have no ID. And do you know why? I am not yet eighteen." I wondered if the police would be called at once. Or whether Finnegan and I would pivot on our heels, sprint to his car, and go to a safe bright place instead, like McDonald's. Maybe we'd have to dye our hair in the bathrooms and don overcoats! Take off on a wild road trip to Queensland!

However, Finnegan led me around the side of the club, and a shifty-looking fellow let us in.

We found ourselves amidst gathering crowds on the dance floor in front of a stage.

Finnegan was polite.

"Something to drink?" he said.

I shook my head quickly, in a panic. Something to *drink*! Was he serious?!

"You want to go up to the balcony," he suggested, "where we can talk?"

This time I nodded, coolly.

There were only three or four tables lined along the balcony, and we were alone. It was much quieter here. My heart began to thud. I had scarcely said a word since I got into his car — but now he would expect me to speak.

"The band won't start for another half hour," Finnegan

explained, elbows on the table. The table wobbled violently, and he lifted his elbows and began to shift it around. "So, how's things?" he said, as he battled with the table.

He was giving me an opportunity to talk!

At once, it seemed ridiculous.

That I had phoned in the middle of the night to discuss a family situation!

Was I mad?

I felt faint with horror — then: a flash of inspiration.

"I invited you to this meeting," I began (and felt pleased with my official tone), "because I am concerned about some members of our FAD group."

He raised his eyebrows, sitting back, gazing at my face. I thought there was the slightest smile at the edges of his mouth.

"As I'm sure you know," I said, "Sergio and Elizabeth are — seeing each other. But earlier this week, while at Castle Hill Library, I clearly saw Sergio with *Astrid* — and they were — behaving like — *they* were together."

Finnegan's eyebrows again. But he leaned forward, serious.

"You think Sergio's cheating on Liz?"

We discussed the issue for a while — at least, I expressed my views on cheating, its prevalence in the schoolyard, the responsibility of the third-party observer, my shock at seeing Sergio with Astrid — and Finnegan appeared to accept what I was saying.

Then he tilted his head at me and said, "Are you sure that Sergio and Liz are together? I know they're friends, but I thought I'd heard something about Liz being with a guy from Brookfield."

Now I stared at him in shock.

"I was kind of thinking of asking Liz out myself a while back," he explained. "but then I heard about this Brookfield guy. Em's got a guy at Brookfield too. Someone named Charlie? I guess it's the place to get guys if you're an Ashbury girl."

"Sergio and Elizabeth are not *together*?" I whispered. "I've been wrong about that *too*?! How many mistakes can a single person *make*?!"

And suddenly I found that I was telling him the story of my day.

How I had been making mistakes all day, thinking the phone ringing was my dad and it was really just the piano teacher, or the bookshop owner ringing to tell me I'd lost my job, thinking that a postcard for my cousin was actually for me, when it wasn't, and *then* I told him how I had made the mistake of sending an e-mail to Dad a few weeks ago, saying that my brother was downstairs, at the same time as my brother was phoning him from the other side of the city.

"Huh," said Finnegan, frowning ferociously — that is, trying really hard to understand what I was saying.

I told the Anthony story. He shook his head rapidly, now and then, as if to clear away confusion. His face was serious. It was as if he *knew* that this was the real reason for my call.

"So," he said, drumming two fingers on the table, "your brother wanted to go to a performing arts school, and your mother wanted him to go to this school, and your mother was happy to pay the fees — but *still* your dad wouldn't let him go?"

"Right," I said. "Right, so that's why — "

"So that's why you all decided to pretend that your brother was still going to Ashbury with you, and living with your Auntie Veronica like you, when he was actually living with his friend, Sam, in the city, and going to this school?"

Such a sharp mind!

To remember all those names!

To pinpoint the issues!

I nodded in awe.

"You weren't worried that your dad would come by to see you guys at your Auntie Veronica's sometime, and — I don't know, ask to see your rooms?"

"Well, no, see, my dad isn't the type to — to visit — and he'd never — I can't imagine him asking to see our . . ."

"So your *dad*," began Finnegan, slowly, "your *dad* is the kind of guy who — "

Maybe he saw panic in my eyes, because he changed direction.

"Well, what I think," he said, "is that was an unfair situation for you to be in." And he seemed genuinely angry!

But he calmed down almost immediately, and said, "I betcha it'll all be better now that it's out in the open. And I bet your dad forgives you right away. What else could you do? If you'd told him about your brother you'd've been a dobber? Does he want a dobber for a daughter? Besides, it's three against one."

He smiled a dazzling smile.

"We'll be going to the mountains tomorrow, so that's good. You'll be out of town while your family sorts this out, and by the time you get back, it'll be fixed."

I was not so sure.

"Well," I said, "it's my birthday today, or I guess it's over now because it's after midnight, but it was my birthday today, and Dad didn't even say happy birthday! That's how mad he is with me. Unless he just forgot."

Finnegan breathed in sharply and let his elbows collapse on the table so that he leaned closer to me. "It's your birthday," he said. I think his voice was tender. I was having trouble concentrating on tone: His face was so close to mine.

"Well, not really, not anymore."

"It's still your birthday," he asserted. "It stays your birthday until you fall asleep." He sat back in his chair. "Happy birthday."

I felt desperately embarrassed.

I thought: *Enough about me! I must ask about him!*

What are his interests? Should I ask about his hometown in Queensland? That cousin he used to play imaginary games with as a child? How the cousin died last year? His family? Siblings? What he thought of Ashbury compared to his old school?

"Isn't it amazing," I said, "that the city of Cincinnati is built on a foundation of pigs?"

At that moment, the lights dimmed and the band ran onto the stage.

It was after the band had finished performing that it happened.

First, Finnegan went to get drinks for us — I had seen someone at another table with a Coke and realized that soft drinks were allowed. I was not sure what to do while waiting for him, so I opened my computer and typed transcripts.

I was so busy typing that I did not hear Finnegan return.

I did not realize he was standing behind me.

I did not realize, that is, until two glasses were placed on the table — and *I felt two hands in my hair.*

Now, I wear my hair in tightly coiled plaits, pinned to either side of my head.

Finnegan's hands, to be perfectly honest, were not quite *in my hair.* They were, however, slowly taking the pins from my plaits.

I did not know what to do.

I sat very still and quiet.

His fingers worked away gently, taking one pin at a time, and dropping them onto the table. He then began unwinding my plaits, pulling them apart.

After a moment, he spoke.

"What are you always writing on that thing?" he said, meaning my laptop.

I explained that I like to type transcripts — that I record the conversations of people around me.

"So that's what you're doing," he said, "when you sit on that seat outside the library?"

I nodded, which was a mistake, as he had a finger tangled in my hair. He apologized for pulling my hair, and I sat still again.

"I wonder why you like to sit in the shadows," he said after a moment. "Is it that you prefer to be on the outside, watching other people?"

I didn't know what to say, so I just shrugged one shoulder.

He said, "And when you're on that seat, do you ever hear anything surprising?"

I thought about telling him about the substitute teachers who turned out to be computer programmers, and how useless I had been with the lawyer, but decided I'd bored him enough with the errors of my life, so I shrugged my other shoulder.

He shook out my hair with both hands then, and I felt the flash of his fingertips brushing against my neck. Then he sat at the table.

After the burning in my neck, face, and heart had calmed down, I realized that my head felt strange.

Hair was falling on either side of my cheeks. I could feel it on the back of my neck. I never wear my hair out! Except to bed!

"I hope you don't mind me doing that." His chin tilted towards my hair. "I just thought — because it's your birthday, you might — " He smiled. "Look at the color," he said. "You can't see that red in your hair when it's tied up in plaits like you do it."

And he reached out and touched a strand of my hair, winding it around his finger, and then letting it spring back.

My hair has a natural wave, and it had been plaited all day. Hence, the ringlets and curls.

"Ringlets," I tried, my voice sounding strangled. "Another word for a ringlet is a *cincinnus*. It's a good word, isn't it, *cincinnus*? Like *cinnamon*. Or *cineraria*. Huh, that's funny! It's a lot like Cincinnati! Isn't it weird about Cincinnati and pigs? I mean, that pork was Cincinnati's biggest industry? So then they used the pork fat to make candles and soap, so that candles and soap became their —"

"What is it with you," said Finnegan, "and Cincinnati?"

He touched another curl, and I was dumbstruck.

$$\times \quad \times \quad \times$$

And so, now, I am home again.

On the drive back, we listened to music, and Finnegan asked which songs I liked best tonight. I mentioned that one song had reminded me of Handel's "Overture to Joshua," then I wondered what was wrong with me. But Finnegan knew what I meant! It turned out he is extremely musical, and plays three instruments (piano, guitar, and trumpet), and would like to write reviews of bands for music magazines.

Then I got brave enough to say: "Um, and your cousin, was she musical too?"

He didn't raise his eyebrows at me, or say something cruel like "What cousin?" so I'd have to remind him of what he'd said in FAD in the park. He just started talking about how his cousin was a couple of years older than him so she was the one who first got him into clubs to see bands, but she loved techno and was kind of into drugs, and he used to worry about her hurting herself but she always told him to take a chill pill, which really pissed him off, but otherwise she stayed like herself. She had moved to Sydney to work for a year before she went to university, and had this job in computers, and it was while she was riding her bike home from work one day that she got hit by the car that killed her.

I said, "Was the driver drunk?"

"Well," he said. "The driver didn't stop. And they never found him."

At this I became outraged, that a person could hit someone

and then drive away. I found myself almost shouting. And the angrier I got, the more he relaxed his shoulders and loosened his hold on the steering wheel. So I really started ranting furiously until he reached over and touched my hand. (He touched the middle knuckle of my right hand.)

Then I said, "Sorry," about having been so mad, but I meant sorry about everything: his cousin and everything in the world that is wrong.

We were quiet then until we drove into my street.

"Happy birthday," he called, as I closed his car door. "Don't forget it's your birthday until you fall asleep."

Still, I suppose I should get some sleep.

It's 4 a.m. I have to take a train to the Blue Mountains in exactly three hours.

It is now 5 a.m., and it's still my birthday.

Something amazing just happened.

I was lying in bed, staring at the ceiling, thinking through the night. It was like walking slowly through a tangle of spiderwebs, hands out trying to shield me, because I was flicking through everything I'd said and done, and anything embarrassing was a spider. The spiders sank their fangs into my heart when I found them, leaving me writhing for a while, but I tried to brush each one away and move on.

And then I came to the image of Finnegan standing behind me, taking down my hair, and I rested at that part for a while because it was like his fingers were pulling spiderwebs apart on my behalf, and saying, gently: *See, there is nothing to fear.*

But when his fingertips brushed the back of my neck, it was like he was holding a match to dry leaves.

I kept replaying the scene, letting it lull me to sleep.

I remembered he had wondered why I like to sit in my shadow seat. "Is it that you prefer to be on the outside," he had said, "watching other people?" But his voice was almost admiring, as if that were something the world needed, people who watched. I thought about the surprising things I hear on the shadow seat, such as the two computer programmers walking by, and I thought about myself typing trans —

It was exactly like that.

I thought about myself typing trans — . The word "transcript" stopped halfway.

Because I was sitting straight up in bed, thinking: *Was I typing a transcript when those two women walked by?*

And right away, I thought: *I was!*

I got out of bed, and I didn't even switch on the light. I just sat at my desk in the moonlight, opened my transcripts file, found the right period, and started scrolling through.

And there it was.

It seems I have the transcript.

4.

Friday

3:55 p.m, still on my shadow seat. Two young substitute teachers are approaching, one a redhead, the other blonde. Their voices are raised and tumbling together — they speak in half-sentences only —

Redhead: . . . Edna Lbagennif, I mean, for a start, what kind of a pass— but, come on, what are you thinking? You have to —

Blonde: Brilliant. I mean f . . . , just spectacular. And you knew this all —

Redhead: You're being so totally — This has nothing to do —

Blonde: But you knew, I mean, with that trap — she can do *anything* —

Redhead: Don't be ridic— as if she — it's just basic mainten — I mean, right off you know, I'm going to have to say you think — I'll have to tell Mr. —

   (*The blonde just SLAPPED the redhead!!! I'm going over there!!*)

5.

Nighttime Musings of Bindy Mackenzie

Katoomba, Blue Mountains, Saturday

Let me tell you how I feel right now.

I feel as if I have erased the pencil marks from my sheet music, ready for a piano exam. So that when I look at the music, I see something familiar *yet completely new*. Cleaner, whiter, sharper pages than before, the notes blinking brightly back at me.

I see my face reflected in a picture window: brighter, happier, fresher than ever before.

I feel like weeping gently, with this happiness.

It is 11:30 p.m., and we are in the living room of Try's house in the Blue Mountains.

I am in a rocking chair in the corner. Sergio and Elizabeth are kneeling at the fireplace. The fire has almost gone out. They have been trying to save it: lighting matches, adding paper, prodding at the wood — and now I see they have decided simply to blow. Side by side, they blow and the charcoals glow.

Astrid is lying on the couch, reading a *People* magazine —

Scarlett Johansson smolders on the cover. On the opposite couch, Emily is flat on her back, also reading. She twists her wrists now and then, as if to ease the strain of holding her book aloft. Both Emily and Astrid are frowning intently as they read.

Toby and Briony are nothing but sounds: *click-clop . . . click-clop . . . click-clop . . . CLICK.* "Ah!" "Ha ha!" and so on. They are playing table tennis in the recreation room next door.

We met at Central Station this morning, yawning, clutching pillows, kicking backpacks and sleeping bags around the platform.

Finnegan chose to sit next to me on the train.

He behaved as if there was nothing odd in what had happened last night. We talked about the band. I opened my laptop to show him the transcript I had taken — the bass guitarist and drummer discussing the meaning of life. Finnegan laughed and pointed out that it wasn't tobacco they were smoking. I laughed too, pretending I knew what he meant. We talked about the rain that slipped languid against the train windows, and about Try's plans for bushwalking all day — and then I fell asleep.

I had only slept an hour the night before.

When I found that old transcript of the computer programmers' fight, I felt as if my bloodstream were rapids. A sensation of rushing and crashing! Tiny whitewater rafters squealing down my arms!

I wanted to phone the lawyer at once, to wake him at 5:30 a. m. I still cannot believe that I must wait until business hours on Monday. Of course, I suspect the transcript will be useless to him — there seemed to be no talk of copyright. (Nor did there seem to be talk of a Polish exchange student — I can *almost* see why I jumped to that conclusion, but, really, who knew *what* they were talking about? All those half-sentences: They were talking over each other so I couldn't hear everything clearly. And that name was not Polish at all! Edna is an Irish/Scottish name. Also an Old Testament name meaning "pleasure" in Hebrew.)

Nevertheless, I would now be able to speak in a voice of pride to that pompous lawyer. I would be able to announce: "I know precisely what those women said as they passed me that day." *Precisely.* (Or, at least some of what they'd said.)

At last, I would be praised. I would redeem myself and move on.

Hence only an hour of sleep last night.

There are enormous picture windows in Try's house, and these were full of rain and mist today. (She assures us there's a spectacular view of the escarpment when the mist clears.) The house has a rustic yet cozy atmosphere, with wide floorboards and brightly colored scatter rugs.

There's a covered verandah, and Try, Astrid, and Sergio barbecued sausages and hamburgers for lunch. I sat between Sergio and Toby to eat, and they talked about how different I look without glasses, and tried to figure out the color of my eyes. I kept saying, "They're just dark blue," and they kept shaking their heads dismissively: "No. That's not it."

After lunch, we played games directed by Try, such as getting tangled together and then untangling ourselves. Also, we sat in a circle and massaged the shoulders of the person in front.

(I was rubbing Emily's shoulders, while Toby massaged mine. His hands are steady and firm.)

Dinner was the same as lunch, except that Sergio and Toby did not discuss my eyes. And, as I spooned onions onto my hamburger, I reflected sadly on the following: There was, in general, a restrained sort of politeness in the group's conduct towards me. Perhaps they were a little less cold than they had been, but still this remoteness. I grew depressed. What more could I do? I'd pointed out their positive features, but nobody had even *mentioned* the memos from me.

It was the same with my Life: Try had *never* referred to it.

It was just as if I'd never existed. Had I become invisible, a shadow of a person? How could I make my FAD group see me?

After dinner, Try said she was going to leave us some space. We should sit in a circle, she said, and take turns saying how our year is going.

I found myself following Try upstairs. I noticed she was humming quietly to herself, and hoped it wasn't because she thought she was free of her students for the night. Here I was behind her: a student. She stopped abruptly at her bedroom door and I almost bumped into her. She let out a small scream.

"I'm sorry," I said. "I was just wondering if I could ask you something."

"Of course!" She backed into her room, looked around briefly, then leaped onto the bed. She sat right in the center of the bed, cross-legged, and waved both hands indicating that I should do the same. But I stood, nervous, just inside the doorway.

She bounced a little and the bed creaked quietly. "What can I do you for?!" she exclaimed, her accent reminding me of the Midwesterners in *Fargo*.

"It's about that project I did for you over the holidays," I explained. "*Bindy Mackenzie: A Life*? I was just wondering if you ever got a chance to — look at it — and if you thought there was anything — if you noticed anything you wanted to — "

"Oh!" She bit her lip. "No, I read that *ages* ago! It was great, Bindy. Really — useful. I learned so much about you! I'm sorry, I should have said something to you. I'm *hopeless*! You wanted — a *grade*? I'm such a terrible teacher." She was scrambling off the bed. "Here, look, I even carry it around with me!"

Her blue basket was on the dresser, and she drew out my (slightly crumpled) *Life*.

"I'm hopeless," she repeated, pressing the *Life* into my hands. "I'm really sorry, Bindy." Now she was solemn. "I should have given this back sooner. You go downstairs now, okay? I'll bet that your FAD group is missing you." She rested her hand lightly on my arm, looked into my eyes — were there *tears* in her eyes? She glanced down at my hands, and my glittering, ragged-edged fingernails.

"You should stop biting those," she murmured distractedly, and turned away.

Downstairs, the others were already strewn about on couches in the living room, looking at one another, maybe embarrassed to be following Try's instructions while she was upstairs in her room. I sat on the floor and put my *Life* on the carpet beside me.

I was completely confused: I hadn't wanted her to *mark* my *Life*, nor to give it back. So what had I wanted from Try?

Astrid was talking. She was having a bad year, she said, because of her parents' divorce, and she'd never told anyone this but her father had walked out on her mother while he was in the middle of waxing her legs. Her mother was lying flat on her stomach on the bed and her father said, "I'll just go reheat this wax on the stove. It's getting gluggy." And he "kind of like never came back."

You could see people trying not to giggle at that.

Astrid said that she was grateful to two people, Emily and Sergio, for being such good friends to her this year? And they were always, like, giving her hugs when she needed them?

At that comment, Emily threw her arms around Astrid, Astrid cried, and I caught Finnegan raising his eyebrows at me.

Hmm, is what we were both thinking, *was Sergio just being a FRIEND to Astrid when I saw them together in Castle Hill?*

After Astrid had been comforted, it was Elizabeth's turn and she said she was *also* glad that Sergio had been around, and a good friend, because she's been thinking about breaking up with her Brookfield boyfriend, but they've been together for almost two years. But he never seems to understand that she needs time apart to train; it's like he wants her to choose between running and him. But she really loves him. So it's been hard. And now, she's finally done it, she broke up with him yesterday. Sergio looked startled at this news, and he moved closer to Elizabeth.

I glanced at Finnegan again, and he was sending me a very small smile. I returned the smile.

I had not seen betrayal in Castle Hill! Sergio had not been cheating because he was not yet together with Elizabeth! (But perhaps soon . . .)

But, as I smiled my relief at Finnegan, I thought: *He looks tired.* And seconds later he announced that he was going up to bed.

I wondered if I should mention that he'd been out all night, but I didn't say anything.

I felt a thudding disappointment at Finnegan's departure.

Also, however, I felt a strange relief.

We went back to going around the group.

The strangest thing happened when it got to my turn.

I'd been planning to say something like: "I feel lucky that my parents are still together, and that I don't have relationship troubles. Overall, my year has been fine." Then I was going to nod my head at Briony, beside me, for her to take a turn.

I had the nod rehearsed inside my mind.

"I feel lucky," I began. "I mean, my parents are together — but I guess it hasn't been such a great year because I crashed my uncle's car and I'm kind of sick all the time and I think I'm going to fail Year 11."

My head tried to catch up with my voice. What had I said? I looked around the group, tried to smile with nobility, and nodded at Briony.

But Briony did not speak. Nobody spoke. There was silence — and then a deluge.

"You crashed a car?"

"What do you mean, you're sick all the time?"

"You're *failing* Year 11?"

I turned to Astrid, who had asked this last question. "I haven't done any homework for weeks," I said. "I've got seven overdue assignments and five overdue essays."

"Seven overdue assignments," she whispered.

At which, I burst into tears and began to babble: "And I wrote you all memos! But you still won't forgive me! Except Astrid! I didn't write a memo for — ! But the green ribbon! But the Name Game! I couldn't! And I *was* unforgivable! So how can I — ? And Sergio, I can't believe I — ! I was never coming back! But Mr. Botherit! And someone *moved* me! And the nail polish! And I felt so guilty! And I'm *so, so* sorry!"

I stopped talking and simply sobbed, wrenching sobs — and then something happened. I sensed the strange, sweet melodies of comfort. A careful shifting of people toward me. Somebody's hand gently stroking my hair. Somebody's arm, hesitantly patting my back.

Warmth and relief overcame me. I did not want it to stop, this comfort, this touching, and so I kept my head buried and cried on.

Eventually I had to look up. The stroking hands paused. They were all around me, watching carefully, confusion like giant spotlights in their eyes.

"Bindy," said Toby, in the sweetest voice. "What the FLAX are you talking about?"

I laughed shakily. It was Toby's hand on my back. He kept it there, and feeling its warmth gave me strength.

I took a great breath and told the story of my year.

I began with the first Name Game. I know it by heart. I recited all their comments, how upset I'd been, how I'd chosen poisonous animals as revenge. I told them how it had gone too far, and how guilty I'd felt, and how I'd planned to leave, but Mr. Botherit had said someone hacked in and moved me into this FAD group. I said someone from FAD gave me nail polish. I told them how sick I'd been, about my strange dreams and hallucinations and insomnia, how I'd stopped doing schoolwork and somehow didn't care. That I thought it would fix things if I gave them good animals. That I didn't understand why it hadn't worked.

Once I had finished, they were all thoughtful and quiet for a few moments.

Then someone asked what the doctors said about my health.

I had to admit that I had refused to see a doctor. The confusion lights switched back on.

"I think it might be glandular fever," I whispered. "If a doctor thinks that's what it is, I'll have to take weeks off school. I can't do that, especially not now that I'm so behind. Besides — " I avoided Astrid's eyes. "I don't believe that glandular fever exists."

Now Astrid became very professional about my symptoms. She fired rapid questions at me and actually felt the glands in my neck. "Trust me," she said, "glandular fever exists. I used to want it until I, like, got it? 'Cause I thought you'd just watch TV and that? But you feel like SPURGE. You can't even watch TV, you feel, like, so SPURGEY. And you're not supposed to kiss anyone for, like, a *year,* but I ignored that bit."

Everyone else wanted to check my glands too, and there was disagreement about whether they were swollen or not.

"I didn't throw up when I had glandular fever though," Astrid said. "Plus I didn't get those hallucinations you've got? Maybe you've got something, like, fatal?"

"Have you got an eating disorder?" said Emily. "Why do you keep throwing up if you haven't got an eating disorder?"

"Whatever's wrong with you," said Briony, "you should go to the doctor. What if there's just one pill you need to take to get better? And if you don't take it, you'll get worse and end up having to take even more time off school."

Everybody agreed.

"Plus," said Astrid kindly, "how do you know you're not contagious? Maybe you've got, like, typhoid or that FOXGLOVE chicken flu, whatever it's called, and you're giving it to all of us? No offense."

But the others doubted I was contagious because I'd been sick for such a long time without anyone else catching it.

"Anyway," Sergio said, shifting subjects. "You've got to get a doctor's certificate so you can give it to your teachers and get extensions for the overdue assignments."

They all agreed about that too, and assured me I would not fail. All I needed, they said (knowledgeably), was a doctor's certificate. They were pleasingly dismissive about my schoolwork worries.

But then they moved into the more difficult territory of my attitude towards them.

"Okay, so you've been feeling sick and that," said Astrid, "but it's kind of like no excuse for slagging us all off, and like putting posters up with our names on them, and what you said to Sergio and that?"

"I guess she's been delusional," Toby pointed out.

"And the *Name Game*," Elizabeth said. "If people said all those things about me, I'd be upset too."

"Well, the *Name Game*," Emily leaped in. "I wanted to say something about that. How you said what everyone said about you? Like you'd figured it all out. Well, there's an injustice there, because I *didn't* write what you think I wrote. That you have long words in your huge head. I wrote that you can't help who you are and maybe you'll change. And I said, 'Good luck with Year 11. I think you'll change.' Something like that. Which was meant in the greatest and most compassionate sense and was my effort to be kind, Bindy, as you know that we hadn't got on well in the past, but I wanted to start fresh."

"I'm the one who said you have long words in your head," Briony confessed. "Sorry. But I was just trying to make it funny by talking about your big head. I was really just praising you, Bindy, for having a good vocabulary."

"Yeah," said Astrid. "And I was just praising you too, Bindy. I just said you wear your hair weird which means you've got guts, and I actually meant that about taking guts, cos a lot of people, like me, for example, kind of like choose clothes that are fashionable? And I admire people that don't. Even if it hurts my eyes to look at them. So that wasn't that bad of a thing to write, was it?"

"I didn't say you were a bit too smart, either," Elizabeth put in. "I said you're a fast typist. Which you've got to admit, you are. I don't know who wrote that you're a bit too smart."

"I did," said Sergio, and then, to me, defensively, "but you *are*."

Toby sighed deeply. "Okay," he said. "I did write that you talk like a horse. It was a humorous reference to the way you say 'nay' all the time. You know, neigh. Like a horse. But your voice is just fine, Bindy, it's not like a horse. It's a very nice voice."

"Well, except when she gets, like, hysterical, I guess?" Astrid said. "Toby, you've gotta admit, sometimes Bindy goes off and then her voice has this scre—"

Sergio interrupted at this point. "You said you crashed a car?" he prompted me.

But I had to take a moment to look from face to face, and readjust my views of each of them. Except for Toby and his "talks like a horse," none of them had written what I thought they had. And the way they explained themselves now: Maybe the comments weren't as serious as I had thought? Maybe I'd over-reacted? I began to smile a little.

But then I described my driving lesson, and how my uncle had told me to be "one with the car"— and as I spoke, I remembered.

"My piano teacher said that too!" I exclaimed. "She said I wasn't one with the piano! I'm not one with the piano *or* the car! Because I drove straight into a parked car! I'm not one, I can't be one with *anything* — I don't — I just don't belong."

Suddenly, I was crying again.

"See, that's your fault," Astrid said. "Because when you act like the teacher you can't be part of the class? If you want to be *one* with us, you've got to —"

But Sergio was talking over Astrid's voice again.

"You just crashed straight into a parked car?" he said. "That's it? You drove out of your driveway and hit a parked car? Forget about it." (He used his mafia accent at the end.)

Then he described the three accidents *he'd* had. He included squealing-tire, shrieking-brake, and crunching-metal sound effects. Next thing, almost all of them were telling car crash stories. Running over letterboxes. Putting the car into reverse instead of drive. "The road took a right-hand bend," I heard Toby say, "but the car did not."

I looked around, astonished.

"See?" said Emily. "We're all the same. None of us can drive!"

"Well," said Sergio slowly, "Maybe *some* of us can *dr*—"

"If you want to be *one* with us," Astrid repeated, "you've gotta stop acting like you're better than us."

"And you've gotta try to learn the difference," said Sergio thoughtfully, "between an animal and a human being."

Astrid stood up and left the room.

Toby put his arm around my shoulder. "And look at your beautiful indigo eyes," he murmured. "All red now with your crying."

"Indigo," scoffed Sergio. "Indigo means purple. Her eyes are not purple. They're midnight blue."

They argued mildly until Astrid returned with a tray of hot chocolate for everyone.

And as I looked down at the little white marshmallow bob-bing about in my hot chocolate, I thought: *This is what it's like to have friends.*

It soon emerged that Astrid had put Kahlúa in everyone's hot chocolate. I have never really drunk alcohol before, so I believe it had an effect on me. In fact, I found myself *accepting* her offers of *more* alcoholic beverages. Tall alcoholic beverages in glasses! Colorful alcohol! Alcohol mixed with soft drinks! They were all surprisingly delicious.

Everyone was drinking, and some people even smoked mari-juana! Not I.

Someone put music on, and it was a song I recognized from the hip-hop class. Forgetting myself, I stood up and tried out some of the "hip-hop" moves I had almost learned in the class.

At which, Astrid and Elizabeth began to do the same moves! They did them *beautifully* — those girls can dance! Only, they did not seem to be trying to show me up. Oh no, they did not seem to judge me for my inabilities! They were just happy, they said, to be reminded of those dance moves. They had forgotten them!

Now everyone was dancing!

Even Briony! (Toby made her.)

Everything was music, shouting, and leaping!

Try appeared at the door, dressed in her pajamas, rub-bing sleepy eyes. We looked at her guiltily, and somebody turned the music down. Try simply smiled, turned, and went back to bed.

And that is why I am here now, in this rocking chair, typing at my computer. (I felt such a wave of creativity! Such a desire to write!) Now we are all quiet — we are all reading, blowing on flames, playing games.

And there is my reflection in the mirror, sharp as a musical score.

There am I, one with this room.
One with this group of people.
And there is something about crying,
About dancing, and drinking,
About talking
That makes me feel so very
Happy so very
Tired
And now I might fall asleep
I might just
fall
Asleep
On this
Nice Typewriting
Pillow here
This nice
Keyboard
Colored
Pillow
Here
f4 f5 f6 calling to my forehead

6.

Emily

Okay, DO NOT BE MAD, Bindy. This is Emily, and I know I am typing on your computer, but there is a reason for it. So please forgive me right away.

What happened was the best intentions. Astrid and I were reading on the couches, and Sergio and Toby decided we were boring and they lifted up Astrid's couch and kind of rocked it in the air, and she was sitting back with her arms behind her head, enjoying the ride, and

Astrid

Just tell her, Em. Okay, while my couch is in the air, Emily sees some paper on the floor *under* the couch and she goes, "What's that under there?" and Sergio effin' drops his end of the couch trying to see where Em's pointing, which gave me a concussion, I swear, it was like a JOLT? And it's these papers stapled together with your name on the front. So, we look over at you, kind of like, "What's this?" But you were passed out on your rocking chair and face-first on your laptop.

So we read the papers. Em starts reading it aloud, and then we start passing it around, taking turns reading it aloud until it's done. And for your information the papers were called: *Bindy Mackenzie: A Life.*

Emily

Right, exactly, okay, but I would have explained it more tentatively than Astrid just did and maybe less blame on me. So, basically, we read your whole life story, Bindy, and PLEASE DON'T BE MAD. We felt guilty, but you say in the introduction that it's a FAD assignment, so we are actually FAD. We ARE your life raft, Bindy, so we thought the LIFE raft should read the LIFE story. In case it would help with all those issues you were telling us tonight.

So, after we read it, we were all quiet, thinking, wow, kind of interesting life. And we wanted to talk to you about it, and make comments, and that, but you were still comatose on your computer. So, we're staring at you, and Briony goes, "I wonder if she'll get cancer with her face on the computer like that?" And Toby goes, "Maybe we should shut it down for her?"

So we slid your computer out and put a big atlas under your face instead, so you wouldn't notice, and you stayed passed out. And I really quickly hit Save and closed the document you were working on, without looking at it, to show to you that I don't usually read people's private things, just your life story, that's it. But then I had this idea, and I go, "Maybe, we could just put a message on her computer screen telling her we read her life story and what we think about it, so she sees that when she wakes up?"

And everyone agreed. I think because it's easier to confess in writing than to tell you in person. So, we just opened a new document and that's what this is. So, now everyone wants to say something about your life story.

Astrid

Okay, I want to say something first which is that your problem is very clear from this life story. It's that you think you're like a scientist and the rest of the world is like your experiment? Your life story is full of watching other people, and being scientific about them. It's like you think you're above other people, and maybe even grading us for an exam going on inside your head? It's weird, Bindy. You've gotta learn that you're not necessarily above us, just cos you're smarter than we are.

Sergio

Astrid and Emily are being hogging of the computer. Other people should get to speak. I say this about your life story, Bindy: I was right when I said you are too smart. You are, Bindy. There's something wrong with your brain, you're so smart.

Astrid

But it was really interesting how you say it's hard to be Number One? I'm kind of like tripping about that now, because it's so interesting? I never thought of it like that. That you'd be scared all the time? It's a lesson for me, I'll confess that.

Briony

This is Briony. I liked your life story, Bindy. I hope you forgive us for reading it. You sure have to move houses a lot. You must feel very confused.

Elizabeth

Well, I just want to say sorry that we read your life story, and I hope you don't mind. We all felt bad but we also felt like we were getting to know you in a way.

And I've been thinking about how you said you've tried to change and see the positive things about us, instead of being critical. So you sent us those memos giving us "good animals." I guess I'm thinking that that was nice of you, and you were trying hard, but there's not much difference between deciding what's bad and deciding what's good. Either way it's judging people. And maybe you'd feel more "one with your world" if you just relaxed and stopped trying to judge? And I'm thinking maybe

Emily

Sorry about grabbing the computer, Liz, I just really had to write this before anyone else did, which is that, Bindy, it's your DAD'S fault that you feel superior to everyone!!! And it's your DAD'S fault that you're always judging!! Because he MADE you into a judge! Or anyway he encouraged that tendaciousness in you. Because he said to you that you are the shepherd and the rest of us are sheep. And he says that terrible thing when you're going to Ashbury where he says those other kids are "nothing" and you are "Number One." And he always wants you to rip us off to make money.

Elizabeth
That's kind of what I was about to say.

Emily
Okay. Sorry, Liz. And also, Bindy, we think your dad doesn't sound all that nice and maybe you should realize that? Because it seems like you think he's great, but he's always making you do the painting and sanding, and don't get offended, but he sounds a TINY bit pleased with himself. Whereas, however, I KNOW your mum is nice because I know her. And she comes out better in your life story than your dad does.

Now, also, this will be a cruel truth maybe, but your parents' marriage is not in a perfect situation there. It sounds like they were happy once when you were really little, and your dad fell over and everyone was laughing except you? Only, since then, we kept hearing stories about them fighting, and we were all looking at each other, kind of grimacing, and I think there is doom on the horizon.

Briony
Yes, no wonder you're feeling so sick, really, with your parents' fighting all the time, and moving all the time, and now you have to live with your aunt and uncle. I wondered why you were living there.

Emily

I think she's sick because she's stressed out all the time. Because I *noticed*, Bindy, that you got sick when you were in fifth grade and you had a history test the next day? I noticed that. Actually, we all did. But I said, maybe you get SICK whenever you worry about school? And Year 11 was too much for you because it's senior school so maybe it became like a vicious cycle, where you get worried, get sick/go crazy, get behind in schoolwork, get more worried, get more sick/more crazy hallucinations, get more behind, and so on.

Sergio

I don't mean to sound f—ked up and depressing, but I'm just thinking about this hallucination issue, seen as I'm watching over Em's shoulder, and I'm thinking about this second cousin I've got who got schizophrenia. And I've gotta say his symptoms were stuff like hallucinations, and not being able to sleep at night, and feeling kinda helpless and f—ked up the way you've been, Bindy. And another thing, I know it can get smart people like you, and around your age. Anyway, that's not what you've got, but if it is, you've gotta get to a doctor and get treatment or you get completely f—ked up.

Elizabeth

Okay, but she told us she's got other symptoms as well, I mean physical symptoms, so it's probably part of some bigger thing. I mean, not just her brain. So, don't let Sergio scare you too much, Bindy, but you'd better go see a doctor. Astrid wants the computer. I think she might get a few more turns at your computer than most oth

Astrid

BINDY HAS A DRUG PROBLEM. I should have seen it before. It explains EVERY single symptom. She's addicted to hallucinogens. Maybe LCD, PSP, maybe GHB? Not sure which. Or she's like hooked on amphetamines. Which, Bindy? I can send you some material on addiction if you like, my mum keeps leaving it around the house.

Briony

Well, that makes me think, maybe she's being *poisoned* by something?! (I don't think she's the drug-taking kind of a girl.) I read about this family who were all getting sick and crazy like you, and they discovered it was from the wood they were burning in their fireplace, which had some kind of chemical in it. And also some families get lead poisoning from old pipes! SO. THINK, BINDY. Where might you be getting accidentally poisoned? You live with your aunt and uncle: Do they have an old house? Old pipes?

Emily

Briony is right. For sure it's poison because now everything makes sense! Why has Bindy been thinking that *we're* all poisonous? It's because her subconscious is trying to *warn* her that *she* is being poisoned. It keeps sending her submarinal messages but all she hears is the word: *poison!* so she gets her head confused.

But why does it have to be accidental? It's probably someone trying to murder her.

Astrid

If someone is trying to murder Bindy, it would be that guy she talks about in her life story. The one named Joshua Lynch who went to her lunchtime session, and then she writes to the principal about marijuana in his backpack? Which by the way should be legal anyway. I remember when they did that search of his stuff, and he got expelled like the next day. Who knew that was cos Bindy told the principal? He's been waiting to get revenge ever since and now he's getting it.

Briony
But

Astrid

Joshua would know about *drugs* because he was a drug lord. He's probably poisoning her with drugs (i.e. hallucinogens — *as I said above!!!*). He was only at our school for like a week but I remember him. He was like totally old school.

Briony

But what about the people who were using the school intranet to share music files, and Bindy wrote to the principal and it got shut down?!! Or maybe some of the people who were using the reserve to drink, smoke, etc., and Bindy wrote to the principal to tell him about them?!!! It could have been them.

Sergio

It was the principal. Couldn't take any more of your correspondence, Bindy.

Toby

No, you have to look close to home. It's always someone the victim knows.

I think it's that little cousin of yours, Bindy, the one named Bella. You've gotta learn to leave her toys alone.

Emily

No! It's Auntie Veronica and Uncle Jake because Veronica's pregnant, right, so they want to make room for their new baby and they are too kind to hurt Bindy's feelings by asking her to move out and therefore it's easiest to kill her! It makes perfect sense.

Toby

And then they can bury her in their garden and KEEP TAKING RENT FROM HER PARENTS!!!

Emily

But do we know that her parents are paying anything for her to live there? Her dad seems pretty cheap (who makes you do a business proposal before you can get pocket money?). Along with all his other faults of character. And I think to myself: Maybe the *dad* is killing her so he doesn't have to pay for her university education? I suppose that is upsetting to hear.

7.

Nighttime Musings of Bindy Mackenzie

Sunday, 10:30 p.m.

Here I am at home again: very calm, very philosophical.

Such a strange day!

Yet I am content.

I have yet to speak to my parents or Anthony — but even on that issue I am calm. I will defend myself, and Anthony. I will try not to let my father condemn us.

I woke this morning, with a start, in the rocking chair! A sudden rock backwards woke me! (That was Toby.) I screamed, then stopped. He looked funny in his pajamas.

I felt fine. It turns out I am not the sort of person to get hangovers. I am so glad to discover that about myself. Astrid said she is the same, so we have that in common.

Well, but Toby wandered out of the living room again, and I saw my laptop on the coffee table. It was open, and I could see words on the screen. Immediately, I felt uneasy. I recalled typing in a frenzy last night, in my hazy, ecstatic state. But then what? I had no memory of shutting down. What if I had deleted the whole file?! Worse, what if they had read it?!

And so I checked, and lo, I discovered that my FAD group had created a document of messages. Further, they had found my Life, and read that. I was so relieved that they hadn't read *this* document that I didn't really mind the intrusion of privacy with respect to my Life. The Life is just my old diaries and merit awards, really, from childhood. Whereas in *this* document, which *includes* the Life, I have scanned in all my philosophical musings and memos; I've typed in the most intimate nighttime musings! And these include much about the FAD group itself that would perhaps have reversed their newfound fondness for me. (For instance, I seem to remember referring to Emily as a drama queen, a vampire, swinging double doors, the death of debating, and a person who will never do well at school.)

I was a little annoyed by their suggestions that my dad is not a nice person, and that my parents' marriage is in trouble. That is just the misrepresentative nature of those diary entries. My father is a good, strong, creative, noble, and ambitious man. And obviously, I'd only ever written in the diary at times of distress! Such as when my parents were fighting! My life story was not accurate, and at some point I'd have to explain this to the FAD group.

But then I began to laugh at their outlandish comments — ideas about me being poisoned, suspects from my past, and so on. Before I had quite finished reading, a voice called me into the kitchen.

Breakfast was ready!

Everyone was there except Finnegan, who, it seemed, was

still asleep upstairs. The table was set with cereals, milk, juice, toast, and jams, and Try was standing at the stove, looking very tiny in a white bathrobe, making pancakes! She was gazing at her frying pan earnestly.

The others looked up guiltily as I entered, but I smiled my forgiveness upon them, and there was a general sigh of relief.

"Okay, Bindy," Sergio said. "We've gotta give this to you straight. We have something important to tell you."

I sat down at the table, and turned to him.

"You are slowly being murdered," he declared.

"Poisoned," Briony asserted.

Try swung around from the frying pan. I sat on my hands.

"Are you ready for this?" said Sergio. "You want to know who it is?" He dropped his voice to a hoarse whisper: "It's Mrs. Lilydale. With the carob-coated energy drops."

I reached for the Special K, laughing.

Then I looked up again. There was silence in the room but for the sizzling of Try's pancakes. Her back was turned again, but the rest of the group was staring at me.

"Mrs. Lilydale?" I said, straight-faced. "With the carob-coated energy drops. *Interesting.*"

Suddenly, they were all talking.

It seemed that after writing messages on my computer, they had talked late into the night. And this was their conclusion.

They almost seemed to believe it.

"It's cos we read in your life story that you *saw* something in her office," Astrid explained. "She wrote that note to you about the papers on her desk, and she wanted to know exactly what you'd seen? They must have exposed Mrs. L., somehow. Like maybe she's in a criminal conspiracy or something."

"Or maybe she's a stripper in her spare time," Sergio suggested.

"Don't make me throw up my breakfast, Sergio!" Emily seemed very angry.

"And Lilydale sent you the carob-coated energy drops," Toby said, turning back to me, "and told you to come back for more."

"I see you eating them all the time," Emily pointed out. "I thought they were chocolate for the longest time, and I was so pissed at you for not offering me one."

Now, I am ashamed to say, a strange sensation overcame me. A tingling excitement. Because, although they were only joking, perhaps they were right! I had been feeling so unwell, so unlike myself all year. And Mrs. Lilydale *did* keep pressing those energy drops on me. Why? Then, of course, I had overheard her one morning, talking to someone at school, earlier this year. "I *lied* in mine," she had said, "but the rest should go through." What did she mean? Should a teacher be *lying*? Were her lies connected to the mysterious item on her desk? Would she really murder me?

"But why?" I said. "Why would she want to kill me, instead of, I don't know, *bribing* me not to say what I saw on her desk? She's not insane! And I think she *likes* me!"

"Exactly!" cried Astrid.

The others turned to her and she shrugged.

"Are you *sure* you didn't see anything insinuating on her desk, Bindy?" Emily demanded.

"I didn't see anything at all," I said. "I never knew what Mrs. Lilydale was going on about."

"It's such a tragedy," said Astrid happily. "She has to die for, like, no reason?"

Try was silent throughout this discussion. She flipped pancakes, moved around the table, tipping pancakes onto plates, and returned to the stove and made more.

I noticed, as a pancake slid onto Sergio's plate, the faintest hint of a smile. But she remained silent.

Until Astrid said, "Try! Don't you reckon this is serious and we should, like, get Lilydale arrested?"

The others clamored, "Yeah, why aren't you saying anything, Try? This is, like, one of your FAD group being murdered and all you can do is *bake*!!" Although, she was not technically baking, of course.

At this, however, she finally switched off the stove, and turned around. She stood with a hand on her hip, a querying look on her face.

They all took this as an invitation to explain, and began to tell Try how sick I had been, that I'd been having hallucinations, that it was Mrs. Lilydale trying to poison me. In a frenzy, they listed my symptoms, and Toby explained that they were the symptoms of someone being poisoned.

Try raised an eyebrow at that.

"Ask Briony!" cried Toby. "She told us the symptoms. She *knows* them because she did this biology assignment about contaminated water in Bangladesh. Tell Try about it, Briony."

Briony said that wells had been dug in Bangladesh, as part of a world aid project, to get fresh water for the people. Only, they didn't realize they were digging into soil and rock full of arsenic, so now the water is full of arsenic and the people are being slowly poisoned.

"And it is true, Try," Briony insisted. "Bindy does have some of the symptoms of chronic arsenic poisoning."

"Don't you think we should *tell* someone?" Emily cried. "I mean, we've got our semifinal in debating this Friday! We need Bindy *alive!*"

Try turned to me with a concerned frown. "How are you feeling today?" she asked.

Surprised, I replied: "Fine!" And this was true, I felt better than ever! Perhaps I was over my illness!

"Okay," Try spoke in a soft voice — the kind that makes people lean forward to hear. She held the back of a chair and rocked slightly.

"Okay," she repeated. "You all remember I once promised I'd tell you my theory on *teenagers*?"

Not really, most people said.

But I remembered. It had been early on.

"And you remember how Bindy claimed that she is *not* a teenager?"

They all remembered that.

Suddenly Try pulled out the chair she had been leaning on and sat on it. She pushed herself back from the table, so she was surveying us all.

"It's like this," she said, talking fast. "It is my belief that the teenager is a person with three main characteristics. First!" She held up a finger. "First, teenagers get caught up in their own heads. Okay, I don't want to offend you guys, but teenagers think about themselves a *lot*. They obsess about what they look like, what people think of them, what the point of life is. So, number one, too much introspection.

"Now," she held up a second finger, before anyone could interrupt. "Now, number two, the teenager needs excitement — it's a reaction, I guess, to the realization that life is ordinary. In childhood, it's fresh and exciting, but then you start to see that the grown-up world is boring. So you look for hysteria and drama. You scream at concerts, you shriek when you see each other, you ride on roller-coasters, you get into alcohol and drugs. All year I've been hearing you guys use words like conspiracy, compulsion, pathology — you get post-traumatic stress from exams; you're always running from the cops. I mean, you guys are just desperate for excitement. You're looking for *extremes*. You're looking for a *climax*."

There were slight noises from the group — minor, murmured protests. But Try held up a third finger.

"And *finally*, teenagers lose their sense of perspective. They're stuck between childhood and adulthood so they don't know whether they're up or down. One day, they're dressing *up* to look old and get into a bar; next day, they're putting on their cute voice to get the child's fare on the bus. It's like they're in an elevator all the time, so they can't judge where they are."

"Well," began Emily. "*I* think that —"

But Try had not finished. She lowered her voice to an even gentler pitch.

"You guys are just being teenagers," she said. "You think about poison because you're caught up with your*selves* — Briony's studying poison in Biology, so she thinks it must be happening all around her. And you all throw yourselves at Briony's idea because you're looking for the climax. You want there to be something exciting going on behind the scenes. So Bindy's being poisoned — that's why she's sick, that's why she's hallucinating! It's a murder plot! And you don't have judgment or perspective, so you can't say to yourselves: *Well, hang on just a second, why would somebody murder an innocent schoolgirl like Bindy Mackenzie?*"

People were beginning to look uncomfortable. Some frowned, opened their mouths to speak, and closed them again. Some tried to explain that they'd only been *joking* about the poison.

"Which brings me to our Bindy," Try concluded, ignoring them. "I think she might be more of a teenager than she knows herself. I think she's too introspective, for a start — always obsessing about doing well at school, and that makes her tense and unhappy. I think she's looking for extremes, by which I mean, *extremely* high marks, and that makes her stay awake all night, pushing herself to the edge, going for number one in everything. And she's lost her perspective — she can't see where she belongs in the world, partly, forgive me, Bindy, because her parents have gone off to an apartment that has no space for her. And *this*, in my humble view, is what's making Bindy sick. All *this* is making her exhausted and stressed; she feels out of control and lost."

I admit, I was overwhelmed.

I felt like weeping again.

What she said felt so true.

"And today," Try said, looking at me again. "You say you feel okay today?"

I nodded.

"Could that be," she suggested, "because you've finally been honest and open with a group of friends?"

How did she know about last night?!

I felt a wave of serenity. People half smiled at me. They began to eat breakfast again, pour themselves juice, ask for the raspberry jam. They began to talk of other things.

Nobody was trying to poison me. And I was healthy again, for I had found a place I belonged.

As I chewed on my pancake, thoughtfully, I felt a sudden burning in my cheeks. For a memory had come to me complete. That earlier FAD session when Try asked us to list our flaws. I had refused to do so, but, in my mind, I had listed my own three flaws as:

- a tendency towards reverie;
- difficulty coping with anti-climax; and
- occasional trouble judging distances.

There they were! Try's three *teenage* characteristics! *I* was caught up in my own head (reverie); *I* was obsessed with crises (and so could not cope with anti-climax); and *I* had trouble with judgment!

I *was* a teenager, after all!

After breakfast, Try asked me to help her clean up, and sent the others away. We did not say much as we worked, but at one point, Try said quietly, "I hope you don't mind what I was saying there. I didn't mean it to be critical." She was looking away from me, leaning over the dishwasher.

"Not at all!" I exclaimed. "I was just shocked to hear I *was* a teenager."

And *then*, when we emerged from the kitchen, there was a sudden shout of "Surprise!" and do you know what it was?

It was a *surprise party for me*!

Because it had been my birthday on Friday. They had been blowing up balloons and hanging streamers from the walls while I was in the kitchen!

Emily was holding an open carton of ice cream, with a candle in its center. Everyone sang "Happy Birthday," and I blew out the candle quickly, before any more ice cream could melt.

I was so nervous and surprised I could only tremble and smile, not saying a word. But they didn't seem to notice, they were just excited about the party, and wanting to show me how they had pulled together the side tables, and they were now covered with meringues, gingerbread men, Anzac biscuits, chocolate bars, and chips.

"How did you know it was my birthday?" I said, although I suspected that Try had found out, through teacherly methods, and had talked them into this.

But they all explained that *Finnegan* had whispered it to them while I was asleep on the train yesterday! And he had brought along the streamers and balloons! And that's why he hadn't been at breakfast this morning — he'd gone out to buy food for the party!

Someone turned music on, and everyone ate and talked, and nobody mentioned the poison theory again. Toby went into the kitchen and emerged with glasses of chocolate milk. "I was going to make banana smoothies," he said, "but the bananas were black, so these are Kit Kat smoothies." He was quietly proud of blending up the Kit Kats.

Astrid started talking about my hair, and how she'd never seen it in anything but curled-up plaits (nobody had), and she and Emily kept wanting to pull on the ringlets to see them bounce back. (They did it gently.) Then Briony came up and complimented my hair too. Also, Elizabeth said she loved my new jeans.

My happiness was practically perfect.

And now, home again, I have a new set of resolutions: I will stop judging other people. I will recognize that I am not inherently superior. I will ask for help when I need it.

Tomorrow, a new school week. I will begin to catch up! I'll phone that lawyer first thing and read out the transcript to him! I can't wait to hear his reaction.

I may be a teenager but I feel on the cusp of grown-up life. When I saw that lawyer, I *thought* I was an adult, but no ... Tomorrow when he hears my voice, he will sense a change.

I still haven't heard from my family about the Anthony situation, but I'll deal with that in a calm, mature way too. Like the lawyer, my dad will hear a change in my voice.

For now, I'll take an energy drop and get to work on some assignments! (You see! No ill effects.)

For the first time ever, I feel as if I really know myself.

Further Nighttime Musings of Bindy Mackenzie
Sunday, 11:30 p.m.
Just woke up with stomach cramps.

8.

Monday

A Memo from Briony Atkins

To: Bindy Mackenzie
From: Briony Atkins
Subject: Sample
Time: Monday morning

Dear Bindy,

Could you please bring in a urine sample tomorrow?

I'd like to test it for heavy metals, such as arsenic. Just put it in a clean, plastic container with a good, tight (ha ha) lid.

It's best if you give me your first sample of the day. Also, have you been eating shellfish lately? If so, wait a few days before providing the sample — there is (harmless) arsenic in shellfish which would affect the results.

Best wishes,

Briony

P.S. Have you made a doctor's appointment yet? Of course, you

must tell the doctor that you think you're being poisoned. BUT!!!
You might have trouble convincing him or her to do the correct
tests right away!!! (He/she will be wanting to eliminate more common illnesses first.) That's why I want to do some testing myself.

× × ×

A Memo from Emily Thompson

To: Bindy Mackenzie
From: Emily Thompson
Subject: Witnessing
Time: Monday recess

Dear Bindy,
I am writing to ask if you will let me look at your life story again.
The one we looked at without your permission? Only this time,
with your permission.

Because I have remembered something about how you
witnessed something — two teachers arguing? As you can see, I
am not clear on this because I did not really concentrate on
that part.

However! I realized in the middle of Maths this morning that
I SHOULD HAVE PAID ATTENTION. Because you might have
seen something significant, and *that's* why you're getting murdered. It might be nothing to do with what you saw in Mrs.
Lilydale's office. That could be a red herring.

I still think it's Mrs. Lilydale poisoning you with the energy

411

drops, but it's just that the bad guys have hired her to do it, as she has contact with you, and has your trust and so on.

Now, think carefully. What did you see? Did one of these teachers execute the other? Why? That would explain things very clearly. However, I suppose I would have heard if there had been a teacher executed on the lawns of Ashbury last year.

Can I look at your life again? Great. Thanks.

Love,

Emily

P.S. I've invited the FAD group to the debating semifinal on Friday, seeing as it's at Ashbury. I hope that's okay. I don't know what's normal for debating.

A Memo from Elizabeth Clarry

To: Bindy Mackenzie
From: Elizabeth Clarry
Subject: The box
Time: Monday lunchtime

Dear Bindy,
Em told me my job is to work *outside the box*, so I'm thinking up other suspects, in case we've got it wrong about Mrs. Lilydale.

My first suggestion is this: someone who's coming second in one of your classes. Because they want to come first. So, they have to eliminate you.

Or maybe they've been poisoning you just to affect your work and give them a step up?

(But the others want it to be about murder, not just diminished capacity.)

However, THINK CAREFULLY. Have any students given you anything to eat or drink this year?

Best wishes,
Elizabeth

× × ×

A Memo from Toby Mazzerati

To: Bindy Mackenzie
From: Toby Mazzerati
Subject: Update on Surveillance
Time: Monday afternoon

Hey Bind,

Uptodating you: Serge and I have now got a mobile phone concealed in Lilydale's office. It's switched to vibrate and auto-answer, so we'll call in sometimes and listen to what she's saying for the rest of the day. Plus, we're keeping an eye on her every move.

It's surveillance.

So far, we haven't seen any moves as she's never in her office.

Emily has told us we have to send you memos like this because we can't risk talking out loud to each other in case someone surveils and overhears. Also, we can't use technology, e.g.

413

e-mail, IM, texting, as hackers might hear. Finnegan's not at school today so we haven't got him in the loop yet, but we will when he gets back.

Watch your back,

Toby (and Sergio)

× × ×

The Philosophical Musings of Bindy Mackenzie

Monday, around 5 p.m., in my bedroom

Strange! I did not call the lawyer today to tell him about my transcript discovery. I was so looking forward to it! Yet I did not call! Mysterious . . .

Perhaps it was because I was busy reading memos from my FAD group! (Now, there is another mystery. Did they not hear a word of Try's wisdom? I had thought we were all feeling subdued after her speech. And here they are caught up in a fervor about murder! It is funny, I suppose. I guess they're all just playing. But sometimes they seem almost serious about it!)

And then, of course, I was busy at the doctor's this afternoon — what he said will disappoint my FAD group!

5:15 p.m.

Yet, I think the real reason that I did not phone the lawyer is this: The transcript is rather confusing. I keep imagining him saying, impatiently, "Well, what does that all *mean*?" Or: "Why didn't you type out *complete* sentences?"

So, I have spent some time trying to analyze the transcript —

figure it out. And here's something! The first thing the redhead says is this: "Edna Lbagennif, I mean, for a start, what kind of a pass — but, come on, what are you thinking?"

5:19 p.m.

I realize now that I thought the redhead was saying something about how Edna Lbagennif did not deserve to "pass" an exam. But perhaps she actually said, "Edna Lbagennif, I mean, for a start, what kind of a password is that?" It makes sense. "Edna Lbagennif" might be the password. Funny! I might know the password! I could get access to that software and all the "model" answers to essays and assignments! Humorous!

5:29 p.m.

Of course, I will not. That would be cheating. (I wonder if it's the software Mr. Botherit was talking about, that time I was in his office —"newfangled software," he said.) I'll call the lawyer tomorrow. For now, I will get to work! I shall begin with that overdue history assignment! No more reverie ! No more philosophical musings! SIX SOLID HOURS OF WORK BEGINNING NOW!

5:33 p.m.

I hope Finnegan is okay. Strange that he was not at school today. I wonder if I should phone and check on his health?

5:43 p.m.

No. Better leave him be.

5:45 p.m.

He did say he wanted to hear what happened with my family now
that my brother's secret is out. I should call him and tell him! Not
that much has happened — my parents are not speaking to each
other, and my brother is still living with Sam's family and going
to his performing arts school. I haven't heard from Dad, but then,
nor have I replied to his e-mail.

Besides, if he is ill, he should be resting. Finnegan needs his
sleep: He is so often awake through the night. I wouldn't want to
wake him. Hopefully, his eyes are closed now . . .

5:56 p.m.

His eyes are his best feature. Such a beautiful shape. They seem
to swoop. Such swooping eyes . . .

6:05 p.m.

Then, too, there is his voice. He speaks as if he has his foot on
the soft pedal of his voice — all the notes crisply pronounced,
but something so gentle in the tone.

6:25 p.m.

This afternoon, on the way home from school, I bought a "teen
magazine." I have never done that before. I don't believe in glossy
magazines. It was an experiment really: Would it catch my attention now that I know I am a "teenager"? Well, I just took a short
break from my study to find out — and of course, it did not. A lot
of bad grammar and advice about makeup and hair treatments.

Still, I can't seem to stop turning the pages. MUST STOP READING AND GET SOME WORK DONE.

---

7 p.m.

My magazine has advice for those who have never kissed a boy. That is sensible — to acknowledge the innocent readers. I'm surprised that it does. It suggests that I learn to kiss by whispering the word *"who"* into the palm of my hand.

9.

A Memo from Bindy Mackenzie

To: Briony, Emily, Elizabeth, Toby, and Sergio
From: Bindy Mackenzie
Subject: Your Memos
Time: Tuesday, 9 a.m.

Dear All,

First, I would like to thank you for your memos. It gladdens my heart to see you using your stationery.

Next, I must tell you that I have been to the doctor. Auntie Veronica took me straight after school yesterday afternoon.

I mentioned your poison theory to him and I am sorry to say we both laughed. It cheered us up.

But really, what is going on with you all? Do you not remember what Try said?! Why would somebody be poisoning an innocent teenager?! It makes no sense. You all seemed so quiet after Try gave her speech. I thought you were convinced by her

418

reasonableness! But no, your "detective work" continues. It is intriguing.

At any rate, the doctor arranged for some tests — I'll get the results in a few days. He's testing to see if I have food allergies; also, if I'm anemic, as I look pale. If so, I'll need more iron. He doesn't think I have glandular fever. He decided to throw in tests for heavy metal poisons, such as lead, mercury, and yes, Briony, arsenic, because these things do happen, especially in old houses — and the symptoms might actually match my symptoms. (And because he enjoyed the story of my overexcited friends.)

Nevertheless, in his opinion, the only thing wrong is that I'm overworked and overstressed. I need to relax and get more sleep.

I am very sorry to disappoint you, and I'm sorry you've been wasting time with your "detective work."

Lots of love,

Bindy Mackenzie

P.S. Briony, I'm not keen on bringing a urine sample to school. Thanks all the same. I suppose you don't want it now that I've been to the doctor.

P.P.S. Emily, I don't really want to show you my life story again. I hope you understand. The fight I witnessed was not between teachers as I'd thought. I've talked to a lawyer, and it turns out it was computer programmers, arguing about copyright in a computer program. So, you see, nothing important.

P.P.P.S. Toby and Sergio, I think you should get your phone back out of Mrs. Lilydale's office. I think that might be unethical. And imagine your phone bills.

$\times$ $\times$ $\times$

The Philosophical Musings of Bindy Mackenzie

8 p.m.

I can't seem to concentrate on study tonight! You see, by the process of deduction, I have realized something. Finnegan wrote this on my Name Game: "I have never spoken to Bindy Mackenzie but I'm sure that behind her extremely annoying personality, she is a beautiful human being." He thought I had an *extremely annoying personality*. Can't get that out of my head.

---

9 p.m.

I was just reading my teen magazine again, and it said that a boyfriend should like you exactly as you are. BUT: (1) He thought I was extremely annoying. (2) He told me to take a kickboxing class. (Why? Did he think I needed exercise? I'm not fat, you know. Well, I'm not a skeleton either, but if skeleto-girls are his thing, he's a "shallow guy" [as my magazine would say].) (3) He took my hair out of its plaits in the club. (Why? Didn't he like it the way it was? He should have!)

---

10 p.m.

Not that he's my boyfriend, I guess.

He wasn't at school again today. I'm not going to call him to see how he is.

ANNOYING, am I?

I might start wearing my hair in coiled plaits again.

10.

Wednesday

A Memo from Briony Atkins

To: Bindy Mackenzie
From: Briony Atkins
Subject: Food Recommendations
Time: Wednesday morning

Dear Bindy,

Well, I COMPLETELY understand that you feel uncomfortable bringing in a urine sample and I guess we'll just have to wait for your doctor's test results. Often, they test hair and fingernails for arsenic because it stays in those things for years — so, don't worry, they'll be able to test even after you're dead (ha ha, just kidding, you won't die) (hopefully . . .).

I ordered my testing kit off the Internet when I was doing my biology assignment and wanted to check arsenic levels in local streams. (And now I get *so* much junk mail from online pharmacies.)

421

Anyway, can I please suggest that you eat a lot of eggs, onions, beans, and garlic? These foods have sulfur in them, which will help to get rid of some of the arsenic in your body.

Love,

Briony

P.S. None of us were convinced by Try when she made her speech about you not being poisoned. That's just what you do when a teacher gets reasonable like that. You act quiet and serious and wait until the teacher is gone and then you get on with what you were doing. Didn't you know?

× × ×

A Memo from Emily Thompson

To: Bindy Mackenzie
From: Emily Thompson
Subject: Now, it might not seem significant to *you* . . .
Time: Wednesday recess

Dear Bindy,

Now, it might not seem significant to you but copyright issues can involve a lot of money, such as millions of dollars, and therefore maybe you *did* hear something so important that you must die? You just don't know. (And your doctor admitted that your symptoms could be poisoning!! What more proof do you need?!?!?!)

So, now, if it's about software, we need to think about people involved in computers at our school? I don't like to admit this, but maybe it's not Mrs. Lilydale at all. I'm thinking through all the computer teachers, and also, I'm remembering that I *always* see Miss Flynn at the computer in the library! And she wears pastels! Could be a disguise. Could it be her?

Please can you tell me which law firm you went to about this copyright issue? Also, what kind of software it was, and who the parties were? And then I can ask my mum if she knows anything about the case, as she is a copyright lawyer herself. I'm going to ask you in person right now, actually, because I can see you.

Great.

Thanks.

Emily

× × ×

A Memo from Sergio Saba

To: Bindy Mackenzie
From: Sergio Saba
Subject: Update on Surveillance
Time: Wednesday afternoon

Bindo,

Toby and I hereby reportificate on Mrs. Lilydale as follows.

We have dialed in to her office and we have heard her give exactly the same speech to five different students in a row. The speech is about apples. I don't get it and neither does Toby and that's after five goes of hearing it. It's something about Granny Smith as compared to Golden Delicious and I'm sorry. But it makes no sense. Can an apple-obsessed woman be a murderer? I don't have the answer to that question, but I hear that apple seeds have cyanide in them, if you chew them hard enough. So that's relevant.

We have also watched Mrs. L.'s office door and we have noticed that she's often not there. Except for the apple speeches, she's never there.

Don't eat anything.
Sergio

A Memo from Elizabeth Clarry

To: Bindy Mackenzie
From: Elizabeth Clarry
Subject: Nail polish
Time: Wednesday afternoon

Dear Bindy,
You know how I said you should think about people at school who have given you food or drinks this year?

Well, I realized I wasn't outside the box as I was supposed to be. Because you can get poisoned in other more interesting ways, such as bath products, toothpaste, or perfume. I've seen you using a Ventolin inhaler, so, listen, who has access to that

424

inhaler? Also, I was watching you in History this morning and you were biting your nails. I know you wear nail polish. . . .

Also, I notice Em mentioned Miss Flynn as a suspect. I think she's always at the computer because she's editing her online newspaper. *But*, it's interesting to note that Miss Flynn is *new* to the school this year. And she's here to replace Ms. Lawrence who *seems to have completely disappeared.*

Did Miss Flynn murder Ms. Lawrence so she could take her job and murder *you*?

Just some things to think about.

Love,

Elizabeth

✕ ✕ ✕

The Philosophical Musings of Bindy Mackenzie
4:30 p.m.

Finnegan was still not at school today, and my FAD group continues their insanity.

Meanwhile, I slip further behind as I spend my nights in reverie, and there's no point in putting that word into a box. It makes no difference. Nor have I phoned the lawyer yet! I am obsessed with getting the transcript right first. For instance, just now I was looking at the password, Edna Lbagennif, and I thought: *How do I know that I spelled that correctly?* I only *heard* it, after all, and must have guessed the spelling. Why, it could be Edna Lobbagenif, or Edna Lybugenyf, or, for all I know it might have been *Ed Na*lbagennif or Ed *Nolb*anagennif. Who knows? The women were speaking very quickly, words running into one another.

I wonder if I should find a way to *test* the password before I phone the lawyer? Just to see if it works? To prove to him I am no fool?

6:30 p.m.

What does it matter if he called me annoying? He also called me *beautiful*. At least, he saw that I was a beautiful person, behind my personality. Oh, insightful Finnegan. And then, in the second FAD session, he became my buddy! Of course, that was Try who paired us up. But still, if I think back now, perhaps I see his *feet* pointing straight towards mine, his body subtly twisted, so that Try felt *compelled* to put us together! He played a psychological trick on Try and that's how we became buddies! I bet.

9:30 p.m.

Impossible to get any work done. Can't stop whispering *"who"* into the palm of my hand. I sound like an owl with laryngitis. Who? Who? Who? *Who, indeed?*

II.

A Memo from Astrid Bexonville

To: Bindy Mackenzie
From: Astrid Bexonville
Subject: Hill End
Time: Thursday, I don't know what time it is, but it's effin' early, like before school.

Dear Bindy,
Well, I am writing to you today cos I said I would, cos I haven't written yet this week and that's even tho you gave me this pretty nice memo paper while we were at the mountains. We were talking about you in the reserve yesterday cos Sergio goes, okay, enough with the writing, we need to *confer*. He doesn't want to keep doing memos & making copies for the others. You can tell he and Toby and Liz think this is all funny, but Em and me and Briony think it *MIGHT* be real.

Nobody was around to, like, hear us talk, so don't worry.

427

We've now decided that EVERYONE is a suspect, including the FAD group. Because we started talking and, okay, we realized this:

(A) Liz talked about nail polish being maybe a poisonous thing, since you chew your nails, and that was genius. And then Em remembered you told us that someone from FAD gave you nail polish as a present, but *anonymously*. (Briony wants to test your nail polish for arsenic.) So, okay, who do you think gave you the nail polish? We are all sure it wasn't us, anyway none of us can remember giving you nail polish, and I think we'd remember that. But it could be significant.

(B) Also, you told us that Mr. Botherit said *SOMEBODY* had moved you into our FAD group, tho you used to be in another FAD group with more your style of people. Who moved you? Someone from our FAD group who wanted close access to you, so they could give you nail polish and kill you? Don't laugh, Bindy, it *could be*.

So Emily was cross-examining all of us about the nail polish, saying we could be denying it. And since we haven't told Finnegan anything about this situation, she's going to cross-examine him when he gets back to school. (We can't ask Try who gave you the nail polish because she kind of doesn't believe any of this.)

I could tell the others were kind of thinking, if there's anyone in the FAD group who wants to kill Bindy, it'd be Astrid. Because we have a kind of history of hostility. Everyone was going, "Who hates

Bindy most? Oh, look, there's Astrid. Hmm. Coincidence." But I promise I'm not killing you.

Anyway, but now I come to why I have not joined in the memos this week? It's that I feel guilty.

Because in your life story that we read, you talk about how you wanted to be friends with me, and I just laughed in your face.

And you also talk about the trip to Hill End in Year 8 but you don't go into details.

I remember what happened at Hill End exactly, cos I was pissed out of my brain on that trip, tho I was kind of young to be that and someone should really of stopped me. I didn't know *you* would keep it in your mind, but I see you did.

I remember you were put in the same cabin as me and my friends cos you must have forgotten to put your name down for a cabin with your own friends, and we, like, politely asked you to move to another cabin. Cos we knew you wouldn't really fit in with us. But you laughed like you thought we were joking, and you had a cold, so when you laughed there was a bit of snot that came out of your nose. Not too much and I know I overreacted when I got hysterical and started screaming that you were grossing us out.

And then you blew your nose and said it was too late to change cabins. So I went, "Okay, Booger Mackenzie, you can stay here if you like." And that kind of infected everyone, and they called you Booger for the rest of the trip.

And on the last night, I started kind of like chanting, "Booger, Booger, Booger Mackenzie!" cos I was still annoyed with you for staying in our cabin. Kind of like pretending it was a fun game as a tribute to you. And everyone joined in the chant, and you got that asthma attack.

I thought you were just faking it to make us stop.

It was probably just that your cold had moved to your chest tho? But still, it made me feel bad.

So, when I think back, even tho I was only young, I kind of really hate myself for it. You were always so happy back then, I never thought that, like, calling you a name could take you down, plus you were so smart, so you know, I kind of think happy, smart people are indestructible.

But I think maybe people kept calling you Booger for the rest of Year 8. I hope not but I have a kind of memory of you being alone a lot that year, and people making fun of you. I hope that's a wrong memory, but if it's right that must have sucked.

So, I feel guilty and terrible.

But I'm very sorry and I hope you can forgive me one day.

Love,

ASTRID

× × ×

Nighttime Musings of Bindy Mackenzie

Thursday, 11:35 p.m.

Strange, strange, disturbing!

A mystical thing just happened and I must type quickly to know if it is real.

Very well. (Calm my breathing.) Here it is:

I arrive home from school in a state. Astrid's memo leaves me feeling as if I have been plucked from my life and placed into a rattling cage. I feel awry, broken, exposed, taken apart piece by piece. My secret anguish, my secret year, scrawled in Astrid's handwriting.

I pound the piano all afternoon. Veronica and Jake watch me carefully. Bella presses one of her toys into the palm of my hand — a little plastic man who belongs in her toy bus. This makes me cry.

I decide I must have a hot bath. Anthony gave me bath bombs for my birthday: I watch as a strawberry bomb fizzes and dissolves.

Astrid apologized.

That stone of resentment that I carry around in my heart: Should it now fizz and dissolve?

But can I let it go?

I think I've been trying to do that all term. I think that's why I've been wanting Try to talk to me about my Life. I wanted her to *ask* me about the cataclysmic episode in Year 8. It's all there, hinted at in my Life. I wanted to tell Try all about it — a part of me wanted her to hate Astrid as I do.

I lie in the bath and watch the light bounce off the tap like a starburst.

I think about the "name" that Astrid gave me in Hill End — the name that they called me for most of Year 8. I can never write it down.

I forgot who I was that year.

Astrid chose my name for me.

I think of Ernst von Schmerz and how, at his old school, they would not let him choose his name. So now he chooses over and over, to defy them.

Astrid's just a skinny girl who is always running from police. Why did I let her choose my name that year? I see now why she hated me. I was happy. I wanted to be friends with her. I didn't care that she'd been cruel to me the previous year — I had *signed up* for her cabin. Astrid knew my social status but *I did not*. She felt compelled to show me who I was. By naming me, she thought she held a mirror to my soul. And now she takes it back.

This year, I've been just like Astrid. Frantically naming my FAD group, showing them who I think they are. But as my FAD group pointed out, if you name people like that, you place yourself above them. Worse, you give them no room to change.

It was the Name Game that made me do it — when they put my name in the center of the page and described me like that. It was just as if they had renamed me. I think that's why Hill End has been so present in my mind this year.

I think of names, and of choosing who you want to be.

I think of the names of my FAD group. Toby, Briony, Astrid, Emily, Sergio, Elizabeth, Finnegan, and Try.

I stare at the starburst of light on the tap, squint, and the starburst splits into squiggles, like a sparkler shaking in the night.

Names begin to merge and collide.

Try and Toby collapse into one. Briony and Bindy. Finnegan, Miss Flynn.

432

Now my squiggles of light have become two fish, facing each other, almost colliding, almost kissing, whispering: *who who who.*

The starburst, the squiggles, the fish, the starburst, the squiggles, the fish. I move closer to the tap and there is nothing but a tap: a swan's neck, a silver cane. Reflected in that cane is the elongated face of Bindy.

Bindy Mackenzie.

I stare and all I can think is: Finnegan, Finnegan, Finnegan Blonde.

Finnegan A. Blonde.

His signature on that Buddy Contract, all those months ago.

Finnegan A. Blonde.

And as I stare, his name collapses. Fin. Neg. Gan. A. Blon. De. The pieces run backwards. De. Blon. Gan. They reverse within themselves. Ed. Nolb. Nag.

I lift the plug by its loop.

I am standing in the roar of draining bathwater

Ed. Nolb. Nag.

I am grabbing at the towel, running to my bedroom, searching through my notes —

And there it is.

My musings on the password. One spelling of the password:

Ed Nolbanagennif.

It is Finnegan A. Blonde in reverse.

12.

Friday

The Philosophical Musings of Bindy Mackenzie
Friday, lunchtime
The relief is great. At last, it is done.

Of course, I behaved like a fool before I did it.

———————————

This morning, I climbed the steps to the top balcony, and waited outside Mr. Botherit's office until he emerged to go and teach a class. Then I slipped into his office.

I sat at his computer. I seemed to be in a trance.

For, you see, this is what I was thinking: *It is a message.* If the password is Finnegan's name in reverse, it is a message from Finnegan to me. The message says this: *Use the password, use my name, reclaim your own good name!* The message urges me: *Just download the outlines of some assignments and exams, and you will find your way back to your position! Number One.* Finnegan, my buddy, trying to send me there.

———————————

I sat at Mr. Botherit's computer, looking at the icons on his

434

screen, hazy in the light from the office window. But there it was. An icon of an open scroll, with the word *Enlightenment* across it. That was the name the lawyer had mentioned, the name of the software. I clicked on the icon.

Password? it demanded.

With trembling fingers I typed it in: ednolbanagennif

It won't work, I thought, *it's probably another spelling — it's Edna, like I thought, it's —* and then I hit Enter and I was in.

I was in, as they say in the movies. The screen was awash with bright colors and tantalizing options.

I grabbed the mouse, clicked LOG OFF, leaped from Mr. Botherit's chair, ran out of his office door, and burst into tears.

I cannot believe how close I came to cheating.

As it was, I may have come close to getting caught: As I rushed from Mr. Botherit's office, I saw Try down the end of the balcony. I'm not sure if she noticed me or not. Certainly, she was looking my way.

But I swiveled and sprinted to the library.

And here I have been in my shadow seat, pretty well ever since. The sun is warm today but there is a chill in the shadows, and I huddle around my computer and my fingers try to type.

As soon as I got here, I took out my phone, deleted seven or eight messages from my mother asking me to call her, and telephoned the lawyer. Surprisingly, he answered at once.

435

I told him that I had found a transcript of the words spoken by the two computer programmers as they passed me by. I explained that I like to type transcripts. He was taken aback.

But I did not feel proud, I felt ashamed. *I had not phoned before because I wanted to use the password for myself.* I knew that now — the coincidence of Finnegan's name being the password in reverse. That was only the excuse I had been waiting for.

———————————————

At any rate, I read out the transcript to the lawyer, and he made some interested sounds. He wanted to know if I had printed it out or saved it to disk or shown it around. "It's highly confidential," he explained. "That's one important document you've got there." I felt some stirrings of comfort. He wants me to bring my laptop into his office on Monday.

I ran into the library and printed out a copy of the transcript, even though he didn't want me to. He was a fool — anything could happen to my laptop! You should always have a backup.

Good grief! Do you know who that is?
That is Auntie Veronica!
Walking through the front gate of my school!!!

A Memo from Bindy Mackenzie

To: Briony, Emily, Elizabeth, Toby, Sergio, and Astrid
From: Bindy Mackenzie

Subject: Your Memos
Time: Friday, 5 p.m.

Dear Everyone,

I am going to give you this before the debate tonight. I hope, once you have read it, you will understand why it was easier for me to write than to explain this in person.

Auntie Veronica came to the school at lunchtime today, and took me to a café with her for the afternoon. She had news.

She had heard from the doctor. He had some of my test results back. And it seems there are traces of arsenic in my system: more than there should be.

And that explains so much of what's been happening this year. The doctor gave Auntie Veronica a list of symptoms of chronic arsenic poisoning, and they include things like feeling physically and mentally exhausted, and sick, and numb, and getting headaches, and it can even cause these calluses on my palms that I thought were from the rowing machine. Also, you can get "visual disturbances" and "impaired mental activity." No wonder you all turned into animals.

Auntie Veronica had spent some time talking to the doctor, my mother, and the doctor again. The three of them think they know the answer: I have been going to an old house that my dad owns. It's on Gilbert Road in Castle Hill. And I've been tearing down the wallpaper for him. My mum has been to the house before too, and remembers that the earliest layer of wallpaper is green, and could date as far back as the 1870s.

Well, at that time, people sometimes made wallpaper green by putting arsenic in the paint.

They're going to check this, of course, and I have to go to the hospital tomorrow to get more tests done.

But, as you can see, there's no mystery.

It's just that my dad's been poisoning me.

Oh, and Auntie Veronica also let me know that my parents have decided to separate. My mother's been trying to reach me for the last few days, but I hadn't returned her calls. She's going to tell me all about it tomorrow.

My friends, you were right about so much.

See you after the debate tonight. And thanks for your work — you're all amazingly smart and very special.

Lots of love,

Bindy

PART EIGHT

I.

Dear Finnegan,

When you said good-bye this evening and pressed that envelope into my hand, I had a curious feeling that I would never see you again.

But that is idle foolishness.

It is now about 9 p.m., and I am writing to you on my laptop while sitting in Mr. Botherit's office.

It was kind of you to come to the debating semifinal tonight — I couldn't believe the whole FAD group turned up, including Try! All of you cheering so enthustically when we won.

Your giving me that envelope made me think of writing to you now. I want to tell you what's been going on.

Tonight, Emily almost missed our debate. We have an hour of preparation beforehand, and Ernst and I were alone for that hour. We wrote Emily's speech for her, panicking that we'd have to forfeit. But she sprinted in at the last moment.

As you know, when the debate was over, we all hung around in the classroom, up here on the top balcony. You gave me your letter and left.

Mrs. Lilydale appeared beside me. Together, we watched you hurry from the room.

"Who is that nice young man?" she said. I explained that you were Finnegan Blonde, a new boy this year.

Gradually, people began to leave. Teachers and parents drifted away. Sergio suggested we go to the Blue Danish to celebrate, and offered to drive me home afterwards. Auntie Veronica and Uncle Jake asked to speak with Try. The three of them stepped onto the balcony.

That left only the FAD group and Ernst von Schmerz in the classroom.

Immediately, the others gathered close around me.

It seemed they were in a frenzy.

Finnegan, I'm very sorry, but they think you have been poisoning me this year. You see, I've been sick for a lot of the year, and today I discovered that there's arsenic in my body.

They think you've been giving me the arsenic. This is why:

1. You're new this year, so you're a stranger.
2. Somebody hacked into the school system to move me into our FAD group. You're really good at computers so they think that must have been you.
3. Somebody from FAD gave me nail polish anonymously — they all deny it was them, so that must have been you too. They think there's arsenic in the nail polish. (But there's no proof of that.)
4. You always get the coffee at the Blue Danish: They think that's an opportunity for you to slip the poison into my drink. (That's if it's not the nail polish.)

5. Toby and Sergio have been watching Mrs. Lilydale's office this week, and yesterday, they saw you slip into the office three times.

6. Emily's boyfriend has a brother who's a police officer, and he did some checks on a few different Queensland lists for you. He can't find any record of your existence.

I didn't believe a word of what they're saying. I know you're not the kind of person to murder me. Besides, the doctor thinks the arsenic probably comes from wallpaper I've been taking down for my father. But no! The FAD group would not accept that. They're sure it's more sinister. Besides which, I started getting sick *before* I started working on the wallpaper.

I told them it was irrelevant that your name doesn't come out on any Queensland lists. Maybe you don't have your driver's license, I said. (Although you drive as if you do.) Maybe you've changed your name? Also, I explained what you had said to me a few weeks ago, that you're doing an independent study with Mrs. Lilydale for your Ancient History class. That's why Toby and Sergio saw you in her office.

But then I stopped.

Finnegan, Mrs. Lilydale *asked me who you were* tonight. "Who is that nice young man?" Surely she would know you if she'd been working with you. . . .

What are you doing in her office?

I did not say this to the others — anyway, I didn't get a chance. Emily had something to say. It seemed she had been frantic to speak, but had waited for her moment. She had an important announcement.

"There is no such lawyer," she breathed dramatically, "as Blake Elroy."

That is the name of a lawyer I have spoken with about an argument about computer software that I overheard last year.

Emily had asked her parents, who are lawyers, to check on Mr. Elroy's firm for me. They said there was no such firm. This afternoon, Emily had traveled into the city, to the office where I had met with the lawyer, to find out what was going on. That is why she had run late for the debate.

The office was completely empty.

Now, I admit I was somewhat shocked by this. I had spoken to Mr. Elroy just this morning.

"He must have moved offices," I said. "That place was a dump!"

But Emily was insistent — Mr. Elroy does not exist.

Now the group was hysterical. There was something illegal, they said, about the software. It must be more than a copyright dispute. I must have overheard something vital. It was a fake lawyer and a fake meeting, set up to find out what I knew. And you have been planted in the school to eliminate me as a witness. It was so clear to them! (They see too many movies.)

"Think," said Astrid. "Is there any connection between Finnegan and this software?"

And then it came to me.

444

Finnegan, just last night I discovered that the password used at Ashbury to get access to that very software is *your name in reverse.*

Is that a coincidence? An amazing coincidence? Or is there a connection?

Once again, however, I laughed at them. I took out my transcript of the conversation I had overheard, to prove it contained nothing vital.

I gave the transcript to Ernst, who had been listening to all this with serene bemusement. He's a computer expert like you.

At that moment, Auntie Veronica and Uncle Jake leaned back into the classroom to stay good-bye. Try approached us. She was looking at me with concern.

"I wonder if you and I can have a chat?" she said. She suggested the others go into Castle Hill. She and I would join them shortly.

I left my school bag, keys, notes, and so on behind, but brought my laptop with me. As you know, it is always on my shoulder.

Try suggested we not waste any time. As Mr. Botherit's office is on the top balcony, and the door was open, she led me in here.

The others whispered, "We'll talk more later," as they walked along the top balcony, saying good-bye.

And that is where I am right now. In Mr. Botherit's room.

Try asked me to wait a moment while she took a phone call out on the balcony — I can hear the low murmur of her voice. She's taking a long time!

Oh, the door.

× × ×

It's me again. Still here in Mr. Botherit's office.

Try came in and apologized for the delay, and asked me how I was feeling. It's good of her to care, but I don't think I'm ready to talk about my parents — I don't know *how* I feel — so I just stammered and mumbled for a while. She nodded, looking compassionate, and stepped straight back out to take another call. I've been waiting at least half an hour! Still, I don't mind so much as I feel like I'm talking to you. Although Mr. Botherit must have had garlic in his lunch today. I think I can smell it in his office. And why is it so cold in here? I'm shivering so much it's hard to type.

My aunt and uncle had told Try about my health and my family situation. That's why she wanted to talk to me. She was just offering support, saying I could talk to her whenever I wanted to.

Now I wish she would hurry. I can't hear her voice on the balcony anymore. She's going to drive me to the Blue Danish now, and I don't want to miss the others. I wonder if I should go home, though? I don't feel that well.

I sometimes grow nervous talking to you, Finnegan. I can't imagine what you're thinking as you read this. I just wanted to give you the chance to explain if you can.

I can't believe how thirsty I am. And I'm a bit short of breath — seriously, it's getting — and my head!

The strangest thing, Finnegan.

I'm staring at the window, which of course is black with night and misty reflections. It's a cold night out there.

I'm staring at the window and I *think* what I see is this:

$$\frac{-b \pm \sqrt{b^2 - 8ac}}{2a}$$

Only in reverse.

As if someone had written it in the mist on the outside of the window.

It's my favorite formula. Wait! But it's wrong. It says 8ac instead of 4ac! Who would do that? All the trouble of climbing — and then to get it wrong. I must look into this. I'll just — oh, but my stomach really hurts.

It's —

My head, Finnegan, is so —

You can't even *breathe* in here —

Sorry, I can't really type — I just tried to open the door to get some air and it's locked.

My Ventolin doesn't help at

Finnegan, I really,

Finnegan,

kemwkmksdnafkvknskdkjfwiiiiiiiiiiiiiiiiiiiiiiiiiiiiiiiiiiiiiiiiiiiiii
iiiiiiiiiiiiiiiiiiiiiiiiiiiiiiiiiiiiiiiiiiiiiiiiiiiiiiiiiiiiiiiiiiiiiiiiiiiiiiiiiiiiiiii
iiiiiiiiiiiiiiiiiiiiiiiiiiiiiiiiiiiiiiiiiiiiiiiiiiiiiiiiiiiiiiiiiiiiiiiiiiiiiiiiiiiiiiii

2.

Emily

A black cloth covering Bindy.

That's all I can think of.

And now, I am sorry to say, the FAD group must take over.

The FAD group must now speak for Bindy.

Oh, our poor friend: Bindy Mackenzie.

I will begin by saying what was happening, in the meantime, while Bindy was writing her final words — letters, I guess, her final letters, just up above.

We were all heading down to the parking area, ready to drive in to Castle Hill.

We could not stop talking — we were hovering around in the dark, cold parking area, leaning against our cars, trying to read the transcript that Bindy had just given us. This is the transcript.

—✕—

Friday

3:55 p.m.: Still on my shadow seat. Two young substitute teachers are

448

approaching, one a redhead, the other blonde. Their voices are raised and tumbling together — they speak in half-sentences only —

Redhead: Edna Lbagennif, I mean, for a start, what kind of a pass — but, come on, what are you thinking? You have to —
Blonde: Brilliant. I mean f.., just spectacular. And you knew this all —
Redhead: You're being so totally — This has nothing to do —
Blonde: But you knew, I mean, with that trap   she can do *any-thing* —
Redhead: Don't be ridic— as if she — it's just basic mainten — I mean, right off you know, I'm going to have to say you think — I'll have to tell Mr.—

(The blonde just SLAPPED the redhead!!! I'm going over there!!)

— ✕ —

So, that was the transcript.

Ernst von Schmerz had an opinion about it, but everyone thought he had come to it too fast. He read it once, and then he spoke.

"Check it," he said — pointing to the part where the Blonde says to the Redhead: "But you knew, I mean, with that trap — she can do *anything* —"

He said she must have found a trapdoor in the program. They must have put that in, secretly, so they could hack back into the software later, whenever they wanted or were inclined.

So then the Redhead said, "Don't be ridic — as if she — it's just basic mainten —" and then she says "I'll have to tell Mr.—"

Which, in my humble view, makes no sense.

Ernst, however, said that means the Redhead was claiming the trapdoor was there so they could get back in to maintain the software, but obviously, it was more than that, because (a) it was a secret from the Blonde, and (b) the Redhead was going to tell some mystery person, who must be in charge, that the Blonde had found it.

Therefore, said Ernst, the Blonde must have been trippin' about the person knowing, because she hit the Redhead.

And, furthermore, said Ernst, had any of us located said Blonde to know if she was spry? (I think he meant to find out if she was alive.)

Now, we all thought Ernst had reached his conclusions much too speedily, and with too much in the way of strange language. Also we were a bit annoyed that he was being such an easygoing detective, kind of shoulder-shrugging, as if it were obvious, plus asking if we'd gone looking for the Blonde! When we'd only just found out about the Blonde!

I'm finding it hard to write.

We didn't take much notice of Ernst, but started looking through Bindy's things for clues. Toby had carried them downstairs, and they were now sitting on top of Sergio's car.

This is when we saw a sealed white envelope with "Bindy" written on the front, and *Finnegan A. Blonde* on the back!!

You can imagine our agitation!

We were hysterical.

Finnegan had probably *filled* that envelope with poison! Or maybe some kind of biological chemical.

We were all picking up the envelope and throwing it away from us. And then gingerly picking it up again.

Now Ernst annoyed us again by saying, "Dudes, I do not find your case against Finnegan convictifying."

And he picked up the envelope and *opened* it.

There was nothing in it but a piece of paper. He took it out and read it aloud. And here it is:

Dear Bindy,

I'm writing to say good-bye.

I've decided to drop out of Ashbury, and this is my last day. But I didn't want to go without explaining myself.

Okay, first: I am not who I say I am.

My name is not Finnegan A. Blonde.

That's the imaginary name my cousin gave me when we were kids — I chose it as a kind of tribute to her.

You see, the reason I've been at this school is because my cousin was working here last year. She was doing some computer programming and, as you know, was killed by a car after work one day. The day before she died she had Instant Messaged me a couple of lines. Something about a problem with the software and an argument she'd had with a coworker. She also mentioned that a student named Bindy had overheard the conversation.

I thought that meant the accident was suspicious. But the police down here took no notice of a guy up in Queensland who thought he knew more than them.

So, I moved down to my gran's place in Sydney and enrolled in your school under a false name.

I was here for two reasons: first, to see if I could find out what happened to my cousin. I knew she was working on some new educational software, which was being tested out by the teachers in your school. That's why I've been going in to Mrs. L.'s office, by the way — to see if I could find something in the software connected with my cousin. (Mrs. L. is *never* in her office.) But I knew squat about computers before this year, so I've been trying to learn, doing extra work with the computing teacher, staying up late, etc.

Second, and this sounds insane, I realize now, but I was here to see if I could protect you. I thought that something might happen to you, like it happened to my cousin. Luckily, there was only one student at Ashbury named Bindy.

I got the principal to put us in the same FAD group by pretending I knew you. I kind of twisted my body toward you when Try was allocating those "buddies," hoping to subconsciously influence her so she'd put us together. I even told you to do a kickboxing class, thinking you'd learn to defend yourself. And then I kind of waited to see what would happen.

But you have to understand I lost my mind when I lost my

cousin. I wasn't thinking straight. Over the last few months, I've been realizing this. I didn't find anything sinister in the software. You seemed fine and not in danger. . . .

Anyhow, this week I've stopped coming to school. I did Year 11 two years ago, anyway, so I'm just repeating it now. I should actually be in first-year uni. So I am heading back there.

You're a good friend, Bindy. I hope it's worked out with your family — let's catch some music together one day.

Take care of yourself, okay?

Markus Pulie

P.S. I'm going to see a friend of yours tonight. I guess my cousin used to buy books at a place called Maureen's Magic. Anyway, Maureen herself contacted me the other day and said she'd heard I was here now, and wanted to meet me. She told me that you used to work for her.

— X —

So. (This is still Emily.)

Finnegan Blonde is not Finnegan Blonde but *Markus Pulie.*

And his *cousin* was working at this school just last year. Why did he not say anything to us? Maybe we could have helped him?

But Ernst was keen to get into the software and see if his theory was right about it having a trapdoor. Perhaps he felt injured that we had doubted him.

We decided we'd go into Try's office, to look at the software on her computer, and we thought she would not mind, once we explained.

So! There we all were, crowded into Try's office, being very careful not to touch anything, as Ernst sat down at her computer. We gathered around him, watching over his shoulders.

Astrid, meanwhile, was being rather quiet.

I noticed she was not watching the screen. She was staring at Try's bookshelf. I followed her gaze and saw *The Travellers' Ohio*.

"You know," Astrid said slowly, reaching for the guidebook. "I've just remembered something."

"Shh," said Toby. "Ernst is trying to concentrate."

But Ernst typed away, happily enough. Now and then he made a "tch" noise, and hit the keys harder.

"I've remembered something Try once said," Astrid continued, sounding dreamy. "Okay, she told me she comes from Ohio? And she told me a bit about it too."

Toby said he'd heard that Try was from Ohio, but others couldn't remember.

"She doesn't talk about herself very much," Briony admitted, sounding guilty. "I guess we should have asked her more . . ."

Ernst hit the same key seven or eight times. Astrid opened the contents page of the guidebook.

"And see, this book has Cincinnati, so it must be in Ohio," she said. "But I remember once when Bindy was going on about Cincinnati, at FAD? And she was even wondering what it was like? And Try said nothing. Can you be from Ohio, do you think, and have *nothing* to say about a place there?"

There was some thoughtful breathing in the room.

454

"You could," said Sergio eventually, "if Bindy's the one asking."

"She might be from somewhere else in Ohio," Briony pointed out. "Somewhere far away from Cincinnati."

But Astrid was flicking through the guidebook.

"This is too familiar," she murmured. "This introduction about Ohio — the second paragraph? It's, like, *exactly* what Try said to me when I asked her about her home."

"You think she's not really from Ohio?" said Elizabeth.

"Maybe Try's the murderer," Astrid whispered. "Remember Em thought it was Miss Flynn because she's new this year? And then we thought it was Finnegan because *he's* new. So, Try's new too."

There was quick tapping on the computer keys from Ernst. He certainly has focus.

People started talking — slowly, at first, but then accelerating.

"Her accent changes a lot," someone said.

"And remember in the first FAD session? She didn't remember anyone's name except Bindy's?"

"Still," Sergio said. "Bindy's memorable."

"She's got that big empty house in Castle Hill. What's up with a teacher with a big empty house? Plus another house in the mountains?"

"And she could have given the nail polish to Bindy. She's in the FAD group."

"And *she's* the one who introduced FAD to the school!"

Sergio's hand was on the office door.

"Maybe I'll go check on Bindy," he said.

And he was gone.

The rest of us looked at one another.

Suddenly, it seemed acceptable to look through Try's things. Even if only to clear her name. We opened drawers, tipped out papers, took folders from shelves, flipped through her calendar and diary book.

And then Toby looked at the printer.

He held up a single piece of paper. It was a printout of a photograph.

The photograph was of Finnegan.

And underneath, printed in capitals, the name MARKUS PULIE.

In fine print across the top of the page, the words: "Maureen's Magic." And at the bottom of the page?

"Maureen, take immediate action."

3.

Astrid

I'm taking over now as Emily is getting too upset.

She's crying, tho you can't tell that from the way she's been typing.

What happened next?

Okay, we run down to the car park, kind of falling down stairs together, and even Ernst is running with us?

We're all like: *Finnegan's in danger! We've gotta warn him!*

Now, at this point, Sergio turns up.

"How's Bindy?" we all go.

Sergio says, oh, he just climbed the side of the school building and wrote a message in the window of Mr. B.'s office for Bindy, so she'll be all right.

So now we're all yelling again, like, what? You climbed the *building*? Also, we're going: Why didn't you just knock on the office door?

And he goes, take it easy, he didn't want Try to know we're kind of suspicious of her, so he climbed up the building. And he saw Bindy in there facing the window, and Try talking to her. So he thought he'd better write a message to her in the window steam, but he couldn't write anything obvious like "GET OUT NOW" in case Try turned around and saw it, and right away just picked up a gun and killed Bindy. But if he wrote a cryptic message, he says, Bindy will see it and just be cool and make an excuse, like, say she has to go to the bathroom, but actually get out of there.

So, he says, he wrote a mathematical formula.

We were all like, excuse me? And he goes, "Here's the genius, I put a *mistake* in it! She won't be able to sit there in *Mr. B*'s office with mistakes being made in maths formulae. Trust me, she'll be heading out of there now."

Before we had time to go off on him about that, he goes, "What are you doing down here and not in Try's office?" So we tell him about the Finnegan situation, and next thing he and Liz are in his car, and he must have f/n flattened his foot because he was screeching out the school gate before we even, like, breathed out.

The rest of us go: We'd better get Bindy.

And we all run up to the top balcony.

4.

Briony

And what we found on the top balcony was nobody.

We knocked on Mr. Botherit's door, and no answer. For a moment, we wondered if Try and Bindy had just slipped away, but Emily was hysterical, insisting we get in.

She ran to the administration office and found a key for Mr. Botherit's door, and we got in.

Bindy was on the floor.

The window had been smashed, and cold wind was blasting in.

Her skin was yellow. She wasn't breathing.

We phoned an ambulance.

Now we are at the hospital.

Bindy has been poisoned with arsine gas.

It looks like she collapsed, then regained consciousness long enough to smash the window, but then collapsed again.

Smashing the window may have helped reduce the severity of the poisoning.

But now she's gone into heart and kidney failure.

In severe cases like this, a doctor just said, survival is not expected.

It is difficult typing this. I can see Bindy's parents across from us.

5.

Elizabeth

It's the next day, and the others have asked me to type an entry so we have the complete story.

I'm in the hospital waiting room now. Bindy lived through the night, but she'll need blood transfusions and she might need dialysis. She's still critical and we're basically just waiting for her to die.

I wasn't here last night because I was with Sergio at the bookshop.

It was dark and locked up when we got there, but we thought we could see a light near the back of the store.

We knocked, and there was no answer, and Sergio breaks the window and gets us in.

Maureen was talking to Finnegan in the storage room at the back. I guess his name is actually Markus.

Anyway, they looked up at us in surprise. They were sitting opposite each other at a table.

Between them was a plate of apple and cinnamon muffins, and Finnegan had just reached out to take one . . .

We both kind of shouted, "Hey, Finn, we just need to talk to you, okay?"

So, he got up, confused, and we kind of rushed him out of the shop — and showed him the paper we'd found in Try's printer. We told him the whole story on the way to the police station. We tried to tell the whole story there too. They didn't seem as quick to catch on as Finnegan. But it was around then that Emily called from the hospital, to tell us what was happening with Bindy.

Then the police took it seriously.

At about 3 a.m., they found Try. She was speeding out of Sydney.

They've already found out that Try Montaine is not her real name. She's not American either. She's from Adelaide.

6.

Toby

Now it's the next day, and Mackenzie lives on. I'm not giving up the way the girls are. Same goes for her family, I guess, who sit there every day, and we've all kind of become friends.

The police have been working fast. They've found a trapdoor in the software, like Ernst said they would. The programmers had it configured so they could get back in once it was up and running, go through the Board of Studies and into the State Government payroll, where they were already starting to make up false identities of teachers and public officials. The plan was to collect the salaries of thousands of imaginary people.

Anyway, that's how they got Try's identity as a schoolteacher into the system, along with fake teaching records, and got her the job at Ashbury.

She was there to do damage control, make sure nobody at Ashbury suspected anything, and coordinate the elimination of Bindy.

Try has confessed to everything. She's told the police she had two local women giving arsenic to Bindy: Maureen, the bookshop lady (muffins), and someone named Eleanora (ginger biscuits). There's also arsenic in the pages of some old books on etiquette that Maureen gave to Bindy. Plus in the nail polish that, of course, Try gave to Bindy, pretending it was from one of us.

It was supposed to be brilliantly masterminded so it was just the right quantities of arsenic to weaken and disorient her, so they could set up an accident that appeared innocent. Nobody would ever bother checking her for arsenic, because who gets poisoned by arsenic — was the idea. And if they ever had to move fast, they could increase the poison without throwing suspicion on themselves.

Apparently, Try has told the police she'd grown really fond of Bindy (something to do with finding her eccentricities endearing) and all the FAD group, and had been fighting to let Bindy live. She came up with the idea of getting a fake lawyer to question Bindy, and eventually got the murder called off when it seemed like Bindy knew nothing. But then, Bindy phoned the guy and told him she had the transcript. And on the same night, her aunt and uncle told Try that the doctors had found arsenic — so, I guess Try got orders to take action straightaway. She'd treated a tray of zinc dust with acid (which causes arsine gas to be released) and hidden it in a vent in Mr. Botherit's office.

Her plan was to leave Bindy to die in the office, come back to get the laptop, and disappear. She says she was really upset about it.

Doesn't she break your heart?

7.

Sergio

And now it's the next day and everyone sounds so f/n morbid. She's still breathing. Why are we even listening to what they're telling us about her chances?

Meanwhile, at school, we've got reporters hangin' around the gates trying to talk to us.

Toby goes, "Go home to your families! There's nothing to see here!" in that speaker-voice thing he does. The journos ignore him.

This is the weirdest time that I, for one, have ever experienced. It's weird being here in the waiting room, kind of getting to know Bindy's family. It's weirder being at school.

We all want to hang around the police talking to them but they say they've talked to us enough. Meanwhile, they keep uncovering stuff, such as that Finnegan — I guess his name is Markus — anyhow, the criminal types who set up the software scam, they'd been keeping an eye on Markus because he'd been asking questions about his cousin. So then they realized he'd disappeared from Queensland, and they were kind of wondering where he was. And it was just last week they realized that he was actually Finnegan. The bookshop lady set up the meeting so she could feed him a muffin full of strychnine. That would have killed him pretty fast, if Liz and I hadn't shown up and got him out of there.

He's going back home to Queensland. He's kind of wrecked that he didn't save Bindy's life, even though that was why he was here. Which makes us all feel wrecked for thinking he was here to finish her off, but, listen, he's from Queensland. You never know with Queenslanders, right?

Well, we are supposedly waiting for Bindy to die, and as I said, that is f/n morbid.

Okay, but Emily and Astrid are going on about how this is the time to stop, while she's still alive, so this is how we should end this. They wanted to put the story together, kind of a tribute to Bindy, so that's why we've been typing this. So, they think we've said it all now, and I am supposed to end it.

So, good-bye, Bindy Mackenzie.

We love you.

The End.

PART NINE

I.

Well!

Imagine allowing somebody else to close, nay, to *end* my life! I am fond of Sergio, nay, I adore him, but Sergio! You have greatly mistook if you thought I would permit you the honor of the closing words!

I, Bindy Mackenzie, have awakened from my slumber.

I understand that I was unconscious for a week!

I suppose I needed the rest.

They are going to send me home in a few days. The doctors are full of remarks upon my feistiness, and I am pleased to report that my organs are functioning well.

When I first awakened from my slumber, various events took place. Not necessarily in this order, the events included the following: the discovery of bounteous flowers, chocolates, teddy bears, cards, and correspondence; discussions with police about what they have discovered (imagine — Try was trying to kill me. You know, I'm not sure I ever really liked her); and a meeting with my mother. The next three chapters briefly outline these events.

2.

**BELOW ARE SOME SAMPLES OF THE CORRESPONDENCE
I RECEIVED WHILE UNCONSCIOUS, WHICH WAS WAITING
FOR ME WHEN I WOKE UP.**

My dear Bindy!
How dreadful all this is! I haven't slept a *wink*! Do get better soon, and don't give a thought to the Tearsdale. We've got the final postponed a couple of weeks, in view of the exceptional . . . Do you think you'll be all right by then?

Anyway, the roses are from the principal, the tulips are from Mr. Botherit, and the Violet Healing Crystals with Apple Peel Infusion are from yours truly. I asked an orderly to hang them in various key places around Intensive Care. I do hope he complied.

Here's something else to cheer you up! I have an announcement to make! Ms. Lawrence and I have been secretly setting up a business — The Lily of Arabia — specializing in energy therapies, chakra and aura healing, bubble baths for the soul, and so on. Remember Ms. Lawrence's "surfing" trip to Thailand earlier this year? It was actually a fact-finding mission! She was so inspired she decided to stop teaching altogether, and she's been

470

working on the business full-time. I'm still at Ashbury, of course — do not fear — I just slip away from the grounds whenever I can. . . .

I think you might have happened to see our loan application on my desk last year! I was in a flap about that, as we wanted to keep it a secret until the Grand Launch next month. I also think you might have *seen* me talking to Ms. Lawrence in the school grounds, very early one morning — we were talking about the automated palm reader we're building.

You may be honored to know that you've already tried one of our products: the carob-coated energy drop. I hope it's helped to make your year divine.

Now, Bindy, in the future, if you are being poisoned, please do come and see me.

So long,

Mrs. Lilydale

X X X

A Memo from Ernst von Schmerz

To: Bindy Mackenzie
From: Ernst von Schmerz
Subject: Stationery Order
Time: Saturday

Yo Bind,
Wake up, dude, I'm in needs of you, and plus in needs of your stationery.

Herewith, my FINAL slice of personalized memo from Ernst von Schmerz.

According to which, can you wake up, outta the hospital gown, into civ. threads, and cut me some new stationery in the name of Kee Dow Liang?

Thatta girl.

Whassup, Ashbury? The real me? And if Ashbury cannot accept this me? I'll be back for an order of stationery in the name of Bubble Van Burp.

Nevertheless, have no fear,

Whoever I am,

I will still be:

Your Home Boy,

Ernst von Schmerz

×　×　×

Dear Bindy,

This is a quick note as my flight to Cairns leaves in less than an hour. I'll write again when I get there.

I just want to wish you good health and happy times, and I cannot tell you how sorry I am for letting you down. I was supposed to be there at Ashbury to save your life. And I went and missed it all.

I'm grateful to you because the truth has come out about my cousin, and I knew something was wrong about that all along. It makes me mad that someone hurt her, and now they've hurt you too, but the truth is always better than a lie.

And thanks to you, I now know that the password my cousin chose when she was installing the software at Ashbury was *my* imaginary childhood name, in reverse. That she chose that password is like a gift from her to me. It means she was always thinking of me. And that's something I want to thank you for also.

I want you to come to visit me in Cairns, and I'll take you to the beach and to see some live music. I know just which bands I'll take you to, and you'll love them.

You're a special girl, Bindy, and I hope you will always be my buddy.

Love,

Finnegan A. Blonde

(or you can call me Markus Pulie if you like — whichever you prefer)

Office of the Board of Studies, NSW

Ms. Bindy Mackenzie
24 Clipping Drive
Kellyville NSW 2155

Dear Ms. Mackenzie,

Thank you for your letter.

We are happy to confirm that Friendship and Development (FAD) is a course currently offered at Ashbury High. The course is to be taken by senior students for one lesson each week. It covers personal development issues such as self-esteem, stress management, career planning, and study management.

We understand that Ms. Try Montaine introduced FAD to your school, and is conducting your classes in FAD. We can confirm from our files that Ms. Montaine has several years of experience and an excellent teaching record.

We trust that this has been helpful.

Please do not hesitate to contact us if you have any further queries.

Yours sincerely,

George Sutcliffe

Student Liaison Officer

Office of the Board of Studies

3.

The police have had many questions for me, and have given me much to think about.

I think the following exemplifies what their detective work has uncovered.

It is a copy of some encrypted notes that were discovered on Try's computer and that they asked me to help decipher. The notes had been sent by Try to her "superior" in the relevant "criminal gang." They update him on Try's efforts. His response could not be retrieved.

Note that "M" is Maureen (or Maureen's Magic), "E" is Eleanora, "MP" is Markus Pulie (that is, Finnegan), and "BM" is, of course, me.

- Installed at Ashbury — all well so far — making contact with teachers/students — working on FAD course (my two years of psychology useful at last!) — have ensured BM is in my FAD group.
- Communication lines set up with M and E — as agreed, M has installed BM as baby-sitter / E has installed BM as "pasta companion" (!) — both M and E in serious

need of $$$ — both will deliver quantities of product too small to have any serious effect alone, so believe their role is to disorient B so we can question her. Note: In combination, product will eventually have serious effect.

- Extensive exploration of school grounds/layout — have found alternate entrance to FAD classroom (fire escape) — could be useful? Checked BM's records — seems to be a "super student"/some kind of genius.
- First FAD class — initial contact with BM — paid close attention to her — other kids seem sweet/fun.
- E reports that BM "loves" things historical? Useful?
- Current delivery mechanisms: muffins/pages of historical book/ginger biscuits.
- At your request, alternative, external location for FAD established at Blue Danish café — less likely to be problems with other teachers/students out of school dominion.
- All seems well — no apparent leaks — seems BM has spoken to nobody — maybe didn't hear anything at all? Suggest we delay product delivery until this confirmed? — will keep making efforts to get her to talk to me — software running well.
- Have issued several invitations to BM to come see me — never taken up.
- Tension btwn rest of FAD group and BM — (difficult — feeling sorry for BM — she shoots herself in the foot with that group; she even pointed out Sergio's burn scar today) — decided to *exacerbate* tension by getting them

to do Name Game again, knowing the FAD group would be cruel to her — but might make her more likely to come to me for help/get close to me?

- Relax! I'm not getting "too fond" of anyone — but plan backfired — BM didn't come to FAD after last week's events — says she doesn't want to come back — refuses to talk . . . Had a crazy idea — might just work — will ask BM to do project writing about events she has "seen and heard" . . . Might uncover something?
- As requested, have increased product delivery — instructed M to increase delivery (she says she'll get BM to work in her bookshop over the holidays) — and new delivery mechanism: nail polish.
- M concerned about leaving BM alone with her kids as product takes effect/risks of her own kids taking product — wants to offer permanent job in bookshop instead of as baby-sitter. OK?
- URGENT NOTE — BM did project — REFERS to episode — *SHE THINKS IT WAS 2 SUBSTITUTE TEACHERS ARGUING ABOUT A POLISH EXCHANGE STUDENT (???)* — relevant page of her "life project" attached— PERMISSION TO CALL OFF DELIVERY OF PRODUCT IMMEDIATELY?
- Have arranged for "lawyer" to contact BM — to "prod" her for possible memories — Still think she knows nothing — BM is v. sensitive, and was upset about the slapping — noticed nothing else — this is unnecessary job.

- Product is having extreme conseqs — BM seems ill/ completely changed — not doing schoolwork at all — could lead to suspicions — suggest reduction in product so that conseq slower, less obvious?
- E wants out — concerned about BM's contact with her baby — says she's done e/thing to keep BM away from baby — but can't watch her *all* the time — E thinks BM is going "mad" from the product & she's scared that BM will hurt the kid — or is it just conscience pangs? — enough delivery mechanisms anyway — pressurize or let her go?
- As instructed, have arranged trip to your Blue Mtns property — agree, good location for "accidental fall"
- Understand that the cousin who made trouble w/the police (MP) is "missing" from home — as instructed, have begun "blackmail" of M to get more "help" from her (i.e. told her actual nature of product/threatened her kids & husband etc.) — v. effective — she'll do w/ ever we ask now — have sent M to Queensland to investigate "cousin's" whereabouts.
- URGENT NOTE —"lawyer" confirms — BM knows NOTHING — many prompts, referred to software itself — (called it a copyright dispute) — but no memory — PERMISSION TO CALL OFF DELIVERY OF PRODUCT IMMEDIATELY?
- As instructed, have canceled M and E — (note that product is still being delivered by nail polish/book pages — permission to retrieve these mechanisms?).

- As instructed, have not retrieved mechanisms — mild effects noted but BM is recovering well — Blue Mtns trip w/o incident (rained whole time so hiking & "accident" wld not have been an option anyway) — small false alarm when group talked about poison — (kids getting on great tho — think my FAD course is successful!)
- Received your fax with identity of MP — *he's a student in my FAD group* — seemed so lovely — feel betrayed — but I don't believe he has uncovered anything — have instructed M to take immediate action. Have provided her with product for delivery of extreme dosage.
- *EXTREMELY URGENT* —"lawyer" just contacted me — it seems that BM has phoned him & revealed she *did* hear the conversation. She knows too much. Awaiting instructions.

4.

This is a description of a "meeting" with my mother.

This happened almost in a dream.

I was in the hospital, in recovery, but I did not know that at the time. I had just regained consciousness. My focus was hazy. I saw flowers, windows, some curious violet ornaments. I saw a man in blue rush past my glass and I thought of the giant blue cat.

Then I saw my mother. She must have seen me open my eyes, because she was standing by the bed, crouching, leaning close to me.

I spoke.

"Why did you do it?" I said.

My voice was hoarse and faint, but my mother heard me. She sat on the edge of the bed now, and put a hand on my forehead.

"It's okay," she said, "you've been poisoned, but you're okay now. Don't worry, just rest for now."

"Why did you do it?" I repeated.

She smiled gently. "It wasn't me, darling. You mustn't worry about who it was for now."

"I mean, why did you move out to the city and leave me behind for the year?" My voice broke into pieces as I said this, and I found myself crying into my hands. My mother let out a small cry and gathered me into her arms.

I heard her murmuring, "Bindy, I'm so sorry."

Through my tears, then, I spoke a lot of nonsense.

"You went behind Dad's back for Anthony this year," I said, "but not for me. You stopped loving me, didn't you? Because you spent last summer with the girls from school, Emily and her friends, and not with me. And you liked them better than me. I know you did because they're better than me. And you wouldn't help me get professional driving lessons when Dad said I couldn't have them. And then I crashed the car! And you *agreed* to move out to the city with Dad. Why did you agree to that? Why did you leave me behind? Why did you stop loving me this year?"

My mother kept rocking me, saying, "It's okay, it's okay," and I could feel the shuddering of sobs in her chest.

Eventually, I was exhausted and lay back on my pillow. She looked down at me with her red, teary eyes, and was quiet for a while.

Then, she said, "We thought we were going to lose you, so I wrote you a letter. You can read it if you like. When you feel up to it." She put a pink envelope on the table beside my bed. "But for now," she said, "please rest, and know that I will never let you down again."

She leaned closer and whispered, "I could never stop loving you, Bindy."

Then she brushed her hands over my eyes so that they closed, and sat on the bed watching me.

I think I let my eyes flutter open for a moment, and when I did, I believe I saw my father standing behind the glass, staring in at us.

I fell deeply asleep.

5.

FINAL WORDS

A month has passed since my release from the hospital.

I wish to express my heartfelt gratitude to the excellent staff at the Baulkham Hills Shire Hospital. Apart from their prompt treatment at the critical phase, they have been very conscientious in these last few weeks. I have to return for regular checkups: There is the possibility of complications following acute arsine poisoning, not to mention chronic arsenic poisoning. (Apparently, the chronic poisoning had made me anemic, which made the arsine's effect more extreme.) But so far, there are no signs of long-term ill effects.

Meanwhile, the officers of the Hills District law enforcement are unraveling the wicked scandal! They come by occasionally to ask me more questions. They are still gathering evidence for the prosecution of Maureen, Eleanora, and several other members of this criminal conspiracy. (Apparently, the "gang" extends across the nation, and largely consists of computer criminals.) Try herself was a reasonably new member of this gang, and has entered into a plea agreement: She has given the police as much information as she can about her superiors and their plans in exchange for a reduced sentence. In fact, her information has led them to the man behind the whole scheme. He's a computer programmer named Elias Brandy. I hear he has freckles and a red beard, and he pretends to be extremely perplexed by the allegations made against him. But the police have not fallen for that. They've seized his computers and talked to computer crime agencies around the world — it turns out he's part of a gang of notorious cyber-pirates. They've stolen billions and are implicated in over twenty-five murders. Apparently, Try is terrified of Elias Brandy.

I believe she will serve seven years.

My mother is looking after me beautifully. You see, I am writing these, the final words in this project, in the living room of our old home at 24 Clipping Drive, Kellyville.

Mum evicted the tenants, and she and I moved in. The really marvelous thing about this is that my personalized letter stationery is now valid again!

Anthony is staying with his friend, Sam, in the city, and my father remains, rather tragically, in his little one-bedroom apartment.

Sometimes, in these days of recuperation, I turn to the letter that my mother wrote when she thought I was not going to make it. I'll scan it in below.

— × —

My Bindy,

I just want to tell you how little you look in this big hospital room. I just want to gather you up and take you home with me.

It's too late to write this letter, isn't it? All year you've been sending me e-mails, and each time one arrived, I grabbed my phone and called you. No wonder you ignored my messages. You wanted me to sit down and *write*, to think about you and your questions — all I wanted to do was chat. I wanted to hear your voice.

It was such a little thing for you to ask, and I have failed.

Just as I've failed you all these years. I know how much you admire your dad, and how he takes advantage of that. I should work harder to protect you from that — I've been realizing this all year. How he sent you that cruel e-mail on your birthday. How his wallpaper was almost poisoning you . . . well, it *could* have been.

He does mean well. He's not a wicked man, and he loves you very much. It's just that he doesn't really understand kids. He thinks of you as someone fascinating, but I don't think he really understands you. And he's completely caught up in his own world.

Which is why I agreed to move into the city with him this year. I thought you and Anthony might be better off learning to live your own lives, without being in the shadow of your father all the time. I've been regretting my decision all year. I feel as if I've abandoned you both, rather than given you freedom.

Bindy, you work so hard, you're so creative, and you're unlike anyone else. It's a miracle that a pair of hopeless people like your dad and me created a person as extraordinary as you. I'm so proud of you.

You are the strongest, toughest girl in the whole world. You are so very sick, and they say you might not wake up.

I don't believe them. They don't know who you are.

You're my little girl.

Bindy, please wake up.

Lots of love,

Your Mum

—✕—

So, apart from looking back over that letter, there is plenty to keep me busy here.

My teachers at Ashbury have agreed to send quantities of schoolwork so that I can begin to catch up. I am *devouring* the work! I have got my passion back! It is me again! (My mother comes in now and then to make me stop and rest. It's a real nuisance but she means well.)

I also have numerous visitors.

My father comes occasionally, but of course he is a busy man and often has to travel interstate. He always looks very sheepish. (He can't seem to take in that it was *not* his wallpaper that poisoned me, even though we have confirmed that there was no arsenic in his house on Gilbert Road.) He never stays long, is very awkward with my mother, and he really only talks about his property development. But the other day he kissed the top of my head and gave me the gift of a Mont Blanc pen. I was delighted.

Anthony and Sam also visit often and bring movies to watch. They also bring their movie cameras. They are interviewing me and the members of the FAD group, and plan to make a documentary about the events of my year.

Astrid, of all people! came by the other day. She brought along a gift certificate for me to get my eyebrow pierced. How droll. I think I will do it. She told me many tales of running from the police, and said she now thinks she's not a reincarnated carnation, after all, but a reincarnated dove — something about a rooftop she flew from while the police were in hot pursuit. I admit, my attention drifted.

There was another more precious gift that Astrid brought with her. It seems that my FAD group decided to create another Name Game — just for me. It gladdened my heart.

Other members of the FAD group have also dropped by. They tell me that FAD has been canceled at my school. The old FAD groups have been transformed into Study Groups. Apparently, *my* group has permission to continue going to the Blue Danish. I can't imagine how little study they're doing! Things will have to change when I get back.

I will conclude by expressing my utmost gratitude to my FAD group and to Ernst von Schmerz. Together, they have saved my life.

I have read through the entries the FAD group wrote in the

hospital waiting room while I was unconscious. I must say, I agree with Sergio: Their attitude *was* rather morbid. I considered deleting the entries from this project, but have retained them for their authenticity.

I have nothing but affection and gratitude for that group, but, truly — you think a little arsine gas is enough to finish me off?

You don't know Bindy Mackenzie.

PART TEN

Bindy is my best buddy and one day i hope she'll let me kiss her.

A supernova brain with these gorgeous magenta eyes.

Well, she is so much more COMPLICATED, INTERESTING and ORIGINAL than I ever realized!!! And therefore it's a good lesson for me. I look forward to knowing her further.

BINDY MACKENZIE

BINDY IS VERY FORGIVING, AND SHE HAS A LOT OF KIND OF LIKE HAPPINESS AND LOVE HIDDEN INSIDE HER. AND SHE WAS BRAVE HOW SHE USED TO WEAR HER HAIR UP FUNNY, BUT BINDY, YOU MAY AS WELL KEEP WEARING IT OUT NOW, OK, COS IT LOOKS GOOD LIKE THAT.

I think you are a determined, compassionate, funny, imaginative, and kind-hearted person. I think we are lucky to know you.

Bindy, you are STILL SO SMART!!! And you still have HUGE words in your head, and that's even though you had chronic arsenic poisoning and acute arsine poisoning!

Bindy Mackenzie talks like a horse & I hope she never stops.

Author's Acknowledgments

I am extremely grateful to the extraordinary people at Scholastic, especially Arthur Levine, Cheryl Klein, Rachel Griffiths, Elizabeth Parisi, and Jacky Harper; to my wonderful agent, Jill Grinberg; to Nicola Moriarty, Sean Moriarty, Fiona Ostric, Katrina Harrington, Steve Menasse, Jane Roberts, and Jack Llewellyn, who all shared stories about school with me; and to Frances and Naomi Roberts for Cincinnati information. Thanks, most of all, to my parents, who are nothing like Bindy's parents; to my sister Liane, who wanted to know more about Bindy in the first place; and to Colin McAdam, who was there for me and Bindy, at every single page.

Several texts and articles on poisons were useful in writing this book, among them: John Harris Trestrail, III, *Criminal Poisoning* (Humana Press Inc, 2000–2001); Peter Macinnis, *Poisons: From Hemlock to Botox and the Killer Bean of Calabar* (Arcade Publishing, 2004); Carol Turkington, *The Poisons and Antidotes Sourcebook* (second edition, Checkmark Books, 1999); Agency for Toxic Substances and Disease Registry, "Public Health Statement for Arsenic" (September, 2000); M. Amini, M. D., "Arsenic Poisoning: Not Very Common but Treatable" (Vol. 3, No. 2, SEMJ, 2002).

Try based her "intelligence theory" (very loosely) on the theories of David G. Lazear in his *Seven Ways of Knowing: Teaching for Multiple Intelligences* (IRI/Skylight Publishing, Inc, 1991), and Bindy used the *Shorter Oxford English Dictionary* (Oxford

University Press, 2002) to look up "cin" words. She was also slowly poisoned by *Our Deportment* (John H. Young, Pennsylvania Publishing Co., 1881) and *Twentieth Century Etiquette* (Annie Randall White, 1900).